TRAFFICKED

TRAFFICKED

kim purcell

VIKING

An Imprint of Penguin Group (USA) Inc.

VIKING

Published by Penguin Group

Penguin Group (USA) Inc., 345 Hudson Street, New York, New York 10014, U.S.A.
Penguin Group (Canada), 90 Eglinton Avenue East, Suite 700, Toronto, Ontario, Canada M4P 2Y3
(a division of Pearson Penguin Canada Inc.)
Penguin Books Ltd, 80 Strand, London WC2R 0RL, England
Penguin Ireland, 25 St Stephen's Green, Dublin 2, Ireland
(a division of Penguin Books Ltd)
Penguin Group (Australia), 250 Camberwell Road, Camberwell, Victoria 3124, Australia
(a division of Pearson Australia Group Pty Ltd)
Penguin Books India Pvt Ltd, 11 Community Centre, Panchsheel Park, New Delhi – 110 017, India
Penguin Group (NZ), 67 Apollo Drive, Rosedale, Auckland 0632, New Zealand
(a division of Pearson New Zealand Ltd.)
Penguin Books (South Africa) (Pty) Ltd, 24 Sturdee Avenue, Rosebank, Johannesburg 2196, South Africa

Penguin Books Ltd, Registered Offices: 80 Strand, London WC2R 0RL, England

First published in 2012 by Viking, a member of Penguin Group (USA) Inc.

1 3 5 7 9 10 8 6 4 2

LIBRARY OF CONGRESS CATALOGING-IN-PUBLICATION DATA
Purcell, Kim.
Trafficked / by Kim Purcell.
p. cm.
Summary: A seventeen-year-old Moldovan girl whose parents have been killed
is brought to the United States to work as a slave for a family in Los Angeles.
ISBN 978-0-670-01280-0 (hardcover)
[1. Human trafficking—Fiction. 2. Slavery—Fiction.
3. Moldovans—United States—Fiction. 4. Los Angeles (Calif.)—Fiction.] I. Title.
PZ7.P9744Tr 2012
[Fic]—dc23
2011011530

Printed in U.S.A.
Set in Adobe Garamond
Book design by Sam Kim

TO GAVIN

TRAFFICKED

CHAPTER ONE

Hannah took two small steps forward in the immigration line entering America at LAX. She was in a large white room with a line for people like her and another line for people who belonged. The people who belonged laughed and slouched, wore clothes that fit their bodies, and smelled of milk, dry cleaning, and deodorant. The people who didn't belong stood upright unless they couldn't, wore dressier but older clothes, and smelled of body odor, hot sauce, fish, garlic, and cheap perfume.

Hannah wished she looked like an American teenager. If only she'd been able to change out of these dirty Moldovan clothes. At the airport in Romania, they'd made her check her suitcase, and she'd been so flustered, she hadn't taken a single thing out of it. In the suitcase, she had a brand-new pair of jeans that the good agent had given her to look more American, as well as her T-shirt that said GOOD NEWS with a monkey dancing below the words.

Those clothes would have given her a type of armor, but this dirty white shirt with the frills on the front and the too-blue slacks from her babushka made her look poor and desperate, exactly what the good agent had warned her she must try to avoid.

She squeezed the book with her fake documents inside. Two couples, a family, and an older woman and a man were in line ahead of her. Then it would be her turn.

The line slid forward like a slow escalator, pulling her closer to the grim immigration officers who sat on stools behind a long white counter, separated into glass booths. They were examining people's documents, searching for fakes like hers. They waved most of the people through a large white archway into America, but they sent some through a door with a tiny unbreakable window, which she was sure led to an interrogation room.

She'd never been a good liar. The man in front of her was probably a bad liar too. He kept scratching the back of his hairy neck, above the collar of his ill-fitting suit, turning the skin bright red. She wished he'd stop. His nervousness was spreading to her like a disease.

The man stunk too, worse than she did, for sure, though her own smell embarrassed her. She'd tried to wash in the small bathroom on the plane, but her clothes held the smell of panic and fear and she couldn't wash that off.

There was a faint tapping noise. She looked down and saw it was her black shoe, tapping on the white linoleum floor. Great. If the Americans had a camera on her and they were watching her in some secret room, they'd know something was up. Her mother used to rub her back in slow circles and remind her quietly not to fidget, that nobody needed to know if she was nervous. The memory made her sad.

The man turned around and stared into Hannah's green eyes

and then gazed down at her breasts and her hips as if she were a picture he could just look at for as long as he liked. She cleared her throat, glaring. He looked up in surprise and turned back around.

She wished she were more like her mother. Even when her father used to come home drunk and singing, her mamulya never yelled or got angry. She'd take in a deep breath, let it out, and relax, like her body was an armchair she carried everywhere she went.

Hannah breathed in as deeply as she could and let it out, but it didn't work. Her brain felt fuzzy. From the moment she'd left the bad agent in the taxi outside the airport in Bucharest and walked inside, alone, she'd been in a kind of daze. Her mind drifted to what had happened there, in the taxi, but then she shook her head. She was tired, that was the problem. No sleep for thirty-six hours. Anyone would feel this way.

She looked longingly toward the line for Americans. The family she'd met on the plane was at the counter already. They were all blond. The boy was ten, the girl six. She'd learned this from brief conversations with the mother. Hannah had shared her cookies with the girl, and the boy had done his math homework, of all things. Even though Hannah was pretty good at math, she couldn't imagine an international flight being so boring that you could do your math homework.

The line moved forward. In a few minutes, it would all be decided. If she could get a kind immigration agent, she might make it through, but none of them looked all that kind.

There was an Asian man with a too-large shirt, an Asian

woman with a too-tight bun, two black male officers, and one older white male officer. It seemed odd to Hannah, entering America, that only one of the officers was white. She studied the two black officials with interest. In all of her life, she'd seen only one black man in the flesh, strolling along Ştefan cel Mare Boulevard. People had pointed and yelled, but he'd acted like he didn't see them. Everyone said he was an aid worker.

The white officer crooked his finger at a Moldovan family at the front of the line. The man shuffled toward him, leading his tiny wife and two young girls. They looked hungry. Hannah had seen families like this one when she'd visited the village where her mother had grown up.

The officer slid his glasses down his nose as he examined their papers. This was not a good sign. Anyone who put glasses on the end of their nose was mean. But she hoped they'd make it through. The mother was wearing several sets of colorful clothes, including two bright headscarves, probably to save room in the suitcase, because the husband and children were only wearing one set of clothes each. She was such a contrast to this plain white room that she made Hannah miss Moldova just a little.

The white officer pointed to the door of the interrogation room. The father bowed his head and walked to his fate. His family followed obediently. No! *Anyone but the white officer*, Hannah thought, scanning the others. She picked the Asian man because of his too-large shirt—it made him seem vulnerable somehow, and she figured he'd be softer with her.

Two more people and then it was her turn.

The good agent, Olga, had told her to look the immigration

officer in the eyes so that she'd seem trustworthy. Olga had also told her to smile, and then said, never mind, she was much more beautiful when she didn't smile. Hannah ran her tongue over her crooked top teeth. They made her look less American and more like an outsider than anything else, but there was nothing she could do about them now.

She squeezed together the fanning pages of her novel, *Anna Karenina* by Tolstoy, and looked down to make sure the fake Russian passport and the real student visa were still tucked neatly inside. Her father had given her this book when she was just eight, and it reassured her now to hold it. She felt as if she were a little girl again, holding his hand to cross the street. That was long before he and her mother were killed, when times were good and he still read to her every night.

The older Russian woman was called. Now it was just the man with the scratching problem and then her. Five minutes and it would be over.

The fact that she'd have to lie was the most terrifying part. The new name and the fake passport weren't her idea, but she was doing what she had to do. Along with the fake documents, the bad agent had given her a list of instructions to get through American immigration. She could not mess up her new name. She could not say she was from Moldova. And she had to act Russian. Whatever that meant.

Fortunately, her family was Russian and she spoke only Russian with her babushka and most of her friends, who were mostly Russian too, even though the majority of her schooling was in Romanian. The official state language was Romanian, but because Moldova had been ruled by the Soviets for nearly fifty years, older people spoke mostly Russian, younger people spoke mostly Romanian unless they were Russian, but everybody spoke a little of both for communication. She'd been practicing her English, too, and she wasn't horrible, so she should be able to avoid a translator.

If they got a translator for her, she'd have to slow down her dialect, and make it less clipped and more formal. Every country from the former Soviet Union had a slightly different Russian dialect and a good translator would be able to tell where she was from within seconds.

The bad agent had told her she'd make it through if she wasn't too stupid. Pig. She was smarter than he was, she knew that much.

She repeated her new name in her head like a chant. *Elena Platonov. Elena Platonov. Elena Platonov.* In the tiny bathroom on the plane, she'd stood in front of the mirror and repeated it out loud at least fifty times, but the name had sounded like a lie every time she said it.

She smoothed the frizzy little hairs flying out of her ponytail. *Elena Platonov. I am from Moscow. I want study English. I stay with uncle.*

The man in front of her stepped forward. He got the Asian officer with the big shirt. Panicked, she scanned the other officers, trying to pick another one to wish for, but before she had the chance, she heard "Next." The white officer was bending his finger at her, like she was a bad child. She gulped down the saliva gathering in her throat. Her feet would not move.

Her mother's words came into her head. *Stand up tall. Be*

proud of who you are. Hannah held her chin up, pulled her shoulders back, and stepped toward him.

She cleared her face of any expression: eyes straight ahead, cheeks flat, mouth relaxed but closed. After her parents were killed in the bombing, this was the mask she'd worn to shield herself from all the stares—if she could make it through that, she could make it through this.

Once she got to the counter, she opened her novel, slid out her documents, and gave them to the officer. Her hand was shaking. She looked at him quickly, worried he'd seen, but he was already flipping through her passport. He slid his glasses down his nose and examined her picture. As if suspecting a fake, he rubbed the picture with his forefinger, and then his bluish gray eyes shifted up and he examined her face with an intensity that reminded her of her grandmother, whom she affectionately called Babulya. She would not be able to lie to him.

"What is your purpose for coming to America?" he asked.

Her mind went blank. She understood him but couldn't think of a single way to respond. He repeated the question.

"Study." The word burst out of her mouth, as if she didn't know how to speak English at all. She formed a sentence. "I want learn English."

"You only have a three-month visa," he said.

"Yes." She had practiced an explanation for this with the good agent.

"How do you think you're going to learn English in three months?" he asked.

"I am good student," she said.

"Are you going to stay here *longer*?" he asked.

Longer. This meant something was bigger, like a shirt or nails. She made a guess that he was talking about the length of time and then remembered what Olga had instructed her to say. "If it is necessary," Hannah said, lifting her chin up, "the school will obtain extended visa."

He moved on. "Who will you be staying with?"

"M-my relatives," she said, gulping at the lie.

"What kind of relatives?"

This was not a question she'd studied. She stared at the reflection of fluorescent lighting in his reading glasses on the end of his nose and tried to make sense of his words. Did he want her to describe their personalities or their jobs? He tapped his gray pen twice on the counter. He looked down at her fake passport, then back up at her, and pursed his lips. He was going to get a translator, she thought, and then they'd figure out that she spoke Russian with a Moldovan accent.

"Repeat please," she said.

"Your aunt?" he asked. "Your cousin? Your father?"

When he said her father, she felt her heart pounding like an old woman punching dough into bread, but she finally understood. "I stay with uncle. He have wife and two children."

He looked up. "Where are your parents?"

She couldn't say they were dead. Olga had said this would bring more questions. The trick was to seem as uncomplicated as possible.

"They are in Mol—" She froze. In her attempt to lie about her parents being alive, she'd nearly said Moldova. She felt dizzy with fear. Her face flushed. "Moscow."

He looked her straight in the eyes and seemed to know everything in that moment. Her heart thumped. *Please,* she thought, *please, just help me.*

He gave her a grim smile and flipped back between her visa and her passport. She waited. He lifted a stamp—one that would likely send her to the interrogation room, and then, once they found out who she was, off to a small island in the middle of nowhere for suspected terrorists.

He banged the stamp down on her passport with such force it made her jump. He folded her visa and tucked it in the passport. "Study hard," he said, handing her the documents.

She knew "hard" was the opposite of "soft," but she had no idea what this had to do with studying. It was best to agree. "Yes."

"Okay," he said, as if he was expecting her to do something.

She pointed at the beautiful arched entrance into America and he gave her a quick, impatient nod.

She tucked the fake documents back into her book and continued past the counter, walking as slowly as she dared, even though she wanted to run. Electricity shot through her arms and legs; her whole body buzzed. She wanted to laugh and cry at the same time. Finally her life was turning around. A smile crept to her face, but she covered it with her hand, in case someone was watching.

CHAPTER TWO

Hannah tucked her documents in the handmade pouch around her waist, pulled her dirty white shirt over top, picked up the old brown leather suitcase that had belonged to her father, and pushed on the metal doors to exit the baggage area. She jerked to a stop.

On either side of her was a red velvet rope, like they had for the Oscars, which she watched every year on TV. Beyond the rope, maybe a hundred people were waiting, including several men in suits waving signs with names in big block letters.

People darted past her, shouting and waving at long-lost relatives. An older Russian mother with spiky maroon hair rushed forward and embraced what looked like her grown American daughter. They rocked back and forth, weeping silently. Hannah stared at them for a long moment, despite herself, and then took a step forward. This was where she was supposed to meet the family.

And then she saw it. On a small placard, in among all the others, was her new name—Elena Platonov—in bright red letters. A man was holding the sign. Not a family.

She thought about striding past him to find a bathroom, but he'd already spotted her, probably based on the photo she'd sent. His bright blue eyes shone with recognition and he jerked his hand up in the air and smiled at her like she was a long-lost relative, like he was about to grab her and rock her back and forth.

Hannah walked slowly toward him. At least he didn't look like a pimp or a creep. He had a thick head of reddish blond hair and wide shoulders like an athlete. His smile was Russian, tighter than an American smile, with his teeth clenched together. He was dressed in a black sports jacket, jeans, and a tucked-in blue dress shirt. His nose was on the large side, not perfect, which she always thought was a good sign. People with perfect noses could never be trusted.

But how could she know for sure that he was okay without seeing the family? The first and last time she got in a car with a strange man, it had been the biggest mistake of her life.

She considered her babushka's last piece of advice to her before she'd left Moldova. Babulya had grabbed her hand just as she was going up the steps to the bus. Her grip was surprisingly strong for her age. Hannah had looked down at her, startled. Babulya's once brilliant green eyes were coated with thin white cataracts that threatened to cast her into darkness, and Babulya gazed up at her, drinking her in like she might never see her again. *Don't worry,* Hannah had thought. *I will get your eyes fixed.*

Her babushka spoke: "Listen to your nose, my girl."

"Okay, Babulya," Hannah had said, though she didn't know how this would help her. She had what most people would call a very good nose, but it wasn't an excellent nose; her mother had had an excellent nose. In Gura Bicului, the village where her mother had grown up, she was famous for having smelled the first sparks of a fire in a house halfway across the village. At her parents' funeral, at least ten people had talked about how her mother had saved the village.

It would be cool to have that kind of a supernose, the kind of nose that saved people, but for Hannah, her nose was a bit of a nuisance. It made foul smells so much worse, and even nice smells could be irritating if they were too strong.

She stopped a few feet away from her new boss. He smelled of sweat and cologne that had been applied earlier in the day, which probably meant he wasn't trying to impress her. This, at least, was a good sign.

"Hello, sir," she said in Russian, using the polite form. "I'm Hannah."

"Call me Sergey," he answered. "It's nice to meet you." He spoke in Russian, but he held his hand out to shake hers like an American.

She wasn't used to shaking hands—it wasn't normal for girls or women to shake hands in Moldova—and she worried about the smell that would come from her armpit, but she had no choice. His handshake was warm and strong, though his hand was awfully calloused. How did a businessman get hands like that? She tried to let go, but he kept shaking it, gazing into her eyes.

"Welcome," he said, and she noticed he had a habit of speaking through his smiling yet clenched teeth. It seemed odd. "Welcome to America."

"Thank you."

He still wouldn't let her go. "You are a beautiful girl," he said, shaking his head as if he couldn't believe it.

Her face flushed. People never said she was beautiful. Except for Katya. But she was her best friend, so it didn't count.

He released her hand, laughing. "Let's go," he said, and picked up her suitcase, which she thought was another good sign. He was a real gentleman.

CHAPTER THREE

Hannah felt like she was floating on a cloud. She was sitting in the front passenger seat of Sergey's black BMW convertible. The wind flipped her ponytail around as Sergey dodged other slower cars leaving the Los Angeles International Airport. It blew away the trouble in Moldova, the pain of the last year, everything that had happened. She was flying.

Her whole life, she'd either walked or taken buses that jerked her from side to side, bumping over the hundreds of potholes dotting the city streets of Chişinău like acne scars on a beggar's face. Sergey had even asked her to wear a seat belt, which made it feel more like a gypsy carnival ride than a form of transportation.

If only Katya could see her now, or even better, be here too. A few days before she'd left, she'd gone out with Katya for some trout and cream cheese pizza, which was their favorite. It always made Hannah think of her mother, who used to put everything from the refrigerator on a pizza—carrot salad, crumbly brinza cheese, potatoes, plums—and somehow still made it taste delicious. After the pizza, they'd gone to an American action movie. A little bit of Moldova, Katya had said, tossing her blonde hair, and a little bit of America.

As they left LAX, the BMW sped past a set of blue glowing pillars, which seemed strange and glamorous, because Americans could afford to light up random pillars. In Moldova, most of the streets didn't have streetlights, even in Chişinău, the capital. And here, there were palm trees everywhere—like a tropical vacation. Hannah wanted to pull out the elastic on her ponytail and let the wind flow through her wavy hair, but she worried it wouldn't seem professional.

"Did you have a nice trip?" Sergey asked.

She nodded. "Yes." The flight was good, at least, and she'd left the rest behind.

All the signs on the street were in English. No more Russian. Good. Her plan was not easy, but she knew she could do it. First, she'd take English classes at night and during the weekends. Once she understood everything, she'd finish her last year of high school at a night school in Hollywood that she'd read about on the Internet at Katya's house. She'd get top grades and then she'd get a student loan to go to medical school, and she wouldn't have to be a nanny anymore.

Sergey's cell phone rang from a neat compartment on the dash. He slid it out and answered in Russian. The phone was surprisingly large, and it had a big screen. In Moldova, everyone wanted the small ones.

He drove onto the freeway, darting around other cars while talking fast on his cell phone. It was getting dark and a bit cold. Hannah crossed her arms over her body. Sergey glanced at her, saw her shiver, and turned up the heat. It was such a kind and simple act, it made her want to cry. She leaned into the hot air.

It blasted against her face while the cold wind whipped around her. The car's lights shone on graffiti covering the insides of overpasses, and she remembered a program on television that claimed the excessive graffiti in American streets proved how backward the country was. There was some graffiti in Moldova, but not nearly this much.

She listened to Sergey on the phone; she couldn't help herself, even though she knew it wasn't polite. His Russian accent was clipped, like the accents of Moldovans who spoke Russian, though it was a little different, and then she caught the telltale "h" sound where a Russian would use a "g" sound. He had to be Ukrainian.

"We had some problems at the bank," he said to the person on the other end. "They want someone else to secure the loan. The bank manager says we're overleveraged." It sounded like he was having money problems, but that was impossible with this fancy car.

Sergey exited the freeway and stopped at a light. The air stank of tar and gas and pollution. She spotted three nail shops on different corners of the street, and one doughnut shop. Three young, darker-skinned men were waiting at a bus stop, gazing at the BMW the same way young men in Chişinău looked at elites when they sped past in their Mustangs and their Hummers—with a mixture of anger, jealousy, and admiration.

Sergey pushed a button on the dash and the convertible's soft top slid over them and clicked in above her head. The lock by her elbow slid down. She wondered why he'd put the top up and locked the doors. Perhaps this was a bad area.

"I'm dropping the girl off now," Sergey said into the phone. "You can see her later."

Hannah's breath caught in her throat. He'd just locked her in and now he was going to drop her off somewhere. Where was she going, and who was coming to look at her?

The light turned green, and the BMW tore off down the street. Sergey slid his phone into the space on the dash. She stared at him with her green eyes opened extra wide; she was giving him "the eye," as her ex-boyfriend Daniil had called it. Daniil said it was unnerving the way she could look at someone when they'd done something wrong, and Sergey seemed to feel the same. He glanced at her, and then looked away with a frown. He had the look of a guilty man.

Her heart raced, and her cheeks flushed. She felt ill. He'd been so happy she was attractive because he could get more money for her. He was bringing her to a brothel, just as Katya had warned.

She imagined having sex with twenty men a day. That was the number she'd heard. She'd break in half. She was nearly a virgin.

When they stopped at the next light, she looked down at the lock on the door and considered jumping out. She wondered if she could undo her seat belt and unlock the door before he grabbed her. Probably not.

And what if he was really taking her to the family? Even now, after everything, she still couldn't believe that the good agent had lied to her so convincingly. She decided to ask before she risked her life jumping out of the car.

"You're dropping me off somewhere?" She could hear an edge of hysteria in her own voice, but she managed to keep her face flat and expressionless.

"At home," he said, as if everything was normal. "My wife and I are going out for dinner."

She glanced at the clock. It was eight thirty—late for dinner. "Do you live near here?"

"We are farther north and east. Ten more minutes. This is the south part of La Brea."

"Oh." Hannah let out the breath she'd been holding. She was starting to feel silly. She wondered why he'd looked guilty. Had she just imagined it?

"You can make a sandwich. I think the children have eaten."

She heard the word "children" and dropped back into her seat. He was a father. He did have a family. "Sure," she said. She had to stop letting all the warnings from people back in Moldova get to her.

When she first told Katya she was going to America, Katya had been furious with her. They were walking along the wide sidewalk of Ştefan cel Mare Boulevard near the park and Katya had pointed at a large poster on the side of the office building. "That's going to be you," she'd said, tossing her long blonde hair away from her face and glaring at Hannah.

YOU ARE NOT A PRODUCT, it said. The poster depicted a minia-ture woman in heels struggling in the palm of a giant hand. It had been drawn by a girl at Hannah's school—she'd won a contest as part of a campaign to stop the trafficking of Moldovans around the world.

"Katya, my uncle's wife knows the agent."

"Still."

"The mother of the family is a doctor. And it's not like I'm going somewhere in the Middle East. I'm going to America."

"Why don't they hire someone who lives there already?" Katya asked.

Hannah shrugged. "Maybe there aren't many people who speak Russian who want to do that kind of work. Olga said the mother wants someone who speaks Russian."

"You think all the Russians who live there are too rich to take care of children?"

"Maybe they don't want to live with a family," Hannah said.

Katya stared at her in disbelief. "Even if it's a real job, you're going to hate it. You don't even like to do dishes."

"I'm not going to wash dishes forever." Hannah felt a surge of anger that Katya couldn't be happy for her, but then remembered how Katya had stuck with her after the bombing, when so many others had abandoned her. She had to be honest with her best friend. "I need this, Katya." Her voice cracked. "I don't have anything. If I don't do this, I'm stuck here. I'll be nothing."

"You would never be nothing." Katya's cheeks sagged a little and Hannah had a glimpse of what she might look like in ten years.

"Cheer up." Hannah linked her arm in her friend's. "When I come back, I'll be rich. We'll drive around in my new BMW."

At the time, they'd both laughed at the thought that Hannah would ever be able to afford a BMW. But maybe it wasn't impossible, Hannah thought. After all, she was sitting in one now. Four hundred dollars a week plus room and board sounded like an impossible fortune in Moldova. But not in America. Together, she and Katya had watched endless repeats of *Sex and the City*, so they both knew that lots of people in America spent that much on going out for dinner.

Sergey drove for another five minutes in silence. Elegant streetlights out of some old English storybook replaced the neon signs of a few blocks back. Clothing stores with mannequins and restaurants with white tablecloths replaced the doughnut shops and nail salons.

"What do you think of LA?" he asked.

She tried to think of something to say. All she felt was a tentative relief that he wasn't dropping her off at a brothel. She cleared her throat. "I like the palm trees."

"Developers planted them here. Los Angeles is actually a big desert."

So the palm trees were like her. Transplants.

"Look," he said, pointing up the street at the famous grassy mountainside with the large white block letters: HOLLYWOOD.

"Wow. You live close to here?"

"Not far."

Maybe she could walk to the Hollywood sign. Touch the letters. That would be something to tell people back home.

After a few minutes, Sergey turned down a quiet street with modest houses and green lawns. It wouldn't have been remarkable except for the small spotlights on many of the lawns. If she had a million dollars, Hannah thought, she would not light her bushes.

Sergey stopped in the driveway of a white stucco house with a red Spanish tile roof. It had two stories, but it was smaller than both of the neighboring houses. It had a short palm tree in the center of the lawn, with lights around it, like the other houses on the street. It was strange that he'd parked in the driveway, instead of the garage. It would have been cool to see the garage doors open like in the movies and then drive inside.

The car door unlocked and Sergey got out.

Hannah opened her door and followed him down a path to the steps by the front door. It seemed like a normal neighborhood, not a place for a brothel, but she'd feel better once she saw the family.

A blast of noise came from behind her. She turned around and saw a silver car zipping down the street, rap music blaring. The car screeched to a stop in front of the next-door neighbor's house.

Loud female laughter burst from inside the car. It was a Mercedes.

A blond-haired boy heaved himself out of the car, shaking his head as if he was embarrassed. He wore low-hanging, oversize jeans and a large American football jersey, which didn't conceal the large rolls of fat around his belly. He seemed close to Hannah's age, but it was difficult to tell in the dark.

There was no way a brothel was located right next door to an ordinary American teenager's house. His house was pink, which was a strange color but made it look friendly. They had two floors as well, and on their lawn, there was a tree with bright pink flowers, which seemed to glow in the car's headlights. They did not light their bushes.

"See you later," a girl called from inside the car. Hannah couldn't believe a girl her age could have a Mercedes, even here in America.

"Catch you later," he said.

Catch you later. Hannah repeated the phrase in her head. You can catch a ball, but how do you catch a person? She gazed at the boy. Maybe they could hang out.

The boy glanced over at Hannah. He grinned and lifted a hand like he was taking an American pledge. Hannah lifted her hand in response, but then decided that he couldn't be waving at her because he didn't know her, and quickly dropped her own hand, hoping he hadn't seen.

Sergey was taking her suitcase out of the trunk. He grunted out something that sounded like "hello." Hannah wondered if he could speak English.

The girl's car backed up fast and zipped down the street. The boy glanced at it once more, walked up the drive, and heaved himself up the steps to his house. Hannah knew she was staring, but she couldn't stop herself. The boy was fascinating. He pulled out a set of jangling keys, unlocked the door, and opened it just wide enough to squeeze through. It looked like he was sneaking into his own home.

Sergey came around the BMW and rested one hand on her lower back to guide her forward. The unnecessary touch made her nervous. She took a large step away, though she tried to be casual about it so he wouldn't notice.

Sergey passed her and unlocked the door. Inside, the house

was really dark. He waved his arm to usher her forward. She stepped past him into the house. The front door banged shut behind her.

It was pitch black. Hannah glanced over at Sergey. He was coming at her, reaching for her neck. She shielded herself with her arms and screamed.

CHAPTER FOUR

In the dark, Hannah listened to Sergey's raspy breathing. He stepped back and cleared his throat.

"I was turning on the light."

She could smell his sweat. She'd scared him. Her voice came out of her in a whisper: "Okay."

He reached past her to flick on a switch, lighting up the foyer with a glamorous chandelier. She felt foolish, like when she turned on a light after a nightmare and realized it was a bad dream, nothing more.

Sergey laughed, but it sounded forced to her. "You see?"

She did see. If this was a brothel, it was a brothel for very rich clients. There were no strips of wallpaper peeling off the walls, no cracks in the hallway closet door, no water spots on the ceiling. To her left, there was a large, winding oak staircase to a landing where she could see an enormous bouquet of what she knew were fake flowers because otherwise she'd smell them. Past the foyer, she could see an enormous living room with wall-to-wall white carpeting, a large white sofa and armchair, two matching glass end tables, and a glass coffee table with gold legs. On the far wall, there was a black entertainment center, huge speakers, and a gigantic flat-screen television.

All that white furniture would turn black with two children running around, but it didn't have a single mark on it. "Where are your children?" she asked in a high-pitched voice.

"They are coming now." He glanced at the front door, as if he wished they would appear at that moment. "They were at a friend's house with their mother."

"Oh." She looked around furtively for toys or something that would belong to a child.

"You can find some slippers in there, I think." He waved at the hall closet but kept his distance as if he were afraid to get too close.

She took off her black dress shoes, opened the closet, and crouched down to place them on the mahogany rack beside the other shoes, which were lined up perfectly, toes in, heels toward her. And then she saw them. Tiny blue running shoes and pink sandals with little flowers on them. Slowly, she stood up.

Sergey kicked his shoes off into the closet, not bothering to place them on the shoe rack. She noticed he was wearing clean black socks without holes. Socks told a lot about a person.

She was so embarrassed, acting like a fool, screaming at this nice man. Not all men were like that bad agent. "I haven't slept for almost two days," she rushed, trying to explain herself. "There was a television playing for the entire overnight bus trip from Chişinău to Bucharest." It had played episodes of the popular Russian soap opera *My Beautiful Nanny*, in which the nanny falls in love with the father, so she didn't tell him what she was watching. "And of course I couldn't sleep on the airplane." She wanted to say that she was sorry she'd screamed, but it was so embarrassing now that she hoped he'd just forget it.

He laughed good-naturedly. "I remember those televisions. So loud. You can never get anyone to turn them off."

At least he didn't seem to be holding her erratic behavior against her. She reached in the closet for a fluffy pair of pink slippers. "Your wife won't mind if I use these?" she asked.

It was customary in Moldova to have extra slippers on hand for guests, but she didn't know which ones were for guests and which ones belonged to his wife.

"Go ahead, she's not an ogre," he said.

That was a strange thing to say, Hannah thought, sliding her feet into the slippers. They looked new. Maybe there was an older pair.

"I have to get changed for dinner." Sergey gestured to the living room. "You can sit."

With that, he hurried up a curved oak staircase off the foyer. Hannah stood at the arched entrance to the living room, hesitating. The white leather sofa was so pristine.

A car engine sounded outside. She knew she should wait, but she was curious. She opened the front door and peeked outside. A large navy blue SUV was coming up the driveway. A blonde woman gripped the steering wheel, beautiful in her stoniness. In the backseat were two children. Hannah squinted at the shield on the grille of the car. Was that a Cadillac? Her father would have loved seeing all the cars here.

Hannah stepped back inside the house and closed the door, her heart beating faster now. She felt awkward in this woman's house with her husband upstairs before she'd even met her. It was a backward way of doing things and felt wrong somehow.

One of the car's doors opened and then another, and Hannah heard a shout and little-person shoes running up the outside steps. A curly-haired blond boy, around two years old, burst through the door and stopped just before he slammed into Hannah. He looked up, feet planted together, and stared into her face, his large blue eyes widening.

"*Privyet*," Hannah said, "hello" in Russian.

He let out a loud, terrified scream.

She stepped back. "Ah!" she cried. The little boy ran out.

"*Ah-yai-yai, zaitchik*," the mother said in Russian at the bottom of the steps outside, softly, calling him a little rabbit. Hannah smiled. Her own mother used to call her that too. The woman strode into the house, holding the boy, whose face was buried in her bouncing honey-blonde hair. The woman's nose was one of those perfect noses, not too long like Hannah's. It had no bumps or curves, and the nostrils were evenly shaped. Hannah chose not to see this as a bad sign, because the woman was smiling and she had the most beautiful hazel eyes with specks of amber in them, and laugh wrinkles in the corners. She looked American, not Russian at all, Hannah thought. She wore little makeup, just some mascara and pale pink lipstick. Her yellow blouse was tucked into jeans with a shiny black belt cinched in tightly; black heels matched the belt, and she had a short yellow silk scarf tied around her neck like a movie star.

The mother ran her hand over the little boy's curly hair. "I see you have met Michael. He'll warm up, don't worry," she said in Russian. Then she held out her hand to shake Hannah's. "I'm Lillian." Even though she spoke in Russian, she used the American version of Liliya.

Hannah reached out her hand and tried to squeeze tightly, as Sergey had shaken her hand earlier, but Lillian's handshake was like squeezing bread dough.

"You must be tired from your trip," Lillian said, examining her with the kind of sharp eyes that were perfect for a doctor. "Would you like to have a shower?"

Hannah knew her body was casting off waves of sour odor—she could barely stand herself. "Yes, please, if it's all right with you, ma'am, I would like that," she said, using the polite form of "you" in Russian.

"Don't be so formal," Lillian said, meaning she should use the familiar form. They were so much friendlier than she'd thought they'd be. It was a tremendous relief after all the warnings from people back home.

A girl of around eight or nine marched through the front door. She had hazel eyes just like her mother, and her dark hair was pulled back with two matching fabric barrettes. "Do you like rap music?" the girl demanded in English.

"Uh," Hannah stammered, "y-yes." This girl was so American. It was hard to say why Hannah thought this; maybe it was the relaxed but emphatic way the girl moved her body, or maybe it was her casual yet expensive-looking clothing: jeans and a green shirt with a large ragged purple flower sewn on the front. Hannah hoped this girl was less spoiled and more disciplined than the American children she'd seen on television.

"This is our daughter, Maggie," Lillian said in Russian, and then chastised Maggie. "No English. Elena doesn't speak English." Hannah wanted to correct her about the name, but it wouldn't be polite in front of her children.

Hannah switched to English. "It is nice to meeting you, Maggie."

"I'm eight—how old are you?"

"Seventeen."

Lillian rested a soft hand on Hannah's arm. "Russian only, please."

Hannah looked at Lillian, alarmed that she'd already done something wrong, and switched back to Russian. "Of course."

"She gets so much English in school," Lillian explained. "I'm afraid she'll lose her native tongue. We speak only Russian at home."

Only Russian? She hadn't come to America to speak only Russian, and clearly the girl preferred English.

"Sergey!" Lillian called.

Sergey came into the entranceway and took a pair of black dress shoes from the closet. "Ready?" he asked his wife.

Lillian rolled her eyes in frustration. "We can't go."

"Why not?"

She gestured at the little boy, who was still burying his head in her neck. "We can't leave Michael with her yet. He's scared of her. You know how he is."

Hannah felt terrible that she'd already scared the boy. She'd never been the girl with swarms of children around her. The one time she babysat for her cousin's baby, it was a disaster. The baby cried for three hours straight.

"Come on, Lily." He gave her a look of exasperation. "I'm starving."

"There will be plenty of time for us to go out once he's used to her. Why don't we take him and pick up food? Michael can fall asleep in the car and the girl can take a shower."

Hannah pressed her arms harder against her sides and wished she'd taken a moment to run into the bathroom when she first arrived at the house. Lillian probably thought she always smelled this bad.

"I'm staying," Maggie said, planting her hands on her hips.

"Fine. You can show her around," Lillian said, then turned to Hannah. "Don't give her any candy. It's too late and it will go to her brain."

"Mo-om."

"Russian, Maggie," she said.

Sergey picked up Michael and walked out the door with him. Lillian shook her finger at Hannah and Maggie. "Be good," she said, then closed the door.

Maggie looked up at Hannah and grinned.

CHAPTER FIVE

"You want to see my room?" Maggie spoke English with a perfect American accent. "My mom just had it redecorated."

Hannah nodded, even though she had no idea what Maggie was talking about.

"Come on." Maggie grabbed her hand and tugged her up the spiral oak staircase.

"Your mother said we have to speak Russian," Hannah reminded her in Russian, though she was secretly glad Maggie seemed willing to break the rules.

"She said *you* can't speak English, remember?" Maggie said in English, glancing back, her hazel eyes sparkling wickedly. "She didn't say *I* couldn't."

"True." Hannah decided to stick to Russian for now, at least until the family was used to her.

At the top of the stairs, Maggie pulled her down a hall with a long, expensive-looking Oriental rug, threw open the door to her bedroom, and flung her arms out. "Ta-da!"

She had a real pink princess room, the kind of room girls in

Moldova only saw in American movies. In the center of the room there was a pink canopy bed with sheer pink curtains around the outside, and cozy white pillows and a white duvet inside. And one entire wall was filled with small, pink wooden cubes, each holding a separate doll—there had to be at least fifty of them. It was the biggest doll collection Hannah had ever seen.

"Wow," Hannah said, in English, entranced. She walked across the room and reached for a particularly old doll, maybe even an antique. The doll had pink cheeks and thick blonde hair, curled under and stitched in at the scalp, and a frilly yellow dress that looked handmade.

"Don't touch that!" Maggie screeched in Russian.

Hannah pulled away her hand fast, as if the doll had burned her. "Why?"

Maggie continued in Russian, "You can't move them."

"You don't play with them?"

"I play with them, but I have to put them back in the right cube, and if you mix them up, it's going to take me ages to figure it out, and they can't be messed up." She blinked her bright hazel eyes, obviously upset, though Hannah still didn't understand why.

"They're only dolls," Hannah said.

"My mom doesn't like it."

But everyone's house got messy. Hannah thought of the piles of junk they'd had on the balcony of their old apartment back home.

"I'll show you my brother's room." Maggie grabbed her hand and tugged her out of the room.

"He has his own room?" That was strange. In Moldova, all small children slept with or near their parents.

Michael's room was painted dark blue with a poster of a red Porsche on the wall, and he had his own television and DVD player, like an American teenager.

Maggie waved at a room down the hall. "That's my parents' room."

Hannah glanced through the open door at the biggest bed she'd ever seen. She wondered where she was going to sleep.

"That's my father's office," Maggie said, pointing at a closed door. "You're not allowed to go in there."

"Why not?" Hannah said.

The door looked like an outside door; it was the kind that locked with a key. She'd never heard of such a room inside a house.

"You'll get in trouble," Maggie said.

"No one is allowed to go in?" Hannah asked.

"My mother just said you're not, in case it's not locked." Maggie blinked her long, dark eyelashes. "But my father doesn't usually let me and Michael come in either."

Next to the office, there was a small, pretty room with a single bed covered with a red and yellow flowery bedspread. Hannah paused at the doorway. "Is this my room?" she asked, figuring it must be, since it was the only room left.

"You're going to sleep in the playroom downstairs." Maggie tugged her past the pretty room and down the elegant staircase. "Well, it was a garage and now it's a playroom." That explained why Sergey didn't park in the garage, Hannah thought. Maggie switched back to English. "Cool, huh?"

Hannah nodded, though she'd never been in a playroom, and she didn't really want to sleep in a garage.

"Come on. I'll show you the kitchen," Maggie said, dragging her the opposite way down the hall.

"That's the bathroom." Maggie waved at a closed door next to the kitchen.

Hannah realized she was desperate to pee. She'd been holding it for too long. "Wait," she said. "I have to use the bathroom."

"I'm hungry," Maggie said.

"I'll be fast."

Hannah grabbed her suitcase from the front door, walked down the hall, and went into the bathroom, which she knew her mamulya would love. She'd always wanted a nicer bathroom. Hannah could imagine her mother clapping her on the back, saying, *Good for you, Hannah.* Mamulya had never been one of those people who were happiest when they were miserable. She'd go on about the crisp white tiles and hot water, and she'd laugh with delight at the white American toilet paper. Moldovan toilet paper was brown and stretchy so that ten inches could be expanded to twenty if you were desperate.

Hannah locked the door and sat down on the toilet, amazed at how much extra space she had for her legs. In her old apartment, they had a separate small room for the toilet, and her father used to complain that he couldn't even sit down without his knees banging against the door.

"Hurry," Maggie said in English, leaning against the door. "I'm hungry!"

Hannah stood up, undressed, and folded her dirty clothes beside the sink. Her body was sore from what had happened in the taxi before she got on the flight, and when she looked at herself in the clear mirror, and inspected the damage, she felt the horror of it rush upon her like a blast of city wind filled with the debris of the street. She shook her head. No. She would not think of it.

Taking in a shaky breath, she glanced at the huge bathtub. A nice, long bath was just what she needed, but she'd have to wait. Instead, she washed herself off in the sink and then used one of the hanging green towels with lace to dry herself.

Maggie's body banged on the door and Hannah panicked that she was going to burst in while she was naked. Quickly, she pulled on a fresh pair of underwear and her other bra, which had a tear in the front, but at least it was clean. Maggie let out a long, low groan.

"One more minute," Hannah called, as she took her toothbrush and toothpaste out of her makeup bag and brushed her teeth.

"Are you taking a bath?" Maggie called back through the door in English. When Hannah didn't answer immediately, she asked the same question in Russian. Hannah noticed her Russian didn't seem quite as fluent as her English.

Hannah spit out the toothpaste. "I'm just washing up."

"Don't use the towels with lace," Maggie called. "They're for decoration."

The lacy green towel was now wet and wrinkled. Hannah smoothed it out, hoping it would dry before the parents got home. When she stepped out of the bathroom wearing her new

American jeans and the green button-up shirt that matched her eyes, Maggie looked her up and down, examining her. "Cool shirt. Come on. I'm starving to death."

Carrying her suitcase, Hannah followed Maggie into the largest kitchen she'd ever seen. It had slick granite countertops, new wooden cabinets, a central island, shiny silver appliances, and pristine white tile floors. They even had a dishwasher! She couldn't wait to tell Katya.

Even Katya's family didn't have a dishwasher, and they had the nicest kitchen Hannah had ever seen, with cupboards her mother had ordered from Italy. You could put wet plates on the bottom shelf and the water dripped down into the sink. Very high-tech. But Katya would be impressed with this kitchen for sure. Hannah's family's apartment was rented, so it had old cupboards with fading varnish, peeling wallpaper, and a small counter with a crack running through it. Their kitchen was always clean, though, and the dishes were put away, even though many of them were cracked. Somehow, Hannah doubted this family had cracked dishes.

Maggie opened the refrigerator. It was packed with food. Hannah wondered why Lillian needed to pick up dinner with all this food in the house.

"Do you always eat this late?" Hannah asked.

Maggie began digging past the soda cans. "Only in the summer."

"No candy," Hannah reminded her.

Maggie rolled her eyes. "I know."

Five minutes later, Hannah didn't know how it had happened, but she'd already broken the first rule. She and Maggie were eating coconut-flavored sirok bars: sweet, frozen brinza cheese covered with chocolate. She'd suggested other options—salami, cheese, yogurt, apples, oranges—and all had been rejected. Maggie only wanted the sirok bar, which wasn't exactly candy but was close enough.

"You don't eat it like that," Maggie said in Russian. She switched back and forth between English and Russian as if they were just two different pairs of shoes.

"Like what?" Hannah asked, licking her lips self-consciously.

"You don't bite ice cream," Maggie said in Russian. "You lick it or you suck it."

"That doesn't seem very polite," Hannah answered, thinking how she'd always been taught not to put food into her mouth and take it out.

"In America, it's polite." Maggie switched to English. "You look weird."

Hannah frowned. All the rules, even table manners, contradicted what she'd been taught. She didn't want to seem weird. She knew that word—it meant you were different, in a bad way.

A bang outside made Hannah stop chewing. Was that a car door?

The front door opened. "Hello!" Lillian called.

They were home!

Hannah panicked. She grabbed Maggie's sirok bar and tossed it in the garbage along with her own. Lillian's soft slippers padded down the hall. Hannah looked at Maggie, and her heart thumped. Maggie's entire mouth was covered in chocolate.

CHAPTER SIX

illian strode into the kitchen and jerked to a stop. Her hazel eyes fixed on Maggie, who gave her a guilty smile with her chocolate-covered lips.

"What are you eating?" she asked.

"A sirok bar." Maggie pointed at Hannah. "She gave it to me."

"You know better than that, Maggie." Lillian glanced over at Hannah, annoyed. "Dessert is for after dinner."

Hannah stood up to explain. "I tried—"

Sergey came into the kitchen carrying two plastic bags of food. The smell of rotisserie chicken wafted from them, making Hannah's mouth water. "What's wrong?" he asked.

Michael squeezed through his legs, stretched his arms out like a superhero, and let out a screech as he flew around the kitchen. Sergey and Lillian shared a smile, but then Lillian waved in Hannah's direction, still angry.

"She fed Maggie a sirok bar before dinner," Lillian said.

"Ooh," Sergey said, sarcastically. "That's a first."

Michael stopped. "I want sirok," he said, looking up.

Maggie gulped down the rest of the sirok bar that was in her mouth.

"Did you finish it?" Lillian asked.

Maggie shook her head slowly. *Oh no*, Hannah thought, sick to her stomach. She felt like Raskolnikov in *Crime and Punishment*, waiting for her crime to be discovered.

Lillian tried to look around Maggie, expecting it to be hidden behind her, and held her hand out. "Give me the rest."

"I don't have it." Maggie's eyes widened in fear, which made Hannah's heart start to beat faster.

"Where is it?" Lillian asked.

"In the garbage." Maggie pointed at Hannah. "She threw it there when you came in."

Lillian opened the garbage can and looked down. Her face turned red. She pulled out one of the unfinished bars and shook it. "Is this what you do in Moldova?" she asked, her voice shaking with rage. "You waste good food?"

"I'm sorry," Hannah stammered, digging her nails into the sides of her jeans. "Maggie wouldn't eat anything else."

Sergey cleared his throat. "Don't worry about it."

"Don't worry about it?" Lillian turned to him and barked, "Paavo warned us about her, but you insisted."

Who was Paavo?

"Come on, Lily." Sergey rested his hand on his wife's shoulder. "She's a good girl." He spoke firmly, with conviction, as if he'd known her for more than a few hours.

Lillian shrugged his hand away. "She's already lied!"

"It's not really—" Sergey began.

"Hiding something so you don't get in trouble is lying. You, more than anyone, should know that," Lillian said, glaring at him.

It took only the smallest gesture, just a half shrug with one shoulder, but it was like a lit match to a rag covered in gasoline.

"Goddamn it, Sergey!" Lillian flung the sirok bar across the room toward his head. He ducked. Maggie flinched.

The bar hit the wall behind the kitchen table and slid down, making a long brown streak on the white paint before it dropped onto the floor. Lillian stared at it, as if she'd surprised even herself.

Michael laughed. Everyone else was still.

"I'm sorry," Hannah whispered.

Lillian turned to her. "You are not going to teach my children to lie."

"I won't. Really. I'm sorry." This was terrible. She was just about the most honest person she knew. Just a few months ago, she'd found a wallet lying on the ground with the equivalent of forty American dollars in it, and she'd returned it, even though everyone said she was crazy. Katya said that anyone with that much money in their wallet had tons more and she should give it to her babushka, maybe pay some bills. Hannah had flushed with embarrassment, sure that Katya somehow knew that they hadn't paid the electric bill for two months. Since her uncle Vladi had gone missing, they didn't have enough money, and the power had been turned off in their apartment. They'd had to use candles for the last month and put ice in the refrigerator to keep the food cold. And still she'd given back the wallet.

"I want bar!" Michael yelled, stamping his feet.

Lillian bent down and picked him up, gently smoothing his curly blond hair back away from his face. "Dinner first."

"Bar now!" He flailed and tossed his head back.

"No!" she barked, and put him back on the ground. Michael started thrashing and screaming on the floor.

Lillian opened a drawer, slid out a washcloth, and wet it under the faucet. Then, she took careful steps across the room, around the flailing boy, and slowly wiped the dirty wall in little circles. Michael stopped to watch along with the rest of them, whimpering so they wouldn't forget about him. Sergey rested his hand on Maggie's back. When it was clean, Lillian walked back to the sink, rinsed off the cloth, and hung it in the cupboard below.

Maggie stalked out of the room, looking annoyed, and Sergey began opening the containers filled with potatoes, roasted chicken, and what looked to Hannah like a broccoli and pasta salad, though perhaps she was wrong. That was an awfully strange combination of foods.

"You need to set the table," Lillian said to her, pointing at the cupboards. Her voice was calmer now, as if nothing had happened. "The dishes are in there. You can find the utensils in the large drawer."

Hannah stood up fast. The sudden motion made all the blood rush to her feet, and for a moment, she couldn't see anything but black. Her body wobbled. She reached out to grab the glass kitchen table. Her vision came back before anybody noticed. She'd never been awake this long in her whole life.

She carried the dishes to the kitchen table. Michael was still moaning and whimpering on the floor, but everyone was still ignoring him, so she did the same.

"Not that one," Lillian barked. "Through the door."

There was another room off the kitchen. Hannah opened a sliding wood door and gazed at a beautiful maple dining room table, brand new with no stains or scratches.

Lillian came up behind her with a white tablecloth, which she stretched across the table. "I'll show you where to find everything tomorrow," Lillian said. "I don't want my table to be ruined."

Hannah set the table as Katya had taught her, hoping that she remembered it right. After it looked ready, she stepped back and admired the gleaming, matching perfection. Lillian came up beside her in the doorway, holding Michael on her hip. His cheeks were shiny with tears, but he was smiling because he was eating a sirok bar.

Lillian looked displeased. Hannah followed her gaze to the table, wondering what she'd done wrong. Katya had taught her the Western way to set a table before she'd left, but maybe she'd left something out.

"Elena, I see you didn't understand me."

This definitely wasn't the time to correct her about the name. "I'm sorry?"

Lillian continued, "You'll be sitting in the kitchen."

Hannah's words stuck in her throat like a hard piece of old celery. She could feel tears tugging at her eyes, and finally, she managed to speak. "Of course." She rushed to remove her utensils and her plate, and turned to get out of the room before she burst into tears like a fool.

Lillian was still standing in the doorway. She touched Hannah softly on the shoulder, as if she felt sorry. "We need our private family time. I hope you understand."

Hannah had imagined helping this mother throughout the day and thought she'd be included in all family activities. It hadn't occurred to her that she'd be just a nanny, nothing more, not part of this family, not part of any family. That wasn't how the agent, Olga, had put it.

"I'm sorry I threw out the bars," Hannah rushed. "I don't— that's not normal for me."

Lillian nodded briefly. "It's fine." Michael renewed his escape efforts, wiggling and kicking, and Lillian stepped to the side to put him in his high chair.

Hannah hurried into the kitchen, where she eased her plate, glass, fork, and knife down onto the table, trying not to make a sound on the glass. Since she couldn't seem to stop making mistakes, she stood by the table and waited until they told her what to do.

"Sit," Sergey said.

She sat. He took her plate from the table and she worried that once again she'd made a mistake. Maybe they didn't think she should eat tonight? Then he filled the plate with a large serving of the pasta salad and a leg from the chicken and put it back down in front of her.

"You're too thin," he said. "Eat."

It was unbelievable that he'd served her. Men didn't serve food, and certainly not to their employees. On top of that, he'd given her the leg. In Moldova, dark chicken meat was what everyone preferred, and young people never got it. She'd have to write Bab-ulya and tell her about it. The chicken leg alone would reassure her that she was with a good family.

Sergey headed into the dining room, carrying the pasta salad and chicken. The door slid shut behind him.

The smell of the food was making Hannah's stomach growl. She reached for her fork and was about to take a bite of the chicken when the doorbell rang.

"Who's that?" Lillian asked.

A chair scraped on the hardwood floor. "Paavo," Sergey said, opening the dining room door. "He wants to see her." He looked at Hannah, his brow creasing, and then strode through the kitchen and down the hall to the front door.

She put her fork down. It was like they'd bought a new TV and their friend was coming to see it, except that she was the TV.

She pushed her chair back and stood up so she could look this person in the eye.

CHAPTER SEVEN

The man was a hippopotamus. Sergey had seemed large before, but he looked small compared to this man, whose neck was as thick as one of Hannah's thighs. The man was wearing billowing gray dress pants and a black shirt, unbuttoned to the third button, revealing black chest hairs on sickly white skin. He had on white socks, no slippers, and smelled of French cologne, sweet cigars, and a yeasty body odor.

His little black eyes examined her.

"So, you're the girl," he said in a brusque dialect—not Ukrainian but not Russian either. Siberian?

"I guess," she said with a shrug, trying to pretend she didn't care.

"This is my friend Paavo," said Sergey. "He introduced us to your agent and helped us with the documents."

"Which agent?" Her voice squeaked, but neither man seemed to notice.

Paavo leaned against the counter and looked her up and down. She gave him her cold stare, the same one she gave to any man who couldn't keep his eyes or his hands to himself.

"Elena." He said her fake name like a statement, as if it was permanent, not temporary. She wondered if the fake name had been his idea. He poked a fat finger toward her. "You better work your knuckles off, girl. The Platonovs are good people. You're lucky to be with them."

He reminded her of the bad agent, the way he pointed at her. His nails were just as long. She looked away, trying not to cringe. She'd left the bad agent behind when she'd gotten on the plane to America, but he was following her still.

"I will work hard," she said, making the promise to Lillian and Sergey, not their creepy friend.

"Maggie, how are you doing?" Paavo boomed.

Maggie was peeking out of the dining room. Her face was shy, maybe even scared.

"I brought you something." He rummaged around in the roomy front pocket of his large pants and pulled out a wrapped lollipop.

"Thank you." Maggie took it, then stepped backward fast, leaning into her mother, who rested her hand on her daughter's shoulder. Hannah wondered if Lillian felt protective of Maggie around Paavo.

"Are you staying for dinner?" Lillian asked. Hannah studied her face to see if she wanted him to stay. It was blank, not overly inviting.

He glanced toward Hannah's plate like he was going to take it. "No," he said at last. "Rena is waiting."

The phone rang and Lillian hurried into the living room to answer it. Maggie returned to the dining room, sucking her lollipop. Paavo stood by the counter and Sergey offered him a beer from the refrigerator, which he accepted. From the dining room,

Michael started screaming, and Sergey yelled for him to be quiet. Hannah stayed by the kitchen table, uncertain whether she should help Michael or stay out of the dining room altogether.

Paavo murmured to Sergey in a voice too low for Lillian to hear from the living room, but loud enough for Hannah's ears. "When I saw the picture," he said, "I couldn't believe you wanted her. But now I see, you don't disappoint me."

Hannah was confused. Paavo was implying that Sergey had requested her specifically, before Olga had found her for him. But she didn't know Sergey. She'd never seen him before in her life.

"Come on." Sergey laughed it off. "She's here to clean our house and take care of the children, so Lillian can study."

Paavo gazed at her. "The pretty girls never work as hard."

"She'll be fine." Sergey gave Hannah a tight smile.

Thank God she hadn't ended up with Paavo. He was speaking about her as though she were a piece of juicy meat that he'd like to wrap his tongue around.

"What did Lillian say?" Paavo asked.

"Lillian's a beautiful woman. She can handle it."

"You'll hear about it later," Paavo said.

Michael screamed again from the dining room. "Candy!"

Hannah took this opportunity to hurry out of the kitchen. In the dining room, Maggie was waving her lollipop right in front of Michael, taunting him.

"Maggie!" Hannah said sharply. "Give him a lick."

Maggie glanced at her, as if considering saying no, but then she reached the lollipop out and let him lick. Michael reached forward and grabbed the stick away.

"Hey!" Maggie said, reaching for it.

Hannah let Michael suck on the lollipop for a moment. "That's enough," she said, prying it out of his hands. "Maggie, you can have it after dinner, like your mother says. Eat your chicken."

Hannah stared at Maggie's food, her stomach rolling about. She spooned some more salad onto Michael's plate, intentionally spilling some on the table, which she shoved into her mouth. Maggie watched her but didn't say anything.

Lillian came into the kitchen, having finished her call. "Are you certain you don't want a little food?" Hannah heard her ask Paavo. "A snack?"

"If I don't go," Paavo laughed, "Rena will kill me."

Lillian and Sergey laughed a little too forcefully at that, which made Hannah curious about this Rena. She was glad Paavo was leaving. He reminded her too much of the bad agent. Her foot started to twitch under the table, and she wrapped her arms around herself.

As they said good-bye at the front door, Paavo's voice boomed loud and clear down the hall, as if he wanted Hannah to hear, "Make sure you get her documents. Don't let her rip you off like Alexei's girl. And Lily, you lay down the rules. Be tough at the start or she'll walk all over you."

Hannah listened to the quiet creak of their slippers on the wood as Sergey and Lillian walked back down the hall toward the kitchen, and she discreetly let her hands drift down to the bottom of her button-up shirt, making sure the pouch with her documents was safely hidden.

CHAPTER EIGHT

Hannah ate in the kitchen. In the other room, Sergey and Lillian were talking in low voices, probably about getting her documents. Hannah tried to listen, but she couldn't catch what they were saying. At least she was still wearing the pouch with the documents hidden around her waist.

She'd already made the mistake of giving up her real Moldovan passport, the only document that proved who she really was. If she didn't want to give them the Russian documents, she'd have to lie, though the thought of lying more, especially to Lillian, made her sick to her stomach. Katya was a better liar—she'd know exactly what to say and how to say it. She always said a good lie needed just the right amount of details, and it also had to have some truth in it.

Hannah sighed. Her eyes felt heavy and her whole body ached. Now that she was sitting down, all the traveling and the lack of sleep hit her. She finished the chicken and took a bite of the potatoes, but she was too tired to chew. She pushed her plate away, folded her arms in front of her, and rested her head.

Just for a minute. They'd never know.

The smell of the chicken brought back a memory of her mother cooking in the kitchen in Chişinău, wearing her sunflower apron. She was singing a Russian folk song, flipping a cut-up chicken with potatoes, carrots, and onions sizzling in the same pan. Her long dark hair was swinging down to the small of her back, as her thin body swayed back and forth. Hannah was drinking tea, reading a book, not even really appreciating the moment. She didn't know it would be the last time she'd hear her mother sing.

Hannah was jerked awake by the sound of a door sliding open and male laughter. The whole family was looking down at her. She sat up, blinking.

Sergey laughed. "The poor girl, she is too tired."

Hannah rubbed her eyes. How long had she been asleep?

Lillian was frowning. "All that good food."

Hannah reached for her fork. "I'll eat it."

"We'll save it for you." Lillian took Hannah's plate away. "You need to sleep. But first, why don't you give us your documents and your plane ticket? We'll keep them in a safe place."

"No," she burst out. They stared at her. What had she just done? Her brain felt groggy. She wanted to trust them, she really did, but she didn't want to make another mistake. If she gave them the documents and the plane ticket, she'd have no way to leave if she didn't like it here.

"I can't," she stammered. "I lost them."

"What?" Lillian glanced at Sergey.

Hannah stared at her suitcase, remembering that the plane ticket was in the suitcase, not in her pouch. She felt ill that she hadn't thought to hide it, but it was done now. She had to go on. "I left my purse at the airport. It had everything."

Lillian squinted at her in disbelief, then looked down at the suitcase.

Hannah thought about the truth that must be in any lie. "I went to the bathroom and I left it there. It's a white leather purse with tassels." She really did have a purse like that, but she'd decided it was too old for the trip to America.

"Why didn't you tell us earlier?" Lillian asked.

"I only just realized, after you started eating, and I figured it had probably been stolen by now, so I didn't think there was anything we could do."

"Mom, can I watch TV?" Maggie said, as if this was boring to her.

"Give Michael a bath first," Lillian said, then opened a drawer and heaved a thick yellow phone book onto the counter. She flipped through it and ran a polished pink nail down the page.

A few minutes later, Hannah heard Michael giggling in the bathroom down the hall. The girl was just eight and she helped give her brother a bath. This was a good family. She wished she'd just given them the documents. Why couldn't she trust someone for once?

Lillian picked up the phone and dialed. "Give me Lost and Found." Hannah was impressed at first by how fluent she was, but then, when she continued, her English was slow and halting. "I pick up my husband niece from airport two hours before and she leave purse in bathroom. It have passport, visa, airplane ticket."

She listened and asked Hannah in Russian, "Which bathroom?"

Hannah had to think quickly. "Between immigration and when I came out. By the baggage area."

After a pause, Lillian said, "Elena Platonov." She nodded a couple times as if the person could see her. "Okay," she said, like "ahkay," which didn't sound right. Hannah remembered her English teacher drilling them on that "o" sound, lips forward, like they were kissing.

"Do you want me to talk?" Sergey asked, reaching for the phone.

Lillian stepped back, gave the person a phone number, and hung up. "Don't insult my English," she said, poking him with a smirk on her face. "You speak no better than I do."

"That's true." He laughed. "What did they say?"

"No one has turned it in. They'll call us if they find it."

She believed her. Hannah let out a sigh.

Lillian frowned. She'd caught her sigh. Of course, Hannah thought, she wouldn't be relieved if she were innocent—she'd be disappointed they hadn't found her purse.

Lillian looked down at the suitcase by Hannah's feet. "I need to look in your suitcase."

"It's not in there," Hannah said, mortified that Lillian was going to look through all of her things, especially her old underwear and the pictures of her family.

"If it's not there, you don't mind if I look."

"Here? In the kitchen?"

"Why not?" Lillian said.

"She could unpack her bag in the playroom," Sergey suggested. "Where she'll be sleeping."

"Whatever," Lillian said, glancing at him with irritation. "Come on."

They led her down the hall and around the corner, past a washer and dryer and through a door. It didn't look like a playroom to her—it looked like a garage. It had some old shelves filled with toys and a parking lot of children's riding toys and bicycles. Next to the door was a sofa with a sleeping bag and a pillow, where she was presumably going to sleep. There were no windows, and the two garage doors were chained up. Was that so nobody could get in or so she couldn't get out? It felt like a prison, and the pink and blue braided children's rug in the middle of the cement floor did nothing to soften this feeling.

"I wish I could sleep in the playroom," Maggie sighed from behind her while Hannah stared in horror at what would be her room.

Lillian laughed. "No, you don't. After ten minutes, you would be running up the stairs and coming into our room."

"No, I wouldn't."

Hannah glanced back at Maggie. Hannah had always slept in the same room as her parents and she'd never had a nightmare that she could remember, not until they died. After that, she'd had the same one every night. In the beginning, it had left her shaking and sobbing for an hour or even more, with Babulya rubbing her back the whole time; but now she simply got up, splashed cold water on her face, and went back to sleep.

"That's where you'll sleep," Lillian said, pointing at the sofa. "You can put your things in those boxes."

Hannah saw she was referring to some empty cardboard boxes piled next to the sofa. She couldn't believe she had to sleep in a garage. What about the room upstairs?

"Your suitcase?" Lillian said, trying to take it from her.

Hannah glanced at Sergey, embarrassed that he was going to see her underwear and fabric sanitary pads, and looked back at Lillian. "I have private things."

Sergey spoke up: "I won't look."

Reluctantly, Hannah put the suitcase on the sofa and unzipped it, hoping Lillian wouldn't see the front pocket where she'd foolishly put the flexible return plane ticket because it was too bulky for the pouch under her clothing. Lillian sifted through the suitcase with the tips of her fingers as if Hannah's things were too disgusting to touch. Maggie and Michael crowded in. Hannah sat on the sofa beside her suitcase and bit nervously on her lip. Michael grabbed at Hannah's shiny blue belt, and Lillian swatted at his hand. "Dirty," she said.

"Nothing's dirty," Hannah said, insulted. "Except for my traveling clothes."

"We will get you new things."

Hannah wanted to say that her things were just fine, thank you very much, but she kept her mouth shut. It was true that the hems of her pants were pretty dirty from when she'd stepped in a mud puddle before she got on the bus. Lillian winced as she picked up her traveling clothes and placed them on the rug. *Do you want to get your surgical gloves?* Hannah thought. *It's just a little dirt.* Moldovan dirt. Without realizing it, she'd brought Moldova with her. She wondered if she should flake it off and keep it somewhere, though of course that was silly.

Lillian flipped the suitcase shut in frustration.

Sergey came in. "Nothing?"

"No."

Sergey didn't say anything, but he smiled that tight smile of his, as if to say *I told you so.*

Hannah held her breath, hoping she wouldn't think about the front pocket. No luck. Lillian unzipped it and reached inside.

Hannah felt her insides groan like an old building.

Lillian pulled out the picture of her parents first and glanced at it briefly before handing it over. Her parents were sitting on the large granite steps that went up to the National Opera House with its large concrete pillars. Her papa had his arm around her mama, who was smiling that wide smile of hers. They were happy back then. Papulya used to be a mechanic, but he was so much more than that. People joked he was the most literary mechanic they knew. When she was just six, he'd started reading all the great Russian literature to her: works by Chekhov, Dostoyevsky, Gogol, and Tolstoy. At first she didn't understand the words, but she loved to hear the passion in her father's voice. Then, when she was just twelve, her father's father died in police custody—beaten to death by the police for no apparent reason—and her sweet Papulya had abandoned his books and turned instead to the bottle.

"Can I see?" Maggie asked.

Hannah handed her the photo, even though she didn't want to. Maggie looked at it, her eyes opening wide. "That's your mother?" she asked.

Hannah nodded, wondering if Maggie knew her parents were dead. She dreaded having to answer more questions, but then Maggie handed the picture to her father, who gazed down, longer than she would have expected, out of politeness, probably.

Lillian handed her the picture of Katya. "Pretty girl," she said, then pulled out the picture of Daniil at the Black Sea. He looked sexy wearing his Speedo. On impulse, Hannah had taken it from her desk and slid it in her suitcase, though she regretted it now.

"Boyfriend?" Lillian asked.

Hannah shook her head. She and Daniil had been together for three years, and he'd told her he wanted to marry her, but when her uncle Vladi disappeared, she had to finish school at the end of eleventh grade instead of twelfth. It was a perfectly acceptable grade to graduate, but all her friends were continuing to twelfth, which would count as a first year of university. She would have liked to do the same thing, but she had to go to the market every day to help her babushka. It was the responsible thing to do, and she planned to take night classes, but Daniil told her he wanted someone more ambitious, like he didn't know her at all.

Lillian handed Daniil's picture to her, and Hannah pressed it facedown on her lap.

Next, Lillian pulled out Hannah's keys to her apartment and dangled them in the air. "What are these for?"

Hannah shrugged. "I forgot I had them." She knew it was

crazy to bring her keys for the apartment, since Babulya was moving to her uncle Petru's house in a couple of days, but she'd carried them everywhere she went for as long as she could remember.

"Why didn't you have them in your purse?" Lillian asked.

"That's why I forgot about them," she stammered.

Lillian tossed them on the sofa and Hannah snatched them up. The keys were familiar in her hand and calmed her.

The plane ticket was near the bottom. Hannah held her breath. Lillian pulled out *Anna Karenina* and raised her eyebrows at Hannah. "You're reading this?"

"It's my favorite book," Hannah said, her voice shaking. The only thing left was the plane ticket. Lillian reached back inside.

Hannah had to distract her somehow. She waved the book in the air. "Have you read it?"

"Of course I've read it," Lillian muttered, reaching deep in the pocket. Hannah cringed as she pulled out the plane ticket. "Look what I found," Lillian said to Sergey, raising her eyebrows.

"I forgot about it," Hannah rushed to explain. "Now I remember it was too big for my purse, so I put it there."

"It must have been a small purse." Lillian gaped at her. "Now I see what Paavo meant about slippery Moldovans. Why didn't you tell us you had the ticket?"

"Honestly, I thought it was in my purse." It sounded lame, even to Hannah's ears.

"Where are the passport and visa?" Lillian planted her hands on her hips.

"In my purse. Definitely." She licked her lips and then

remembered that Katya said you should never lick or bite your lips. It looks like you're lying. Her face flushed and her eyes watered, giving her away again and again. It was so clear she was lying that she wanted to give up, but she stumbled on, like a runner whose legs have cramped up. "You can see I don't have them."

"Empty your pockets."

Hannah reached into her pockets and felt the pouch through the thin fabric. If Lillian tried to check in her pockets, she'd feel the pouch, so she turned the empty pockets inside out.

"Let me see your bra," Lillian said. "Sergey, turn around."

"Who wants to play with Legos?" he said, walking away and pulling a box of toys from the shelf. Michael ran up and they sat down on the pink and blue rug. Maggie stayed, staring up at Hannah, blinking. Hannah didn't blame her. It had to be fascinating for an eight-year-old.

"Undo your top."

Hannah hesitated, looking down at Maggie. "Can she—?"

"Maggie, go to your father." Reluctantly, Maggie walked over to the rug, and Lillian stared at Hannah, waiting.

This was her body, Hannah thought, her eyes watering. This woman had no right.

But still, she undid the top buttons on her blouse, revealing her old beige bra, which was one size too big and had a hole in the lace, and once again she felt ashamed.

"More," Lillian said.

She gulped down the saliva gathering in her throat and undid two more buttons, all she dared. Any more and Lillian would see the top of the pouch above the waistband of her jeans. Hannah slid the few sweaty lei out of her bra. In Moldova, lots of girls kept spare money in their bras, babushka style.

"You can see I don't have them."

Lillian cupped the outside of her bra, feeling for the documents. She was just inches above the pouch. Hannah sucked in a nervous breath.

"It's okay. I'm a doctor," Lillian reminded her, speaking softly as she dropped her hands.

Hannah promised herself that when she became a doctor, she was never going to use that as an excuse to touch someone. "The documents are in my purse," she said, stepping back to do up her shirt, glaring at her. "If I had them, I'd easily give them to you."

Lillian was staring at Hannah's hands as she fumbled to do up the buttons.

"What do I need them for?" Hannah said, her voice shaking. "I'm already in America."

"My wife thinks she is a lie detector," Sergey said, laughing from his spot on the pink and blue rug. "She should have been in the secret police. She is always looking for the lies."

"I am not," Lillian said, rolling her eyes. Then she looked back at Hannah and spoke to her in a quiet voice, too low for Sergey to hear. "Did someone hurt you?"

The question was so out of the blue, it startled Hannah. She blinked at her.

"You are bruised." Lillian pointed at her chest, above her bra, where there were purple and red marks on her skin.

Hannah's eyes teared up. "I'm fine," she said, stepping backward. Her hands shook as she forced the buttons into the too-tight buttonholes, covering herself up. She didn't want to talk about that.

Lillian was silent for a moment. Finally she said, "We'll call again about your purse in the morning." Lillian picked up the plane ticket and frowned, turning to Sergey. "Didn't you pay a lot more than this for the ticket?"

Hannah, dizzy from exhaustion, found it hard to follow what Lillian was saying. How could they have paid even more? The plane ticket was over eight hundred dollars.

"The fees included the ticket, the agent's fee, and the documents," Sergey said. "It was cheap, really, considering."

"Cheap? Besides the fee, he charged extra for everything, even the ticket."

Was she talking about the bad agent?

"You are in charge of the money," he said, shrugging as he sauntered out of the garage.

"Come on, children. We have to let Elena sleep," Lillian said, waving them out.

She was still holding her plane ticket. Hannah tried desperately to figure out what she could say to convince Lillian to leave it with her. There was nothing.

"G'night," Maggie said to Hannah.

"Russian," Lillian barked.

"Mo-om," Maggie said, heading out to the hall.

Lillian flicked off the light and walked out, carrying the plane ticket with her. Hannah climbed into the sleeping bag with her clothes on, rested her head on the musty-smelling pillow, and looked around the too-dark garage. She was with a good family, she told herself. It didn't matter if they had her plane ticket. She could have done worse, she thought, thinking of the bad agent and that hippopotamus, their friend Paavo. A lot worse.

CHAPTER NINE

Two weeks ago, America was just a place where rich people lived, not a place Hannah would go anytime soon. She'd been working at her grandmother's booth at the open-air market in Chișinău, picking at the red pepper paste stuck under her fingernails, thinking about her ex-boyfriend Daniil, when she'd heard an unusual buzz in the market. The older woman selling strawberries a few stalls down was craning her head to look at something, but the narrow aisle was packed with babushkas in colorful head scarves, teenage girls in micro miniskirts, housewives with square bodies, and men in business suits that had seen better days.

Hannah breathed in and smelled a foreign perfume mingling with the sweat and old cardboard of the open-air market. The crowd cleared and she saw a beautiful Russian woman with auburn hair and Western clothing. The woman was talking gaily to an older man who sold things like coffeemakers, toothbrushes, and towels. The man said something and the woman tossed her head back and laughed. Even though he was one of the most serious people Hannah had ever known, he actually laughed with her, pinching his bulbous nose.

Hannah felt what she called "the ache"—a very real, physical pain in her chest—which happened whenever she saw something she wanted but feared she'd never get.

The woman was one of those people who drew others to them, like bees to plum jelly, the kind of woman Hannah had always hoped to become. She wanted to be one of Moldova's success stories, but she was starting to worry it wouldn't happen.

Just over a year ago, her parents had been killed in a bombing in the breakaway republic of Transnistria. It was predominantly Russian, and its people longed for the days when they had been part of the Soviet Union. Many people thought they'd be better off if they separated and rejoined the motherland, but of course the rest of Moldova didn't want this, and the rebellion had begun. Hannah hadn't wanted her parents to go to the wedding, but it was her father's brother and they didn't have a choice. Hannah had exams, so she didn't go, or she would have died in the café along with her parents, the Minister of Internal Affairs, two of his security guards, a cook, a waiter, and two teenage girls.

When her parents died, she'd gone from being one of the smartest girls in her class, someone with real possibilities, to just another poor girl who worked in the market. She feared that all her friends would eventually leave her, as Daniil had, and she'd be stuck there, selling carrot salad until her hands turned yellow and the expression on her face shifted into a permanent frown.

The woman strode toward Hannah, gliding around the other shoppers, not taking her eyes off her. Hannah swallowed and her heart beat faster. She stepped backward into her booth and rested her hands on the black garbage bags she'd stretched over the old wooden table to make it look cleaner.

"*Privyet.*" The woman smiled at her, a little wider than was normal in Moldova, especially for strangers. "It's nice to finally meet you, Hannah."

Hannah had never seen this woman in her life. She stared at her in confusion.

"I'm Olga, Valeria's friend?" the woman said.

The agent! The night before, Hannah and her babushka had been visiting her uncle, Petru, and his new wife, Valeria, along with her two snotty girls from a previous marriage, who were twelve and fourteen and acted like they were better than everyone else. Valeria had been gazing at herself in the mirror by the hall, primping up her curled-under short blonde hair, and then she'd glanced back at Hannah and told her she knew a reputable agent who was looking for a nanny to go to America. "I recommended you," she'd said. She hadn't given her any more details—she'd just tossed it in the air like a petal plucked carelessly from a flower—and Hannah hadn't taken her seriously because Valeria was the type of person who said things like that to make herself seem important.

"Yes, she mentioned you," Hannah said, crossing her arms over her dirty apron. She wished Valeria had told her that Olga was coming to the market. She would have worn something nicer, maybe even some mascara and a little red lipstick. Daniil had always claimed her eyes didn't need makeup, but Katya said he just didn't want her to realize how stunning she was. Hannah loved her best friend—she always said the right thing, even if it wasn't true.

Olga's jacket didn't have buckles or zippers or bumpy skin, and it smelled of real leather. "Would you like to touch it?" Olga asked, reaching out her arm. "It's from America."

How embarrassing. Hannah realized she'd been gaping at Olga's jacket like some peasant. She reached out to touch it briefly with one finger before dropping her hand back down by her side. "It's very nice."

"You can buy many things like this in America," Olga said. "I hope you know what an opportunity this is."

"I didn't know it was a real thing," Hannah answered, feeling shy, despite herself.

"Well, I'm doing a favor for Valeria," Olga said. "She told me last week your babushka got an eviction notice and she's worried because she and Petru can't afford to subsidize your income, not with two other children to care for."

An eviction notice? Olga was telling Hannah things she didn't even know about her own family, right here in the bazaar where anyone could hear. It was true that money had gotten tighter in the last few months, but Babulya hadn't said anything about an eviction notice. She glanced at the woman in the booth beside her, who sold lettuce, cabbage, and radishes. The woman was staring straight ahead, but Hannah could tell she was listening.

Olga went on, "Ever since your uncle Vladi took off, Valeria says it's been too much for your babushka, going back and forth to the village."

"He didn't take off," Hannah said, her eyes narrowing at the woman.

"Of course not," Olga said softly. "But he's gone."

Hannah's uncle Vladi had disappeared two months ago. One day he hadn't shown up at the apartment with the weekly delivery of carrots and vegetables for the carrot salad. She and Babulya had gone to Gura Bicului to see what had happened, but nobody in the village knew anything. At Babulya's house, they found a terse note on the old table by the woodstove: "I am working in Italy. I'll send money. Vladi." It was in his handwriting, all right, and he'd taken some of his clothes, but it wasn't like him to leave so suddenly, especially after what had happened to her parents just a year before. He was her sweet, funny uncle. He juggled to make the old people in the village smile. He'd taught her how to make Ukrainian eggs and decorate the frames they sold at the booth next to the carrot salad. He had a secret that only she knew, and she had kept it for him. He wouldn't leave her like this.

They'd called the police, but the police couldn't do anything if he wasn't in the country. There wasn't much she and Babulya could do either—just pray that he was all right. Life went on. They still had to eat. Since then, Babulya had to go to Gura Bicului a couple of times a week while Hannah worked in the market. One day a week, they closed the booth and went together to tend to the garden and do whatever was too difficult for Babulya to do alone. Every time, Hannah hoped he'd be there, but the once warm, welcoming house was always empty and cold.

"Your babushka can move in with Petru and Valeria, but they

don't have room for you too. If you stay, you may have to move to the village alone," Olga said.

The village? She was a city girl; Babulya always teased her about wearing gardening gloves when they pulled up the carrots.

"Unless you plan to marry?" Olga asked.

Hannah shook her head. Not anymore.

Olga bought a bag of carrot salad and dipped her finger in to taste it. Hannah rushed to give her a plastic fork, embarrassed that she'd forgotten and Olga had had to use her fingers. A small voice inside said that it wasn't very good manners to use your fingers, but she ignored it.

"Mmm," Olga said. "This is good. But do you really want to spend your life making carrot salad in the village and bringing it to the market every day? Or shall I tell them you are interested in starting an exciting life in Los Angeles?"

Hannah's voice croaked. "Los Angeles?"

Olga gave her a queenly smile and nodded.

This was the first time anyone had said Los Angeles. It sounded too good to be true. She could run on the beach and feel the wet sand between her toes, like she'd seen in the movies. She'd never been to an ocean before, and she'd always wondered what it smelled like.

"They'll pay four hundred American dollars every week." Olga paused to let it sink in. "What do you think?"

Four hundred dollars? "It sounds wonderful," Hannah said, though she was having a hard time believing it might really happen. "I'll have to talk to my babushka, though," she added, knowing Babulya wouldn't want her to go. She'd already lost her husband and two of her children.

Olga frowned. "Perhaps you are not so interested."

Hannah rushed to reassure her. "No, I am. Really."

"We need time to get the documents ready for your travel. You can tell me tomorrow?"

Hannah hesitated, noting how Olga was pressuring her. "That's pretty soon."

Olga continued, "I am doing a favor for Valeria, but you know, if it is not for you . . ."

Hannah told herself that she shouldn't be so paranoid. Valeria knew Olga, and this was a job in America. Not Turkey. Not Israel. Not anywhere in the Middle East.

"Okay," she said. "Tomorrow."

"Good," Olga said brightly, and gave her a wide smile. It was a smile of victory, a smile that made Hannah worry she might have lost somehow.

But before she had much time to think of it, Katya came up to the booth. "Hi," she said, looking curiously at Olga, running her hand back casually over her blonde hair.

Hannah introduced them, and Olga gave Katya a long look before saying, "I'll see you tomorrow, Hannah!"

Hannah told Katya, and of course Katya thought it was a crazy idea. She said Olga seemed sketchy to her, but Hannah figured it was just that her friend didn't want to lose her.

That night, when Hannah was having her tea with her babushka, Hannah asked her if it was true about the eviction notice.

Babulya nodded. "We will do something. Don't worry. How did you learn of this?"

Hannah told her about Olga.

"Valeria told me about this possibility." Babulya nodded and pursed her wrinkled lips. "Do you want to go, my girl?"

Hannah shrugged. "They're going to pay four hundred dollars a week. It's America."

Babulya looked out the window into the courtyard fourteen stories below them for a long time. Then she tightened her bright purple and yellow scarf around her neck. "A stone cannot roll if it is planted to the ground. America will be good for you." She smiled her toothless grin, her face cracking into a hundred wrinkles so deep that it looked like the outside of a walnut shell.

It took only two weeks for Olga to prepare Hannah for the trip. She helped her get her passport, gave her new clothing to wear on the airplane so she'd look more Western going through American immigration, and drilled her with questions the immigration agents would ask her when she entered both Romania and America.

Before she knew it, Hannah was on an overnight bus from Moldova to Romania, staring out at the dark countryside while a television blasted above her head. She'd noticed one other girl, maybe nineteen, who was glamorous looking with long chestnut hair, deep brown eyes, and more makeup than Hannah ever wore, even to the discotheque.

At the border, the passengers were forced to get off the bus and file into an empty warehouse with a central glassed-in office area. They waited and waited. An hour. Two hours. Hannah's legs started to ache from standing so long. She wished she had her book, but she'd left it on the bus.

"Hello." The glamorous girl came up to her and blinked her mascaraed eyelashes. "I'm Ina."

The girl was wearing blue jeans that hugged her long legs and looked just faded enough to be real American jeans, Levi's probably. Hannah wondered if she was a daughter of one of the elites. Her hands were tucked in the pockets of a short, light fur vest, which looked real. Underneath it, she wore a tight tank top, revealing some cleavage, but no more than most girls.

Normally Hannah wouldn't talk to someone she didn't know, but it was different when you were the only two girls at a border stop and you were leaving Moldova for the first time. "I'm Hannah."

"They are taking a long time today," Ina commented.

"This is my first time out of Moldova," Hannah said.

"I go all the time. My fiancé lives in Bucharest. He works at a four-star hotel." Ina raised her sculpted eyebrows. "Do you want to see his picture?" Before Hannah could answer, Ina reached into her purse to pull it out. Hannah looked down. He had dark hair, brown eyes, and olive skin, quite typical looking for a Romanian.

"Nice," Hannah said.

"This is the hotel." She pulled out a flyer with a picture of a crystal blue pool and a bar surrounded by red stools. "I could get you in if you want to hang out."

"Thanks," Hannah said, standing up proudly, "but I'm flying to Los Angeles today." As the words exited her mouth, she nearly gasped at her mistake.

"Los Angeles?" Ina looked impressed.

Hannah felt sick to her stomach. Olga had specifically warned her not to say anything about Los Angeles at this border. She wouldn't have documents for America until she met the second agent. She looked at her watch, hoping the border people would get on with it before she made any more mistakes.

"Do you know why they're making us wait?" Ina asked, like she knew the answer.

"No."

Ina tossed her hair back. "If they delay the bus long enough, they get a bigger bribe."

Hannah watched a robust village woman who was talking to a pregnant woman from the city. The villager bent over and spit on the pregnant woman's belly, three times, for good luck. A British woman standing nearby brought her hand to her mouth, out of shock or humor, Hannah couldn't tell which. Hannah groaned and wished she could tell the British woman that it was something only villagers did.

"What are you doing in Los Angeles?" Ina asked.

Hannah hesitated but figured Ina was just a girl her age. She wasn't going to say anything. "I'm going to be a nanny," she said, lowering her voice, though she was proud she didn't need to tell her that she was working at the bazaar. She had a future now. She had possibilities.

"Oh, well, that's good if you like that sort of thing." Ina stroked the front of her fur vest, over her breasts, as if it were a pet.

"What do you mean?" Hannah asked, insulted.

"Cleaning snotty noses is not my idea of a good time." Ina

looked Hannah up and down. "Listen, you're a beautiful girl. You could make a ton of money as a dancer at my boyfriend's hotel."

Hannah noted that he was her boyfriend now, not her fiancé. "No, thanks." She laughed lightly, even though she felt her chest constrict. "I can't dance." She didn't add that she was going to be making four hundred dollars a week in America for cleaning snotty noses and that it would shame her family if she were dancing half-nude in front of a room of men.

At last, the official came back and turned on a light in the office area. The bus driver's assistant brought the plastic bag with the passports to him and began calling passengers through the glass door, stamping their passports and sending them behind him, through a gate that led outside.

As Hannah waited for her name to be called, she started to get more nervous about Ina. Something about how she'd come up to her and told her she could be a dancer seemed too forward when they didn't know each other.

"Oh, Ina," Hannah said casually. "Don't say anything to the official, okay? About me going to America?"

Something flickered behind Ina's gaze before she smiled. "Don't worry about it."

The immigration official didn't even look at her. He stamped her passport and she got back on the bus, then waited anxiously for Ina to return. Several passengers came before her, but finally Ina got back on, ran her finger over Hannah's shoulder, and continued to the back.

Stupid, Hannah thought. She had to be more careful than

that. A few minutes later, the bus driver got back on and they continued into Romania.

Just after ten in the morning, the brakes on the bus squealed like a chicken with its foot caught in a fence, and the bus turned into a rocky parking lot in a residential area on the outskirts of Bucharest where other buses were parked. They'd arrived at the main bus terminal, where the agent would meet her. Outside it was bright and sunny, a perfect day for flying to America.

Everyone remained seated, waiting until the assistant said they could get off. Ina crept up from the back and plunked down into the empty seat next to Hannah.

"Are you going to the airport right now?" Ina asked.

"I think so." She scanned the faces of the ten or so people who were waiting by the brick bus terminal building, but didn't see any man wearing a leather jacket with a Romanian pin.

The bus driver's assistant yelled for everyone to get off the bus. Ina jumped up in front of the rush of passengers and tugged on Hannah's arm. "Come on."

Hannah picked up her father's suitcase and hurried out of the bus.

The assistant started taking larger suitcases out from under the bus, but Ina didn't step forward to grab a bag, which was surprising because she had only a black purse. Perhaps her boyfriend had all her things. The passengers started heading off with the people who had come to meet them, but nobody approached Hannah.

"It doesn't look like anyone is here to meet you," Ina said.

"No." Hannah looked around, feeling anxious.

"Maybe he's gone," Ina said. "We're over two hours late, you know. What did you say his name was?"

"Volva?"

Ina shrugged.

They stood for another moment and waited. Hannah started biting her lip.

"Are you sure you don't want to come with me? The hotel has a swimming pool."

Hannah thought about all the work Olga had gone through to prepare her for the trip. They wouldn't have done that if they were going to leave her here. "No, thanks. I'll wait."

Ina gave her a quick smile, spun around like a fashion model, and strode toward an expensive-looking black car. An older man sat behind the steering wheel, watching her. He wasn't her boyfriend, that was for sure, but this was a land of complicated relationships. He could be her father, her uncle, her pimp.

Hannah had to go to the bathroom after being on the bus for twelve hours, but she had no idea where it was. The black car was still there, and she could ask Ina, but she didn't want to. She hoped they weren't waiting for her. If the agent didn't show up, she'd just go back to Chişinău.

On the way to the bus depot in Chişinău, her uncle Petru had sat next to her on the minibus and he'd slid her forty American dollars. She'd stared down at it in stunned amazement. She'd never held that much money. He told her to put it in her pouch, and once she'd done that, he rubbed one hand on his balding head and told her it was for any emergency she might have, either here or in America. He'd cleared his throat then and told her she was always welcome at his home. It had been nice for him to say it, even if his wife didn't agree.

An older taxi driver was leaning against his taxi, watching her, a cigarette pinched between his forefinger and his thumb. She didn't like the feeling that everyone was just a little too interested in her. Finally she asked the cigarette seller where the bathroom was.

He pointed to the side of the main terminal building. She picked up her father's suitcase and hurried around the building to a set of crumbling concrete steps that led down to the public toilets. The stench made her stomach turn. At the bottom, two bathroom attendants were playing cards at a small table.

She paid the men four lei out of her bra, went into a tiny room with a toilet, and locked the door with the hook lock. She crouched and started to go to the bathroom.

Mid-pee, she heard a man calling her name outside. "Hannah?"

She hurried to finish, made sure her pouch with the documents and the rest of her money was hidden under the waistband of her pants, and then threw open the door. A man stood at the top of the stairs. He had a regular lean build, hazel eyes, dark brown hair, and white Russian skin. He was wearing a denim jacket. On his lapel was a small Romanian flag pin. The taxi driver came up next to him, smoking a cigarette.

"You Hannah?" the man with the pin asked.

"Yes," she breathed. "I'm Hannah."

"You were supposed to be waiting for me out here." He spoke

in a rough Russian accent and sounded irritated. He had to be the agent, even though he was wearing a denim jacket, not a leather one. She couldn't imagine most people wore Romanian pins on their lapels, and he did know her name. "Let's go."

She ran up the stairs. "What's your name?" she asked, trying to be careful for once.

"Volva," he said, giving her an appraising look.

He had one of those perfect noses. It had no bumps or curves, and the nostrils were evenly shaped.

They walked back toward the terminal. The black car was still there. Volva lifted his hand and Ina waved out the half-lowered darkened window. Hannah lifted her hand, confused, as the car drove off. It was like they were passing her off. From Olga to Ina to Volva. But perhaps it was just a coincidence.

"You know her?" Hannah asked.

He grunted an affirmative response. "Ina went on the bus from Moldova to make sure you arrived safely."

"She didn't tell me that," Hannah said, hesitating once they came up to the yellow taxi.

"It was safer this way," he said, opening the back door for her.

"Why was it safer?" she asked, ignoring the door.

"If you knew it, maybe you would tell the authorities something." He shrugged. "And you didn't need to know."

She looked toward the black car disappearing down the road and back at Volva. Her heart was beating fast. Something felt wrong. Volva jerked his head impatiently toward the door. She hesitated, then climbed in the taxi and sat down on the cracked seat.

At least it was a taxi and not his own private car. A taxi was a luxury she'd never been able to afford in Moldova. Even taking a minibus cost too much for her family. The driver started up the car, turned on some traditional Romanian music, and headed down the road, not waiting for instructions. He already knew where to go.

"You have my documents and the plane ticket?" she asked, gulping down her fear.

"I do." He flattened his hands out on his lap and stretched out his fingers, like a cat flexing its claws, and she noticed his fingernails were long, which was unusual, but at least they were clean and well groomed. She told herself this was a good sign.

While they drove, Volva told her what she should and what she shouldn't do when she was going through immigration at LAX. He bobbed his knees back and forth, and it distracted her, those knees jumping around, hitting her own legs on occasion. She barely paid attention to what he was saying.

At one point, he asked for her Moldovan papers, and she reached into her pouch and gave them to him. He didn't even look at them before shoving them in his pocket. Instantly, she regretted it, but there wasn't anything she could do to get them back until he was ready to give them to her.

The taxi stopped at the back of a long line of taxis outside the Romanian airport. Some of the drivers were leaning up against the taxis, chatting and smoking.

She felt nervous, but she knew she'd keep going. It would be too hard to go back to Moldova and admit to everyone that they were right. She held out a shaking hand. "You have the documents? My plane ticket?"

"First you have to pay me for my troubles," he said, looking down at her waistband where her pouch with the forty dollars from her uncle was hidden.

"I have nothing."

"I saw the money when you gave me the Moldovan passport," he said. "Don't make me take it. Give it to me like a good girl."

She hesitated and then reached into her pouch and handed over the money, praying that he'd give her the plane ticket and she could get out of the taxi, fast.

"Forty dollars? That is all?" He looked incredulous.

"I was told the family would pay you."

He clucked his tongue, shaking his head. "If you want to go to America, you will pay." He unzipped his zipper. "But there are other ways to pay."

CHAPTER TEN

The next morning in Los Angeles, Hannah stood in her loose underwear next to the gleaming white bathtub. She yanked out her elastic and shook out her hair. Still in her underwear, she stepped into the bathtub and examined the nozzle, trying to figure it out. It was an odd, high-tech thing with a lever.

She couldn't wait to have a hot bath. Plenty of people in Moldova had bathtubs, but her bathroom had had only a nozzle out of the wall. Maybe it had once had a bathtub, because there was a small hole in the wall where one could have been bolted long ago, but there hadn't been one as long as Hannah could remember.

The second most exciting part was the hot water. In Moldova, they'd had cold running water, like most other people. Some people had a boiler, but most people had a bathtub, so they could boil the water on the stove and fill it up. In her house, the cold showers she took in the summer were a rushed, panting experience that gave her chicken skin but left her feeling refreshed. In the winter, she didn't attempt showers. Instead, she heated up water in the kettle for warm sponge baths.

Ugh. Stupid nozzle.

The door rattled. "Elena?" Lillian was shaking the door. The pouch that held Hannah's documents was lying on top of her green blouse, right out in clear view.

Hannah hid the pouch under her blouse. "Yes?" she called.

"Do you know how to work the shower?"

She felt disappointed. A bath would have felt really luxurious, but a hot water shower would be a treat too. "I think so."

"Unlock the door," Lillian said. "I'll show you."

"I can figure it out."

"Open the door," she ordered.

"I have to put on my clothes."

"We're both girls," Lillian said, laughing outside the door, with an edge of impatience in her voice.

"One minute." Hannah tied the pouch around her waist and put on her blouse and jeans. She opened the door, and then realized, too late, that the pouch felt a little loose.

Lillian glanced at her hair—probably because it was dirty and the waves were all knotted from the ponytail she'd had her hair in for two days. Hannah walked to the shower to show her that she could figure it out—and to get Lillian out of the bathroom before the pouch fell off. Guessing, she tugged at the lever and water burst out from the shower. As she leaned forward, her pouch loosened. It was falling off! She jerked up and pinned her arms to her sides to hold it in place.

"Oh," said Lillian, oblivious for once. "You know what to do. I thought maybe you would have had to bring water from the well."

"I'm not from the village." Lillian's brow furrowed, and Hannah realized she'd been terse. She felt a bead of sweat form on her forehead. "I mean, in the villages they use wells, but in Chişinău we have running water."

"I forgot you were from Chişinău. Wasn't your father from a village in Transnistria?"

"Yes, he was," she said. "How did you know that?"

"Sergey told me."

But Olga hadn't known, and therefore Sergey couldn't know either. Hannah specifically remembered that Olga had assumed that her father was from Gura Bicului, just like her mother, and Hannah hadn't corrected her.

The pouch slid lower. Hannah held her breath.

Lillian backed out of the room. "Don't take too long."

When the door closed behind her, Hannah locked the door and checked the pouch. It had come untied. That was close. If it had fallen, Lillian would probably have gotten rid of her on the spot, and then what would she do? She'd be in a strange place with no friends, no money, and nowhere to go.

She wondered what else they knew about her and how they knew it. Paavo had implied that Sergey had picked her out. But how? Olga had approached her with the job. She'd never applied for one, and she'd had her photo taken only to get her documents after she'd already been offered the job. It didn't make sense. Perhaps she'd misunderstood.

She put the pouch on the counter and glanced at the door, worried that Lillian had a way to unlock the door and that she'd burst in and see it, but then told herself she was paranoid. Still, when she took off her clothes, she put them on top of the pouch, just in case.

She got into the shower, and hot water pelted down on her skin like a massage in one of those European spas. The last thing she wanted to do was get out, but after a few minutes, she made herself turn off the water, get dressed, and put on some light makeup. She looked at her reflection and smiled. At last, she looked like a normal human being.

In the kitchen, she found Lillian sitting alone at the table, holding a single sheet of paper. "Better?" Lillian asked, with a kind smile.

"I was dirty after all that traveling."

"You have very wavy hair," Lillian said.

Hannah touched her wet hair. "I always wanted straight hair, like yours."

Lillian waved her hand. "Oh, it takes forever to blow-dry so it doesn't look limp. Wavy hair, you can let it dry by itself and it looks beautiful."

It sounded like this stunning woman had just complimented her, but perhaps she wasn't referring to her hair, just wavy hair in general. Hannah couldn't figure things out as quickly as normal. Her brain felt dull, maybe from the jet lag.

Lillian pointed to a plastic garbage bag by the entrance to the kitchen. "I found you some clothes that are more appropriate for work."

Hannah glanced down at the bag and saw a large gray sweat suit on the top. For the summer?

Lillian continued, "And from now on, you won't need makeup. People here are very relaxed; they don't wear it, especially when they're taking care of children."

Hannah nodded, confused. Was Lillian forbidding her to wear makeup or merely saying it wasn't customary?

"There's an alarm clock in the bag to help you wake up by six. Michael wakes up between six and seven. Have a seat." Lillian gestured to the chair across from her, and Hannah sat down. "Eat," she said.

In front of Hannah, there was a piece of toast on a plate. She looked at the toast, worried it had been left there from Sergey's breakfast. "Thank you," she said finally, picking up the cold toast and taking a tentative bite. The toast was dry, like crackers. She'd never had toast like this before—her family didn't have a toaster, so they dipped bread in eggs or butter, when they had it, and fried it in a pan. "Where is everyone?" she asked.

"Sergey took the children to the park." Lillian pointed to a small jar. "There is jam."

Hannah put some jam on the toast and found that it was much improved. "Thank you."

"Can you pour the tea?" Lillian said. A white porcelain teapot had been placed between two small white teacups on saucers.

"Oh yes!" Hannah jumped up too fast and her legs banged on the table, causing the empty teacups to clatter about in their saucers.

"Careful," Lillian said.

Hannah reached for the teapot. It was heavy with tea and hard to hold because the handle was too small. She tilted it over

Lillian's cup and the tea spilled all over the cup, the saucer, and the table. Lillian held the paper in the air, eyebrows up.

"Sorry," Hannah said, rushing to get some paper towels from the hanging roll by the sink. "It must be the jet lag. I'm not ordinarily so clumsy." She said this even though she was actually this clumsy. Her friends always joked about it and moved their beers away from her so she wouldn't knock them over.

"I called the airport. They didn't find the purse."

This time Hannah made sure to look disappointed. "Oh no."

"It's gone. Nothing we can do about it." Lillian tapped her long pink fingernail on the glass table and lifted up the paper. "I've written down some rules. I think they are quite reasonable."

Hannah wondered if she should be taking notes.

"Number one," Lillian said. "You must wake up before Michael so that you can keep him quiet until we wake up at seven, and then you can make breakfast. We eat at eight in the summertime, seven thirty during the school year. I need to study all day, so you'll need to do the cleaning and occupy Michael at the same time."

"What are you studying?" Hannah asked.

"I'm studying for the USMLE, the test that foreign doctors must take here in America," Lillian said, rolling her eyes. It was a haughty gesture that Hannah didn't much like. "There are two tests I must pass, the USMLE Step One and the USMLE Step Two. Once I pass them, I'll get a residency at a hospital and I'll be paid as a doctor in America."

Hannah felt disappointed. "I thought you were a doctor already."

"I am," Lillian said icily. "And I will soon be practicing in America."

Hannah realized she'd touched a nerve and tried to make up for it, gushing, "I think being a doctor is the most honorable profession. One day I hope to get into medical school and become a doctor too."

"What?" Lillian squinted at her, and the edges of her mouth curled up like something was funny. Had she assumed Hannah was some stupid village girl? "What kind of doctor do you want to be?"

Hannah lifted up her chin proudly. "Pediatrician, I think. Maybe emergency room."

Lillian said, "Hmm," and looked down at her list. "Number two," she said, clearing her throat. "The entire house must be cleaned every day, including the laundry. I like a shiny floor and a lemon smell in the house, and I don't like clothes to pile up."

Hannah wondered how she'd get this lemon smell in the house. Her babulya used water to clean the counters and the floors, nothing more.

"Okay," she said, even though she was getting worried. It wasn't that she was lazy, but she'd never done much housework or even noticed whether the apartment was clean or dirty.

"Number three—nobody is permitted to eat outside of the kitchen or dining room." With that, she swept a few crumbs up from the table with her hand and dumped them onto her saucer. Hannah didn't know much about cleaning, but cleaning anything with your hand was bad luck. Her babushka and her mamulya always used a piece of paper or a cloth.

The list went on. "Number four—no telephone use. You don't have friends here, and it's too expensive to call Moldova."

Surely she'd make friends, Hannah thought, but whatever. She'd find a pay phone.

Number five—she could not take the children out of the house without permission, and she had to get permission if she wanted to leave the house herself.

That was crazy. She should be free to go if the work was done. "Why?"

"We don't want you wandering around the neighborhood, announcing your presence. You are illegal, remember? If the police find out about you, they'll put you in jail."

If she'd known about the fake documents from the beginning, she never would have come. "Will I be able to go to school?"

"School? The student visa was only to get you in the country, and anyway, you've lost it. You didn't really think you'd have time to go to school, did you?" Lillian asked.

"Yes," she said quietly.

"Believe me, I've been trying to study for the last eight years. It's impossible to do anything when you have to clean a house and take care of children."

Surely she'd have some time off. "But this is why I came to America."

"I was under the impression you were here to work," Lillian said, a wrinkle forming in the center of her forehead.

"I am," Hannah said quickly, not wanting to upset Lillian. She thought of the four hundred dollars she'd make every week, money that would fix Babulya's eyesight. "But I could take classes at night."

"Maybe. Let's see how you adjust." Lillian took a slurpy sip of tea and continued. "Number six—turn off the air-conditioning when the children are not home. We're adults and we can sweat, but the heat is too much for them. And the garage doesn't have insulation, so you need to keep that door closed. I don't want to waste electricity."

Hannah had never had air-conditioning in her life, so this wasn't a big deal. "Okay."

Number seven. Stay out of the office.

Number eight. Speak only Russian to the children.

"Maggie speaks English very well," she said tentatively.

"Exactly. We don't want her to lose her Russian." Lillian gave her a firm look.

Hannah nodded. Maybe Lillian would relax over time.

"Rule number nine. We don't want any friends coming over, and we absolutely forbid boyfriends. Or boys you say are just friends."

Hannah wondered how she'd make friends anyway, if she couldn't go to school and had to ask for permission to go anywhere. She thought of the boy next door. "Why not?"

Lillian looked up sharply. "A lot of you girls say you want to work, but you spend all your time looking for a husband."

"I'm not looking for a husband." This was the whole point of coming to America, so that she could support herself. If she married one day, it would be for love.

"And finally . . ." Lillian placed the paper on the glass table and flattened it with her hand. "Rule number ten. I don't want you hanging around Sergey. If he talks to you, answer him but look at the floor. He's a man, like any other, and he has male instincts."

Look at the floor? "You don't have to worry about me. I'm not like that."

"I'm not worried."

Hannah thought of Paavo's warning to Lillian the night before and decided that must be why she was being so hard on her.

"The biggest part of your job is keeping Michael away from me. He's too attached, and I can't get anything done. I don't need any extra stress." She cleared her throat. "I have to pass Step One in two months. You don't know how hard it is to relearn microbiology after you've been cleaning diapers and wiping noses for eight years."

"I'll keep him occupied," Hannah said. "Don't worry. You'll pass your test."

"Thank you." She relaxed into her chair and smiled. She looked more beautiful than ever, but Hannah couldn't get rule number ten out of her head. That was definitely strange. *Look at the floor?*

"It must have been difficult for you to leave your babushka," Lillian said.

Hannah nodded. "She's all I have."

"How have you made a living since your parents died?" Lillian asked.

"Working at the market."

"Did you have enough money for food?"

Hannah lifted up her chin proudly. She'd never starved. She

wasn't a street kid. "My babushka grew vegetables in her garden in the village, and we traded the carrot salad she made for whatever we needed."

"But the winters were hard," Lillian said, as if she'd been through them herself.

"We had canning," Hannah answered. "I didn't go hungry." When the canned cabbage, beets, meat, eggplant, and plums had run out at the end of last winter, Babulya traded carrots for bags of beans and they ate beans, carrots, and potatoes for weeks, but she never went hungry.

"Don't worry, we'll take care of you now." Lillian stood up and patted her arm. "Come. I'll show you all my picky little cleaning details."

CHAPTER ELEVEN

By noon, Hannah had already written three pages of notes about things like how to cook broccoli so Michael would eat it and how to work the coffeemaker in the morning. And Lillian still wasn't finished.

In the master bedroom, Lillian plunked down on the bed. She patted the spot on the bed next to her. "Sit down. Relax."

Hannah sat down. She was already exhausted.

"I have a favor to ask," Lillian said, shifting on the bed, running her hand over the down comforter, and crossing her legs in a way that seemed almost flirtatious.

Oh no. "Yes?" Hannah's voice croaked out of her.

"Sergey thinks it's too much to ask."

Hannah inched away, trying not to be too obvious about it. She felt like she had little rocks rolling about under her skin. This was the moment Lillian would ask her to do some sick sexual thing, and everyone back home would be right.

"I stayed in this beautiful hotel in Japan once with Sergey on a business trip when we were still living in Moscow." She paused and let out a nervous laugh. "Every morning, a girl came to clean my room. She brought my breakfast and washed my hands with warm washcloths. And then–" Lillian hesitated, licking her lips, as if she was uncertain about whether to go on.

Hannah was ready to vomit. She'd heard men sniffed girls' underwear in Japan and did all kinds of weird things.

Lillian continued, "She put a chocolate on my pillow."

Hannah waited for more, but when Lillian didn't continue, she said, "I don't understand."

"A chocolate." Lillian strode to her long dresser, pulled open the top drawer, and took out a box of wrapped truffles. "I want you to put one of these on my pillow after you make my bed each day. Just one. And hide the box somewhere."

Only a chocolate.

"Under no circumstances do I want you to tell me where you've hidden the box."

"I can't hide it from you."

"I insist. I will thank you later, believe me."

"What if you're hungry, and you eat your chocolate before you go to bed?"

"That's too bad for me, isn't it?" Lillian flashed Hannah her pale yellow smile. "That's all I get. Just one."

Hannah could see some problems with this situation, but at least she didn't have to wash Lillian's hands with warm washcloths. Then she'd really feel like a servant. Lillian had listed so many cleaning jobs that Hannah had no idea how she'd have time to babysit. Olga had told her that most of the time she'd be babysitting and she'd do some light cleaning. But it looked like the opposite was true.

Later, Hannah was scrubbing the bathtub in the bathroom off

Sergey and Lillian's room, her fingers all wrinkled and raw, when she heard Sergey drop on the bed with a loud groan.

She thought he might start undressing, so she called out, "I'm in here."

The bed creaked again as he stood up and walked to the bathroom. "Yes?"

She glanced back at him standing in the doorway. "I just wanted to warn you."

"Why? Are you going to beat me?" He grinned.

Hannah looked at him in confusion and then realized he was flirting with her. Katya would say something sassy back, but Hannah felt embarrassed and didn't want to give him the wrong idea. What was he looking at anyway? She was wearing the baggy gray sweat suit, possibly the most unflattering clothing known to mankind.

He cleared his throat and seemed embarrassed. Maybe he hadn't meant anything by it. "Lillian has put you to work already?"

"Yes." Hannah continued scrubbing, remembering that she wasn't even supposed to look at him. But if Lillian thought she was going to stare at the floor, she was out of her mind.

He didn't leave. She could smell his sports deodorant right behind her. He was still watching her. Maybe he was looking at the strap on the back of her pouch. The sweatpants were a bit loose. She touched the back of her sweatshirt. The strap was covered, but what if he'd seen her check? She had to find a place to hide the documents, a place where no one would look.

"Sergey!" Lillian said.

Hannah stiffened.

"What?" he said, stepping away.

"Let the girl clean," Lillian said, her slippers slapping across the hardwood floor. She appeared in the doorway and stared down at Hannah as if it was her fault. "Why do you have so much soap? And why are you using the sponge? I said to use the scrub brush."

Hannah stood up, wiping the sweat off her forehead with the back of her soapy hand. The sweat suit was too hot. "I guess I forgot. There are so many things."

"You've only done the upstairs. You need to work faster than that or you'll be up all night." Lillian turned and stalked out of the room.

Hannah cleaned all day. At night, after Michael's bath, she was picking up the bath toys, which he'd thrown around the downstairs bathroom, when a burst of male laughter came through the bathroom window. It was so loud, it felt like someone was in the room with her.

She peeked past the frilly green curtains and looked out. There was a high green fence between the two houses, but from above, she could see a few feet into the kitchen next door. They had no curtains or blinds, just windows wide open with the lights on for the whole world to see.

The blond-haired boy was sitting in a yellow chair at a round, bright yellow table, with his mother and a younger brother, around fourteen, who was the opposite of his brother: skinny with longish dark hair. Probably took after his father. Hannah wondered where the father was. Maybe he was dead too. Maybe he died in one of America's wars, she thought, noting a picture on the wall of a man in a military costume. She wouldn't wish that on anyone, but at least then they'd have something in common.

They were eating a brown dessert, maybe chocolate pudding. "Mom, you've got to lick the spoon," the older boy was saying. He stepped out of view and then came back in, licking his spoon with his whole tongue. "Look." He tilted his face up and hung the spoon on his nose. He wasn't holding it or anything. Hannah leaned in, mesmerized. She'd never seen anything like it and wondered if it worked better with some noses than others. The whole family seemed to have upturned noses and oversize nostrils.

The mother was licking her spoon with her whole tongue. There was no way Hannah's mother would have done this, and it amazed her that any mother would. In Moldova, mothers were too busy or too serious, and sticking your whole tongue out like that, well, it wouldn't be polite. Hannah kind of liked it that Americans weren't so worried about being polite or doing what everyone expected, but it also made them a little unpredictable.

The mother's spoon stuck to her nose. "I got it," she screeched. "I got it. Hurry."

The younger brother got his spoon up too. Yes! They had it— all three of them had spoons on their noses. It was miraculous. Then the mother's spoon fell and they all burst into laughter. The older boy laughed with his whole body, clapping one hand on his thigh again and again, head down, belly shaking. Hannah grinned.

Lillian came into the bathroom and looked over her shoulder, tisking.

"They're funny," Hannah said, glancing back at her.

"Strange, you mean. They make so much noise, it drives me crazy."

Hannah released the curtain. Lillian looked at her firmly, as if she didn't want her to start acting too American. "You still have to wash the kitchen floor and take out the garbage."

Hannah nodded, glancing at the clock on the wall in the bathroom. It was nine thirty. All the rooms had clocks.

"The rest of the house looks clean," Lillian said, smiling briefly, before she walked out of the room. Hannah listened to the laughter coming from next door. She couldn't remember ever hearing her neighbors' laughter in Moldova.

It was eleven thirty before she finished working. She climbed into the sleeping bag on the sofa in the hot, windowless garage and stared at the haphazard shelves of toys. This job was going to be much tougher than she'd expected, but it would all be worth it when she got her first four hundred dollars. It would be a glorious thing, that moment when she held the crisp American bills in her hand. She wondered how they would pay her—with four one-hundred-dollar bills or maybe twenty twenty-dollar bills. After three weeks of work, Babulya would get her operation.

She smiled to herself. Just when it seemed like life wasn't going to get better, it did. She closed her eyes and fell into such a deep sleep, it was as if she'd been hit on the head by a good old American baseball bat.

CHAPTER TWELVE

I t was after midnight. Hannah had been in America for one whole week. She wanted to collapse on the musty-smelling sofa in the garage, but there was something she had to do first. She'd stayed up an extra hour to make sure everyone was asleep.

There were no sounds coming from the bedrooms upstairs. It was safe. She reached under the sofa for the packing tape she'd hidden earlier in the day and then crept across the garage. After Lillian had told her that she really didn't like playing with the children's toys, Hannah had decided the toy area would be the best place to hide something. Everywhere else was risky because everything was super organized, but Lillian didn't like to come in here. Toys made her cringe, she'd said, and not once in the last week had Hannah seen her sit down on the floor with Michael to play with him.

Hannah took a small board book called *Goodnight Moon* from the bookshelf, taped the passport in the back, and closed the book. Nobody would ever guess it was where she'd put her documents. She lifted the seat of a fire engine riding toy, which

Michael never rode because the wheels didn't work, and placed the book inside with a small ball on top to grab Michael's attention if he ever looked there.

Was that a creak? She listened, holding her breath, but didn't hear anything else. She wished she could lock the door to the garage.

Now she had to get rid of the money pouch. If Lillian found even that, she'd know that Hannah had been lying. All week, Hannah had been terrified her shirt would come up while she was cleaning and someone would see the strap. She opened the door to the garage and tiptoed past the washer and dryer, then peeked around the corner, down the hall. The house was quiet. All the lights were off. As long as she could make it to the kitchen, she'd be fine.

She took off her slippers and held on to them while she slid down the dark hallway in her socks. In the dark kitchen, she dropped the money pouch into the garbage under the sink.

There was a creak, the sound of a footstep on wood. She smelled the vodka on Sergey's breath and his overly strong sports deodorant. She spun around. He stepped into the kitchen, from the dining room, wavering a little.

He gripped the wall. "You are working in the dark?" he slurred.

Immediately she thought of her socks and how she'd taken off the slippers to be quiet. She put them on the ground and stepped into them, figuring he wouldn't notice since he was so drunk. "I'm almost finished."

He flicked on the switch and stared at her, as if she'd startled him. "You look so much like—" he slurred, stopping suddenly as if remembering himself.

"Who?" she asked, thinking he was acting strangely.

"Nobody," he murmured. "Just someone I knew in Ukraine."

A lot of Ukrainians looked like Moldovans if they had Russian in them, but Hannah knew she looked more Moldovan than Russian, even though she was three-quarters Russian, one-quarter Romanian. Her grandfather on her mother's side had been Romanian, and that was perhaps the reason her olive skin tanned so well, rather than burning like Katya's, though the bright green of her eyes came from the Russian side. Her mother, her uncle Vladi, and Babulya all had the same eyes.

Sergey stepped back into the dining room, where she heard the glug of alcohol being poured. She hated that sound. It reminded her of the man her father had become. The brandy her father used to make from sweet beets would fill their house with a rotting, sour odor that she'd never forget. More than once, the pressure cooker he'd rigged to make the alcohol had exploded and burned him. Her mother used to treat his wounds with a leafy plant called plantain that she found in the woods near their apartment on the edge of Chişinău, but Hannah wouldn't have anything to do with it. She thought the pain served him right.

Hannah heaved the garbage bag from under the sink. But she wasn't fast enough. Sergey stumbled out of the dining room, spilling a glass filled with an amber liquid, and stopped, blocking her path to the door.

She looked up, worried he knew what she was doing. Maybe

he wasn't as drunk as he seemed. His hand was steady as he placed the glass of whiskey on the kitchen counter. She'd seen a bottle in his collection, one that looked a lot like the Moldovan brand her father used to drink when he had money.

"This is for you," he said, pushing the glass an inch toward her. "Good job."

"I don't drink alcohol."

When her father had started drinking, she'd promised herself she'd never drink, no matter what happened to her, and she never had, not even after her parents were killed. Her friends drank, and she'd hang with them but drink Cola instead.

"Good," he said, lifting the glass and gulping down the alcohol, fast.

She lifted the garbage bag, turned away from him, and took a step toward the back door.

"Where are you going?" he asked.

Was he suspicious? It would be horrible if he looked in the garbage at that moment and found the pouch. She licked her lips. "I'm taking out the garbage," she said.

He gave her one of his toothy smiles. His jaw always seemed a little tight, even for a Russian, like he was nervous around her, though that was impossible. "It's after midnight," he said. "You've worked hard. I'll do it." He tried to take the bag from her.

"Please," Hannah said, holding on to the bag and trying to keep her voice even. "You're so good to me, but you need to relax. This is my job."

"For years I have been taking out the garbage," he slurred.

She didn't know what to say to that. She heard Lillian's voice in her head. Rule number ten. Maybe there was a good reason for this rule.

Finally he laughed and waved his hand forward. She picked up the bag and carried it outside into the hot night air, where she took in a shaky breath.

Her slippers sank into the wet grass. The sprinklers were off. The automatic sprinkler went on every night around dinnertime, making a sudden, if quiet, machine-gun noise. The first day, she'd run to the window to watch, beef stew boiling on the stove behind her. It was incredible, water shooting up from the ground like that. Even elites in Moldova didn't have automatic sprinkler systems. She'd gone for a walk one day with Katya near a gated community in Chişinău and they'd seen a gardener putting out a sprinkler with a long hose. They'd admired the grass, breathing it in, until the gardener made a sharp hissing noise to get them to leave. They'd run off, laughing, and declared that one day they'd have a lawn with real grass.

Hannah swooshed her feet through the grass to the side of the house. Her slippers crunched on the gravel walkway. From the neighbor's house, she heard some loud bangs like shooting, combined with rap music. She recognized the sounds from the video game system Daniil had bought on the black market. A male voice yelped and then shouted, "Yeah!"

She couldn't keep herself from grinning. It reminded her of Daniil. Even though she tried not to think of him, sometimes she couldn't help but miss the way he used to look at her.

She reached the garbage bins, which had wheels, of all things. There was no limit to American luxuries. Holding her breath, she reached into the garbage can and pulled out an older, full garbage bag, and dropped the one from the kitchen to the bottom of the can. She stuffed the older bag on top. If Sergey suspected anything, she hoped he'd look in the wrong one.

When she came back in the house, the kitchen was dark and Sergey seemed to have gone to bed. Her heart was beating so fast, she could hear it pounding in her ears.

She went down the hall to the garage, dropped down onto the sofa, and glanced at the glowing yellow numbers on the alarm clock. It was almost one o'clock in the morning. She wondered where her uncle Vladi was and in what time zone. She was sure he was still alive. He had to be.

It was eleven in the morning in Moldova. Babulya would be ironing clothing for Valeria's horrible girls. Katya would just be waking up since it was summer, and Daniil would have already finished his morning soccer practice and might even be at the appliance store where he fixed rich people's dishwashers.

She'd gone out with him for three years, but they'd had sex only once, just a month ago, though so much had happened since then, it felt like more than a month. After she had told him she couldn't continue on to twelfth grade, he had been so angry he hadn't come to see her at the market for the next three days. Finally she'd told her babushka she couldn't work because she had her annual checkup.

She'd called him from a pay phone—her home phone had

been disconnected months before. "We need to talk," she said. "Can you meet me for pizza at eleven?"

There was a pause over the phone, a pause that made her heart stop.

"We'll go to my apartment after," she rushed, even though she knew she sounded too desperate.

"Okay," he'd said at last.

She'd dressed carefully, wearing her green button-up shirt with a white skirt that stopped modestly above her knees and two-inch black heels. In the summer, many girls in Chişinău wore half tops and super miniskirts with just enough fabric to hide their underwear, but when Hannah wore anything too revealing, she couldn't stop tugging at her shirt or her skirt the whole time.

When she walked into the pizza shop, she could tell immediately he liked how she looked. He gazed down her body at her legs, which had gotten skinnier over the last few months from all the standing on her feet and pushing the heavy cart back and forth to the market.

He wrapped his arms around her. She looked over his shoulder toward the door, worried her babushka would be standing there with her hands on her hips.

"I love you," he murmured, kissing her ear, as if nothing was wrong between them.

After a quick pizza, which he paid for, they hurried to her apartment. It was hot and humid, but they headed up the open-air concrete staircase. Even though her apartment was on the fourteenth floor, they didn't take the elevator because they had to avoid the curious neighbors, especially the older ones who took the elevator.

He pinched her behind and she swatted at his hand. He laughed and pinched her again. She started running and he chased her. By the time they reached the fourteenth floor, they were drenched in sweat and laughing their heads off.

She grabbed his hands. "Shhh," she said. "Wait here."

He stayed out of sight while she walked up the remaining steps to her floor to make sure no other tenants were leaving their apartments. She unlocked her door and then she hurried him in before anyone saw. His hand was warm and sweaty as he pulled her into the main room, where he started to kiss her with a strange hunger. Laughing, she folded her convertible armchair down into a single bed. He wanted to use the blue sofa, which folded down to a double bed, but it had been her parents' bed and it was the one Babulya now used, so she said they couldn't. She was always worried that her parents would be able to see her somehow.

He pulled a small square cardboard box from his pocket. On the front, there was a knight with a sword. Inside, the condom was green. She hoped it could be trusted.

It was over sooner than she had thought it would be. It was three minutes of pain and wrestling, and nothing more. Afterward, he gave her a quick kiss, like one you'd give a sister. This was supposed to be their moment of reconnection, their moment to realize that they could make it through this tough time together, that it didn't matter if she had to delay school; all that mattered was that they were together. After all, he'd said he loved her.

He got dressed too quickly. Maybe he was worried about her babushka, she thought, and she got dressed with him. But at the door, he burst out, "I can't do this."

"What do you mean?" she cried.

He mumbled that he had to focus on school and didn't want to get more serious. He couldn't even look her in the eye. And then he ran.

Half an hour later, Hannah stood in a line of people outside her apartment waiting for the pay phone. She clenched her hands together to keep them from shaking. The rule was you were only supposed to talk for two minutes if people were waiting, but Hannah took longer. The moment her best friend answered, she started bawling. Long, wrenching sobs came out of her, making it difficult to breathe. Finally, she explained.

Katya said she'd be right over and Hannah hung up and hurried past the people in the line to wait next to her building, wiping her tears in embarrassment. When Katya came, they talked for hours in the courtyard, crouching on their heels. Katya said all the right things, how he was a dog and Hannah was wonderful and he was lucky to have her, but she still felt miserable.

When Katya left, Hannah made her way upstairs. Babulya had come home and already knew what had happened. Probably a neighbor had told her that Hannah was crying in the courtyard and Babulya figured it out. She made Hannah some tea and said it was for the best, though of course she didn't know exactly what had happened in the apartment that afternoon, only that Daniil had left her.

Hannah only spoke to him one time after that, to tell him she was going to America. She met him after soccer practice as he came off the field. He looked beautiful in his green uniform, his hair sticking to his sweaty brow, his blue eyes shining with exertion.

When she told him about the job in America, she saw the relief in his face. She asked him what he thought and stupidly hoped he'd tell her not to go.

"I don't know, Hannah. You're too naive," he said, his blue Russian eyes blinking sharply, as if he were the smart one.

It bothered her, him saying she was naive, but she hoped he was only saying it because he wanted her to be near him. "You think I shouldn't go?" If he begged her to stay, she would.

He shrugged and looked away, like he didn't care.

"What?" she asked sharply.

"You could get hurt," he said.

"Since when did you care about that?" She heard the pain in her voice and cringed at it.

"Hannah." He cupped her chin in his hand, pinching her skin with his thumb and forefinger, and made her look at him. "You know I love you," he said. "I want what's best for you."

She leaned forward, raising her lips to him. At first, she thought he was going to ignore her, but then she felt his soft lips. It was exactly like before, as if they'd never broken up. Suddenly, he pulled back, glancing up at the stands. She looked up and saw that girl Lera standing there. Hannah rubbed her lips with the back of her hand while he stared at her, like he was deciding something. "Maybe America is a good idea," he said. "You could get a new start."

She'd hated him then, hated him for wanting her to have a new start, hated him for choosing someone else.

In the dark basement room in America, Hannah rolled onto her side and wrapped her arms around herself. She'd show him, she thought. She'd come back speaking perfect English, wearing a green suit made by Versace or Gucci, and she'd be irresistible and he'd want her back and she'd say, "Too bad."

CHAPTER THIRTEEN

"Elena!" A woman's voice woke her up the next morning. The room was pitch-black and Hannah didn't know where she was. At first she thought that Elena, the annoying girl in her class at school, was in her apartment in Moldova. But then she smelled coffee instead of the hot red pepper and vinegar sauce Babulya put in her carrot salad, the smell she'd woken up to every morning since her parents had died, and she remembered she was in the USA.

She sat up and rubbed her eyes. "My name is Hannah," she muttered. She'd been here for a week and three days and Lillian still called her Elena.

She glanced at the alarm clock and realized she'd forgotten to set it for the second time. It was already seven thirty. She jumped up, put on her bra and gray sweat suit, and hurried down the hall.

The family was sitting at the glass table in the kitchen. Sergey was reading the paper. The children were both eating their particular mixture of cereals. "Here comes the vacation girl," Lillian said with a quick laugh, then took a sip of tea.

"I'm sorry," Hannah said quickly, thinking that working

twelve to sixteen hours every day was hardly a vacation.

"You're still getting over your jet lag, I suppose," Lillian said, standing up. "Why don't you sit down and eat? You've got a long day ahead of you."

"Oh no, I couldn't." She took a step back.

"Go ahead, I'm finished." Lillian took Hannah's arm and guided her to her chair.

She sat down in front of Lillian's dirty bowl and spoon while Lillian continued. "It is natural that your body hasn't adjusted to the time difference, but in the future, Elena, I would like you to set your alarm. I have a lot to do without having to wake you up too."

"Sure, no problem," she said, and then, because she couldn't stand to lose the first thing her mother had given to her in this world, she added, "Could you please call me Hannah?"

Lillian looked up. "Elena is the name on your plane ticket."

She explained, "The agent in Bucharest took away my Moldovan passport and made me use a Russian one with a fake name."

"What are you talking about, Elena?" Lillian laughed, lightly, then raised her eyebrows at Maggie, urging Hannah to play along. "The documents were not fake. You simply had the wrong ones for coming into America from Bucharest instead of Moscow."

Sergey glanced over his newspaper at Hannah. Of course, the lie made sense. Children couldn't be trusted not to tell friends. She felt sick that she'd made such a foolish mistake.

She fumbled to make up for it. "Yes, of course, you're right about the documents. But everybody calls me Hannah."

Maggie was watching, her spoon hovering over her cereal bowl, her eyes dancing back and forth between them.

"We'll call you Hannah. Why not?" Sergey said, smiling.

Lillian glanced at him and looked annoyed. "If it's your nickname."

Hannah felt her insides clench, because Hannah was her real name and it was special to her because it had been the name of the American doctor who'd delivered her. This woman had befriended her mother and convinced her to become a nurse, once she learned of the natural remedies she gave to the poor people in their neighborhood, remedies she'd learned from Hannah's babushka, and which she'd taught to Hannah. She'd made her mother believe in herself. Her mother had often said that Hannah would be a great doctor like the woman she was named after.

Everyone was looking at her.

"Yes, it's my nickname. I don't like the name Elena."

"You said Moldova," Maggie pointed out.

Lillian looked at Maggie and then back at Hannah, with a look of fury.

Hannah scrambled to explain. "I passed through Moldova to get to Bucharest. The flight was cheaper from there." She hoped Maggie's knowledge of geography was not as good as her hearing. Nobody would go from Moscow to Moldova to Romania.

Maggie squinted. "You're Papulya's niece, right?"

"Yes." Hannah glanced at Sergey and wondered how he'd explained this to her. Didn't Maggie know her own family? He looked down at his paper, as if he wasn't listening.

Lillian cleared her throat. "Do you want more cereal, Maggie?"

"You don't look like him," Maggie said to Hannah.

"No."

"Maybe we could give you a new nickname," Maggie suggested. "An American one."

"No, thank you," Hannah said, thinking that her name was already American.

Lillian placed a clean bowl and a spoon in front of Hannah, who'd never eaten cold cereal before coming to America.

"I don't care what we call you," Lillian said, "as long as you start working a little faster. I've never seen anyone move so slowly."

"We could call her Turtle," Maggie said in Russian, giggling.

"Turtle," Michael repeated. "Turtle."

"No, thank you," Hannah said firmly.

"Turtle," Lillian repeated, laughing along.

"Oh come on. Stop teasing," Sergey said, taking a sip of his coffee. He put it down and added another scoop of sugar as he talked. "Hannah was working until midnight last night."

"How do you know that?" Lillian asked. Hannah looked away from Sergey, nervous about the suspicion in Lillian's voice, and yet she couldn't help but admire how sharp Lillian was—she didn't miss a single thing.

"I was up," he said, adding more sugar, which was very strange for a Russian man. Most drank coffee black. "I had to make a call to Moscow." He tried his coffee again and, finding it to his liking, placed it down on the table. He raised his newspaper in front of his face.

Lillian glanced from him to Hannah, whose face was turning red, even though absolutely nothing had happened. She told her face to stop it, that she hadn't done anything wrong, but it never listened to her. It made her look guilty even when she was not.

"Maybe you should go to bed when I go to bed," Lillian said.

"I would love to go to bed earlier," Hannah said, choosing her words carefully. "Aren't people supposed to work just forty hours a week in America?"

"Forty hours?" Lillian tossed her head back and laughed.

Hannah looked from Lillian to Maggie, who was staring at her mother, a crease forming between her own hazel eyes. She seemed worried, as if she'd heard this laughter before.

"Nobody works forty hours a week," Lillian said, grabbing her used teacup. "I certainly don't, and Sergey doesn't. It's just one of those lies about America. You can't get anything done in forty hours a week."

Hannah reached for the cereal box—"Cheerios," it said—and poured it before Lillian could take it away. "I thought I would have time to take English classes."

"She wants to be a doctor," Lillian announced, like it was the craziest idea ever.

"Good for you," Sergey said to Hannah. His eyes crinkled kindly, forming deep creases in his tanned skin.

Lillian grabbed his bowl, even though he wasn't finished. "It's good for her, but for me, you say it's a waste of time, that anybody with brains can make more money in business."

He let out a bark of a laugh, as if he'd been caught. He reached up and wrapped his arm around his wife's waist, stopping her.

"Lilichka, sweetheart, I meant that you could do anything you wanted in America. You're smart and beautiful. Why not make more money?"

"Being a doctor is a respectable job," she said. "It's good, honest money."

"You're right," he said. "You'll be a great doctor."

Hannah wondered why he said she'd be a great doctor if she was already a doctor.

Lillian squinted down at him, as if to see whether he was patronizing her, and then bent down to give him a quick peck on his nose. "Thank you." She grabbed the cereal boxes and carried them to the cupboard. Then she stopped and threw her hands in the air. "Why am I clearing the table?" she asked, more to herself than anyone else. "I have to study."

Hannah felt guilty all of a sudden for eating.

"You don't have to do this anymore." Sergey stood up, wrapped his arms around her, and gazed into her beautiful face. "Now you can focus on your studying."

"You're right. I'm not used to this," she said, and kissed him slowly on the lips. Hannah looked away, embarrassed. After a moment of kissing, the children started giggling and Lillian broke away. "Elena—I mean, Hannah," Lillian said. "The laundry is piling up. After you eat, you can bring Michael to the playroom while you fold the clothes." Lillian always referred to it as a playroom, but to Hannah, it was just a garage, not unlike the one where her father used to work on cars. It even had an oil stain on the concrete floor, which was what Lillian was hiding with the pink and blue children's rug.

"I have to go," Sergey said, tousling Michael's hair, then bending down to kiss Maggie's forehead.

"Bye, Papushka," Maggie said.

"Have a fun day, little rabbit," he said, and then strode out of the room, holding his paper.

Lillian followed him out of the room.

Maggie blinked at Hannah with those big beautiful eyes of hers. "You can eat with me," she said in English.

"Okay," Hannah answered her in English, then glanced at the door, worried about Lillian. She switched back to Russian. "Do you know how to hang this spoon on your nose?"

CHAPTER FOURTEEN

Hannah stretched her legs out and felt the hot sun on her skin. She'd been in Los Angeles for two weeks and was finally getting a chance to tan. In Moldova, that was what people her age did all summer. She wasn't officially tanning, though. *Officially*, she was babysitting Michael and Maggie together, for the first time, and she'd come up with the great idea of going in the backyard and playing with buckets of water.

It was already ninety-five degrees Fahrenheit at ten thirty in the morning. Ninety-five was thirty-five degrees Celsius. This was one of the unexpected things about America. Without converting things like Fahrenheit to Celsius, dollars to lei, and pounds to kilograms, she had no idea how much anything was. She knew twenty dollars was a lot, but it wasn't until she converted it to lei and thought about how long it would take her to make that much at the market that it really sank in.

She took a sip of the compote, a Moldovan drink she'd made with water, sugar, and mashed strawberries. Michael was mixing water in his buckets, pretending it was soup, and Maggie was being a good sport and pretending to eat it. "Michael, could you dump some water on my legs?" Hannah called.

He ran over, giggling, holding a bucket full of sloshing water, and dumped it all over her legs and her shorts. She screamed. The water was freezing. "Okay, that's enough."

"Do it to me," Maggie said. Michael hurried back to Maggie, giggling.

Hannah heard a lawn mower start up next door. She loved that sound. It was one of the sounds of America, a sound she never heard in Moldova. In the village, people let the ducks and the chickens eat the grass, and in the city, the few people with lawns had gardeners who cut the grass with long curved machetes.

The lawn mower turned off. She glanced at the tall green fence. Was it the boy? Whoever it was started pushing the lawn mower along the fence to the front yard.

Lillian was out—now was a good time to meet him. Once they were friends, Lillian would see that it was harmless. She felt nervous all of a sudden; maybe he wouldn't be interested in meeting her. After all, she was just a nanny.

She glanced at Michael and Maggie. Michael was dumping water on Maggie's feet, giggling. She hurried across the lawn and down the gravel path beside the house, past the garbage cans, to the gate, but she was too late.

The boy was crossing the street with the lawn mower. He pushed it up the neighbor's driveway and a short, older man met him and handed him some bills. Then the boy began mowing his lawn. She couldn't believe it. He had a job, just like she did.

"Hannah!" Maggie yelled from the backyard.

She remembered how Lillian had said to be careful, that a child could drown in a bucket of water, and she sprinted back up the walkway. Michael was sitting cross-legged, pouring water from one little bucket to another.

Maggie was standing, hands planted on her hips. "Where did you go?" she asked in Russian. She always spoke Russian when she was upset.

"I had to throw something out," Hannah answered.

"I thought you left us."

Hannah gave her a funny look. "Why would I leave you?"

"Mama said if you left, I should call her."

"I'm not going to leave you," Hannah said.

"Alexei's girl left."

"Who's Alexei?"

She shrugged. "Paavo's friend."

No wonder, Hannah thought.

"One day, she just left the kids all alone in the house and she never came back."

"I'd never do that, don't worry." Hannah walked over to the hose and picked it up, hoping to distract her. "Are you ready for a water fight?"

She turned it on full blast and let the water stream up like a fountain, falling on their heads. Maggie seemed shocked at first, but then she screamed and charged at Hannah. She grabbed the hose away, giggling, and sprayed Hannah and Michael and even the back windows of the house, like she was an action hero in a Hollywood movie.

Michael jumped in a mud puddle that was forming. Hannah

worried about that puddle, briefly, but then Maggie turned the hose on her, spraying her in the face. Hannah grabbed the hose, laughing, Michael threw himself at them, and they all fell down, giggling in the mud.

"You are a mud monster!" Michael yelled. Hannah looked at Maggie and they started laughing so hard, Hannah's belly hurt.

And then she heard a car engine on the road.

Her heart started pounding and she jumped to her feet.

"Quick, let's get cleaned up."

As they were toweling themselves off, Maggie glanced at her with admiration. "I've never heard you laugh," Maggie said in Russian, then switched to English. "You're cool."

Hannah realized she hadn't laughed, not in a long time. This was the most fun she'd had in ages. "You are cool also," she answered in English, helping Maggie up.

An hour later, when Lillian's Cadillac SUV came up the driveway, Hannah was sitting with the children on a blanket on the dry part of the lawn. The children were still wearing their bathing suits, but she'd hosed them off, and they were eating a snack of sliced-up apples and drinking strawberry compote.

The side gate opened. Lillian's heels kicked up the gravel along the path. When Lillian came around the corner of the house, she gasped, bringing her hand to her face.

Hannah looked around. The children were clean. She'd even dried off the water on the windows with a newspaper, like Babulya had shown her.

"What?" she asked.

"You have made a swimming pool on my lawn."

There was a fairly large mud puddle—she hadn't been that concerned about it before.

"Mommy, it was so much fun," Maggie gushed in English.

"Russian, Maggie," Lillian said automatically.

Maggie switched back. "We played restaurant with the buckets and we ran through the hose. I got to wear my new bathing suit." She stood up and posed, sticking out her behind, which made Lillian smile at least.

"Did you put sunscreen on them?" Lillian asked Hannah.

"Yes, she did," Maggie said, grinning. Thankfully, Maggie had reminded her.

"Well, it's not a total disaster," Lillian said, tossing back her blonde hair. "I had a good meeting and it looks like you had fun. Even if our lawn is a mess." She looked at Hannah and nodded. "Good job."

Michael let out a shriek and tackled Hannah and she fell back, tickling him, and they all laughed, even Lillian.

CHAPTER FIFTEEN

It was eleven at night, three weeks and four days after Hannah had arrived in America. She heaved the garbage bag from the kitchen into one of the bins and stood outside, enjoying the one quiet moment of her day. The air was cooling off, finally.

She looked up at the crescent moon in the sky and wondered if her mother was looking down on her. In Moldova, Hannah had hated taking out the garbage. The smell was vile, especially in the summer, but the worst part was touching the grimy handle on the garbage chute.

Here, garbage duty was a brief moment when she could go outside alone and relax. She'd never worked so hard in her whole life, but once she got paid, it would be worth it. She'd send a thousand dollars to Babulya to pay for her cataract surgery and then she wouldn't have to worry about her babushka falling into a manhole. They'd pay her soon, any day now.

She unlocked the side gate, tipped the garbage container onto its wheels, and rolled it to the curb. Normally there was no one on the street, but today she saw an older couple hobbling down the sidewalk toward her—and there appeared to be a duck waddling behind them. She stepped to the side and squinted. Yes, it was a duck.

The man's hair swooped up, not unlike the fluff of feathers on the duck's behind. The wife plodded on, eyes ahead. She was looking at Hannah, but not smiling. Hannah had heard Americans always said hello in the streets, and she waited for that now. Already she could smell their sweet, dusty old-people smell—it reminded her of Babulya minus the hot pepper. She wondered how her babushka was doing at Petru's house. She'd given Lillian two letters for her babushka and one for Katya, but she hadn't received any letters back yet.

They were passing her. Not saying anything. Maybe she was supposed to say it because she was younger. "Hello," she said in English.

The man and the woman didn't even look at her, and the duck marched past, ignoring her too. A gate opened behind her. She heard the bumping sound of a garbage can on wheels rolling down the driveway. Her breath caught inside her. The boy next door was pulling a garbage can toward her. It looked like she'd said hello to the duck. How embarrassing. She wondered if the boy had heard.

"Quack," he said to her.

She didn't know this word. She stepped backward, her mind rushing with things to say, but it all came to her in Russian. "Yes?" she asked, which didn't make sense at all.

"Just taking the garbage out." He sucked in a breath that

stopped halfway into his mouth and then tucked his head down in embarrassment.

She'd seen the boy many times, moving around the upper rooms of his house or walking down the sidewalk in the oversize baseball jerseys he always wore, that she felt like she knew him. She had to introduce herself at least.

She opened her mouth to speak, but he hurried away so quickly she didn't have a chance to say anything. She couldn't very well run after him, yelling, "My name is Hannah. What is your name?" And it was strange to say good-bye when they hadn't really said hello, so she just watched his back, her tongue sitting in her mouth like an overcooked carrot.

CHAPTER SIXTEEN

The next Thursday, Hannah vowed she'd talk to the boy next door when he took out the garbage, so he wouldn't think she was crazy. It was the perfect day, because Lillian and Sergey had gone out to celebrate Lillian taking her Step One test for the USMLE, the first test for a foreign doctor in America.

Lillian had been studying constantly for the test over the last two weeks and still hadn't paid her. Hannah planned to remind her soon, but Lillian was in such a good mood today, Hannah hadn't wanted to ruin it.

She'd do it tomorrow. Or in the next week, definitely.

She checked the clock on the oven. Ten o'clock. She opened the back door and looked out across the lawn to the neighbor's house.

She grabbed some paper towels and a spray bottle. One more room to clean. She went into the master bathroom. It looked spotless, except for a few hairs, but every day she didn't clean it, Lillian knew. She sprayed the counter and wiped the hairs off.

Good enough. She went into the bedroom and looked at Lillian's bookshelf, at the medical textbooks and the Russian-English dictionary Lillian had warned her not to touch. She'd tried to read one of the textbooks when Lillian left them in the dining room to pick up Maggie, but she hadn't been able to understand even a single sentence with all the medical terminology. She had to work up to it. Despite everything, she couldn't give up. One day, she'd be a doctor.

She pulled the dictionary off the shelf and dropped down on the bed with its soft white duvet comforter. It made a puffing sound. She lay back and stretched her arms out. This was what it would feel like to be Lillian.

She flipped over, opened the dictionary, and started looking up words she could use on the boy next door. The chocolate sat on Lillian's pillow, just inches from her head. She could smell the dark chocolate and imagined the truffle melting in her mouth. Lillian was probably counting them, she thought. She looked up another word.

The chocolate sat there, calling to her. It was Swiss chocolate, in a shiny red wrapper. Everyone knew how delicious Swiss chocolate was.

She reached over and grabbed it. One chocolate. Lillian would never know. The tinfoil paper crinkled as she ripped it off. The chocolate filled her mouth and melted into the space between her lips and her gums.

"Hello!" Lillian was downstairs.

Hannah leaped from the bed, licking her lips.

"Hannah?" Lillian called.

"I'm up here." She grabbed the dictionary, shoved it onto the bookshelf, then ran back to the bed to snatch up the chocolate wrapper and stuff it in her pocket. Lillian was almost at the top of the stairs. She wiped at the corners of her mouth. The duvet looked like she'd been sleeping under it. She bent over, smoothed it down in one quick sweep, and turned as Lillian came into the room.

She could still taste the creamy truffle in her mouth. Did she have chocolate on her teeth? Did her breath smell of chocolate?

Lillian stood in the doorway, wearing a low-cut red dress. Her blonde hair fell softly around her bare shoulders, and she shook her head like she was a model. "What are you doing?" she asked, smiling. Not accusatory. Just happy.

Hannah ran her tongue over her teeth in case they were covered with chocolate. "Just finishing up. I have to get your truffle and then I'm all done. Sorry I didn't do it earlier."

"They're delicious, aren't they?" Lillian asked, as if she knew Hannah had just eaten one.

"Are they?" Hannah's voice squealed at the end of her question, and her heart started to beat faster in her chest.

"You haven't tried one?" Lillian asked.

Hannah hesitated, worried it was a test. "I—um—I didn't think I was allowed," she said, which was true enough.

"I wondered why they lasted so long." Lillian's eyes shone, cheeks aglow. "Why don't you get two and we can have our chocolates together?" She gave Hannah a queenly smile, revealing lipstick on her teeth. "Go on," she said, and waved her hand in a condescending way that itched at Hannah as she ran down the stairs.

She dragged one of the metal kitchen chairs over to the refrigerator and stood on it.

The tinkling of ice in a glass startled her. Sergey had wandered into the kitchen from the living room, drinking cola with whiskey, his favorite drink when he was alone and had no one to impress. The smell of alcohol reminded her of pee, maybe because her father peed himself when he drank too much. Her mother always cleaned it up, like everything else, but Hannah sure wouldn't if she were his wife. She'd make him clean up his own mess. At least Sergey wasn't a drunk, she thought. He drank no more than an average Russian.

She reached into the upper cupboard and took two chocolates from the truffle box.

"What are you doing?" he asked, as if he was just curious, but his eyes were jumping from her face to her breasts. Why did men always think you didn't see them looking at your breasts? She'd even caught teachers looking at her.

"Getting a truffle for your wife," she said, emphasizing "wife."

"Ah," he said, and took a swig of his drink.

She crossed her arms over her breasts so he wouldn't see them bounce, jumped from the chair, and hurried out of the room. When she got upstairs, Lillian was taking off her nylons in long sweeping motions. Her red dress flipped up, revealing black lace panties. There would be sounds coming from upstairs tonight.

Hannah glanced at the clock—five minutes before eleven. Last time she'd met the boy at eleven. She wondered if he was hoping she'd be out there again.

Lillian gave her a genuine smile. "You have the chocolate?"

Hannah handed her one truffle and kept the other for herself. She peeled the paper off the truffle and popped it in her mouth.

"Good?" Lillian said.

"Very good. Thank you." Hannah sucked on the chocolate, but didn't enjoy it nearly as much with Lillian watching her like she was a poor village girl. She glanced at the clock on the nightstand. It was eleven. "Well, I'd better let you change."

"We're both girls." Lillian laughed. "Don't you want to hear about my night?"

She was trapped. "Yes, of course."

Lillian took out a bottle of moisturizer from her vanity and rubbed it on her legs while she told Hannah about the restaurant. "It was really upscale, you know, like New York. It was a dark gray building, no sign out front, but in back, we went through some industrial doors. It looked like a warehouse. I wondered where he was taking me." She laughed, massaging the moisturizer between her perfectly manicured toenails. Hannah saw a flash of her black lace panties and looked away as Lillian continued. "But then there was a doorman and we were in this magnificent place with an open skylight and a garden with a brook running around the tables and the prices—wow—they were high. It was twenty dollars for just the salad." She laughed, then added quickly, "Not that we have to worry. Sergey's new business is doing well. I'm so proud of him."

That was a good opening. She could ask about the money, Hannah thought, but then she heard the unmistakable sound of a garbage container rolling down the driveway next door. She jumped up. Lillian gave her a questioning look as she closed up the bottle of moisturizer and placed it back on her vanity.

"I have a few more things to do," Hannah said.

"Always working," Lillian said, clicking her tongue. "Sometimes, Hannah, you're a little boring. Now that you are in America, you should develop some interests."

Develop some interests? Lillian didn't even care enough to ask what her interests were. If she did, she'd know that she'd love just an hour during the day to sit down and read a book. Or maybe go for a walk up to the Hollywood sign. Anything but work all day long.

"That's a great idea," Hannah said, trying to keep the bite out of her voice. "Maybe I could start going to English school at night."

She listened to the boy's footsteps back up the driveway. There was one more container for the trash and then one for recycling.

"Every night?" Lillian asked, perfuming her breasts with little finger dabs. "You don't even speak a word. Why don't you study by yourself from an English grammar book? I think one student in the family is enough. When I'm finished, perhaps you can take a class."

"Do you have a grammar book I could read?"

Lillian looked annoyed. "Of course I do. I'll give it to you tomorrow."

Another garbage container rolled down the neighbor's driveway. "Thank you very much," Hannah gushed. "I'll let you finish up. Good night." She turned to go. If she didn't run, the boy next door would be gone.

"Why are you in such a hurry?" Lillian asked.

Hannah stopped. "I have to take out the garbage," she said, making one last attempt.

"I'll get Sergey to do it tomorrow morning."

"It has leftover fish in it." Hannah shrugged like it didn't matter to her. "It will make the kitchen smell."

Lillian hesitated, then said quickly, "I'll deal with it. You go to bed. I want some time alone with my husband." Lillian flashed her a wicked smile.

Hannah headed out of the room, disappointed. In the garage, she plunked down on the sofa. Her stomach ached, she was so desperate for a friend. It had been over a month since she'd had a normal conversation with anyone. And she needed to learn English, to feel like she was improving at something other than cleaning. Sometimes when Lillian wasn't around, Maggie read to her in English and explained the words to her. But without practice, she'd never be fluent.

She picked up one of the children's English books and read it a few times, until finally she realized the house was silent. No television, no stairs creaking, no laughter, nothing. Perhaps they'd gone to bed and she could sneak outside, maybe go for a walk if the boy wasn't there.

She opened the door to the laundry area to listen. The house was quiet. She took off her slippers, slid down the hall, and peeked around the entrance to the living room, just in case. She froze. They hadn't bothered to go upstairs.

Lillian's red dress had been flung on the white carpet and shimmered like a pool of blood. She had a zit in the middle of her back. Sergey groaned and looked up at Hannah.

She yanked her head back around the corner. He'd definitely seen her. Maybe he'd think she'd been watching them. That was disgusting.

She slid down the hall in her socks, hoping, at least, that Lillian would not hear her. She hurried around the corner, past the washer and dryer, and through the door to the garage, where she jumped into her sleeping bag on the sofa.

Her heart pounded. She was breathing hard. And her foot was twitching inside her sleeping bag. She made it stop and slowed down her breathing. There was no reason to be afraid. They were having sex. She'd been warned to stay in the playroom, but she hadn't listened. It was her own fault.

Through the door of the garage, she heard a moan. Her stomach twisted and she was back inside the taxi with the bad agent, outside the airport, waiting to see if he would give her the plane ticket. He was undoing his zipper, telling her she could pay him for his troubles in another way. She clenched her teeth together. *Stop thinking about it.*

She could not listen to their moans. It was too much. She covered her ears and started to hum an old village tune her mother had loved. She heard her mother's voice in her head: *Spin, turn around, up and down. Spin . . .*

CHAPTER SEVENTEEN

It was the middle of the night. Light drifted into the garage from the hallway. Sergey was standing in the doorway, holding his hands behind his back. Hannah closed her eyes so he'd think she was asleep. Even from the sofa, she could smell the vodka on his breath.

She heard his footsteps cross the room, and then he crouched by her and brought his face close, as if he was about to kiss her. She jerked back and let out a short scream. He pressed a calloused hand to her mouth.

"Shhh," he said softly. "It's only me."

Only *you*? Her heart pounded in her chest. Why did he think she wouldn't be afraid of him?

"Don't scream," he said. "Promise?"

She nodded, fully intending to scream if he tried anything.

He lifted his hand. "I'm sorry I scared you."

"What are you doing in here?" she asked, tears in her voice, despite herself.

"I have a present for you."

She sat up on the sofa, holding the sleeping bag up over her chest. She was wearing a T-shirt, but she'd taken off her bra to sleep. "Can't you give it to me tomorrow?"

"No."

"Turn on the light then," she said, thinking that it had better be a real present, not the present of his middle-aged body. Maybe he was going to pay her.

He pulled the long cord on the bare fluorescent lightbulb in the center of the room. She blinked and pulled the sleeping bag even higher. He walked back and picked up a pink rectangular box from the floor next to the sofa, not unlike a cake box, and handed it to her.

It was surprisingly light. She opened the lid. Under a mound of pink tissue, she discovered seven pairs of cotton underwear, all with different colors and designs. She rubbed the fabric between her fingers. It was soft, not scratchy, and had a thick elastic band with a brand name written on it. Not cheap. But she would have preferred money.

She thought of how Lillian would react if she learned he'd bought her underwear and tried to hand back the box. "I can't accept it."

He stepped back, refusing to take it. "I saw your panties hanging on the rack."

Hannah glanced over at the old wooden rack where she hung delicate clothes, including her own underwear, not because they were fancy like Lillian's, but because the dryer had already destroyed four pairs and she had only two left.

"They are not the kind of panties for any girl to wear."

If these were the sexy kind, lace or silk, or even bikinis, she'd refuse, but they were simple cotton underwear. She picked up the striped pink pair and stretched out the thick elastic band.

At least these panties wouldn't slide down while she was cleaning the floor.

"What will I tell Lillian if she sees them?" she asked.

"Tell her that you bought them," he said. "The store is by the Russian store on Santa Monica Boulevard across from the Whole Foods grocery store."

"Good luck getting her to believe that," she said sarcastically. "Lillian doesn't let me leave the house or the yard. Ever." Despite her attempt to act like it didn't matter, her eyes started to tear up. "And she hasn't paid me yet, so I wouldn't have the money to buy anything."

Understanding dawned on Sergey's face, and he seemed to feel a little guilty. He cleared his throat. "Tell her you brought money from Moldova, and I'll try to arrange for you to go out of the house, maybe to do an errand."

"Okay." She waited for him to say more about the money, but he hurried to the door and turned off the light.

"Wait!" she said. "What about my pay?"

He cleared his throat. "Lillian deals with all the household expenses, but I'll talk to her."

To him, she was just another household expense. Soap, toilet paper, Hannah.

"Thank you," she said, hoping that if she seemed grateful for what he had given her already, perhaps he'd give more. "Thank you for the underwear."

"Good night, Hannah," he said, speaking her name through the dark with a tenderness that surprised her. She realized he cared for her, at least a little bit, and she wondered why.

CHAPTER EIGHTEEN

The next day, Hannah was standing at a bus stop with a bench. She wanted to sit, because it was so odd to have a bench at a bus stop, but she didn't, for fear that the bus wouldn't stop. She couldn't mess up this opportunity. She wasn't going anywhere exciting, just to a store, but it was more freedom than she'd had for the month and a half since she'd arrived in America.

She'd been sent to buy madeleines, little vanilla sponge cookies. Paavo's wife, Rena, loved them, and since she was coming over in half an hour, Sergey had been able to convince Lillian to let Hannah go.

It was her first time standing on the sidewalk of a busy street in America. Cars were buzzing past her, but the sidewalk felt ghostlike compared with the crowded sidewalks of Chişinău. All she could see was one homeless man with a shopping cart full of cans half a block away. Lillian had warned her not to talk to anyone, because people might try to steal her money or she could be arrested if anyone suspected she was illegal, but there was no one to talk to anyway.

The number 14 bus came up. *A female driver? Strange,* she

thought, and started to walk past her, but the woman held up a hand with long painted nails to stop her. "Money?"

In Moldova, on the big buses, a money collector came around and gave change, and on the small buses, people would sit down first and pass their money up to the person in front of them. The money would travel over many sets of hands until it reached the driver, and the driver would pass the change back in the same way. Hannah looked down at her map and instructions. Lillian had written only that it cost one dollar thirty-five, which seemed like a fortune, compared with two lei, the equivalent of seventeen cents, which she paid at home.

Hannah fumbled in the small silver change purse Lillian had given her and tried to give the money to the driver, but she waved her hand in front of her face. "I can't take that. Here." She pointed one of her long fingernails at a metal contraption.

Embarrassed, Hannah searched for a place in the side to put the money, but she couldn't see any holes. The driver tapped a long, obvious slot on the top and gave her a look like she had to be the stupidest person who ever lived. The money slid down, made a couple of beeping noises, and the driver raised her eyebrows as if to ask why she was still standing there.

Hannah continued down the long aisle and the bus rolled forward. She sat down in the middle of the bus and shrank down into the seat. She'd thought taking a bus would be no problem, but nothing was familiar. In Moldova, the bus always held a blend of businesspeople and students, Romanians and Russians, young and old, poor and middle class. But on this bus, everybody looked poor with old clothes, and they all had dark skin. She was the only light-skinned teenager, and it seemed dangerous to stand out.

At the front of the bus, in the seats for old people, a Latino man with a strange fishnet stocking on his head was staring at her. What if he sat next to her? She slid her hand in the wrist strap of Lillian's change purse and looked out the window. The bus was passing houses now, but ahead it looked like there were more stores. She looked back at the man with the fishnet stocking, but he'd lost interest in her and was now looking down at his basketball shoes. Above his head, a bee was crawling along the window. Its behind bent in and kissed the glass. Hannah winced, worried for him. She hated bees more than anything. In the village, there were so many bees that it was scary to go to the outhouse.

The bus stopped at the corner of Santa Monica Boulevard and Highland. There was a doughnut shop on the corner called Donut Time. A tall, muscular woman strode out in a short, hot pink dress. Hannah stared at the woman's square jaw and realized she was a man. Her first transvestite.

She thought of her uncle Vladi. When she was just eight, she'd gone with her parents to visit Vladi and Babulya in Gura Bicului. Hannah had been so excited to see them that she'd run from the mini bus stop, like she always did, down the dusty road, and through their front door, yelling, "I'm here!"

Vladi was standing in the middle of the living room next to his Ukrainian egg art table, kissing a skinny dark-haired man, his gentle fingers clenching the man's jeans. He stepped back quickly, but Hannah had seen everything. Her mouth hung open. Vladi held up a shaking hand, as if he was stopping a bus that was about to run him over. Perhaps he thought she was about to scream. She could hear her parents outside, talking to her babushka as they came toward the house. The other man hurried out the back door.

"Please don't say anything," Vladi had begged.

"I won't," she'd promised, and she never had, not even when he went missing.

The bus honked at someone. Hannah looked at the street sign outside—La Brea. Up the street, she could see the Hollywood sign.

Hannah sighed. The bad agent's words came into her head. "You don't know how to listen, do you? You're just like your uncle." She had been opening the door to the taxi at that moment, her whole body shaking, and she blinked back at him. "Petru?" Volva gave her a look. "The other one. The sick one." Then he told her to get out of the taxi.

She looked back at the bee. It was crawling toward her. Someone had found out about Vladi, that was for sure. If Volva knew, that was a bad sign.

"Hi," a voice said.

She looked up to see the neighbor boy standing right next to her, smelling of baby powder deodorant. He looked down at her and smiled. She gave him a quick smile back, making sure to keep her lips closed and her teeth covered.

He was so close, she could see every detail of his face. His nose curved to the side, just a bit, something she hadn't noticed from far away. His blue eyes were framed with long blond eyelashes, each separated and glossy, and his cheeks were red as if he'd just been running, maybe to catch the bus.

She forced herself to speak. "Hello."

"What's up?" he said.

She really didn't know how to answer that. She stared at him, feeling foolish.

"You live next door to me," he said, as if he were reminding her.

"Yes," she said, surprised that he'd said she lived next door, instead of that she worked next door. She realized he didn't know she was just a maid. For all he knew, she was still a girl with possibilities. She moved over into the empty seat beside her, and to her relief, he sat down.

"Where are you headed?" he asked.

She didn't know what "headed" meant, but he'd said "where," so she figured he was probably asking where she was going. "Store," she said, making sure to keep her lips curled over her crooked teeth as she spoke, well aware that American girls did not have teeth like hers.

"Oh," he said, glancing out the window. The street was lined with restaurants, banks, shops, and grocery stores. Her mind was clogged with Russian, and she feared if she tried to speak in English, he wouldn't understand her at all. In Russian, she wasn't as talkative as Katya, but she certainly knew how to have a conversation.

She thought of a question in English. "You go to school?"

"Not in the summer," he said.

Of course not. She winced at her own stupidity.

He continued, "I thought I'd go to Santa Monica, maybe hit the beach."

Almost nothing made sense. *Hit the beach?* She couldn't even have a basic conversation. There was an uncomfortable pause. His nose twitched and his cheeks turned red. She realized he was just as nervous as she was, and this realization helped her find the words. "The beach? I no go to beach. I—"

The bee zipped around his head, straight toward her.

"Aaah!" She waved her hands in front of her face.

It landed on the window by her head. She jumped up in her seat and fell backward onto the boy's lap. His hand fluttered near her, as if he was afraid to touch her, and then he patted her arm tentatively. "Take it easy." He let out an embarrassed laugh.

"Oop, sorry." She slid back into her seat, but the bee came back, buzzing around her head. She screamed, waving her hand in front of her face.

"Come on." The boy pulled her by the elbow, she jumped up, and they ran down the aisle, away from the bee.

The bus jerked to a stop. He grabbed a pole and steadied her. Through the window, she saw the Russian store across from the Whole Foods Market where Lillian bought all her organic things. This was her stop! She had to get off. The doors started to close and the bus rolled forward.

She ran to the front. If she got lost, she'd be in a lot of trouble. "Stop!" The driver put on the brakes. The doors opened and she ran out.

The silver purse—had she left it? The bus was pulling away

from the curb. She yelled to stop the bus and then realized the strap was still twisted around her wrist.

She searched for the boy on the bus. He probably thought she had mental problems after that. He was standing by the window, grinning at her. He lifted up a hand in a wave and made a face.

She still hadn't introduced herself, but maybe it didn't matter. She waved and laughed with him, forgetting for a moment to hide her teeth.

CHAPTER NINETEEN

The moment Hannah stepped into the Russian store, she felt comfortable, safe even, because everywhere she looked, she saw something familiar.

A thin layer of smoke filled the room from the lack of air circulation. She gazed through the smoke at the cookies and orange juice with Russian labeling, and above her head, at the New Year's garlands, pink fabric flowers, and Russian dolls. She breathed in the smells of vinegar eggs and salty fish and lard and felt for a moment she was back in the market of Chişinău.

A pretty woman in her mid-thirties with dyed blonde hair, dark roots, blue eyes, and thick makeup was setting out trays of sea bass and skewered chicken. Lillian had told her not to say anything to this woman. Apparently she was a busybody who would cause her trouble. "You don't want to get arrested," Lillian had said. "The INS could pick you up anywhere. Or they might knock on our door one morning and we'll have no choice but to give you to them."

Hannah found the madeleines and placed them on the counter. The woman finished organizing the trays and finally looked up. "What do you want?" she asked in Russian.

Hannah ordered the salami and coleslaw that Lillian had put on her list.

"Nothing more?" the woman demanded.

Hannah had spotted the spicy carrot salad, the same kind her babushka made, in the glass refrigerator case. "Can I have some carrot salad?" she asked.

The woman put her hands on her hips. "Do you think I'm going to take it out for you?"

Hannah opened the refrigerator and pulled out the smallest container of carrot salad. Lillian would want a receipt, but if she complained about the extra three dollars, it would give Hannah a good opportunity to ask about her wages.

The woman gave her a fork. "I've never seen you before," she said.

Hannah remembered Lillian's warning not to speak to this woman. "It is my first time in this shop," she confirmed, stepping away from the counter. She opened the lid to the carrot salad, took a bite, and immediately regretted spending the money. The salad was at least three days old, and the woman had added too much vinegar and not enough sugar or red pepper spice.

"You are Lily's girl," the woman said, as if it was written on her forehead.

Hannah forced herself to swallow. She wiped the corners of her mouth with the tip of her finger and shut the container. "How do you know?"

"She brings this purse," she said, waving her hand at the purse Hannah held. Hannah had never seen Lillian use it, but maybe

this woman had an amazing memory. "I'm Berta." She continued, "Your name?"

She started to say Hannah, but then remembered, "Elena."

Berta asked, "Where are you from? Not Russia. Ukraine?"

"No," Hannah said, not thinking.

"Her husband is from Ukraine. Sergey. He is your uncle?"

"Yes," she said, realizing her mistake.

"You don't sound like him." Berta narrowed her eyes suspi-
ciously. "You're not Ukrainian."

Hannah thought she could just say that she'd grown up in
Moldova but decided it was best to nothing.

Berta continued, "He said he's going to bring your whole
family."

"Who said that?"

"Your uncle." Berta gave her a funny look.

Why would Sergey have said he was bringing her whole
family? Was it just a lie for this busybody? Or was he going to
bring her babushka too? Maybe her uncle was already here. Then
she remembered what the bad agent had told her, that her "sick
uncle" had not listened.

"You don't look like your uncle either," Berta said, blinking her long eyelashes, which had so much mascara on them
that they stuck together. At first Hannah thought Berta was
talking about her real uncle, but then realized she meant Sergey. "You're a beautiful girl," she said, gazing up and down
Hannah's body. "Good thing he's your uncle. Otherwise, that
Liliya, she would never let you stay."

Hannah wished she'd worn her sweat suit instead of the monkey T-shirt and blue slacks Babulya had bought her. She crossed her arms over her breasts. "Why?" she asked.

"You must know your uncle, he's got eyes for the women."

Hannah rolled her eyes like she knew. "Oh, that."

Berta leaned in, whispering, "Last year, he had a very open affair with a socialite. Not as beautiful as his wife. I don't know why Liliya stayed. Must be the money." She shrugged. "I haven't heard anything lately, but these men, they don't stop once they start. One cherry is never enough." She laughed.

Lillian's extra cell phone started to ring from the little purse. "Excuse me," Hannah said, unzipping the purse and pulling out the phone. It said "Home." Lillian was calling her. Hannah's face turned red. Now that she knew all these things, she didn't know how to act. If she answered in the store, Lillian might suspect the woman had been gossiping. Best to go outside and say she was waiting for the bus.

The phone rang insistently in her hand. She hoped she remembered how to answer it. Lillian had told her that all she had to do was push the talk button, but she'd never had a cell phone. She wondered if she could call Moldova on it, but figured it was probably blocked like the home phone. In any case, Lillian would know if she tried. Best to use a pay phone once she had her wages.

It rang again. Berta looked at her curiously.

She hurried toward the door, but before she got there, a sign on the bulletin board by the door grabbed her attention. Free English classes! On the sign, there was a phone number. She stared at it, memorizing it. Lillian had to let her go. After all, it was free.

She ran outside and answered the phone.

"Where are you?"

"I'm waiting for the bus."

"Well, hurry," Lillian barked, then hung up the phone.

CHAPTER TWENTY

Hannah rushed through the front door of the house, placed her shoes in the closet, and put on her slippers. Feeling like she'd accomplished something big, she hurried down the hall with the madeleines outstretched in one hand.

At the entrance to the kitchen, she heard Lillian and Rena talking in the dining room, and it sounded serious. Hannah slowed down. She'd met Paavo's wife just once before, and she knew why Paavo had joked that Rena would kill him if he didn't come home for dinner. She was a tiny Russian lady, but she was as sharp as a paring knife.

"I won't put up with it," Lillian was saying. "If he cheats again, I'm leaving him."

Hannah froze. This was not a conversation Lillian would want her to overhear.

"That's ridiculous," Rena said. "How will you support yourself?"

"As soon as I pass the USMLE, I'll get a residency. Doctors make a lot of money in America. Why do you think I'm studying all the time?"

"You've been studying for years." Rena laughed. "Anyway, Lilichka, I wouldn't worry about her and Sergey. If he cheats, does it really matter? He's not going to leave you for *her*."

Lillian hummed in semi-agreement. "Still," she said.

Who were they talking about? Had Sergey found a new woman?

"But I wouldn't trust her with my children," Rena added.

Children? Why would this new woman be with their children?

"What do you mean? She's good with children. You can't argue about that," Lillian said. A teacup clanked in a saucer.

"She's illegal and she's gorgeous. Those eyes?" It sounded as though Rena were attracted to this woman. "If she decides she doesn't like cleaning your floors and wiping snotty noses, maybe she wants to make more money, she can go to any escort service, you know. And then she can take your children and sell them. You might never see them again."

They're talking about me!

"Sell them?" Lillian's voice rose. "What do you mean?"

Hannah's mouth dropped open with indignation. It was outrageous. She would never sell a child—what did they think she was?

"I don't want to say it, but Maggie is a beautiful child. If the wrong man saw her, I don't know, maybe he could talk to the girl, become friends with her, you know. Then your Maggie, she would be in danger."

Hannah gripped the counter. She resisted the urge to go in the dining room and shove that woman off her chair. How could anyone say that?

"Rena, the girl isn't all that bright, but she wouldn't sell a child," Lillian said, sort of defending her.

"I'm not saying she would, but she's already shown you that she's shifty."

She hadn't done anything "shifty" since the first day, Hannah thought, since she threw out the sirok bars. She wanted to burst into the room to defend herself, but then they'd know she'd been eavesdropping and she'd look even shiftier.

"I don't know," Lillian said uncertainly. It sounded like Rena was convincing her.

"You don't really think a girl like that is going to want to clean and watch children for very long, do you?"

Hannah frowned. She wasn't some kind of supermodel. She'd never been all that remarkable. Katya had the blonde hair and the tall, skinny body.

"Maybe not," Lillian agreed.

"Paavo would pay a lot of money for her," Rena said. "And you know, it's dangerous to have an illegal working for you right in your home. If the police come . . ."

Couldn't Lillian see what she was doing? This horrible woman wanted Hannah to work for them so they could make money off of her.

"Sergey would never agree."

"Of course he wants her," Rena said, laughing that mean laugh of hers.

"Come on, Rena. He promised he'd take care of her if anything happened," Lillian said.

Who had he promised? And when? If anything happened? Plenty *had* happened. Too much in the last year. Her parents had been killed. Her uncle had gone missing. They had gotten an eviction notice. Maybe Vladi was working for Sergey in Ukraine and Sergey had promised that he'd take care of Hannah if anything happened. Or maybe it had nothing to do with her uncle. Maybe Olga had taken pictures of her and other girls, secretly, and he'd picked her from them, but then who would he have promised? Babulya would have told her if she'd talked to him.

Rena continued, "You can handle having a beautiful girl in your house?"

Lillian cleared her throat. "I'll deal with it." She sounded annoyed. "She's not a fast worker and she's terrible at cleaning, but the children like her and Michael's finally taking his naps. Already, I've gotten more done in the last two months than I did in the last two years since Michael was born. This is why I haven't passed the test yet—I need more time to study."

"Mmm," Rena said, as if she didn't believe her.

"Soon I'll be a doctor in America," Lillian declared, reminding Hannah of herself in that moment. "Then I'll have freedom, you know? If he cheats again—"

"Well, if you change your mind, you can always talk to Paavo. He'll be happy to take her off your hands."

Suka! She couldn't be passed along from person to person like a television set.

"Thank you." Lillian's voice was muted, and Hannah couldn't tell from her tone if she was getting annoyed or if she actually felt grateful.

"And don't let her out of the house. That's what happened with Alexei's girl. They gave her a key, let her come and go when she wanted, and she took advantage."

"You're right," Lillian said, almost as if she were resigned to it.

This was her life they were talking about! Hannah couldn't let this conversation go on. If Rena kept pushing, Lillian might agree to hand her over before the end of the day. She pulled a plate out of the cupboard and banged it down on the counter. Their voices stopped. She opened the bag of madeleines and decided she would pay that woman back, in the only way she could.

A few minutes later, Hannah slid open the dining room door. "Please excuse me. I have your cookies," she said, making sure to use a more formal Russian, as she always did when someone outside of the family was visiting.

Rena looked up expectantly, but Hannah gripped the plate, holding them hostage.

"Thank you," Lillian said, examining her curiously, as if she was wondering whether Hannah had heard anything. "There were no problems?"

"No problems," Hannah said.

For once, she felt more powerful, standing above Lillian like this. Lillian didn't know what she'd heard, what she knew, what she was planning on doing with that knowledge.

Rena cleared her throat.

"Lillian told me you like these," Hannah said, looking down at Rena.

"Yes." Rena's eyes narrowed as if she suspected something, or maybe she was only irritated that Hannah was still holding them.

Finally, Hannah put them down in front of her. "Lillian sent me out to buy them from the Russian store for you. I've heard they're delicious. Have one," she said, as if it was her house and she could actually invite her to have one.

Rena placed her teacup in her saucer, carefully, and it reminded Hannah of when guys in Moldova took off their dress shirts to show they were ready to fight. "Why don't you have one, baba?" Rena said.

Had she just called her baba? It was a derogatory name for a girl, less than a maid, really, but it was hard to tell if this was on purpose, or a term she always used. Hannah kept the mask on her face so as not to show her displeasure. "I would love one," Hannah said.

Rena waved her hand at the plate and waited.

In the kitchen, so angry she was trembling, she'd spit on every single cookie. Hannah picked one up and ate half of it in one bite. With a full mouth, she spoke enthusiastically, just like the country girl Rena seemed to think she was. "They're delicious. Thank you. I've never had anything like this."

The suspicion washed from Rena's face like dirt from the sidewalk after the rain. Rena picked up a cookie and bit it delicately, as if to show Hannah how to eat a cookie. She rolled it around in her mouth. Hannah had to stop herself from smiling in triumph.

"Now run along." Rena flicked her hand in the air like Hannah was nothing more than an irritating fly buzzing too close. Hannah stepped out and slid the door shut. She'd had the last word, and as soon as she could talk to Sergey alone, she was going to get some answers.

CHAPTER TWENTY-ONE

A few days later, Hannah got the chance she was looking for. Sergey was in his study. Lillian was outside, sitting in a lawn chair, underlining portions of a textbook she was reading. Michael was asleep, and Maggie was having a playdate at her best friend Roberta's house. It was the perfect opportunity.

Hannah carried the broom to Sergey's study, rested it against the doorjamb, and listened at the door. He was talking to someone on the phone about an order. He gave the person some numbers. Said it was late. Boring stuff. She waited until he hung up and then knocked softly.

"Yes?" he asked.

"It's Hannah," she said, pressing her cheek against the wood, talking quietly into the crack. "Can I talk to you?"

His office chair creaked and he swung open the door. "Come in," he said.

She'd never been in this room before. There was a huge mahogany desk by the window, which took up half the room. On the desk, he had a cordless phone, a few yellow lined papers, a dirty coffee cup, and a jar covered with painted ice cream sticks—probably Maggie had made that.

There were also two huge bookshelves filled with all the literature she could want in both languages. She walked toward the books and ran her hand along the spines. He had her favorite Russian books by Tolstoy, Dostoyevsky, Gogol, and Chekhov. And he had some books by Hemingway and Faulkner, which were hard to find in Moldova. She wondered if he'd read them.

Sergey cleared his throat and she jerked her hand back. "I'm sorry," she said.

"Don't worry about it," he said, sitting down in his office chair, which creaked in response. "If you want to borrow one, go ahead."

She couldn't get distracted—she didn't have much time. "Can I ask you a question?"

He nodded that she should go on, his eyes flicking down for the briefest of moments at her monkey T-shirt. Was he reading it or looking at her breasts?

"Lillian said you promised someone you'd take care of me." She paused to see his reaction. He seemed startled. "Who did you promise?" she asked.

His blue eyes squinted with what looked like pain, then turned hard, even a little cold. He looked out the window, through the half-closed blind. "I, um, I don't know what you're talking about."

She'd heard Lillian say it plainly. "Did you promise my uncle?"

Sergey's forehead wrinkled. "Your uncle?" he asked, looking right at her, with clear, guilt-free eyes.

"My mother's brother, Vladi. He disappeared two months before I came here. After my parents were killed, he was the one who helped me and my babushka with the farm and the bazaar. He helped us survive."

"You said he disappeared two months before you came here." Sergey seemed sincerely puzzled. "How would I talk to him if he'd already left before I met you?"

"The agent . . ." Hannah hesitated. She hated saying his name. "He said that my uncle wouldn't listen. So he knew something about him, and I thought maybe you talked to him. . . ." Her voice trailed off as she realized how ridiculous it sounded.

"The agent said this?" Sergey asked, stroking his chin with his thumb and forefinger, deep in thought. "What was the agent's name?"

Her insides tensed and the name she didn't want to say croaked out of her. "Volva."

"Volva," he repeated.

"Yes."

His face was losing color. It wasn't good news. "He told you that your uncle wouldn't listen?" Sergey asked.

She bowed her head and nodded, tears coming to her eyes. She couldn't think of that man and her uncle at the same time. One was evil. The other was the sweetest, most loving man she'd ever known. He'd been her mom's best friend. He knew how to make them all laugh, even when there was nothing to laugh about.

"Hannah, I don't know what happened to your uncle, but I'll try to find out. I'm sorry he disappeared." Sergey stood up and reached his arms out as if to pat her shoulders.

The stairs creaked. Hannah stepped back suddenly, tripped

on a lump in the rug, and crashed to the floor.

"What are you doing in this room?" Lillian boomed from above her. She had her hands on her hips and was wearing a new red silk jumpsuit with a gold belt.

Sergey spoke up. "Lily, she brought me this." He pulled a fifty-dollar bill out of his pocket. "She found it in my jeans while she was doing laundry and thought I might need it."

Lillian pasted a fake smile on her face. Her teeth had red lipstick on them. "Well, isn't she an honest girl?"

Hannah stood up slowly, reached for her broom, and hurried past her, realizing too late that Sergey still hadn't told her who he'd promised. If it wasn't her uncle, then who was it? And certainly, if he'd promised someone, it meant she hadn't been brought to America randomly. They'd picked her before she knew anything about them. But how?

CHAPTER TWENTY-TWO

Hannah still hadn't figured out how they'd picked her, but she knew why. Lillian had clearly wanted her because she thought she could treat her like some stray dog.

Hannah dusted the top of the black entertainment center, whipping her hand back and forth angrily. That day, the whole family had gone to the beach and come back with the smell of what had to be the ocean on their bodies, leaving a trail of sand everywhere in the house she'd just cleaned. They'd gone to celebrate because it was the end of summer and the next day, Maggie would start fourth grade, but they'd left Hannah at home.

Maggie followed her from room to room, jabbering away, oblivious to her anger. "I ran through this super huge wave, and it almost carried me away," she said. "You wouldn't believe how big the waves were. Tons of people were bodysurfing on these small surfboards. I really want to do it. Did you ever go surfing?"

"No," Hannah said. "I've never been to the ocean."

"Why not?"

"I was too busy studying," Hannah said, unable to admit the truth. She'd always dreamed of seeing the sea. Smelling it.

Moldova was landlocked, but lots of people went to the Black Sea in the Ukraine, and for years, her parents had promised to take her there. It was where they'd met, on vacation, and they'd always wanted to go back. But there was never the money, especially after her father started his drinking.

Michael came dancing in the living room, shaking his sandy body all over the place. Hannah glared at him. He shouted, "I go in the waves and I jump." Then he threw himself at Hannah, hugging her leg.

"You did not," Maggie said.

"I did," Michael argued.

"He didn't," Maggie said. "Mommy didn't let him. He made a sand castle."

"I make a castle," Michael went on, tugging at Hannah's shirt to get her attention.

Hannah pushed her anger away. She'd seen what anger could do, how it destroyed the person who held on to it. Anger had made her father drink, and it was probably the reason her parents had been killed in the bombing. She couldn't become one of those angry people.

She bent down and gave Michael a hug. "You made a castle?"

He nodded, grinning. "It was big!"

"I know how to swim," Maggie said. "But Mama wouldn't let me go deep. She said the sea would be too strong. Anyway, it was lots and lots of fun."

Hannah rested her hand on Maggie's back. "I'm glad you got to go, my *belka*." This was the nickname she'd given Maggie because she reminded Hannah of a squirrel: always curious and a little tricky.

"You should come next time," Maggie said, as if it were Hannah's choice.

She couldn't help it—the anger came back. "Tell that to your mother," she said, and stalked into the kitchen before she said too much.

They still hadn't paid her. She'd given them a million excuses in her head: Sergey was waiting for money to come in, they'd forgotten, they were busy, Lillian was holding on to it for her. But now she had to admit that the real reason she hadn't asked was that she was afraid of what they'd say.

She went into the kitchen, dropped the chicken in the frying pan, and started to cut up the carrots. Lillian strode in, wearing a flowing silk dress that Hannah had never seen before. "Smells good," she said brightly, and poured some cold cola into two glasses for her and Sergey. She still smelled of sand and fishy salt water. It wasn't asking for too much, Hannah thought, to smell the ocean for real.

Michael was watching *Sesame Street* in the living room, Maggie had gone outside and was reading a book in a long wooden lawn chair, and Sergey was taking a shower. Hannah told herself there was no better time. *Do it, just do it.*

Lillian picked up the spatula and turned the chicken, which Hannah had just turned. Now it would be dry. And she would be blamed. Lillian would say something like, "You can't cook the chicken on such high heat," or "You should marinate it for longer." Lillian picked out a slice of fried onion from the pan and began to hum. The humming made Hannah more nervous.

She continued chopping carrots. It was never a good time. She'd even told herself to ask that morning before the beach so that Lillian would have time to cool off before she came home, but then Lillian had yelled at her about hairs in the upstairs shower—Lillian's own hairs, which Hannah was sure she pulled off her head every time she showered, and deliberately stuck on the tile walls for her to clean up. Every time Hannah's finger touched one of those knotted up bunches of blonde hair, she gagged.

Do it, she told herself. She stopped cutting and held the knife still, sharp point down on the cutting board. Lillian gave her a funny look. The chicken sizzled, all the moisture escaping from it.

"I was wondering about my wages."

"Yes?" Lillian said sharply.

"I haven't been paid," Hannah said.

Lillian tossed back her extravagant blonde hair and flipped the chicken again. "You still owe us money."

"What?" Hannah pushed the knife down hard on the carrot, and a piece flew off the board onto the white tile floor.

"You have to pay us back for the plane ticket, the agent's fee, and the passport." Lillian flipped another piece of chicken as if it was no big deal. "You're cutting those up a bit small," she said, referring to the carrots. "And the chicken is getting dry," she added, pouring more oil into the pan; too much, Hannah thought.

"But Olga said that was included."

"Then she lied."

"Why would she lie?" Hannah turned toward Lillian with the chopping knife pointed up.

"Put that down, baba. You're making me nervous."

Now Lillian was calling her "baba." Hannah placed the knife on the cutting board. "She's my uncle's wife's friend."

"Only to meet you," Lillian said, then pressed her lips together, as if she realized she'd said too much.

"What do you mean?"

"Volva gave her a commission to find someone."

Volva. He was the one they'd used; he wasn't merely Olga's connection in Bucharest. He was the one who'd mentioned her uncle Vladi. And Sergey had almost slipped up when he was drunk that one time. He'd said she looked like someone he knew. Was Sergey lying about Vladi after all?

"Someone? Anyone?" Hannah asked, thinking that it was clear they were after her, but she couldn't figure out why.

"Anyone who wanted to come to America. If the woman didn't succeed, she wouldn't have gotten a commission."

"But you said she befriended my uncle's wife to get to me."

Lillian shrugged. "Maybe you looked desperate." Then Lillian handed her the spatula, a little too fast, as if she were in a hurry to leave. "I have to take a shower. Get this salt off my body. You can finish up." She strode out of the room.

"Wait!" Hannah ran after her with the spatula. "How much do I owe?"

Lillian looked back. The light from the entryway shone from

behind and made her blonde hair light up like a halo around her head. "I have to do some calculations."

"I've been here for two months. I was promised four hundred a week. That's thirty-two hundred dollars." It sounded impossible, even to Hannah's ears, and she wasn't surprised when Lillian laughed.

"Thirty-two hundred dollars?" Lillian exclaimed. "Do you think we are millionaires?"

"That's what I was promised," Hannah insisted, her voice choking up.

"Use your brain, girl. We could have hired someone here if that were the case."

Hannah blinked back the tears. Now was not the time to cry. She needed answers.

"Why are you complaining?" Lillian asked. "You live in a beautiful home and you've got all the food you can want. Be grateful."

"I am," Hannah rushed, not wanting to be thrown out into the street with nothing.

Lillian disappeared into the foyer. Hannah heard her firm steps moving up the staircase, as if that was the end of the conversation.

"Wait!" Hannah ran down the hall, turned into the foyer, and gripped the banister at the bottom of the stairs. "How much are you going to pay me?"

Lillian paused halfway up the stairs and looked down at her, annoyed. "The wage was four hundred a month. But you have to pay off your debt first."

"Four hundred a *month*?" Hannah was devastated. This was a quarter of what she'd been promised, though many times more than she'd made in Moldova. "How much do I still owe?"

Lillian hesitated, then rolled her eyes. "More or less? About four thousand." She said it like it was nothing.

"*Four thousand?*" Hannah screeched, despite her desire to remain calm.

"The agent charged almost five," Lillian said.

"Do you have a receipt?" Hannah asked.

Lillian seemed indignant. "They don't give receipts."

"How do I know you're telling the truth?"

Lillian placed one hand on her elegant hip. "Are you calling me a liar?"

"I would never have come if Olga had told me that. It'll take almost a year to pay that off." She'd hoped to save up enough in a year to start college in America. Now she would be at zero in a year, like she hadn't done a single bit of work. She'd never felt so poor in all her life.

"Did you have so many other choices, baba?" Lillian asked, and then her voice softened. "After you pay it off, you can start saving four hundred a month. This is a fabulous wage."

If Lillian actually paid her. "But I need money now," Hannah said, a tear rolling down one cheek. She swiped it away.

"Why?" Lillian asked.

Maybe she'd have some compassion as a doctor. "I need to pay for an operation for my babushka's cataracts. She can't see. I'm worried she'll fall and—"

Lillian was already shaking her head. "Don't be ridiculous. That's too expensive."

"There is a doctor in Moldova who will do both eyes for a thousand dollars."

"He'll botch it at that price." She rolled her eyes and sighed as if the conversation was making her weary. "You have to think of yourself, Hannah. Relatives will take and take and take."

Hannah stared at her in disbelief. How could she be so selfish?

"I need some money for myself too," Hannah said. "I need to buy clothing and—"

"Clothing? You and I both know that you are lucky to be here. If Sergey hadn't saved you, you might be in the streets right now."

"Are you saying I'd be a prostitute?" Hannah's face flushed with anger, thinking back to the conversation between Lillian and Rena. "I would never do that. I'd rather starve."

Lillian tossed her hair back. "Never say never. You'd do what you had to do to survive." She spoke like she had some knowledge of this world herself.

Hannah swallowed down her fear and thought of how Lillian had said that Sergey had saved her, not that *they* had saved her. She thought about how he'd greeted her at the airport and given her that open smile you'd only give to someone you knew.

Lillian continued up the stairs. Hannah had to ask her one last question. "Please, just tell me one thing—do you know where my uncle Vladi is?"

Lillian looked down over her shoulder, gripping the shiny oak banister near the top of the stairs. "Your uncle Vladi? Why would I know that?"

She actually seemed to be telling the truth, but clearly they had some connection to her. "You said Sergey saved me. Did he ask Volva to get me specifically?"

"Come on, girl." Lillian rolled her eyes again. "Why would he want *you*?"

Hannah tried to replay their conversation earlier in her head. Had she misunderstood?

"Mommy!" Maggie was screaming in the kitchen.

Hannah looked back. Elmo was saying something in Russian on the television in the living room. Michael was sitting quietly on the sofa. She stepped into the hall. Smoke was drifting out of the kitchen.

"Mommy!" Her screech was louder the second time. It was a panicked sound. Hannah sprinted down the hall, thinking, *Please let her be okay!*

Red flames were billowing up around a cloth in the pan, reaching up to the ceiling fan, licking the white paint, turning it brown.

What is a cloth doing there? Maggie was too close. She was waving her hands in front of the fire, screaming. The oil popped in the pan.

"Ow!" Maggie yelled.

Hannah grabbed Maggie by the waist and tugged her back. Lillian flew into the kitchen and threw her arms around Maggie. Lillian was screaming at Hannah, "Put it out!"

An image of her mother's charred remains came into her head from the nightmare she'd had every night since she died, and she hesitated. Her mother's body had been so badly burned in the terrorist bombing, Hannah hadn't been allowed to identify her. She'd never seen her, but her mind had imagined it instead, which was perhaps worse.

"What are you doing?" Lillian screamed.

Hannah jumped forward and turned off the stove. The fire was still shooting up to the ceiling. She had to put something on the flames. Her mother's voice came into her head: *Never add water to oil.* On the counter, she spotted the big tub of flour she'd used earlier to bread the chicken. She picked it up and flung the flour onto the fire.

It worked. It was out. Just like that.

But the kitchen was filled with smoke and Maggie was crying. "The chicken was burning and I tried to move the pan," she sobbed, "but the cloth caught fire."

Hannah worried the flames would jump back up again, that they were stopped only momentarily under the flour. She threw the metal lid on top, grabbed another towel to protect her hands, and holding on to the handle, ran it outside and placed it on the concrete steps.

She ran back inside and propped open the door to let out the smoke. Maggie was sobbing, standing by her mother at the kitchen table. Lillian was stroking her hair, repeating, "Shh, *zaitchik*, shh."

"Is she okay?" Hannah asked, stepping toward them, filled with terror. *Please don't let her be burned.*

"No, she's not okay," Lillian snapped.

"Did you get burned, Maggie?" Hannah asked.

Maggie nodded. "My hand."

"The oil sprayed her," Lillian said. "Get the ointment."

Hannah reached above the refrigerator and pulled out a white first aid kit, where she found some ointment for burns, which she gave to Lillian, who put it on Maggie.

"It still hurts," Maggie cried.

Hannah felt terrible. She should have been watching the chicken, not asking Lillian about the money. "I'm sorry. It's my fault." Quickly, she grabbed a potato and cut it in half.

"Of course it's your fault. You're the most incompetent person I've ever met," Lillian said, pulling Maggie in tighter to her chest. "Believe me, you will pay for the damage."

Hannah glanced at Lillian, wondering briefly how she thought she'd pay for it, and then handed Maggie half of the potato. "Put the raw part on your hand. It'll feel better."

Maggie put it on the small red circle on her hand. "You're right."

"What are you doing?" Lillian asked Hannah, taking the potato away. "No, Maggie, we don't put potatoes on our hands."

"It cools the burn," Hannah said.

"How ridiculous. That's village talk."

It had always worked fine for her, Hannah thought. Michael came into the room, coughing. Hannah picked him up and brought him to the open kitchen door. "Maybe they should go outside," Hannah said. "I'll take them if you want."

"No, I'll take them," Lillian said, holding her arms out for Michael. "You clean up the mess. Come on, Maggie."

"I want the potato," Maggie said.

"No!" Lillian barked. "You'll get an infection."

She wouldn't have given Maggie the potato if she thought she'd get an infection, Hannah thought indignantly. She grabbed a wet cloth and started cleaning the mess. No money for a year. And now she'd have to pay for the damage to the kitchen as well. Once she started getting paid, she'd have to save up for three more months to get money for her grandmother's operation. By then, Babulya would be completely blind.

There had to be a way to get money before then.

CHAPTER TWENTY-THREE

That night, Hannah was writing a letter to Katya when the door to the garage cracked open. Sergey peered in, then opened the door wider. "Are you awake?" he asked.

It was an odd question because the light was on. "I can't sleep," she said.

He stepped inside and walked across the concrete floor to the sofa. His eyes wandered down to her breasts, and she realized she'd already taken off her bra under her T-shirt. She yanked the sleeping bag up.

He wore a sheepish expression. "Are you okay?"

His kindness made her nervous. Even though she'd never had a reason to question it, today was a day he should be yelling at her. "I'm sorry about the fire."

He shrugged. "It was just chicken."

"Maggie got burned," she said, reminding him.

"A tiny mark, that is all. I used to get burns like that every day working in the kitchen at the hotel when I was a boy. Kids here are too soft." His eyes crinkled kindly. "Hannah, you put out the fire. Who would think to use flour? You're the hero."

"I don't feel like a hero," she said miserably.

"Lily told me you were upset about the money," he said.

She nodded, though she barely felt like she had a right to ask for money when Maggie had been burned due to her carelessness. She was lucky she hadn't been fired. Where would she go if they tossed her out? She didn't even have her plane ticket.

"I'm sorry," he said. "The agent got a commission and would've told you anything. I had no control over this."

"You didn't ask for me?"

He blinked. She stared at him. His blue eyes darted away and he shook his head. "I told Paavo what I needed, he got the agent, and the agent found you. I had nothing to do with it."

He's lying. "What about my uncle?" she asked.

"I made some calls. We'll have to wait and see." His jaw tensed as if he was angry, but he didn't seem angry at her.

It all left her feeling so—dissatisfied. Sergey knew things she didn't know. That was for certain.

"If it wasn't my uncle, who did you promise that you'd take care of me?" she asked. "I heard Lillian say it."

He hesitated. "I promised your babushka."

"My babushka?" She hadn't even thought of her babushka. Why hadn't he told her that in the first place?

"She was worried about letting you come to America. I called her and said I would take care of you if anything happened to her."

"Oh." It made sense, but she felt like something was missing. Babulya would have told her, wouldn't she?

Sergey sat next to her outstretched legs on the sofa and rested his hand on the sleeping bag near her hip. "I'm happy you're here. You've really helped us, Hannah."

At least he used her real name, instead of baba. Her lip quivered. "I can't work forever with no money."

He reached for her face with his thick hands and wiped the tears away from her eyes with his rough thumbs. She let out a tearful laugh, and pulled back, embarrassed. "I'm okay."

He opened his wallet. She gazed at the wad of money inside— what did he need all that for? He handed her a fifty-dollar bill. "I don't want to see you cry. Everyone should have some money. You might want to get a coffee or something when you are out."

Hannah snatched it from his hand and instantly felt like one of the scrawny little beggar children who knocked on her apartment door in Moldova and took the heels of old bread.

"Thank you," she murmured, looking down at the bill in her hand.

"You found it in the first place," he said.

She looked up in confusion and he winked. She grinned back at him, remembering the lie he'd told to protect her from Lillian's wrath.

"So?" he asked, as if he expected something in return.

She was giving him days of her life. That's what he got in return. "Are you going to pay me fifty dollars every week?" She worked it out in her head. That was two hundred a month, and in five months she'd have enough for the operation.

He cleared his throat. "That is a lot, Hannah. I was thinking here and there, when you need it. Maybe once a month."

He had a beautiful house and two fancy cars, and all he could give her was fifty on occasion, when she begged him for it? "My grandmother is nearly blind. She needs a thousand dollars for her operation. That's nothing to you. Can't you give that to me now? I'll pay it back."

"That's not nothing, Hannah."

"You must make a lot from your business."

He seemed surprised by her statement. "Not a lot."

"What do you actually do?"

He cleared his throat. "I import things from Russia. Machinery parts. But business is slow with the economy."

"Lillian buys so much food we have to throw a bunch out every week. And she's always buying new designer clothes. She has a Gucci handbag she never uses. It just sits on the shelf. You could sell that and pay me the money for the operation. She'd never know." Hannah saw the edges of his mouth jump up and knew what he was laughing about. Lillian would kill him if he sold her handbag.

"It's true my wife likes to spend." He ran his hand through his thick reddish blond hair. "She'd better become a doctor before we have to go into foreclosure."

"Foreclosure?" She listened to the Russian news playing in the living room while she made dinner every night and she'd heard lots of Americans had lost their homes recently, but she was shocked to hear him suggest that they might be at risk.

"I hope not." He wandered to the large white bookshelf in the garage where Hannah had put her personal things—the picture of her parents, the picture of Daniil, facedown, her copy of *Anna Karenina*. He picked up the picture of her parents and stared at it.

"What?" she said.

"You take after your mother."

"Yes."

"She's beautiful."

"Was," Hannah said. She didn't know why she had to correct him, but she did.

He looked at her, his eyes shiny, as if he felt sorry for her. She lifted her chin and turned away. She didn't need his sympathy.

He cleared his throat. "I don't want you to worry about your babushka. We'll figure something out." He gazed at her, like he was waiting for something.

What did he mean by that? Was he suggesting some other kind of arrangement? "Thank you," she said hesitantly.

"Is there anything else you need?" His eyes were cloudy, desire masked with kindness.

Hannah realized that she was going to have to fight a little harder. She wouldn't do what he wanted her to do, but it was her against Lillian and if he thought he had a chance, maybe he would give her more.

"There is something I have to tell you." She let the sleeping bag drop and pointed at her T-shirt with the words GOOD NEWS printed on it, aware of her unencumbered breasts pressing through the thin cotton. Her cheeks heated up, despite herself. "Do you see these words?"

"Good news." His voice croaked when he spoke. He cleared his throat and gave her a weak smile, one that reminded her of boys her age, despite the wrinkles all over his tanned face.

"I bought this T-shirt in Moldova when I learned I was coming here because this was a new life for me, a new chance." She paused to let it sink in, hoping he might now realize she was more than a maid, or wanted to be. Her eyes filled with tears as she thought of her mother and how she'd told her that English was the key to her future. All doctors need to speak English, she'd said. "My mother wanted more for me than this."

"Hannah," he breathed. This was definitely breaking rule number ten, Hannah thought ruefully.

She cut him off before he said something that would push this too far. "If Lillian won't let me speak English, I have to take English lessons." He opened his mouth to say something, but she jumped up and strode across the garage in her T-shirt and her cutoff jean shorts. "There are free classes—I saw it on the board of the Russian store. I will give you the number to call." She picked up a crayon, tore out a page from one of Michael's coloring books, and wrote the number she'd memorized onto it. She pressed it into his hand, holding it there for a second longer than she knew she should. Was it so wrong to manipulate him a bit?

He gazed at her. "You are one of the most determined girls I have ever met," he said.

She waited.

"I'll talk to Lillian and see what I can do."

"Thank you." She climbed into her sleeping bag and rested her head down on her pillow. "Good night."

"Good night." He wandered out of the garage, as if it was the last thing he wanted to do. This was going to be a dangerous game, Hannah thought. She'd have to be very careful.

CHAPTER TWENTY-FOUR

It was eleven o'clock on Thursday night—the same time Hannah had run into the boy next door last time. Hannah opened the back door and shut it quietly behind her.

If Lillian saw her, Hannah planned to tell her she was taking the garbage to the curb for pickup, but it would probably mean a punishment, like scrubbing the hardwood floors on her knees.

From the other side of the fence, Hannah could hear a fan blowing and American rap music playing quietly. A door opened and closed. Was he in his bedroom?

Listen to your nose. She breathed in and held the odors of America inside her. She blocked out the garbage smell and breathed in the pepperoni pizza the neighbors had ordered that night. She smelled night jasmine blooming in the neighbor's backyard. She smelled soap.

Soap?

She stood next to the fence and stared at the weathered wood with the peeling green paint. The last time she'd spoken to the boy was that day on the bus, a day of freedom that now seemed such a long time ago, even though it had been just two weeks.

There was an expression in Russian: *Your elbow is close, but you can't bite it*. And that was exactly how she felt. America was her elbow.

When she'd seen the boy that first day, she'd thought that they could do things together: go for pizza, visit each other's homes, listen to music. But she'd been here for over two months and they'd talked a total of two times, if you counted the time he quacked. They were brief moments and probably meant nothing to him. She didn't even know his name.

Every morning, she cleaned the front living room windows to catch a glimpse of him walking to school. At night, while she was making dinner, she opened the back door off the kitchen and breathed in the smells of his dinner, usually pizza or hamburgers or Chinese takeout. Sometimes, if she was lucky, she saw him moving around his house and heard English drifting out of the windows.

It was pitiful, really, she thought. Katya would never believe she'd stooped to spying, but she felt like a mute. She needed to have someone to talk to, even about stupid things, like music or movies.

She leaned her head against the fence, as if she were resting it on his shoulder. The fence creaked and started to fall in. She jumped back.

One of the slats had slid to the side and now there was a tiny opening in the fence. It wasn't big enough to see anything, but maybe she could open it more. She was pretty sure his bedroom was on the other side of the fence. She looked up at Lillian and

Sergey's bedroom window. It was the kind that opened out with a crank, and they never opened it because they liked to keep the air-conditioning on at night—air-conditioning that was supposedly for the children only.

She pushed on the old wooden slat. It squealed as it rotated on the one rusty nail that kept it in place. She winced and glanced up at the window, expecting to see Lillian's face looking down at her, but the blue curtain lay still. She took in a ragged breath, pulled her sweaty hair away from her face, and leaned forward to look through the opening into his large bedroom window, which had no curtains.

He was standing on the other side of his enormous room, wearing a dark blue towel around his waist, half naked.

That explained the soap smell. He must have just come from the shower. His short blond hair was dripping wet and his wide back was spotted with droplets of water, as if he'd forgotten to dry off.

She looked in the full-length mirror on his wall to see him from the side. He had rolls of fat down his back and belly. His shoulders were surprisingly large, muscular even, and his calves were strong looking too.

Could he see her face if he looked in the mirror? Maybe. Luckily he was avoiding the mirror, just as you'd avert your eyes from something disgusting, like an old man picking his nose on the bus. But he wasn't disgusting. She wished she could tell him that.

He crouched over a white plastic basket of clean laundry, pulled folded clothes out, and scattered them across the floor of his room, mixing them with the CDs, books, and football gear strewn all over the place. She'd never seen a room this messy, not even in American movies. In Moldova, most teenagers slept in the main room, so nobody left clothes on the floor.

She knew she should leave now, but she couldn't. His back was to her and he was still wearing a towel. In the worst case, she'd just see his behind. But this was different from accidentally spotting him in the kitchen or dining room, where their blinds were always up and they were practically inviting you to watch them. Yet she couldn't tear herself away. As long as the towel stayed on, she wasn't hurting anyone, was she?

He pulled a huge white T-shirt over his head and tugged it down with frustration when it stuck on his belly. Hannah always put on her panties first, and her shirt second, but he did it the other way around. He stepped into his boxers and the towel fell away, but she still couldn't see anything because his shirt was so long. And then he stumbled, his foot catching on the boxers. She giggled, despite herself. He tugged the boxers all the way up and glanced toward the window.

She panicked. If he came outside now to see who was there and found out that she'd been watching him, he would never want to hang out with her. He'd think she was creepy. She certainly would, if the situation was reversed.

She closed the slat in the fence and hurried down the walkway.

CHAPTER TWENTY-FIVE

Sergey and Lillian were sitting at the glass kitchen table reading their newspapers while Hannah cooked eggs at the stove. Maggie was upstairs getting ready for school, and Michael was watching Russian *Sesame Street* in the living room.

"What do you think about Hannah taking some English classes?" Sergey asked.

Hannah couldn't believe it. Finally. It had been weeks since she'd asked him to help her. She fumbled with the spatula and nearly dropped it, which would have been another opportunity for Lillian to say, "Don't burn down the house."

"I don't see any reason for her to take English classes." Lillian took a slurpy sip of tea and opened her newspaper. "She hasn't shown any interest. If she was motivated, she could have been studying the dictionary."

Hannah wanted to protest. Every time Lillian was out of the house, she opened the dictionary and looked up words she didn't know, but she didn't have her own dictionary and Lillian had never given her that grammar book she'd promised.

"It would be good for the children," Sergey said.

"She's supposed to speak Russian to them," Lillian said.

Hannah could feel Lillian glaring at her back, but she flipped the eggs for the third time and pretended she wasn't listening.

"She could help Maggie with her homework," Sergey said.

Lillian sputtered out a laugh. "Right."

Hannah had been one of the smart kids all her life and she wanted to defend herself, but she knew if she said anything, it would ruin any chance she might have.

"There are free classes," Sergey continued, and Hannah couldn't help but admire his persistence.

"Did she ask you to talk to me?" Lillian asked.

Hannah flipped the eggs again to keep her hands busy, even though they would be overdone and Lillian would complain.

"No," Sergey lied. "I think it would be good for her. One of Paavo's girls took them."

"He let her?" She sounded incredulous.

"Yeah."

"He was probably screwing her," she said, waving her hand in the air as if to discount what Sergey had said. "It's not safe for Hannah to talk to other people, Sergey, you know that. It's too risky for our family and too risky for her."

"Have you been talking to Rena again?" he asked.

Hannah couldn't help grinning at the eggs as she slid them out of the frying pan and onto a plate. She wiped the smile off her face and walked toward the table with the plate of eggs. "Michael," she called, poking her head into the living room. "Breakfast." He stared at the television, mesmerized. Hannah put the eggs on the table.

Lillian waved the newspaper in the air. "Didn't you see the article about the arrests?"

"What?" Sergey asked.

"A group of illegal Russian women were caught yesterday—fifteen of them."

Sergey looked back at his paper. "Paavo mentioned something."

"All of them were put in jail." Lillian gave Hannah a meaningful look, eyebrows raised. "They don't get lawyers because of that terrorism bill."

Hannah walked up to the table and tried to see the article over Lillian's shoulder, but Lillian closed the paper.

"Were they terrorists?" Hannah asked.

"No, but they don't have any documentation, so they fall under the same category," she said. "This is why you have to be careful, Hannah."

Sergey looked over his paper. "That's ridiculous, Lily. They're whores."

Hannah glanced back, surprised at the disgust in his voice.

"Rena told me Paavo is worried," Lillian said. "There's a crackdown happening. They're taking everyone into custody."

"What do you mean, everyone?"

"Police are asking any foreigners for documents. It's that new mayor, what's his name?"

"Hmm."

"It's serious, Sergey." She reached over and poked him.

"Ow," he said. "Okay, it's serious."

"I don't want her to leave the house. Do you hear that, Hannah? I don't want you to go out." She shook her finger at Hannah, like she was a dog. "The neighbors shouldn't see you. You need to stay inside. Sergey, you should start taking out the garbage."

He nodded and looked back at his paper. Hannah glared at Lillian. Did she really think with the snap of her finger she could take away the best part of the day? Forget it. She wouldn't give it up, not for anything. If Lillian wanted to pick a fight with her, she'd fight.

CHAPTER TWENTY-SIX

Hannah crept along the old green fence. She was holding a heavy bag of stinky garbage to use as a reason for coming outside. Small stones poked her feet through the thin soles of her slippers.

A droplet of sweat snaked down the side of her face. It was hot outside, especially for eleven o'clock at night in October. Los Angeles was having a heat wave—everyone was worried about fires after the dry summer. Hannah's mouth felt parched no matter how much water she drank. At night, she always had a glass of water by her bed, and she kept the door open whenever she thought she wouldn't get caught, so that the air-conditioning would drift into the garage.

She pushed on the wooden slat in the fence. *Creak.* Her hand hovered in the air as she looked up at the master bedroom window. Her heart was ramming about in her chest. The curtain didn't move. She let out the breath of air she'd been holding and thought she should pour some oil on that nail.

The boy was in his room, dressed this time in a Lakers basketball jersey, sitting at an old wooden desk in the corner of his room, which was as messy as the last time. He pulled a sketch-book and a skinny black felt pen out of the drawer and smoothed the blank page with one hand.

He began to draw, and his back curved as he brought his face closer to the page. She could see a thick, arching line he was fill-ing in with his pen, but couldn't tell what he was drawing. His whole body seemed to relax as he drew, like he got lost in it.

His door burst open and his mother flew into his room. The boy shut his sketchbook. "Mom!"

His mother had curly blonde hair and a big laugh, just like his, but unlike him, she never stopped moving. As soon as she got home from work, she was cleaning, folding clothes, making phone calls, always walking around the house, putting things away. She looked around his room. "Did you throw the clothes I just folded all over your floor again?"

Hannah mouthed her words just like she always did. The family's windows were always open, so if Hannah opened the back door while she was cooking or cleaning up, she could hear them talking in their loud voices. She repeated everything they said, gulping down their words like the watery soups from those last few months in Moldova.

The boy dropped his arm with the pen to his side, as if he was waiting for the lecture. She seemed to get angry at him a lot lately.

"What the hell, Colin . . ." His mother shook her head and for a moment looked like she might cry.

His name was Colin! The name rolled like butter over her tongue. "Colin," she whispered, and the darkness held his name like a present.

"I folded everything," his mother went on. "All you had to do was put your clothes in your dresser."

Colin stared at her without saying anything, and for the first time, Hannah saw fury in those bright blue eyes, in that kind face that had smiled at her so brightly when he waved from the bus.

His mother pointed at the mess. "Pick them up."

"I'm busy," he said. "I'll do it later."

Hannah understood nearly everything they were saying, except that word "dresser," which she told herself she'd look up in the dictionary later when no one was looking.

"Busy?" His mother marched up to him and grabbed his limp arm. "Now. Get up. Get off your lazy butt!" When he didn't move, she whacked him on the side of the head. He cringed. Hannah cringed with him.

"Get up!" she yelled again, louder now, and Hannah glanced up at the window above her, worried that the noise would wake everyone up. The curtain didn't move.

He stood up. "Chill out. I'm up."

Chill out?

"When are you taking out the garbage?" his mother demanded.

Now, Hannah thought, *please, do it now.*

"Tomorrow. In the morning."

Hannah felt the disappointment in her stomach, like a hunger she couldn't satisfy.

"It's always tomorrow with you. I'm sick of you sitting around like a fat, lazy pig," his mother said, her voice shaking with fury. Her curly blonde hair quivered like electricity. "You're just like your father. Selfish. Selfish. Selfish." Colin blinked each time she repeated the word, and his fingers curled up slowly, but the rest of his body stayed completely still.

His mother glared at him one last time, then strode out of the room and slammed the door. Colin sank back into his chair.

Hannah felt awful that his mother had said those mean things to him. She'd seen his mother laughing with him and his brother, talking with them at the dining room table, sincerely interested in their lives, and she felt pretty sure she was just having a bad day, but still. How would she feel if that was the last word she ever got to say to him?

Hannah's mother had never said anything unkind to her, while the last thing Hannah had said to her was that she was *tupaya*—stupid. She'd wished a million times she could take back that word. Even worse, it was over something as silly as a curfew. Her friends didn't have one and she didn't think it was fair that she did, so she'd called her mother stupid. She'd never forget that look in her mamulya's green eyes, the eyes that matched her own. It was like Hannah had hit her. Two days later, her parents were killed by the terrorist's bomb at a café in Transnistria, probably while her mamulya was sipping her tea, thinking about how her only child had called her stupid.

Colin stared at the door, as if he was waiting for his mother to burst back into the room. When it became apparent that she was really gone, his whole body sagged like the air being let out of a balloon.

Hannah realized then that maybe Colin needed a friend as much as she did. She wanted to wrap her arms around him and give him a hug, but she was stuck on this side of the fence.

Just ignore her, Hannah thought. *Come outside. Bring the garbage out.*

"Hannah!" It was Lillian by the back door.

Colin glanced back at the window. He'd heard! Hannah jumped away from the opening in the fence and pressed herself against the scratchy wood. Had he seen her? She looked down at the garbage bag in her hand. She'd have to cross the opening to get to the cans. Or leave it here. But if Lillian saw a garbage bag sitting by the opening in the fence, she'd know exactly what she'd been doing. She took one fast step to cross the opening and hurried to the garbage can. She raised the lid and lowered the bag into the can, trying not to make a sound.

"Where are you, Hannah?" Lillian was speaking Russian, which Colin couldn't understand, but she was speaking so loudly he was sure to hear.

Hannah hurried along the gravel walkway and rounded the corner of the house. "I'm here," she said softly.

Lillian was standing on the lawn in a short yellow cotton nightgown and white slippers. "What are you doing?" she asked.

Hannah remembered to keep her voice calm. "I'm taking out the garbage," she said.

"I told Sergey to do it."

"Really, I can do it," Hannah said, managing a casual smile. "Nobody will see me. It's nighttime."

"Go inside."

Hannah bit her lip and walked back across the lawn. There had to be something she could do to make Lillian trust her.

CHAPTER TWENTY-SEVEN

Her chance came a few nights later.

"Wake up," a voice said.

The light in the garage turned on. Hannah blinked her eyes open and squinted at Lillian, who was standing in the door-way to the garage in her white nightgown.

"Michael's sick," she said. "Come."

Hannah jumped out of her sleeping bag and pulled her bra up and under the black T-shirt she was wearing, a new T-shirt Lillian had bought her to replace "that small monkey one." She glanced at the clock—five after two in the morning—and hurried up the stairs after Lillian.

Michael was crying in his bedroom. Sergey was crouched beside Michael's bed, wearing pale blue pajamas, the tips of his fingers fluttering along Michael's forehead. "Shh," he was saying. "Shh, my boy." But it didn't seem to help. Hannah smelled vomit in the room.

Lillian came up. "Okay. Go to sleep," she said to Sergey. "Hannah can help."

He nodded, glancing at Hannah briefly, as if he were afraid to look at her too long, and stumbled out of the room back to the master bedroom.

"Sergey can't stand the smell," Lillian said.

Hannah could barely take it herself. That was the problem with having a sensitive nose.

Lillian pulled Michael's pajamas and overnight diapers off him and handed them to Hannah. They were all wet and sticky. "Clean these and change the sheets. I'll hold him. Get me a wet washcloth." Lillian picked up Michael, who was now naked and wailing even louder.

Hannah didn't know what Lillian wanted her to do first, but figured it was most important to get Michael cleaned up. She dropped his pajamas onto the dirty sheet and then picked up his fuzzy blue blanket from his dresser to wrap around him. "Here," she said.

"Thank you." Lillian took it, wrapped it around him, and sat in the rocking chair in the corner. Michael buried his head in his mother's chest, whimpering. Lillian really could be a good mother when she tried, Hannah thought.

Hannah rushed to the bathroom, wet a washcloth, and hurried back. She ran it over Michael's mouth and face. "Do you want water, little rabbit?" Hannah asked him. "To clean out your mouth?"

He nodded, blinking his teary blue eyes at her. In the bathroom, she filled a glass of water and rushed back in.

Lillian helped him drink it. His crying stopped.

Hannah wiped off his body and arms with the washcloth. She grabbed a new diaper and pajamas, and put them on Michael while Lillian held him. Hannah always dressed him nowadays. Lillian had to chase him around to get anything on him, but he always cooperated for Hannah.

Once he was dressed, Hannah took the blue blanket, which had gotten dirty, and handed Lillian the alphabet one. Then she grabbed the dirty sheets, blanket, and clothes and hurried them downstairs. She wondered if she should rinse them first in the sink, but just threw them in the washing machine on hot with lots of soap. She ran back upstairs.

Michael was moaning in his mom's arms. Hannah felt his forehead. He was hot. "I don't want to give him Tylenol," Lillian said, "but I will if I have to."

"My mother never liked to give me medicine either." Hannah remembered the cold leaf poultices her mother had applied to her forehead and her armpits when she got a fever.

"Why does it smell still?" Lillian asked.

Hannah looked. The rug on the floor was soaked, along with the side of the bed. Hannah rolled up the rug, brought it downstairs, then went back up with a spray bottle of cleaning liquid and paper towels. After she'd cleaned the floor and the bed, the room smelled a little better, but not great. Hannah lit the vanilla candle on the shelf.

Lillian urged Michael to drink more water. Hannah's mother used to do the same, and then Hannah would keep throwing up until she felt better. Michael began to cough. Hannah rushed for the garbage can, but it was too late. Michael started to gag and began to throw up again, all over his mother and his clothes.

Lillian looked so disgusted that if Hannah didn't know better, she would have laughed. Didn't she expect him to throw up again? "Here," Lillian said, handing over Michael with her arms stretched out. "I need to change."

Michael was screaming in distress, and Hannah clucked her tongue while she took off his clothes. Once he was naked again, she used wipes to get the vomit off his body, then put fresh clothes on him. Holding him on her hip, she wiped off the rocking chair and sat back down with him, remembering to lock the rocking chair. It was a little silly to rock a child with a queasy stomach. She put a cold wipe on his head. He whimpered, then wrapped his little hand around her neck and fell asleep.

Shortly afterward, Lillian came back in the room, looked down at her sleeping son, and felt his forehead. Hannah could feel that he was starting to cool off.

"I don't want to wake him," Lillian said.

"Don't worry," Hannah said. "I'll hold him while he sleeps. If he wakes up and needs you, I'll come to get you."

Lillian agreed and left the room. Hannah rested her head back and drifted to sleep.

In the morning, Hannah was in the kitchen with Michael when Lillian walked in. She was holding Michael on her lap, feeding him a murky white liquid that her mother had always called rice soup, though the rice had been strained out.

"What is that?" Lillian asked, walking into the kitchen.

Hannah tensed up, ready for Lillian to call her a village girl again. "It's rice soup, for the diarrhea."

Lillian laughed. "My grandmother used to make that for me. I forgot about it."

Hannah let out a breath of relief.

"Mama, I want sirok bar," Michael said.

"Not today. You're sick." Lillian bent over and kissed his forehead, then looked at Hannah. "No fever. I guess he's feeling better. You held him all night?"

"Yes," Hannah said.

Lillian gave her a long look and then nodded quickly. Hannah grinned and kissed the top of Michael's curly blond hair. Lillian was starting to believe in her, even if she wouldn't yet admit it. Maybe she'd even start paying her early.

CHAPTER TWENTY-EIGHT

Hannah was reading Maggie a fairy book in Russian, as she always did before bedtime. "This is boring," Maggie interrupted her in English. Hannah looked up briefly. She was right. It was far too young for Maggie, something you'd read a five-year-old, and she'd suggested to Lillian that she could read *Anna Karenina* to Maggie, but Lillian had acted as if Hannah had offered to show her a pornography magazine. Her own father had given her *Anna Karenina* when she was eight, and it hadn't scarred her, but whatever. Hannah continued reading. Maggie moaned, rolling her eyes. Hannah shut it midsentence.

"I can't take Russian anymore either," she said in Russian, and then decided to speak in English, despite the risk. Lillian was downstairs, after all. "We can read your English book?" She felt like she was begging. If Maggie told her mother, Hannah would be punished.

But Maggie grinned. "Let's pretend I'm the teacher and you're the student. We'll call it room 116. That's my room at school."

Michael made a *beep-beep* noise from the foot of the bed and ran his train over their feet.

"Ouch," Maggie said, pulling her feet back, and then, speaking in a deeper voice, added, "Mr. Barnes doesn't like that."

"Mr. Barnes?" Michael asked in English and then giggled.

This is dangerous, Hannah thought. If he started speaking English, Lillian might guess that she'd been speaking English around him.

Maggie reached under her pillow for her vampire book. She kept the book under her pillow so Lillian wouldn't find it. Maggie's best friend, Roberta, had loaned it to her, but Lillian didn't know about the book and would never allow it, even for Maggie's own personal reading. She didn't let Maggie read anything with violence. Hannah had never met Roberta, but Lillian dropped Maggie off for playdates sometimes, and Maggie raved about her. She lived in a mansion in Beverly Hills and she was "super cool."

Maggie cleared her throat primly and began to read in her perfect American voice, occasionally making her voice deep, when she remembered she was Mr. Barnes.

"Okay, your turn." Maggie handed Hannah the book.

Hannah read the first line of the next page, speaking slowly.

"No, silly, you don't say it like that," Maggie said in English, laughing. "Say, 'vampire,' not 'wampire.'"

Michael repeated, "Vampire."

"See, he can say it. Good boy, Michael." Maggie readjusted herself and smoothed her long brown hair back. "Try the sentence again."

"The vampire svaggered toward the girl," Hannah said.

"Svaggered?" Maggie flopped backward on the bed and threw her head onto her pillow, laughing.

The door to her room opened. "What is going on here?"

Lillian asked, speaking Russian as she always did, even though she must have heard them speaking English. Hannah leaped off the bed, pressing the book to her side, both for Maggie's sake and for her own.

"Nothing," Hannah said, answering in Russian.

"What are you reading?" Lillian demanded.

Neither Maggie nor Hannah answered.

"Vampire," Michael said in English with a big grin.

Lillian marched around the bed and snatched the book from Hannah. She lifted it up in the air. Hannah flinched, sure Lillian was going to hit her with it, but Lillian just shook it in her face. "How dare you? You are not going to use my children to teach you English. I told you no English books. They need to speak Russian, not bad English."

Hannah knew it was best to be quiet when Lillian got angry. She pressed her lips together even as her mind rushed with things to say, ways to fight, arguments to make.

"But Mommy, I'm teaching her good English," Maggie said from the bed, looking up at her mother with those sweet, innocent eyes.

Lillian read the cover of the book. "What is this? You are not allowed to read vampire books." Lillian turned back to Hannah. "Do you realize that I'm going to have to wake up every night for the next week because Maggie will have nightmares from this book?"

"No, I won't," Maggie said in English. "I haven't for a long time."

"Be quiet, Maggie."

Hannah saw the flush in Lillian's cheeks and prayed that Maggie would stop, but Maggie was just getting started. "I'm not a baby. God. You can't make me speak Russian. You're just jealous 'cause you can't speak English."

Lillian's mouth dropped open and then she marched to Maggie's shelf where Maggie kept all her dolls. She tucked the book under her arm and reached up for Rebecca, Maggie's favorite doll.

"No mamulya, please," Maggie said, switching back to Russian. "Not Rebecca!"

"I'm taking five dolls today," Lillian said, grabbing four more dolls by their hair. "If I hear any more English, Maggie, I'm taking away all of them."

This was a terrible punishment, Hannah thought, and not fair at all when Maggie was just helping her. "It's not right," she spoke up suddenly, reaching her arm out.

"What?" Lillian asked Hannah, hugging the dolls to her body. "Don't contradict me. *I* am the mother."

Hannah looked down at the floor and stepped back. *Hold your tongue,* she told herself. *For once, think of yourself.*

"Those are my dolls!" Maggie yelled, jumping up from the bed and trying to grab at Rebecca.

"Sit on your bed," Lillian barked, yanking the dolls back. Her face was red. Hannah didn't think she'd ever seen Lillian this angry. Maggie swung her hand forward, reaching for the book under Lillian's arm. Lillian jumped back. "Sit," she yelled, and raised her arm as if to strike her. Maggie shrank down on her bed. Lillian shook her finger at Maggie.

"You know the rules. No English. If you don't speak any

English in the house for the next week, you'll get them back. Now stay in your bed!"

Maggie asked in a quiet voice, "Can I have the book, please?"

"No, you can't have the book," Lillian said indignantly.

"But it's not even mine. It's Roberta's."

"I guess you'll have to tell her you lost it."

"No, Mommy, please . . ." Maggie burst into tears and covered her face with her hands.

Lillian glared at Hannah, clearly blaming her. "Put Michael to bed, baba."

Michael wrapped his arms around Hannah's neck, and she knew she should just leave now, before she made things worse, but she felt sick that Maggie was getting punished instead of her. "She didn't do anything wrong. I asked her to teach me. It was just a game to her."

"You, get out," Lillian said, shaking her finger at Hannah. "She knows the rules. I'll deal with you later."

Hannah hurried out of the room, carrying Michael down the hall. Her heart was pounding. She'd deal with her later? What did that mean?

"Maggie, stay in your room," Lillian barked, and shut the door.

"I hate Russian and I hate you!" Maggie yelled in English from inside her room.

Hannah waited for Lillian's response, scared she was going to go back into Maggie's room, but thankfully, she stormed down the stairs. Hannah put Michael in his room in front of the television, turned on a Russian cartoon, *Nu, pogodi!,* and then crept back down the hall to Maggie.

Through the door, she could hear Maggie's long, muffled sobs. It was such a sad, lonely cry. Hannah opened the door, walked over to the bed, and sat down next to her. Maggie was stretched out on her belly, her head buried in her pillow. Her back jumped up with each sob. Hannah clucked her tongue like her mother used to do when she was little.

Maggie let out another wail, and Hannah glanced toward the door, worried that Lillian would rush in and see her comforting Maggie. It was a risk she'd have to take.

"Shh, it's okay," she said, rubbing Maggie's back in small circles.

Maggie relaxed into her touch for a few moments, but then her arm swung back and she hit Hannah hard in the arm. "Get out! You'll make my mother angry."

Hannah stood up and walked out of the room, her arm throbbing. She had some sense of how Anna Karenina must have felt, forlorn and rejected by all, before she stepped off the train platform.

CHAPTER TWENTY-NINE

That night, Hannah awoke to someone touching her shoulder. Maggie was standing in the garage in her frilly white nightgown, looking so small, despite her age. "I'm scared."

Hannah blinked, groggy. "Come here," she said. Maggie climbed onto the sofa next to her, and Hannah wrapped her arms around her skinny, quivering body.

Tearfully, Maggie told Hannah about her nightmare. She'd dreamed that her mother was a vampire, and only Maggie knew, so she had to lock herself in Michael's room at night to protect him, but he wanted to see their mother, so he finally got away and then he became a vampire too and then they were both chasing after her. She sniffed. "It was so scary."

She seemed much younger than eight at that moment. "It was only a dream, Maggie. Vampires aren't real. You know that, right?"

Maggie sucked in a haggard breath and nodded in agreement.

But it wasn't the vampires she was afraid of—it was her own mother. It was no wonder Maggie had a nightmare after Lillian's freak-out. She'd nearly hit her. Over a book. Hannah tickled the back of Maggie's hair by the nape of her neck, shushing her softly, and Maggie wrapped her arm over her chest, resting her head on Hannah's shoulder.

Hannah held her until she fell asleep, then lifted her up and carried her out of the garage and down the hall. At the bottom of the stairs, she paused and listened. All she heard was her own heavy breathing. Even though Maggie was a skinny eight-year-old, she had to be sixty pounds, and it was no easy task to carry her. But she had to get Maggie up the stairs without anybody knowing that she'd woken up. She could just imagine what Lillian would do if she learned that Maggie had had a nightmare about her being a vampire. Slowly, she walked up each step, wincing as the stairs creaked.

Finally, she reached Maggie's room. Fortunately, the door was already open. Her arms were aching. She placed Maggie gently in her bed and shook out her arms, gazing down at Maggie. She looked so young with her flushed cheeks and puffy eyes. Hannah smoothed a strand of dark hair away from her face, surprised and a little frightened about how much she cared about her.

She stepped out of the room. Still, the house was silent. She crept down the stairs. Near the front door, she heard someone yelling outside. Sergey? No, it sounded like English. She glanced back up the stairs. Everyone was asleep.

It would be best to ignore it, she thought, but she was curious; she'd always been too curious. She pressed her head against the crack in the door. Definitely English. Maybe it was Colin.

The dead bolt was cold in her fingers as she slid it open. She paused and listened for any noises coming from upstairs. This is what it would feel like if she were running away. It was tempting, sometimes, but where would she go?

She cracked the door and peeked out. A fancy black Mercedes convertible was in the next-door neighbor's driveway. She took two steps out to the landing at the top of the front steps and peered around the white stucco of the house.

A tall, dark-haired man in a tailored suit was standing at the bottom of the neighbor's steps. He had his hands jammed in his pockets and he was leaning back, unsteady on his feet.

The mother stood in the doorway of her house, holding the metal screen door open with her body. With her other hand, she pulled a short red robe tighter around her flowery nightgown. "We'll talk in the morning, Will."

"Why'd you have to take me to court? I'll give you money for the boys if that's all you want," he said, slurring, looking up at her.

Hannah wondered who this man was. She understood that the mother wanted to talk to the man in the morning and the man was angry that she wanted money.

Colin came up behind his mom, rubbing his eyes, in blue pajama bottoms and a gray T-shirt.

"Dad?" he asked. "What are you doing?"

Dad? Hannah couldn't believe it. This was his father? She'd thought that the picture of the military man in the kitchen was their father, and she'd assumed he was dead like her own parents. She'd kind of hoped it, if someone could hope such a thing without being a horrible person.

"Just having a conversation with your mother," the father said, trying to steady his voice so that he'd seem sober. Parents never understood how smart their children were.

"It's two in the morning."

The father stared at him as if something about Colin displeased him. It wasn't a look of love, like Hannah's own father would give her even when he was drunk. "Son, did I give you everything you wanted for Christmas?" he asked him.

"Yeah." Colin glanced at his mother, as though he were afraid of betraying her.

"And your birthday?"

"I guess."

"You have a roof over your head?"

His mother interrupted. "You haven't paid their September or October tuition. It's almost the end of October. The school won't give us their report cards until you pay."

Tuition. Hannah didn't know that word. If only she could use a dictionary.

"I'll pay it by the end of the month," the father said. "I got a lot of bills right now. We've got only so many pieces of the pie, Izzy."

Her voice rose. "You mean you've got to pay for an expensive wedding when you can't even pay for your children's goddamn tuition!"

Hannah looked into Colin's face, illuminated in the porch light, and noticed the anger in his eyes.

The younger brother came to the door in a T-shirt and boxer shorts. He ran his hand through his messy brown hair and squinted. "Do you have to fight outside at two in the morning?"

"Hey, my man!" The dad took two steps up the stairs and gave him a high five. Colin shifted back. "We've got to take out the ball this weekend."

"Sure, Dad!"

The father stumbled backward down the stairs. The younger boy stepped forward to help, but their father recovered in time. Colin stared down at his father. Didn't step forward to help. Didn't even care.

Colin glanced in Hannah's direction. Their eyes met, and his face revealed a look of pure humiliation. She stepped backward, out of view. No matter where kids lived, nobody liked people to know what a mess their parents were.

She remembered the time she'd been on a school field trip to the National Opera House when she was fourteen and her father had been passed out on the steps. She'd noticed him right away. So had Katya. Hannah had looked straight ahead. Katya had glanced at her in alarm, but Hannah had been too embarrassed to acknowledge it even to Katya. Her face had heated up in anticipation. The class had walked in a row past her drunk father, and all she could do was hope that no one would recognize him. But someone did. The girl she hated, Elena, had yelled out, "Isn't that your father, Hannah?" Katya had turned to glare at Elena and then she'd reached over and grabbed Hannah's hand, squeezing it tight.

Hannah stepped back into the house and closed the door behind her. She clicked the lock shut and sighed. Colin's father was a drunk, just like hers had been. He was a rich drunk, but a drunk nonetheless. She walked down the hall into the garage, and dropped down on the sofa.

One of her last memories of Papulya was of him pacing the living room, a glass of vodka jumping in his hand, as he raged on about the corrupt government that stole money from the people. "We were rich under the Soviets. Rich!"

Hannah was sitting on a cushion in front of her mother, who was sitting on the fold-out sofa, rubbing Hannah's neck with a mild smile on her face as if to say, *Yes, yes, we've heard this before.* Daniil was sitting beside Hannah, nodding vigorously, drinking a glass of vodka her father had poured from the bottle Daniil had brought for him.

Papulya bent down, a few inches from Daniil's face, and said, "You know, you know." A dollop of spit flew from his mouth, landing on Daniil's cheek, but Daniil didn't wipe it off. Hannah was grateful for that.

Her father stood and shook his drink at Hannah, spilling it on the floor by her foot. "This is a good man, Hannah. A good man." Daniil was only sixteen at the time, but that didn't matter to her father.

Her mother had squeezed Hannah's shoulders tight then, a squeeze that Hannah had tried to interpret for the last year, because she'd never had the chance to ask her mother about it. She never knew if it meant that she didn't think Daniil was a good man or if it meant she should not listen to her father about anything or if it was just a strange way to show she agreed. A week later, they were both dead.

CHAPTER THIRTY

Hannah was folding clothes on the long narrow table in the garage. If she had her choice, she'd do it at the kitchen table with the back door open so she could listen to the birds and the lawn mowers, but Lillian didn't like a mess in the kitchen.

She folded Michael's pants. All his little clothes took forever. If taking out the garbage had become her unexpected favorite chore in this country, doing the laundry was her unexpected least favorite. She hadn't known to dread laundry, because she'd never had to do it before. Her mother and then her babushka had done all the washing by hand and hung it to dry outside over the balcony in the summer or on a rack next to the heater in the winter.

The washing machine stopped. She banged open the lid and reached in for the white clothes and heaved them into the dryer. At least she had a washer and a dryer.

Dark clothes next. On cold. When anything got ruined, Lillian said, "I'll just add this to what you owe us." Hannah's debt was an invisible number that seemed to be forever expanding. The bill for the new stove and for repainting the kitchen had surely been added to her debt, and who knew what else.

She reached into one of Sergey's pockets. Emptying pockets was one of the many gross parts of doing laundry. She always hoped for something that would be useful to her, like keys to his office or a letter from her family, but instead she found cigarette butts, receipts from restaurants and coffee shops, and spare change. One time she got gum on her fingers that he'd stuck between two pieces of paper. Another time she found an unused condom in its package, and ever since, she'd worried she'd find a used one. That would be even worse than the poop on Michael's pants and the bloodstains on Lillian's underwear, which she'd had to spray with stain remover.

Hannah pulled out a wad of bills and one piece of paper from the pocket of Sergey's jeans. She unfolded the bills and counted them. Four hundred dollars, all in twenties. Was it an accident, or had he left the money there for her? He'd never had this much money in his pockets before, just random change and one-dollar bills now and then. It was especially odd to leave four hundred when that was the exact amount she was supposed to get paid per week or per month, depending on who she believed.

"Take it," Colin said. He was sitting on the dryer. Well, not actually sitting, and he wasn't speaking out loud, just in her thoughts. She liked to imagine him hanging out with her, so that if she wanted to share her opinion, someone would respond.

"I thought you were a nice boy," she chastised.

He laughed his big American laugh. "They owe you," he said. In her daydream, Colin was speaking Russian because that's what came naturally to her and she couldn't imagine him speaking broken English. Anyway, daydreams didn't have to be realistic.

"They say *I* owe them," Hannah said.

"It's for your grandmother. What are they going to do once you've sent it?"

"I can't just mail this. Someone at the post office in Moldova will take it. I have to transfer it into her bank account. I asked Babulya to send me her account number in my last letter, but she hasn't written back yet."

"Do you really think Lillian sent your letters?"

"Sure," Hannah said, stuffing Sergey's jeans into the washing machine. "Nobody would be that awful." She glanced at the money and thought that maybe the doctor would do the surgery for less, or at least do one eye.

"You should look for the letters," he said.

"They're probably in the office," she said, picking up the piece of paper. Maybe it was a note to her, telling her to keep the money.

No such luck. Just some scrawled notes in Sergey's messy handwriting.

She tried to read it. There were a bunch of numbers and words, but they made no sense—it was almost like a code, and then a number—24,388—with a dollar sign in front of it. Maybe the cost of a shipment. That was a lot of money. Near the bottom, one word made her heart stop. Tiraspol. It was the name of the capital city of Transnistria, the breakaway republic of Moldova, the place where her parents had been killed.

"Hey, Hannah!" Maggie loped into the room, speaking English. Colin disappeared.

Hannah quickly dropped the note on the money and placed a folded towel carefully on top. She hadn't decided to keep the money, but she needed a few minutes to think. Her head was swimming with that one word, the place of her parents' death. She'd left that word behind her in Moldova, and yet, somehow, it had followed her here.

"Whatcha doin?" Maggie was holding a book.

"Hello, belka," Hannah answered in Russian, keeping her face neutral. "You'd better speak Russian."

"Mama doesn't care. She even gave me back my dolls and the book." Maggie held up the vampire book. "She said I could read it as long as I don't start biting anyone." She giggled.

Hannah smiled. Lillian was the one who was more likely to bite. "Are we allowed to speak English now?" she asked, hopeful.

"I don't know. Probably," Maggie said, but then switched to Russian anyway. "What are you doing?"

"Folding laundry," Hannah said, then paused. Maybe Maggie could help. "I was thinking of my family."

"Yeah?"

"Did your mom or dad ever tell you anything about my family?" she asked.

"Your mom and dad live in Moscow and you don't have brothers and sisters."

She didn't know much, clearly. "Did they ever say anything about an uncle?" she asked.

"I know Papa isn't your uncle. It was just something they said."

"How do you know that?" I asked.

"I told him you must be my cousin if he's your uncle. He said he wasn't really your uncle, not biologically. But he said he was friends with your parents, so he was *like* an uncle."

Hannah's breath caught in her throat and her chest constricted. It was hard to breathe, like someone had just clamped a hand over her mouth. Maggie had no idea what she'd just revealed. Finally, she found her voice. "When—when did he tell you this?"

"I don't know." Maggie stretched her arm around Hannah's shoulder and stood on her tiptoes. "I'm almost as tall as you."

Hannah made herself smile, because she didn't want Maggie to suspect she'd just told her something she shouldn't have. "I'm shrinking, that's why. I'm becoming a babushka." She curved her back and hobbled around, changing her voice into a babushka's. "Don't worry about me. I'll just clean."

Maggie laughed, then rested her head on Hannah's shoulder. Normally Hannah loved these bursts of affection from Maggie and Michael, but at that moment, she could only think about what Maggie had just told her. Maybe it wasn't true. If Sergey really knew her parents, she would've heard his name at some point. Maggie continued, "You should come out and do something fun with us. Papulya was talking about going on a picnic this weekend to this park where they play polo on horses. You could come."

Not if Lillian has anything to say about it, Hannah thought. Lillian's paranoia was even stranger if Sergey was a friend of her family. And why wouldn't they have told her? It wasn't something they needed to hide. It had to be another lie.

"Can you come? Please?" Maggie honestly believed it was Hannah's choice.

"I'm very busy."

"You have time. Mama will just say you have a day off. People do that here."

Hannah wanted to tell her that people had days off in Moldova too. Her mother had always worked long hours, but on rare days, she stayed home with Hannah. They'd gone for walks through the woods on the edge of Chişinău and Mamulya had shown her the mushrooms that could calm the stomach, the berries that were good for eating, and the ones that were poisonous. Even when her father had worked at the garage, he'd had Saturdays off. They used to sit on one of the park benches and he'd read to her. She could still see that misty expression in his face when he read Dostoyevsky's *The Idiot*; he was so in love with that book.

"Maybe," Hannah said, folding a towel. She wondered if her parents could see her now. Had they seen her hiding the money that had been in Sergey's pocket? Did her mother see the piece of paper with "Tiraspol" written on it? What did her parents know that she did not? Maybe she could get Sergey alone and ask him.

"It'll be so much fun. You'll like it," Maggie declared, as if Hannah needed to be talked into having fun. "We can play soccer on the big field. Please?"

If only she could say it was going to happen. She ran her hand over Maggie's perfectly brushed hair. Maggie didn't see what was happening right in front of her.

"I would love that." Hannah looked at the towel covering the money. If Maggie found out that Hannah was a thief, she'd lose all trust in her. Hannah lifted the towel and thrust the money at Maggie before she could change her mind. "Give this to your father. It was in his jeans."

"Wow," Maggie said, taking it from Hannah, and running out of the room.

Sorry, Babulya. I couldn't do it.

CHAPTER THIRTY-ONE

At the kitchen table, Lillian gasped. It was morning, when she typically opened the mail. Hannah glanced up from the dishes she was washing and saw Lillian staring down at a typed letter, her hand covering her mouth.

Hannah took the butcher knife out of the soapy water, rinsed it, and placed it in the dish rack before she dried off her hands. "Is everything all right?" she asked.

"Does everything look all right?" Lillian barked.

Hannah waited for her to go on. Perhaps Lillian had received a letter from the government saying that they knew all about her. Perhaps it had something to do with her family. Or what had happened in Tiraspol.

"My life is ruined," Lillian said, standing up, gripping the letter in one hand. "That's what this letter means." Her lip quivered.

Hannah wondered if they were going into foreclosure and would all be thrown into the streets. She waited to hear more, but Lillian's jaw tightened as she clenched her teeth together. "For the next week," she said, her voice wavering, "you will do nothing but clean. Thanksgiving is coming next Thursday, and Rena and Paavo will be our guests. He's very allergic to dust.

Last time he came over for a drink, he said his eyes got puffy from the dust."

Hannah stared at Lillian with barely concealed contempt. Couldn't she see that Paavo was trying to make it look like she was doing a bad job? "I dusted everything the day before he came. It must have been pollen."

Lillian's eyes flashed with hatred. Hannah had seen that look before and her instinct was to run, but she couldn't get out of there fast enough. Lillian marched toward her, grabbed her arm, and dragged her to the back door. "Do you see that dirt?" She pointed at the white tile floor.

Michael had run outside that morning without his shoes on and he'd left two dark footprints right by the door before Hannah had stopped him. "I'll clean that up," Hannah said, trying to pull her arm away. "I haven't washed the kitchen floor yet."

Lillian's fingers pinched tighter and Hannah winced, despite herself. "You will clean on your hands and knees every little corner, every wedge, every molding, every ledge, the ceiling, everything," Lillian said, her eyes wild. At that moment, it was clear to Hannah that Lillian didn't see her, not really. Something else was making her act this way. "I don't want to see a speck of dust. If he sneezes even one time, I'll hold you responsible."

"I'll clean it," Hannah insisted.

Finally, Lillian released her. Hannah rubbed her arm. "Why do you care so much about Paavo?" she asked.

"What business is it of yours?"

"It's none of my business," Hannah said. "I don't even care. But it might help if I knew."

Lillian hesitated. "Sergey has borrowed some money from him. We owe him."

"What does that have to do with me?" Hannah asked.

"It has everything to do with you. If you don't help, you'll never see a dime. And that means you have to do everything that is asked of you. Do you understand? You bow to him if you have to. Paavo can do things to you and your family that will make you wish you were never alive."

Hannah stared at her, her mouth open. Lillian paused, realizing she'd said too much. "Put Michael in front of the television. I'll be in my bedroom," she barked, and then fled the room, clutching the letter in her hand.

Hannah listened to her trot up the wooden staircase into her bedroom. The door slammed behind her, shaking the house. A moment later, Lillian started to sob.

Good, Hannah thought. Sergey wouldn't be home with Michael for at least half an hour. Now was a good opportunity to start searching for an extra set of keys to the office. She might need that plane ticket sooner than she'd thought.

CHAPTER THIRTY-TWO

Hannah didn't find the keys. Not in the pockets of a random pair of pants. Not in the hall drawers. Not in the entertainment center. They were probably in the master bedroom, but Lillian was in there all day. Sergey came home briefly. He went into the bedroom, where Lillian screamed at him. Then he left and stayed out all night.

In the morning, Lillian greeted Hannah with a stony silence, handing her a list of unpleasant chores. Her eyes were rimmed with red. She went into the dining room with her textbooks and slid the door shut behind her.

Hannah waited until she heard a chair slide out and Lillian sit down. Then she hurried out of the room and up the stairs to the master bedroom.

She stepped into the room and looked at the bedside tables. She'd been curious about these drawers in the past, but it had seemed wrong to look in Lillian and Sergey's personal things when she had no legitimate reason, like putting away clothing. But she was finished with worrying about what was wrong or right. They weren't telling her everything, so she had to find out herself.

The drawer on Sergey's side opened easily. To her surprise, it was filled with takeout menus. She glanced through them but didn't see anything else. She went over to Lillian's side. There was a kids' brush on the top, a broken teacup, and a few old bills and notices from Maggie's school. She was about to give up, but then, under the bills, she spotted a too-familiar envelope.

She pulled it out. It was one of the letters she'd given Lillian a couple of months ago. It had been opened and read. She searched through the drawer and found the other six letters she'd given Lillian to mail, all opened. The fifty dollars for Babulya had been removed.

The fact that Lillian had read the letters seemed worse to Hannah than the fact that she hadn't sent them, which she'd already guessed. It was a violation of her mind, of her thoughts, which, until now, Lillian hadn't been able to access. And still worse than that was taking the money for Babulya. How could a doctor do such a thing?

Hannah ran down the stairs, holding the letters in her shaking hand. She didn't care about the consequences. She was going to tell Lillian what she thought. There was no reasonable explanation for what she'd done. As she reached the bottom of the steps, she heard Sergey and Lillian arguing in the kitchen.

"I can't do it, Sergey!" Lillian yelled. "Can't you understand?"

Hannah crept down the hall and stood next to the kitchen to listen.

"It's Saturday tomorrow, Lily. Why don't you take it easy for one day? Come with me and the children on a picnic. It'll be fun."

"I have to volunteer at the doctor's office. He needs help on Saturdays, not other days."

"Does it matter now?"

Hannah wondered why it wouldn't matter now.

"Of course it matters." Lillian let out a sound of frustration. Hannah could imagine her rolling her eyes in that haughty way of hers. "You don't want me to be a doctor, do you?"

Sergey swore. "What do I have to do? I'm ripping the seams of my pants so you can go to school and study. I even got you a goddamn nanny."

"You never liked it that I was more educated than you."

"Lillian, give me a break. You sit on your high horse and act like you're a master surgeon. You never even practiced as a doctor."

Silence. The air was still. Hannah wanted to get out of there as fast as she could. If Lillian knew she'd overheard, she'd punish her for listening.

Lillian's voice was low, boiling with fury. "I did not plan on getting pregnant. If I hadn't, I never would have—" She broke off.

"What? You never would have married a man like me?" He made his voice higher, imitating her. "A man who destroys lives instead of saving them."

Hannah wondered what that meant.

"Well," she said. "If the kettle's black . . ."

"You've got to be kidding me." He was mad now. "I cut off all my old connections even though I was making good money. I've had to find new partners and work much harder to get the business going. But I don't see any appreciation."

"You haven't cut off everyone, Sergey," Lillian said, her voice rising. "I hear things."

"I cut off everyone I could," he said. "I have a legitimate business. I'm barely making enough money for us to live on, and you're spending like we're still rolling in cash."

There was silence.

He let out an exasperated sigh. "Listen, I just asked if you could come on a picnic. If you can't, fine. Go to your doctor. Study for your test."

"I'll need to support our family when you get thrown in jail," she spat.

Hannah's mind was buzzing. Lillian had never practiced as a doctor. And Sergey claimed he'd quit what he used to do, which was clearly illegal, but Lillian didn't believe him. Hannah didn't believe him either. He was writing things in code on a piece of paper, which had mysteriously disappeared from the table in the garage, like he had something to hide.

The dining room door slid shut and Sergey was walking across the kitchen toward her. She glanced back down the hall, but it was too late to reverse and not look like she was eavesdropping, so she took a large step forward, intending to appear as though she were just walking down the hall. He strode through the kitchen door and she careened right into him.

"Oh!" she said, feigning surprise.

He steadied her, running his hand down to the small of her back. They were close, too close.

"Sorry," she said, trying to continue on to the kitchen, but he didn't release her.

"Come," he said in a low voice, pressing on her back, guiding her down the hall, away from the kitchen. She walked with him, scared that he knew she'd overheard. At the foyer, he stopped and faced her. "Hannah, would you like to go on a picnic with the children and me tomorrow?"

She blinked with surprise. "Oh no, I couldn't."

"Come on. You can watch polo. Did you ever see the movie *Pretty Woman*? The park is at the same field where they play polo in the movie." He grinned at her. "You deserve it. The house is spotless and I know you don't get many chances to get outside. We'll pick up lunch and relax for the day. I could use some help with the children."

She'd seen the movie and knew exactly what he was talking about. His eyes flickered down to her hand where she held the letters. She pressed them to her side, thinking that maybe if she went, he'd send them.

"What about Lillian?" she asked, pretending she hadn't heard their conversation.

"She's volunteering at a doctor's office," he said.

He was the one who was suggesting it, so she couldn't get into too much trouble. Babulya would be getting worried now that she hadn't heard anything for almost three months. She already had a bad heart—any kind of strain wouldn't be good for her. Soon, it would be Christmas.

As Hannah answered, she felt a kick of fear in her stomach. "Sure. Why not?"

CHAPTER THIRTY-THREE

On Saturday afternoon, Hannah was sitting on a blanket with Sergey on a huge expanse of lawn while Michael and Maggie kicked a ball back and forth. Her belly was full. The leftovers of their picnic were in two paper bags—Sergey had bought enough pickled herring, brinza cheese, and macaroni salad to feed twice as many people.

It was a hot day, even though it was already nearing the end of November. Hannah rested her head back on the blanket, closed her eyes, and breathed in the smell of the manure coming from the polo horses on the adjacent field. Briefly, she worried that she was getting too relaxed, but this was a rare opportunity. She listened to the *clomp-clomp* of their hooves kicking up the grass as they ran back and forth.

"Maggie gave me the money you found in my pocket," Sergey said.

She opened her eyes and looked up at him. He was leaning on one elbow next to her, looking down at her. He wasn't touching her, but it was a suggestive pose. Anyone who saw them would think they were a couple.

"I was surprised you didn't keep it," he said, grinning.

She sat up, resting on her elbows, and cocked her head to the side. "I wanted to."

He laughed. "I like your honesty."

That very morning, she'd slid fifty dollars out of Lillian's purse while Lillian was in the shower. She never would have done it if Lillian hadn't stolen it from her first. Was it stealing if you were just stealing back?

"You like this park?" he asked.

"Very much," she said. "I like the sound of the horses running." She thought of all the books in Sergey's study. Anything she could say to make a connection with him would help her. "It makes me think of my favorite scene in *Anna Karenina* when she's watching the races and her lover Vronsky falls. Remember how she can't stop from showing her horror? It's such a huge turning point in the book because she can't go back from there, and it's so true in life, you know, how sometimes there are things we can't go back from, even something small—" Hannah stopped talking. Sergey's face was blank. He had no idea what she was talking about. "Never mind. It's stupid." She rested her head back and looked down, noticing how large her chest looked. Sergey was noticing the same thing.

He grabbed one of her feet and began massaging it through her sock. "You need to relax." She'd noticed men said these kinds of things when they realized you were just as smart as them, and maybe even smarter. She glanced toward the children, who were still kicking a ball back and forth, and tried to pull her foot away.

"They are having fun," he said. His blue eyes crinkled at her and he picked up her other foot and started rubbing it. "This is a good country to grow up in, don't you think?"

"Yes." It might have felt nice to have her feet rubbed if it weren't by him. But she didn't want to risk Maggie saying anything to Lillian. This was definitely against rule number ten.

"Better than Ukraine," he said. "More freedom. Better schools."

Hannah had never had less freedom in her life, but she didn't contradict him. He had to mail her letters. She had asked both Babulya and Katya to try to find out some information for her. If they could track down Olga, maybe Katya could find out something about her uncle.

Sergey slid off her sock. She didn't like men taking off her clothing without asking her permission. "Please," she said, pulling her bare foot away. Maggie glanced over at the blanket, then looked away as if she were embarrassed.

"What?" he said.

"The children."

"It's just a foot rub." He continued massaging her calf.

Finally, when she couldn't stand it anymore, she jumped up. "That's good. Thanks," she said, noticing his look of rejection before she ran over to kick the ball with Maggie and Michael. She felt bad. Had she led him on? The poor guy was probably just lonely.

A few minutes later, she looked over and saw Sergey packing up the picnic supplies and the blanket, and soon they were driving down Sunset Boulevard, past the restaurants with white tablecloths where Sergey had told her famous people liked to eat.

This was her chance. She made her voice casual, light, as if it weren't a big deal. "Could we stop at a post office?" she said. "I have some letters to send to my family."

He glanced at the clock on the dashboard as he drove past a country western-themed bar with a fake horse out front. "Lillian will be coming home soon," he said.

She was ready with a response. "I can pay," she said, knowing he didn't want to seem cheap. Even if he was.

He took a few turns and then stopped in front of a long white building with an American flag in front.

He held out his hand for her letters. "If the line is long, I'll bring them tomorrow."

Hannah hesitated. If Lillian found out that he had the letters, she might open them again and then she'd know Hannah had stolen from her. But this was her only chance. She reached into the plastic bag she'd brought for her things and handed him the seven letters.

"That's a lot," he said, surprised. "You haven't given any to Lillian to send?"

He doesn't know.

"I—I just wanted to send a lot," she stammered. "Because they go missing. And you know, I haven't received any mail back."

He gave her a long look and the wrinkles around his eyes creased up, like maybe he felt sorry for her. Or maybe he was going to change his mind.

"I'll pay," she said, reaching into the bag, as if she had more money in there.

He cleared his throat and opened the door of the SUV. "Don't worry. I have it," he said, and disappeared into the building, leaving Hannah in the car with the children.

"Aren't those the mailboxes?" Hannah asked, pointing at a row of blue metal contraptions where an older man was dropping a letter.

Maggie shrugged. "Yeah." But she didn't seem to think it was strange, and Hannah realized that of course he needed stamps. A few minutes later, he returned without the letters.

"No line," he said. "I mailed them fast delivery."

She reached over and squeezed his calloused hand. "Thank you. You have no idea how much this means to me." If the children weren't there in the car, she'd even kiss him for that. On the cheek.

CHAPTER THIRTY-FOUR

Back at the house, Hannah chased Michael down the driveway, pretending she was a monster. He'd fallen asleep in the car on the way home from the picnic and sometimes he could be grumpy when he woke up, but the monster game always worked. Giggling and screaming, he ran into the house and down the hall, wearing his shoes. Hannah slid hers off in the foyer, put on her pink slippers, and continued chasing him.

"Mommy!" he said, lurching to a stop at the doorway to the kitchen.

"Michael, your shoes," Lillian said in a sharp voice that left no doubt about her mood. "Come here."

Her heart racing, Hannah forced herself to walk the rest of the way down the hall to the kitchen. Michael was sitting on Lillian's lap as she pulled his shoes off. A pile of the USMLE books sat in front of her on the table, along with a notebook, a pen, and a glass plate with crumbs on it.

"I thought you were working at the doctor's office today," Hannah said.

"I came home early," Lillian said. Maggie and Sergey sauntered into the kitchen. Lillian continued, glaring at Sergey, "I wanted to go on a picnic with my family."

All the laughter disappeared from the house, all the lightness of being outside and having a good time. It was all Lillian's fault. Everyone would be happy if she weren't around. Hannah wished Lillian would just die, but then she felt horrible. She'd never wished for anyone to die in her whole life.

"You're back already?" Sergey glided past Hannah with the paper bag of leftover deli food, acting as if he hadn't done anything wrong, and dropped the bag on the counter.

"I left the office early to go on a picnic with you," Lillian said.

"You did?" He came up to kiss her on the cheek, but she jerked back. "You should have called my cell."

"I did," Lillian said.

He looked down at the phone and shook his head. "Didn't hear it."

"I can't believe you took the baba," Lillian said.

"You should have met us there." Sergey patted Maggie's back, as if enlisting her support. "It was fun, right?"

Maggie didn't answer—she understood her father was in trouble.

Lillian's whole face was tight and pinched, her fury just under the surface, waiting to explode. "Whose idea was it for her to come?" It was a calculated question—she'd clearly been thinking of how to start her interrogation since she'd arrived home to an empty house.

Hannah knew she was the one who'd be punished, not Sergey.

But if Lillian had mailed the letters, she never would have agreed to go.

"It was difficult for me to take the children alone," Sergey said. "And I thought it would be good for her to get out."

"It's hardly appropriate for the girl to go on picnics with you and our children."

"Well," Sergey said, looking away, "Hannah had an errand to do."

"It was her idea?"

"Lily, it's nothing."

Lillian stood up, strode across the room to Hannah, and spoke to her in a cold voice. "I told you to stay away from him."

"I didn't—"

Lillian raised her hand, preparing to slap her.

Sergey grabbed Lillian's wrist. "Stop it."

"Let go of me," Lillian said, struggling to yank her hand away.

"Just because you didn't pass your doctor exam doesn't mean you can be a bitch to everyone." He flung her hand down and looked disgusted with her.

Lillian pressed her hand to her chest as if he'd just wounded her. She'd failed! Hannah felt a smile pushing from behind the mask she always wore around Lillian, who tried so hard to make her feel stupid. *At least I've never failed a test,* Hannah thought.

"It was a difficult test. Half the people failed." Lillian bit off each word as she spoke. "I'm taking it again."

Sergey gave a shrug and turned away. Lillian glared at Hannah, furious. Hannah looked out the kitchen window, but it was too late to pretend she hadn't heard.

"Did you tell her about your secret when you went for your little adventure? I bet she wouldn't think you were so wonderful then. Why don't we tell her now?"

Secret?

"Don't," Sergey barked, warning her.

"What?" Hannah asked.

"There is no secret. Take the children to the playroom."

Lillian gloated. Michael jumped off his mother's lap and ran to Hannah, but Maggie stayed next to the counter, watching her parents in alarm. Hannah hesitated. She wanted to know the secret, especially if it had something to do with her.

"Hannah," Sergey snapped.

She pulled the children out of the room and walked slowly down the hall, hoping she'd hear something.

"What was the errand?" Lillian demanded.

Hannah couldn't hear his answer because he was keeping his voice down, but then Lillian yelled so loud that the neighbors must have heard. "You mailed her letters?"

"Of course not." He lowered his voice, but Hannah could still hear. "I threw them out."

Maggie stopped at the doorway to the garage and looked up at her. Hannah's eyes filled with tears. All she wanted was to let Babulya know she was okay.

"Come on," she said, nudging Maggie into the garage. "We'll do a puzzle."

She couldn't believe Sergey had lied to her so convincingly. Daniil had said she was too naive to go to America. Maybe he was right.

CHAPTER THIRTY-FIVE

Hannah snuck down the hall and put on her brown leather shoes, which still had bits of grass on them from the park that day. They weren't really for running, but they were the only shoes she had besides her black dress shoes, and they were good for walking—she'd used them every day in Moldova to walk to and from the market. Fortunately, her feet hadn't grown much in the last six months.

It was after midnight. Everyone was asleep. It had taken her a full week to get up the nerve, but she'd decided she had to do it, no matter what it cost her. She'd do it for Babulya.

She opened the front door, closed it quietly, and crept across the grass, rather than the driveway, to avoid any sound. She stepped around the bush with the lights and hit the sidewalk, sprinting away from the house before someone saw her leaving. She hadn't dared to lock the door because of the noise, but she had Lillian's front door keys in her hand, just in case Sergey came home and locked her out.

In her hand, she clutched two letters, one for Katya and one for Babulya, nearly identical to the ones Sergey had thrown out, but without the fifty dollars. There had been no other chances to sneak money out of Lillian's purse. Lillian watched her every move. But she did find a pack of twenty stamps in the groceries and she'd split them between the two letters, hoping it was enough.

She sprinted down the sidewalk. Once her letters were safely sent, she'd be able to relax a little. Hannah had seen the blue mailboxes in front of the post office, and if she had to run there, she would, but maybe there'd be one that was closer.

She was out of shape. Her legs felt leaden and her body was clumsy. It had been a long time since she'd run. She remembered running in Gura Bicului through fields of sunflowers, the large flowers thwacking against her sides, and feeling like she could run forever. She'd hear her mother calling for her and she'd duck down to hide by the stems. Her mother would say, "Hannah, I can see you." And she'd giggle.

She loosened up and stretched out her stride. Tomorrow she'd be sore, but for today, she needed to run at full speed, to feel like a kid again.

A couple was walking toward her, holding hands. She ran past and they didn't even glance at her. She was anonymous here, and it was a good feeling. In Moldova, everyone thought of her as the girl with the father who'd set off a bomb and killed six people, even though they never proved he'd done it. It didn't matter how much Hannah insisted on his innocence, how emphatically she swore that he'd never kill anybody, especially not her mother—nobody believed her. And because her father was guilty in their eyes, she was too. Everywhere she went, people stared at her.

Katya told her that in time, people would forget, but in Chișinău, people never forgot.

A blue mailbox stood there on the corner, waiting for her. Maybe she should drop one letter in this one and one letter in another, she thought, but then told herself that in America, all the mailboxes worked.

Her letters slid inside. She opened it up again to make sure they'd gone down and then took in a shaky breath. If just one letter arrived, they'd both have a way to reach her. Katya had promised to visit her babushka and take her for walks to the park until Hannah could pay for the surgery.

She hesitated there for a moment, wondering whether she should return to the house now. Someone might have discovered she was missing, but if they had, she might as well stay out a little longer while she could. She continued down Santa Monica Boulevard, past the small restaurants and boutiques, picking up her speed, leaping over curbs and sprinting across empty streets. Her hair flowed down her back, the cool night air flowing through it, as if she were a deer running through a field of Moldovan sunflowers.

"You go, girl!" someone yelled, followed by laughter. There was a group of white and Latino transvestites, with styled hair and glossy lips, wearing leather tops and jean shorts outside the donut shop, and they were all looking at her. They looked so different from Vladi. She picked up her pace, not feeling quite so anonymous anymore. *There's nothing to be afraid of,* she thought.

She stepped into the street to avoid a large homeless man with a cart on the sidewalk. In Moldova, the homeless people were skinny, wasted even, and it was odd to see someone living in the streets who looked so well fed. She thought of the legless beggar named Pedro who pushed his wheelchair through traffic for a few coins a day near the chocolate factory by her house.

A few blocks farther, she passed Trader Joe's, a grocery store where Lillian went, now closed, but with all its lights on. Inside, she could see some workers restocking shelves.

The Russian store and Whole Foods were the next places she recognized. A group of Russians walked out of a Russian restaurant and Hannah looked away, in case Paavo happened to be with them and recognized her. When she was entering the ritzy part of Santa Monica Boulevard, a police car passed her. She slowed her pace, hoping the police wouldn't notice her. The brake lights went on and the police car pulled over on the side of the road. Other cars drove by; nobody was paying much attention to the police car, except for her. She stopped and turned around. If she started running in the opposite direction, maybe they wouldn't notice her.

"Hey," a male voice said behind her. It was a commanding voice, the voice of a police officer.

Run. She started a casual jog, pretending she didn't hear.

"Hey," he said. "You. Girl. Stop!"

She glanced back. A tall black police officer had stepped out of the passenger side door of the car. He was running toward her with a flashlight pointed down. Through the back window of the police car, she could see the head of another police officer who was sitting in the driver's seat. His door opened. She stopped.

"Me?" she asked, pointing at herself.

The officer slowed down to a trot and came up to her. "You okay?" he asked, raising the flashlight to scan her body.

"Yes. I okay." She squinted into the bright light. Was there a law against running at night? She hadn't seen anyone else running, but then again, she never saw anyone running at night in Chişinău either, and it wasn't illegal there.

He lowered the flashlight and squinted at her, as if he was honestly concerned about her. Maybe he was. But he didn't know she was illegal. "What are you doing?" he asked, in his deep American voice.

"I am running." She looked down at her brown walking shoes and wished she had real American sneakers.

"For exercise? At this time of night?"

"Yes."

"You're wearing jean shorts in November and you're running after midnight. Are you sure you want to stick with that story?" He took another step toward her and looked beyond her, as if to see what or who she was running from.

"Yes." She hadn't thought wearing cutoff shorts would attract more attention. The sweatpants Lillian had bought her were two sizes too big and would fall off if she ran in them. "I no have many clothes."

He stared at her as if something was bothering him. Finally, he said, "Prostitution is against the law." He looked behind her. "Where's your pimp?"

She didn't know the word "pimp," but she understood what

"prostitution" was. It was almost the same in Russian. "I am not prostitution." She felt insulted. She wasn't wearing the clothing of a prostitute—she was wearing the only shorts she had, walking shoes, and her monkey T-shirt. Prostitutes definitely didn't wear walking shoes—they'd have heels on.

He gave her a firm look. "I don't want to see you in the streets," he said. "That's all. You're a young girl. Go home." Then he headed back to the police car.

Go home. Wouldn't that be nice. She didn't even know what home was anymore.

He got into the police car and drove off. She let out a shaky breath and ran back toward the house.

Twenty minutes later, she opened the gate. Her face was red-hot and her chest and throat burned from breathing so hard. It was a beautiful feeling. She hurried along the walkway, pushed open the slat in the fence, and peeked into Colin's room.

He was sitting on his bed, drawing in his sketchbook. By his feet, at the end of the bed, there was a pile of balled-up paper, a giant bottle of Coke, and an empty bag of tortilla chips. He was wearing one of his large football jerseys and a pair of basketball shorts, his standard home clothes. To school, he often wore very baggy jeans that hung down low like he was a rapper and made him look larger than he was.

She wished she could see what Colin was drawing, but the sketchbook was resting on his knees, tilted up. He stopped drawing and swore. Then he ripped the page out, balled it up, and chucked it across the room.

"What are you doing?" Lillian was standing there, looking down the walkway at her. Hannah hadn't even heard her come out of the house. Lillian was wearing a sheer white nightgown, which shimmered in the light from the back porch. She was all angles and shadow. Her cheekbones looked hollow and her eye sockets looked ghostly.

Hannah hurried toward her, hoping she wouldn't see the broken slat in the fence.

"Are you meeting someone back here?" Lillian asked.

"No." Hannah came forward, into the light, still panting from the run.

"You're sweating. What were you doing?" Lillian was getting hysterical.

"I went for a run," Hannah said, lifting her chin up. It was perfectly legitimate. Lillian didn't need to know about the letters.

"A run?" Lillian screeched, as if she'd never heard the word, and then looked behind her, as if trying to find someone.

"I went running down Santa Monica Boulevard. I need exercise."

"Do you really think I'm going to believe you went for a run? *Shlyuha!*" Lillian said "slut" so loudly, Hannah was sure Colin had heard. "You're meeting someone."

"Who would I meet?" Hannah asked, trying to get past her. "Is Sergey not home? Is that the problem? You think I'm meeting him?"

"Of course not." Lillian pressed her lips together. "Maybe you met someone at the Russian shop or the bus. You probably go to meet him every night. This is why you are so slow in the day. Because you are tired."

"I'm not like that," Hannah said. "I would never—"

"Do you know what the police will do to you? Have you heard what the jails are like? If they catch you, you have no rights. You are not a citizen. They put you in with the men and they rape you. They'll let you rot in prison."

Hannah thought about her close call with the police. "This is the only time I've gone out, and nothing happened."

"Do you think I'm an idiot? I've heard you out here before."

"I bring the garbage," Hannah said, her heart beating fast. "Today I decided to go running. You never said I couldn't run. I figured that nobody would see me if I ran late at night."

"You think you can lie to me? You're wearing tight jean shorts for running."

"I have nothing else to wear," Hannah said.

"Whore! Nobody goes for a run at midnight. Tell me the truth and I won't punish you."

Hannah stared into Lillian's sharp hazel eyes. She was right, of course. Hannah had mailed her letters. If she told her, at least Lillian wouldn't think she was meeting some strange man to have sex in the middle of the night, but she didn't owe her anything.

"You're meeting the boy next door, aren't you?" Lillian asked.

Hannah's eyes darted toward the fence before she could stop herself. "No."

"Really?" Lillian looked at her. "His mother asked about you the other day. She said the boy had met you on the bus, that you were welcome to come over anytime. Naive American. She doesn't know you're having sex with him in the backyard like a whore."

"I am not a whore," Hannah spat, brushing past her. *Punish me and you'll regret it.*

She marched toward the back door, expecting Lillian to chase her, but when she reached the back door, she glanced back. Lillian had gone down the walkway to look at the fence.

CHAPTER THIRTY-SIX

The next morning, at the breakfast table, Lillian told Sergey about the broken fence.

"I'll fix it," he murmured, still reading his paper.

Hannah was at the stove, frying up some thickly sliced ham. She squished the ham down with the spatula and it sprayed up fat, sizzling angrily.

"I caught Hannah outside last night," Lillian continued.

He looked up, surprised.

"She claims she was running. After midnight." Lillian laughed and kept her voice light, even though Hannah could hear the tension behind her words. "I think she went out to meet a boyfriend. Maybe the boy next door. Though he's like one of those pink pigs they put on a stick." She laughed. "It's disgusting to think of, really."

Hannah glared, forcing her lips together so she didn't tell Lillian what she thought of her.

"You have a boyfriend?" Maggie asked Hannah, amazed.

"No," she said, then looked back at Lillian. "I don't have a boyfriend and I don't want one either. I was running. I used to love running. When I was a child."

"You're no child," Lillian said, laughing again. "She went running in tight jean cutoffs." Lillian raised her eyebrows at Sergey. Was she trying to see if this upset him?

"They're all I have," Hannah said. "I'm not meeting anyone."

Sergey stared into Hannah's eyes, as if he cared about the truth, and then nodded briefly. "Let her run."

"What?" Lillian asked. "Do you know what you're saying? No, she can't run." Lillian looked at Hannah to make sure she understood who was the boss.

Hannah knew well enough.

"Mommy, you have to look at this collage I did in my art studio class," Maggie said suddenly. "We used dried fruit peelings to create a picture. I made a butterfly." Hannah wondered if she was trying to distract her mother or if she was just bored with the conversation.

Lillian looked away from Hannah, toward Maggie, who pointed at a spot above the kitchen table. "I think you should hang it right there."

Hannah could just imagine old, dried fruit hanging on Lillian's pristine wall.

"Fruit peelings?" Lillian sounded horrified.

"It's really cool," Maggie said, blinking. "Roberta's mom put hers on their wall."

"Uh, I would like to see it," Lillian managed.

Hannah held back a smile. She loved that girl.

Sergey stood up. "Has anyone seen my keys? I can't find them."

"When did you have them?" Lillian asked quickly, pouring herself more tea.

"Last night." Sergey looked down at Michael. "Anybody play with my keys?"

"No, Daddy," he said, shaking his head. "I can't play with your keys."

Sergey patted his head. "I have a lunch meeting. I'll be back later."

"Don't bother," Lillian murmured, grabbing her tea.

Sergey ignored her comment and bent down to kiss Maggie's forehead. "Good-bye, my cherry blossom."

Maggie looked up, her hazel eyes widening. "You're coming back later, right?"

"Of course." He smiled and his face creased into a million lines—it was the most open smile he had, the one he reserved for his daughter, and it always reminded Hannah of how her own father used to look at her. He patted her head and walked out of the kitchen.

A few minutes later, the front door shut behind him. If Hannah could find the keys, she could get into Sergey's office without anyone knowing. She knew she'd be able to find out more if she could just get in there—maybe even find the plane ticket. It was an open-ended ticket, good for up to one year, which meant Hannah could go home anytime. She still had her fake passport. The student visa had expired, but she didn't need it to get out of the country, only to enter. She'd need about fifty dollars to get back to Chişinău from Romania. If things got really bad here, she could leave, and she would. Just watch them try to stop her.

The keys weren't in the pockets of his jeans or in his jackets.

They weren't under their bed. Michael had said he didn't have them, but he did love keys. She decided to ask him casually, when Lillian wasn't around. He was more likely to tell her than his parents.

That afternoon, Hannah picked up the trains strewn around the living room and grabbed Michael's hand.

"Nap time." Upstairs, she read him a short Russian book, tucked him in his bed, and then she whispered, "Were you playing with your father's keys today?"

He looked up at her with his big blue eyes. "No."

Best to try a different tactic. "Did you play any games with Papulya this morning?"

"I was jumping on him!" Michael covered his mouth with his hand and giggled.

"Where?"

"On the sofa," he said.

Hannah's belly tightened with excitement. The keys must have fallen out of his pocket.

Once Michael had fallen asleep for his nap, she went downstairs to the white leather sofa and reached her hand between the leather cushions. She felt the cold hard metal of keys. Her breath stopped. They were right there! But Lillian was studying in the kitchen, just around the corner. It was too risky. Lillian would hear them.

She popped her head around the corner. "Can I vacuum?" she asked Lillian, even though she'd already vacuumed downstairs. It would be the only way to hide the sound of the keys jingling.

"There are some wood splinters from the train set."

If Lillian came to look, she'd be in trouble, but Lillian said, "Yes, stop interrupting me."

Hannah took the vacuum out of the hall closet and turned it on. Standing by the sofa, she dove her hand between the cushions, grabbed the keys, and shoved them in the front pocket of her gray sweatshirt. She turned off the vacuum and made her way upstairs.

At the door to the office, Hannah pulled the keys from her pocket. They jingled and she froze. Lillian was only just downstairs, in the kitchen, where she could hear footsteps upstairs, but Hannah had to try. She unlocked the door to the office, hurried inside, and shut it behind her.

Michael made a noise in the other room and Hannah remembered she didn't have much time. He could wake up any minute.

She glanced toward the bookshelf. Documents could be hidden in the books—she'd heard of people doing that. But then, she noticed the dust on the shelf in front of the books. If he'd moved any of them recently, the dust would be cleared away in that spot, which meant that the plane ticket was probably in one of the desk drawers.

Slowly, she slid open the drawers but found only pens and papers and receipts. No airplane ticket. She went to the file cabinet. Locked. There were only four keys on Sergey's key ring—two car keys, one front door key, and the office key. He had to have the file cabinet key hidden somewhere.

She checked under the desk, on the floor, on top of the

bookshelf. Ugh. Nothing. She lifted up the two yellow lined papers on top of his desk, thinking the key might be under them, but it wasn't. She looked down at the papers she was holding, curious. He had messy handwriting. A check for over eleven thousand dollars was paper-clipped to the bottom sheet. The papers had a bunch of names and some phone numbers, some supplies, but nothing she recognized. It was as if it had been written in code just like the other paper. There were numbers and some large words she didn't know, scientific language. Nothing about Tiraspol. And then she saw something she recognized: AK-47.

She sucked in a quick breath. Wasn't that a machine gun? It was some kind of gun, for sure. Did he import them? Or maybe he exported them?

"Hannah!" Lillian was calling from downstairs.

She dropped the paper with the check onto the desk, under the other one, just the way she thought it had been.

On impulse, she grabbed *Anna Karenina* in English from the bookshelf and shoved it into the front pocket of her sweatshirt before she ran out of the room and locked the door.

Behind her, Hannah heard a doorknob turning. Michael was up. He banged on his door. Fortunately, he couldn't open it yet by himself.

"Hannah, where are you?" Lillian called again.

"I'm coming! Michael just woke up," Hannah yelled, shoving the keys in her pocket. She'd sneak them between the cushions on the sofa later and then "find" them when Lillian was right there.

She opened Michael's door, picked him up, and threw the book in his closet, planning to grab it later. His eyes followed it curiously, but he didn't say anything. He probably thought she was just cleaning up.

"Hannah!" Lillian called again.

She rushed down the stairs.

CHAPTER THIRTY-SEVEN

Hannah stepped out of the hot kitchen onto the back steps and breathed in the smell of turkey cooking next door. Her neck ached from looking down at a chopping board and stuffing the pelmeni with potatoes, meat, and sour cream. She could never get the edges of the ravioli-like pasta pinched together just right, and she'd had to make a second batch when the meat oozed out.

She'd be thankful when Thanksgiving was over, she thought ruefully, but the hardest part hadn't even begun. Paavo and Rena were due any minute.

She'd made eleven dishes total, an uneven number for good luck, and not one of them was turkey or mashed potatoes or corn. It would have been nice to have a real American Thanksgiving meal, Hannah thought, maybe even go over to the neighbor's house and sit at their little yellow table in the kitchen. But Lillian had declared that they were Russian and they would celebrate this day Russian style.

Amazingly, Michael hadn't messed up the house. He'd watched television for eight hours straight so she could cook.

"Smells delicious," Sergey said from the kitchen.

She stepped back into the kitchen and grinned at him, wiping her sweaty hair off her brow. "Thank you," she said, coming up beside him at the counter, where he was drinking a glass of water. He gazed into her eyes over the top of the glass. For once, she didn't look away.

He was tanned and quite handsome, for an older man. He was wearing a gray suit and a white shirt with no tie, a look she'd always liked. He put the glass down and smiled at her.

"Thank *you* for all your hard work." He reached over to tuck a strand of hair behind her ear before heading into the dining room—it was a fatherly kind of gesture, but one he wouldn't have done had Lillian been in the room. Sometimes she caught him looking at her with this odd mixture of sadness and desire. She probably should discourage his random touches, she thought with a sense of guilt. Though it wasn't really anything, and it felt nice. She missed physical touch: Katya's arm in hers as they walked down the street, Babulya's thick, cozy body pressed against hers as they watched their blurry television, Daniil's warm lips kissing her ear.

The timer on the oven went off and Hannah bent down to take the salmon out as Lillian came into the kitchen, wearing a navy blue dress that tied around the neck, leaving her back exposed. It was a beautiful color on her, but she looked frail in it, as if she'd lost weight since she bought it.

As Hannah pulled out the salmon, Lillian strode past her to inspect the dining room.

A minute later, she was back with the butter dish in her hands.

"What is this mess?" she demanded.

There was a fresh stick of butter next to a clump of soft butter from the night before.

"I didn't want to waste it," Hannah explained, nervously.

"This is not how it should be for company. You throw out the old butter and put the stick on a fresh, clean dish." She thrust it at Hannah. "Do it right."

"Lilichka," Sergey said, wrapping his arm around Lillian's shoulders. "You look beautiful." He kissed her cheek, but she turned away. He cleared his throat. "Aren't you concerned about the flowers, my love?" The house was filled with bouquets of pink and red roses in every room, in odd numbers for good luck.

"What?" Lillian's eyes widened.

"He's allergic."

"You didn't tell me he was allergic to flowers. Just dust."

Sergey winced. "It's everything."

Lillian let out an exasperated groan, ran into the kitchen, grabbed a garbage bag, and tossed it at Hannah. "Throw them away."

"All of them?" Hannah had seen the flower bill. Lillian had spent over three hundred dollars. What a waste. Besides, she'd have to clean out all the vases and there wasn't time. "Why don't I put all the vases outside on the deck?" Hannah asked. "It'll be faster. And pretty when you look in the backyard."

Even though it was a good suggestion, Lillian looked irritated. "Fine."

At that moment, the doorbell rang. Hannah ran into the living room, grabbed the bouquet of small yellow roses from in there and then the one from the foyer. She heard the stamping of feet outside. She hurried down the hall and into the dining room to grab a third bouquet, and then put them all on the deck.

Lillian handed her the bouquet from the bathroom down the hall. "Get the ones upstairs without him seeing."

"Come on, Lily," Sergey said, indicating that they had to answer the door. He strode into the living room, turned off the television and switched on the classical music, then headed to meet the guests.

Lillian blinked her hazel eyes at Hannah. "Be careful. This is an important night."

"Okay," Hannah said, rushing up the stairs, where she grabbed the bouquets from the bathroom, the master bedroom, and the stand in the hall.

She made it down the stairs with the strong-smelling bouquets before Paavo and Rena had taken off their shoes in the foyer. She ducked into the kitchen, went through the back door, and placed the offensive flowers on the deck. Her shirt probably had pollen on it now, which she hoped would serve to keep that man away from her. He gave her the creeps. Anyway, she figured he was lying about his allergies just so she'd seem like a bad maid and they'd give her to him to pay off their debt to him. But he didn't know who he was messing with.

Hannah stepped inside. A second later, Paavo lumbered into the kitchen, followed by Rena, whose short hair was now dyed a brilliant shade of maroon. Hannah had never seen the two of them together. He was easily three times her size.

Rena saw Hannah examining them and gave her a haughty look. Hannah turned her back on them and washed the remaining pot in the sink. She could still feel Paavo staring at her.

"Vodka or champagne?" Sergey asked.

"Vodka," Paavo boomed.

"Champagne," Rena said.

"Hannah, can you get two champagne flutes?" Lillian asked.

They had their special glasses in a buffet case in the dining room, but Hannah had no idea what was what. "What do they look like?" she asked, drying off the pot with a dishcloth.

"They're the thin ones," Lillian said, rolling her eyes at Rena.

Sergey opened the champagne bottle with a pop and handed the glasses to Hannah with a brief smile. She poured the champagne, halfway, the same as wine, like Lillian had taught her, and brought them to the women. Everyone moved into the living room, and Hannah took the fresh oysters from the refrigerator and put them on a tray with lemon and vodka chasers, as she'd been instructed.

"Good for the sex drive," Paavo laughed, swatting at Rena's behind.

She laughed. "Stop it."

He dropped down into the sofa and took an oyster and a vodka chaser. His fingers with their long, manicured nails gripped on the glass, and he sucked down the oyster, gazing at Hannah, as if he'd like to do the same to her, but nobody else seemed to notice. At least the children were upstairs. Lillian had fed and bathed them while Hannah made dinner, and now they were in their pajamas, watching a movie in Michael's room.

Soon, everyone moved into the dining room, and Hannah began to bring in dish after dish, making sure to stay far from Paavo. Between courses, she ran upstairs to check on the children and then sat at the kitchen table listening to Paavo monopolize the conversation with lurid jokes.

Once the main courses were done, Hannah cleared the table and brought out coffee and small cakes from the Russian bakery. She poured the coffee, under Lillian's sharp gaze, making sure to keep her hand steady, but pushed Paavo's cup across the table, instead of getting too close to him. Paavo was telling a story about one of his girls who'd gotten in trouble with the police—likely one of his prostitutes at his club. He pushed himself back from the table, and opened his knees out and pressed them back together as he talked. Out and in, out and in.

She clenched her jaw. She didn't want to think about it but she did. Volva, the bad agent, he'd done that too in the taxi while he talked to her about what mistakes she shouldn't make as she went through immigration.

For the rest of her life, she'd probably hate the sound of a zipper opening. It had taken her months to get Volva out of her head, and this man brought it all back.

She had to hold it together. Just long enough to hand out the cakes. Her hand was shaking. She reached across the table with the cake for Paavo and he took it from her, his thumb brushing her hand, on purpose. She pulled her hand back.

Lillian gave her a sharp look. She remembered Lillian's words earlier: *You bow to him if you have to.*

Hannah passed the sugar to Sergey, but he shook his head briefly and took a sip of black coffee. Normally he took his coffee with two or three heaping tablespoons of sugar, but perhaps he was worried Paavo would think he wasn't manly.

Paavo raised his coffee cup. "It's not full."

It was too difficult to reach across the table with a pot of hot coffee. Slowly, she walked around the table to fill his cup to the top. Rena started telling Lillian about a sale at Barneys. Nobody was paying attention. Even Sergey was looking at his BlackBerry.

Hannah gripped the handle of the coffeepot and took Paavo's cup from him. Just as she started to pour, his hand rested on the back of her sweatpants, where no one else could see. She stepped away quickly and the hot coffee spilled on her hand. She let out a cry from the pain.

"Hannah," Lillian barked. "Be careful. We don't want you burning our guests."

Paavo was looking her up and down, even though his wife was right there. His nose twitched and he squeezed it. His nose twitched again and then his eyes opened wide and he looked at the chandelier over the table. Sergey and Lillian exchanged a look.

Paavo held a finger up in the air as if everyone should wait for him. And then he sneezed. Probably got the pollen from her clothes on him. Served him right. If she could cover him in pollen, so he'd be itchy and coughing and sneezing, she would.

Hannah put the coffeepot down before she was tempted to pour it in his lap, and strode around the table, trying not to run.

"Maybe you're allergic to the girl." Rena laughed. "She probably never washes."

Hannah glared at her as she picked up the butter dish that she'd left earlier.

"You know what they say about those Moldovans," Paavo said. "They're so stupid, they have to jump up and down to see if there are any matches in the matchbox."

Everybody laughed, except for Sergey. Stupid. It was just a word, she told herself, but she heard Volva in her head. "If you're not too stupid." Hannah wanted to throw the butter dish at Paavo's head and see the butter slime down his face, but instead she turned to go.

"That is why they are the garbage collectors and whores of Russia," Rena said, lighting up a cigarette, even though no one smoked in the house. "They can do nothing else."

Hannah was furious. How dare this woman speak like this about her family, her friends, all the people she knew and loved? Hannah looked around the table. Lillian was smiling. Sergey shifted uncomfortably but didn't speak up for her. She opened her mouth, then shut it, and walked out of the room.

Her hands were shaking as she gripped the butter dish. No matter how much she tried to forget, Paavo reminded her of the bad agent, that Volva, with his long cat fingers, his sharp nails.

"What do you think, girl?" Paavo asked, calling Hannah back, like he owned her. Hannah continued into the kitchen, the memories chasing her.

In the other room, Paavo's voice boomed. "Hey, girl!" Hannah placed the butter dish on the granite countertop. It clattered down, making so much noise it startled her. Her hands were shaking. She was clumsy in her fear.

She'd called Volva a pig when he ran his hand over the front of her white shirt.

He'd choked her, pressing one hand to her neck. Those were the bruises Lillian had noticed on her first day. "Who are you calling a pig?" he'd said, while his other hand popped open the snap on her jeans, undid her zipper, and dove down inside.

His fingernails had been sharp like little mice claws. "You want more?" he'd growled. Tears had run down her face and she'd shaken her head, trying to breathe.

The taxi driver had stared straight ahead. The Romanian music played louder. Two women had strode by the taxi at that moment, pulling their suitcases on the pavement. One of them had commented on what a nice day it was for flying.

"Hannah?" Sergey was calling to her from the dining room, forcing her to answer these people.

She took two long, stiff steps back into the dining room and pasted a fake smile on her face. "Yes?" She pressed her shaking hands against the sides of her sweatpants.

Sergey's blue eyes creased apologetically and he tilted his head toward Paavo and Rena at the other side of the table.

"Is it true?" Rena asked, blowing smoke into the air. "Are you Moldovans too stupid to do anything but whoring and garbage collecting?"

Hannah couldn't stop herself. She stretched her shaking hands out. "I think I remembered to wash the garbage off my hands before rolling the pelmeni, but I'm really not sure."

Silence. Rena's face whitened. Sergey smiled briefly, just long enough for Hannah to notice. "Hannah!" Lillian gasped.

Paavo let out a guffaw. "She has a mouth. But she doesn't know how to use it."

Hannah glared at him. He probably knew what Volva had done.

Lillian reassured Paavo and Rena. "Don't worry. I made the pelmeni."

Hannah didn't stop in the kitchen, but ran down the hall and up the stairs before Lillian could force her back into the room to apologize. She went into the upstairs bathroom, locked the door, and pressed her back against it.

She waited for Lillian to follow her, but there were no footsteps up the stairs. In Michael's room, the movie was still going, which meant it wasn't yet nine o'clock.

Volva had let her out of the taxi then. It could have been worse, she thought, staring at Lillian's white wallpaper with the perfect blue flowers. She told herself to breathe. It could have been worse.

Through the open bathroom window, she heard music blasting from a car in the street with that *boom-boom-boom* noise Sergey had told her was the bass. It made the air inside her ears vibrate— she couldn't believe people thought that was music. There were female voices. The screen of the next-door neighbor's front door squealed as someone stepped outside.

"Not too late," Colin's mother said from the front door.

"It's just for a little while," he said.

"By eleven," she said.

"It's not a school night," he said.

"Fine. Midnight."

The front door shut. Colin kicked a stone down the driveway. Hannah peered out the window to see him, but she couldn't see the front yard, just the side of his pink house.

The car roared down the street.

CHAPTER THIRTY-EIGHT

Hannah stood next to the old green fence in the pouring rain, looking into Colin's empty bedroom. She'd been waiting for over an hour. It was after one in the morning and he still wasn't home, even though he'd told his mother he'd be back by midnight. He had a curfew too. And he'd broken it. Just like she had, that last night she'd seen her mother alive.

Hannah tilted her face up to the rain as it beat down on her. It was cold, but her tears were hot, and for once she gave into them. Her chest clenched with pain and she crouched down and hugged her knees. Her body shook as she cried silently. She'd tried to leave Moldova behind, but the misery had followed her. First, Volva, whom she'd tried to forget, and now Paavo, who made her remember.

Blyat! She grabbed a handful of gravel and threw it angrily across the lawn, but it didn't satisfy her urge to destroy or fight back. She couldn't live like this.

A car slowed on the street and then the backyard lit up from the headlights shining down the walkway, the light distorted from the rain as the car pulled into the neighbor's driveway.

Hannah crept down the pathway along the fence and peeked over the gate. With a start, she realized that it wasn't any old car. It was a police car with bright flashing lights but no siren.

LAPD was written in large block letters on the side of the car. She crouched down low. A police car coming to your house at this time of night was bad for anyone in any country. What if Colin was dead?

She remembered the knock on her family's apartment door at ten o'clock at night when she and Babulya had been waiting for her parents to come home. Four police officers had stood in the doorway, and they'd looked at her with grim faces. Her first thought was that at least their hats were still on. If they were off, it meant someone was dead. But she'd been wrong.

A tall, white police officer got out of the LAPD car, with his hat and uniform on, and opened the back door of the car. Someone was getting out. She saw a flash of blond hair before she saw his body. Colin was alive, but he looked sadder than she'd ever seen him. He was staring at the ground, wearing wet jeans and a Lakers jersey splattered with paint.

The front door of his house swung open and his mother ran out. She ran down the stairs, her blonde curls bouncing, mouth clenched tight, eyes furious.

Colin took a step back. His mother flew toward him. At first Hannah thought she was going to strike him, but then she pressed her two hands against his large cheeks. "How could you do that?" she cried.

"I'm sorry, Mom."

She dropped her hands. "Why would you spray-paint a school?"

He looked down at his feet. "I didn't actually spray anything. And it wasn't my idea. They bought the paint because we lost the game to the other school. Anyway, I thought it would wash off with the rain."

"That's so stupid!" His mother spat. There was a moment of silence. "You're wet. Are you cold?"

"Yeah."

Rain dripped down Hannah's face, into her mouth. She licked her lips and brushed the water out of her eyes.

"He's a good boy," his mother said to the officer. "I don't know what happened. I can't believe he would vandalize a school. Will they—will they press charges?"

"It sounds like he was the sober one and got pressured into driving. We impounded the car and we'll bring him in for more questioning when we talk to the other kids."

More questioning. Hannah knew that word and remembered the ten hours of interrogation she'd endured after the bombing. What did "sober" mean? And what did they say about a car? There was so much she didn't understand.

The officer continued. "But you know, he didn't run off and he answered all our questions. He'll get off easy."

The crank on the window squealed above her and the police officer looked toward the gate. Hannah froze. Did he see her or was he just looking in the direction of the window? They must have all heard it. If Lillian looked down by the gate and saw she was outside, she'd be in big trouble, but if the officer saw her and suspected she was illegal, she'd be sent to jail. She didn't dare breathe.

She waited until the police officer got into the car, and then, crouching low, she hurried along the walkway, little pebbles flying into the air, chattering out her escape. She ran into the house, took off her slippers, tiptoed to the garage, and then waited.

CHAPTER THIRTY-NINE

Nobody came. Hannah lay on the sofa in the garage, waiting, adrenaline coursing through her. Finally, when she realized the house was silent and nobody was getting up, she closed her eyes, but she was too wired to sleep. So she'd reached under the sofa for Sergey's English version of *Anna Karenina* and started to read.

After reading until sometime past three, she fell asleep with the light on. That night, she had a bad dream, the same old one, about her mother's body burning. In the dream, Hannah ran through the flames to save her, and when she got to the body, it didn't have a head. But something new happened at the end. She felt a windy heat on her forehead, so hot, like it was happening in real life, not in her dream, and she heard Babulya say, clear as anything, "Listen to your nose."

She woke up, gasping. It had felt real, but she was here and Babulya was far away. She glanced at the alarm clock. It was seven thirty.

Breakfast was supposed to be ready and the table set by seven thirty, but if she hurried, perhaps she'd beat Lillian to the kitchen.

She jumped out of bed wearing the gray sweat suit, which she'd fallen asleep in, ran out of the garage, down the hall, and into the kitchen. Miraculously, she was the first one there. As fast as she could, she put a frying pan on the stove and began melting butter for eggs.

A few minutes later, Lillian came into the kitchen wearing another new red suit. "We won't be needing eggs. We're going out. While we're gone, you will wash all the windows in the house. I expect them to be finished by the time we return." She gave Hannah a cold stare as if she was contemplating further punishments.

"Where are you going?" Hannah said, opting to pretend the night before had not happened—she had not talked back to their friends and she had not gone outside to meet Colin.

"That is none of your business."

Maggie ran in. "We're going for brunch."

Lillian interrupted her. "Don't speak to Hannah. She needs some silent time to think about her actions yesterday."

"What did she do?" Maggie asked, glancing at Hannah with a mixture of awe and fear.

"Every time you *do* talk to her," Lillian continued, "I will throw out one doll."

"What?" Maggie said in English. "That's totally unfair."

"Maggie," Lillian barked sharply. "Russian."

Maggie rolled her eyes at Hannah.

So that was her punishment. The kids couldn't talk to her. That sucked, but Hannah wasn't too worried. It wouldn't last. If they couldn't talk to her, she couldn't take care of them. Soon, they'd drive Lillian crazy and she'd be begging Hannah to take them. Hannah grabbed the window cleaner and a rag and began spraying the windows in the kitchen.

Sure enough, an hour after they got back from brunch, Lillian was sitting at the dining room table with her books, Michael was scooting his train by her feet, and Maggie was interrupting her every few minutes with another question or request for food.

"Maggie," Lillian said, in a low, barely controlled voice. "You can talk to Hannah now. She'll get you what you want."

Maggie skipped into the living room where Hannah was vacuuming. "Can I have strawberry compote, with some cheese and crackers?" They shared a smile, and Hannah went into the kitchen to make her the snack. "And take them outside," Lillian shrieked. "I can't get anything done."

Hannah went outside to play soccer with the children, relieved but also worried about her minimal punishment. She worried Lillian had something else planned. After they'd been playing for half an hour, it started to rain, and they came back inside.

Hannah glanced into the open dining room. Lillian wasn't at the table studying. There was a stack of her textbooks next to an open pad of yellow paper, half-filled with notes.

The book. She'd forgotten to hide the book.

She hoped Lillian was in the bathroom, but she heard sounds coming from the garage. Something being thrown. The sound of fabric tearing.

Maggie ran ahead of her down the hall. She lurched to a stop at the doorway to the garage. "Oh my God, Mom," Maggie said in English.

Hannah came up behind, filled with dread. Lillian was ripping out the inside of her father's suitcase. The garage was in shambles. Hannah's things had been thrown all over the concrete floor, which was never clean no matter how much Hannah swept it. The toys had been pushed off the shelves. The pictures of her parents and Katya were missing too. Sergey's book was next to Lillian's foot, along with a stack of the underwear that he'd given her. Evidence.

Michael ran into the garage and grabbed a truck from the ground, as if nothing were wrong. He vroomed it across the floor, over the stack of Hannah's clothing.

"What are you doing?" Maggie asked her mother.

"I'm looking for Hannah's documents," Lillian grunted, tearing at the fabric. "She's a liar, Maggie. Don't believe anything she says."

Maggie glanced at Hannah, raising her eyebrows at her to show her that she thought her mother was acting crazy.

Hannah could smell the old dust that had made its way to the inside of her father's suitcase. It was one of the few things she'd had that had belonged to her father in the end, but if she got angry, Lillian would win. If she acted like it didn't matter, Hannah figured she'd win. So she sat on the sofa and watched Lillian impassively. He was already dead. Nothing Lillian did would change that. Actually, nothing Lillian did could hurt her, really. The worst had already happened—her parents had been killed. No matter what anybody did, nothing was worse than that.

She looked for Michael's fire truck and saw it in the corner of the garage, next to the chained-up garage doors. It was turned upside down and the seat was up. The ball and *Goodnight Moon* were missing, but Lillian must not have noticed the documents in the book or she wouldn't still be looking.

Lillian lifted her head, lips pressed together, and surveyed her damage. "Maggie, take Michael upstairs. Hannah, stay here." Her tone left no room for argument, but Maggie gave Hannah a quick, scared look before she pulled Michael out of the garage.

Hannah listened to their footsteps going down the hall as she scanned the mess, searching for *Goodnight Moon*, and her documents.

Lillian snatched up the stack of underwear and shook them. "How did you get these?"

"I bought them," she said.

"A village girl from Moldova does not go to a lingerie shop in America to buy eight-dollar underwear."

"I'm not from a village. I'm from the capital city of Moldova, in case you forgot." She paused. "Sergey gave me fifty dollars." She realized too late that Sergey gave her that fifty after the bus trip, but Lillian didn't catch on.

"You sent that fifty dollars to your grandmother."

Which you stole. "He gave me another fifty," she said.

"Why would he give you another fifty?" Lillian asked.

Hannah shrugged. "To be nice."

"My husband is not nice," Lillian said. "He only acts nice to a woman if he's screwing her or he wants to screw her." She flung the panties to the side and they landed near *Goodnight Moon*. It was closed, her documents safely hidden. *Ha,* she thought. *My documents are right there, out in the open, and you're too stupid to see them.*

Lillian lifted another book from the floor—*Anna Karenina,* in English—Sergey's book. Hannah's stomach clenched. "When did he give this to you?" she asked.

Hannah stared at the book, trying to think of a plausible excuse, besides admitting she'd snuck into the office.

"He didn't give it to me. I found it," she said. "It was on the coffee table downstairs."

"Are you trying to tell me he was reading it?" Lillian asked. "My husband doesn't read."

Hannah shrugged.

"What did you give him for his little gifts?" she asked.

"He didn't give me anything," Hannah said.

"Don't lie to me," Lillian roared.

"I haven't done anything with your husband. He didn't give me the book—I found it. My panties were ripped and falling off of me, so I asked him for money. He gave it to me, and the next day, when I went to the Russian store for the madeleines, I bought the panties at the store across the street. It's not a big deal."

Lillian's eyes bugged out of her head and made her look like the cockroach in Kafka's *Metamorphosis.* "He convinced me to allow you to go on the bus that day," she said, her voice filled with betrayal. She stepped toward Hannah and grabbed her arm. "I know something happened between you. Stop lying to me!"

Maggie ran into the room. "Mama, stop!"

Lillian's voice was shaking, barely under control as she spoke. "Maggie, go back upstairs. Now."

"She's not lying, Mama. She's had those panties for ages. I saw them a long time ago and she told me the same thing, that she bought them at that store."

Hannah gaped at Maggie. She was sticking up for her. Lying for her.

"This doesn't have anything to do with you, Mag—"

Maggie rushed on, her large hazel eyes blinking. "Papa didn't do anything to her at the park. They didn't even, like, touch or anything. She just helped, like she does at home."

Maggie thought she was helping, but she really wasn't. Lillian hadn't even mentioned the park and now it was clear that Maggie thought something had happened. Hannah remembered how embarrassed Maggie had seemed about that silly foot rub, and she wished she'd stopped Sergey earlier. Her face began to heat up.

"Nothing happened in the park?" Lillian's face was set in an expression of ill-masked fury.

"She wouldn't do that, and Papa loves you, Mama," Maggie said. "I think you're just imagining things 'cause of that other woman."

Lillian stiffened. Hannah worried for Maggie then, scared that Lillian would strike her, and if she did, Hannah knew she'd protect her.

"How do you know about this?" Lillian asked slowly, an odd tone to her voice.

Maggie's eyes widened. "I heard you and Papa arguing."

Lillian let go of Hannah's arm and lifted her chin proudly. "Maybe you're right, Maggie. Maybe I am paranoid because of that other woman." She strode out of the room, her back stiff, but Hannah wasn't fooled.

Lillian was just biding her time, until Maggie wasn't watching.

CHAPTER FORTY

It didn't take long.

The next day, Hannah was scraping the grout in the downstairs bathtub with an old kitchen knife. Earlier, Lillian had made her iron all the bedsheets. On top of her other work.

All day, while she was cleaning, she talked to Colin in her head, asking him his favorite color, favorite sport, favorite food, favorite everything. She was trying to entertain herself, but it only made it more obvious to her that she'd never been so lonely in her whole life. She wasn't the kind of girl who normally needed an imaginary friend.

She put the knife on the side of the bathtub, grabbed the rag, and sprayed it slowly with cleaner. No point in hurrying. Finally, she understood the Russian expression that it didn't matter how fast you pushed the broom, there was more work all the same. If she worked fast, Lillian would just find something else for her to do.

She moved the rag in slow circles across the bathroom floor, unable to avoid the homesick ache in her gut any longer. She thought about the regular things her friends were doing every day. Passing notes in Russian lit. Laughing about Madame Volchuk's purple bouffant hairdo. Getting felt up under the secondary stairway. Going out for pizza after school. Talking about what classes they were going to take in university. Copying one another's math homework. She used to be the math expert. Now what did her group do? Daniil wasn't bad, but he didn't let anyone copy. Maybe his new girlfriend let them—Lera was good at math too. That thought was so depressing, Hannah stopped cleaning and stared down at the too-clean floor.

An out-of-place smell drifted into her thoughts: Paavo's cologne. That yeasty body odor. She twisted and looked up. Paavo's square frame filled the doorway. His shirt was tucked in tight to hold in the mounds of flesh, and his silver belt buckle in the shape of a bull shone down at her.

She looked past him, down the hall. Lillian had left home a little while ago. Usually the door was locked.

"What are you doing?" He leered down at her, as if she'd gotten on her hands and knees for his benefit.

"I'm cleaning." She wanted to add, *What does it look like, you pig?* "Did you come in with Sergey?"

He stared at her. "No."

Her face flushed. "How did you get in?" she asked, standing up, clinging to the rag.

"The door was open. Lillian said you'd be home."

This was Lillian's punishment. She cleared her throat and stood tall. "Sergey will be back soon. I'll tell him you were here."

"I didn't come to talk to him." He stuck out his belly, blocking her exit. "Lillian said you're misbehaving; I offered to talk to you."

She gestured with her chin toward the hallway. "I have to get something in the kitchen. You can talk to me in there."

"I don't think so," he said, the corner of his mouth curling up.

A quiver of fear passed through her. She searched for a way to escape. The kitchen knife she'd used to scrape the grouting was still on the edge of the bathtub. Maybe she could grab it in time. He might rip it away, but at least she could injure him—right where it would hurt the most.

"What's a girl like you doing cleaning floors?" he asked, stepping toward her. She glanced toward the tub and realized she wouldn't get there in time. He continued, "You could be making a lot more money dancing. More for your family, more for yourself. You could buy some nice clothes for that pretty little body of yours."

Hannah was wearing her monkey T-shirt with her sweatpants, and he was staring at her as if she were naked. She wished she was wearing the black baggy T-shirt, but it was dirty.

"I'm not interested in that. Excuse me. I need to get the bleach." In fact, she didn't use bleach because Lillian was paranoid about Michael getting poisoned. Instead, she used an organic, orange-scented bathroom cleaner, which barely worked. Her hand tightened on the rag. Even if it was earth-friendly, it would probably hurt if it got in his eyes.

He didn't move. "That little shirt. You are trying to tease Sergey, I think. Does he come down to your room at night so you can give him a little pleasure?"

"That's disgusting," she said, even though it was true that Sergey had come down to her room. But she hadn't done anything with him. "I am here to take care of their children and clean their house. Now, if you will please move, I can continue with my work."

"I'm willing to pay," he said.

Hannah stood very still. "I don't want your money."

"Really? I can help you," he said. "In other ways."

"I would never do that for anything."

"Lillian told me about your little adventure the other day. Who'd you meet?"

"I didn't meet anyone."

He hummed. "Sergey didn't want me to help him find a girl. He said he had one already. You two have something on one of his business trips?"

So Sergey really had requested her. She wondered if Lillian knew. "I never saw him before I came here. I'm not that kind of girl. Now will you please let me pass?"

"What were you doing the other night? You came home sweaty, smelling of sex. You have a night job?" He leered.

"I went for a run," she said. "I told Lillian, and it's the truth."

"Whatever you say." He stepped to the side and waved his hand out, as if he'd always been intending to let her pass. She hesitated. His belly filled most of the doorway and she didn't want to come any closer to him, but anything was better than being trapped in this bathroom. She took a leap past him. His arm swung out and stopped her. His fat belly pushed in, squishing her against the door-jamb. "Maybe you can show me the underwear he bought for you."

She lifted the rag with the cleaner and rubbed it on his face. He grunted and yanked it out of her hand. "Suka!"

Panicking, she wiggled into the hall, but he forced her back against the cold wall. "Please," she said. "I don't want trouble."

"You didn't worry about insulting me and my wife. You put a stinking rag in my face and then you say you don't want trouble. Would you like me to shove that rag in your mouth? Or perhaps something else?"

His belly squished around her and his hard belt buckle pressed into her, cold through her T-shirt, right above the top of her pants. Her heart beat in her ears and she struggled to breathe as all his weight crushed against her.

"No," she said. The word was quiet, barely escaping from her lips, and she remembered Volva and how she didn't yell.

"Sergey will be angry," she said.

Paavo stepped back.

"I knew you two had something." He sneered. She thought of the knife. It might be her only chance. She leaped toward the bathroom, but he grabbed her shoulder and pinned her against the wall, his thumb digging into her armpit. "Not so fast. If he wants my money, he can share."

She struggled to get away, but his hand on her shoulder was as solid as a nail pinning her to a board. "Stop!" she yelled, shoving him, but it was like pushing a wall of fat.

"Behave," he barked, undoing his belt buckle, and shoving her back against the wall. "Your uncle didn't do what we asked of him and look what happened to him."

"What?" she breathed, shocked. "What did you do to him?"

"He's alive, for now. In a work camp. He's my insurance."

"Where is he?"

He ignored her. "Next we'll go for your babushka. She's old.

She wouldn't be able to handle much of a shock. Maybe we'll push her around a little, or maybe it will only take the suggestion that you are a prostitute."

"She'd never believe it," Hannah said, though her voice was shaking.

"Your friends will. Your old boyfriend, Daniil. And I know about that pretty friend of yours, Katya. Olga sent me pictures. Many men would pay for her."

"You wouldn't," Hannah gasped.

"I would," he said. "People don't cross Paavo Shevchenko."

She didn't know what to do. Her whole body sagged. His hand snaked under the bottom of her T-shirt.

"Hello?" Sergey called from the foyer.

Paavo shifted away from her and did up his belt buckle.

Thank God. Thank God. Thank God.

"Remember what I said," he murmured under his breath. "Tell him you invited me in."

Sergey cleared his throat. He was looking down the hall at them. Paavo gave her a warning look before he sauntered down the hall, swinging his legs wide.

"Hello, my friend," he boomed.

Sergey stepped into the hall and shook his friend's hand. He looked past Paavo to Hannah standing next to the bathroom at the end of the hall. He seemed angry.

"Any news from the bank?" Paavo asked.

"No," Sergey said abruptly. "How did you—?"

"Your girl let me in," Paavo announced, and turned to look at her. "Right?"

The injustice of it all made her want to scream. She wouldn't say she'd invited him in. She glared at him, her arms and legs shaking from adrenaline.

Paavo's face turned to stone. *We know where your babushka lives . . . your old boyfriend, Daniil . . . that pretty little friend of yours, Katya.*

Hannah never should have come to America. Not only had she put herself at risk, but she'd put everyone she loved in grave danger.

She nodded and stumbled into the kitchen, blinking away the tears.

CHAPTER FORTY-ONE

Hannah crept along the fence. The crickets were chirping in the backyard like they did in the village in Moldova. It had always been such a peaceful sound to her, but today it was like they were warning her. It seemed no matter what she did, things kept getting worse.

She was hoping that just seeing Colin would make it all better. She pushed open the slat in the fence, slowly, so it wouldn't make any noise.

Colin was in his bedroom, awake, even though it was after midnight. He was sitting on his bed, counting a large pile of coins and bills. Crying. Into all that money. How could a person cry when they were sitting in front of a pile of money? What did he have to cry about?

He wiped his red, wet cheeks with one hand, put the wrinkled bills into a wad, and shoved them into a black wallet. The mountain of coins remained. He stared at them for a moment and then took large handfuls of the coins and dropped them in the olive duffel bag. Then he walked across the room to the desk, which was cleared of papers and books, and put the bag on the floor.

She realized the room was different. The bed was made, the

garbage and balled-up papers were gone, and all his clothing had been picked up from the floor. He took an envelope out of the desk drawer and placed it on the desk. It said, MOM.

He was running away. It was unbelievable, but it was the only explanation she could come up with. He was taking all his money and leaving. He'd written a letter to his mom. Her heart twisted inside her. He couldn't leave. He didn't know what he had. His mom wasn't like her mom, but she was a better mom than Lillian. She was better than lots of moms. His dad was a drunk, yes, but he wasn't beating him. Colin had food. He had his own room. He had a brother who loved him, for sure, even if he didn't hang out at the house much. Hannah had heard them laughing, playing video games, joking around the way boys did.

She had to stop him. If she called to him, Sergey and Lillian would hear, but they wouldn't notice a rock. She bent down to pick one up. The window was half open. She could hit the glass lightly and then when he came to the window, she could whisper for him to come out. He could even climb out the window.

He stood up from the desk and grabbed a basketball jersey, some pants, and underwear from a drawer, and shoved it all in the bag. Was he running away right now?

She pulled her arm back, preparing to throw the rock at his window. It was open halfway, so she'd have to make sure to hit the glass, not the screen, or it wouldn't make a noise. She launched the rock forward. It hit the side of the building and made a plunk.

He looked at his closed bedroom door.

Not there. Over here.

Then he moved. Fast. He grabbed the duffel bag and shoved it in his closet. His mother burst through the door.

"Why are you awake?" she asked.

He stepped back, hands up. "What?"

"Why are you awake?" she repeated.

"Why are *you* awake?" he asked.

"You have the SATs tomorrow, young man. You need to do well so you can get a scholarship. Your father isn't going to pay for college," she said. "Especially now."

"I know, okay?" he said.

"Are you trying to destroy your life? Vandalizing a school! Staying up all night before your SATs? What kind of a kid have I raised?"

"I told you, it was the other kids."

"You need to get it together, Colin." She planted her hands on her hips. "Go to bed. This is just dumb. You don't want to be a failure your whole life, do you?"

He stared down at his bare feet and looked like he was going to cry. Hannah wished she could clamp her hand over the mother's mouth, stop her from talking and making things worse. This was the last thing he needed.

His mother paused then, looking around the room. "Thank you for cleaning," she said. Then she turned off the light and left the room, closing the door behind her.

Colin went to his bed, sat down, and dropped his head in his hands. He stayed still like that for a moment, and then lay down on his small bed, curling into a large ball on his side, not bothering to cover himself with his comforter. It was as if he was punishing himself.

Katya always told Hannah she wanted to help everyone else before she helped herself, but Katya didn't understand. After Hannah's parents had died, in those black weeks when her body did not feel like her own, when her arms had weights on them and her chest felt sick with poison, Babulya had brought her eucalyptus tea in the morning and tickled the nape of her neck like Mamulya always had, and at night, made her chicken soup when she got home from working all day at the market. It was only when Babulya thought she was asleep that Hannah heard her muffled sobs and knew it wasn't easy for her either. One day, she asked Babulya how she could go on when her own daughter had been killed. Babulya had told her she'd learned that the only way to overcome a great sadness was to help someone else who was sad too.

Hannah bent down to pick up another rock, stood up, aimed, and threw it. Crack.

"Oh!" It was Colin's voice, just a peep and then silence.

Hannah jumped away from the slat in the fence. *Oh my God.* She couldn't believe she'd just broken his window.

A back door opened. Hannah closed the slat, fast, and stood still, pressed against the fence. There were footsteps down the neighbor's back steps, around the house, to Colin's half-open window. Hannah could hear his mother breathing.

"Colin honey?" his mother said through his window.

"Yes?" His voice sounded scared.

"Are you okay?"

"Yeah."

"There's a crack in your window."

"I think a bird just hit it." He sounded like he was lying, even to Hannah.

"I thought I heard someone out here."

"No, it was a bird. I heard a squeak."

Had he heard her?

"I don't see the bird." His mother paused another moment, probably looking around for the bird, and then walked along his concrete pathway to the back door. It opened and closed.

Hannah crept along the gravel walkway, trying not to make a sound. She hurried across the lawn, opened the back door, and snuck into the dark kitchen. She locked the door and pressed her hand against the smooth white wood, listening.

Behind her, the tinkling of ice in a glass made her jump.

CHAPTER FORTY-TWO

"**Y**ou keep surprising me," Sergey slurred, leaning up against the counter. In the dark, it was difficult to read his expression, but he wasn't smiling. "I didn't think you'd go for a boar."

"I don't," she said, wondering if he was referring to Colin or Paavo. Or both.

He shrugged. "It's your business." He took another sip of his vodka on ice—he only drank it that way when he was alone.

"Your friend—" she began, unsure of how to proceed, worried he would get angry if she told him the truth. "He tried to force me."

"That's not what he said."

"He lied," Hannah spat.

"You didn't want it?" He stepped toward her, coming closer with his breath that reeked of vodka. He actually looked surprised.

"I was cleaning the floor and he walked into the house," she said. "I only said I let him in because he threatened my family if I didn't."

Sergey frowned. "You are a beautiful girl, Hannah. You should lock the door when you're home alone. This isn't the village."

Hannah blinked at the sting of that statement. She wasn't a

village girl! "Lillian had just gone out with the kids," she said. "I don't know why she didn't lock it." This was as far as she could go. If she told him what Paavo had said about Lillian sending him to talk to her, he'd ask either Paavo or Lillian and they'd say she was lying.

Sergey squinted at her, like he didn't know what to believe. How could he doubt that she was telling the truth? Paavo was a disgusting, mean man. No matter how much money or power he had, she couldn't imagine any woman going with him willingly. But it had looked bad when Sergey came into the house. "I said no, but he wasn't going to stop. Not if you hadn't come back." She let out a shaky breath. "I don't want you to think, you know, that I'm that kind of girl. Because I'm not." She pulled her hair away from her shoulders and dropped it behind her back.

Sergey reached for her shoulder and brushed back a few errant strands of hair. "I know."

She flinched and he pulled his hand away. She couldn't take any more men touching her, even if it was Sergey, who wasn't anything like Paavo or Volva. "He said my uncle wouldn't cooperate and look what happened to him." Her voice shook as she thought of Vladi, silly Vladi as she used to call him.

"What?" Sergey looked sincerely shocked. So he really didn't know.

"He said Vladi's in a work camp somewhere. He said it was his insurance. He told me to cooperate or something would happen to Vladi."

"You don't have to cooperate with Paavo," Sergey said, his jaw tightening. "You work for me."

"Can you help my uncle?" she asked quietly, afraid to hear the answer.

Sergey sucked in a sudden, worried breath of air. "I don't know. I'll talk to Paavo. But believe me, Hannah, I never asked him to do that."

She stared at him, trying to see if he was telling her the truth. He gazed into her eyes. She couldn't tell.

"I'm going on a business trip to Russia soon," he said softly. "If he's in a work camp, I'll try to get him out."

This small promise meant the whole world to her. "Thank you."

He rested a heavy hand on her shoulder and squeezed it.

"Paavo told me that you chose me. Is this true?" she asked, searching his face.

He hesitated. "Yes."

Her eyes teared up. "Why?"

"I wanted to help you." He licked his top lip and looked away, as if he felt guilty about something.

He definitely hadn't helped her so far, but it was something else. "Maggie said you knew my parents?" she asked.

He nodded slowly. His eyes twinkled as he stared at her through the darkness, ran his hand down her shoulder, caressing her upper arm. Hannah stood very still. "You look just like your mother. You have her eyes, her feet, that beautiful hair."

There was the loud *bang-bang* of someone running down the hallway. Sergey dropped his hand. Hannah stepped backward just as Lillian burst into the kitchen.

"What is happening here?" she demanded.

Sergey put his hands in the air. "Nothing."

"Why are you two standing in the dark?" Lillian said.

"Lillian, give me a break," Sergey said, brushing past her. "She's a child."

Lillian glared at Hannah like she wanted to murder her. Hannah listened to Sergey's hard-soled slippers bang up the stairs. He went into the office and slammed the door, which woke up Michael, who started crying. Hannah expected Lillian to go after him, but she didn't.

"What are you trying to do to us?" Lillian demanded.

"I'm not doing anything," Hannah said, her heart pounding.

"Do you think you can steal away my family?" Lillian's voice cracked, and she swallowed, her hazel eyes filling with tears.

Hannah felt sorry for her. "No," she said, shaking her head. "No, I would never. Honestly, nothing has happened." Then, she added, sincerely, without thinking, "He loves you. He only needs a little affection."

"Affection?" Lillian grabbed her hair and pulled her backward. Hannah couldn't stop her, unless she wanted her hair pulled out. When they got to the counter, Lillian grabbed the scissors out of the knife block. "*Affection?* Is that what you're giving him? You and your beautiful hair?"

"He wasn't talking about *my* hair," Hannah cried, trying to pry Lillian's fingers off of her hair. "He was talking about my mother's!"

Silence. "Your mother's?"

Lillian lifted the scissors and her voice turned cold. "Stand still or you'll get hurt."

CHAPTER FORTY-THREE

When Hannah woke up the next morning, she lifted her hand up to feel her head, hoping that the whole previous night was all a bad dream. But it wasn't. Her hair had been butchered. In some places, she could feel her scalp.

She glanced at the clock. It was ten after eight in the morning. After Lillian had chopped off her hair, Hannah had been so angry, she hadn't set her alarm, but now she regretted it. She put on the gray sweat suit and hurried into the hall, where she could hear the banging of spoons in bowls. Lillian was sitting with the children, eating cereal. The table was silent. Lillian's eyes were red. Sergey was not home.

She wondered how she could check on Colin, make sure he was still here, maybe even talk to him for a minute.

Maggie was staring in horror at Hannah.

"What happened to your hair?" she asked.

"She cut it," Lillian said abruptly.

"But it was such beautiful hair," Maggie said.

Hannah lifted her chin, determined not to let Lillian think she'd hurt her. "It's lighter this way," she said, glancing at Lillian for her reaction. "A lot of models cut their hair short nowadays."

Lillian's lips pressed together.

I got her, Hannah thought.

"You slept in," Lillian said.

"I was tired," Hannah said.

"Clear the table," Lillian said, glaring.

All day, Lillian watched Hannah. There wasn't a single moment she could have snuck outside. A few times, Lillian caught her looking out the living room window for Colin. One time she'd asked, "Who are you looking for?"

"Nobody," Hannah had said.

By dinnertime, she was getting worried. She hadn't seen him go to school or come home, and she'd purposely kept the living room curtains open, even though it annoyed Lillian, so that she could see him. She'd even vacuumed the living room for twice as long as usual so she could watch for him coming home from school. But she didn't see him. Maybe he was already gone.

Hannah stuck the roast with carrots and onions in the oven for dinner and opened the back door. There hadn't been any sounds from next door all day. She breathed in through her nose, hoping to catch some smell of Colin's dinner, but all she smelled was the dampness in the air. It was going to rain again. When she saw movies set in Los Angeles, it was never raining, but it had rained here every day for the last week.

She had to look in his window, but at this time of day, she couldn't go outside. Lillian was studying three feet away in the living room.

Maybe she could see him from upstairs. If she peeled the potatoes first and put them on the stove, she'd be clear to check on

Michael and Maggie, who were watching a movie upstairs. She hurried out of the kitchen.

The dining room door slid open and Lillian called after her, "Where are you going?"

Hannah closed her eyes in frustration. *Keep your voice light,* she thought. *Don't let her suspect anything.* "I have to organize Michael's dresser," she called, as she continued down the hall. "He pulled all his clothing onto the floor this morning."

The children were watching a Disney movie about robots in Michael's darkened room. Hannah sat on the bed next to Maggie and glanced at the red curtain. She could hear the pounding of rain outside.

"Can you play with my hair?" Maggie asked.

Your thick, uncut hair.

Hannah slid behind her, reminding herself that it wasn't Maggie's fault. She tickled it at the base of her neck, the way her own mother used to do to her. She waited for a scarier scene in the movie, and then, casually, she let go of Maggie's hair, got up on her knees, and peered past the red curtain at Colin's house.

He was home! He was in the upstairs study, which, as far as she could tell, was next to his mother's bedroom. Probably the brother had his bedroom upstairs too, on the other side. The kitchen, the living area, the television room, and Colin's bedroom were all on the main floor.

Colin was sitting at the desk in the study with his back to her, and he was typing on the computer. She studied the screen— Facebook. She had a Facebook account, but she'd accessed it only a couple of times when she was at Katya's.

She pressed her hand flat against the window, reaching for him through the pouring rain. *Look at me. I'm here. You are not alone.*

Then, as if he'd heard her thoughts, he turned in his chair and looked through the window, right at her. They were both in upstairs rooms, probably six meters—twenty feet—from each other, but he seemed confused, as if he didn't know who she was. Then she remembered her hair. He didn't recognize her.

"What are you doing?" Maggie asked.

Was Lillian getting Maggie to spy on her now?

"Nothing." She let go of the curtain, sat down on the bed, and ran her hand along her butchered hair. A tear snuck out of her eye and rolled down her cheek. She wiped it away with her palm, fast, before Maggie could see. She hated Lillian. She hated her more than she'd ever hated anyone in her life. She hated her so much, she wished she'd die.

CHAPTER FORTY-FOUR

That night, at five minutes after eleven, Hannah was in the kitchen cleaning when she heard Colin's screen door slam shut once and then twice, and the familiar sound of him walking around the house, his sandals slapping the wet ground.

He was leaving!

Sergey was out. Lillian had gone upstairs to bed five minutes before. She could do it, if she was quiet. She opened the back door and ran out of the house, into the pouring rain in nothing more than her slippers and gray sweat suit. Colin's side gate opened. Hannah sprinted along her side of the fence and burst through the gate.

Colin jumped back, a few feet away on his own driveway. He wasn't holding his duffel bag. Just the garbage can. He was wearing sandals, shorts, and his basketball jersey. In the rain. He wasn't going anywhere, at least not right at this moment.

"Oh my God. You scared me," he said.

"I am sorry," she said, trying to keep her voice low, just in case Lillian was listening from her bedroom window, though she figured the rain would block some of the noise. "We do not meet properly. My name is Hannah."

"Colin," he said with a quick smile that didn't seem forced. How could he smile if he was planning on running away from the only family he had?

"It is nice to meeting you," she said, realizing then that her hands were too empty. She hadn't grabbed the garbage can.

"Same."

She didn't understand what that meant. Same what? There was an awkward pause.

"Your hair is different," he said.

"It is short," she said.

"It's nice," he said, looking down at his feet, clearly embarrassed.

"No," she said, not wanting lies between them. "It is not." She wished she knew how to make a joke of it and say that it looked like someone had taken a lawn mower to her head, but she didn't know enough words.

He glanced at his house, as if he was thinking of making a run for it. Then he blurted out, really loudly, "How old are you?"

It was one of the questions she'd practiced, one she'd planned to ask him. "Seventeen," she said. "How old are you?"

"Same."

She didn't understand. "Excuse me?"

"I'm seventeen too," he said, clearing his throat, like he was embarrassed.

"I am sorry. My English no is good."

He grinned and she knew she'd made a mistake. "Don't worry about it. I can understand you," he said, again practically scream-ing. Hannah couldn't stop herself from glancing up at the master bedroom window, but it was still dark and the blue curtain was closed. If Lillian saw her outside, she'd come out and kill her.

"Where are you from?" he asked, squinting at her through the rain.

Lillian had told her to say she was from Russia if anyone asked, but she couldn't, wouldn't, lie anymore. "Moldova."

"Moldova?" He didn't know where it was, which wasn't surprising. It was the poorest country in Eastern Europe, small and insignificant.

"Near Romania," she said.

"Ah-ah-ah. Transylvania."

Transylvania was in Romania, but she didn't know why he made that noise. "Yes."

"You know—vampires?"

"Vampires." She felt thankful she'd learned the word. "No vampires in Moldova."

Colin seemed uncomfortable, like he didn't know what else to say. A helicopter pounded in the sky above them and he looked up, as if to say, *Rescue me.*

"You are bringing garbage to street?" she asked, hoping to keep him with her for as long as possible. So far, Lillian hadn't come out, which meant she was probably still asleep.

He shrugged. "Yeah, might as well. It's Thursday, right? My mom will freak if I forget."

He reached over his gate, unlocked it, went on his side of the fence, and rolled the garbage can down the driveway. Hannah walked with him, pulling her garbage cans, hoping Lillian didn't hear. "Freak?" she asked. "My English, I am sorry."

"She'd get angry," he said, giving her another look, more direct this time, like he was actually seeing her and maybe didn't feel so shy. They walked back up to their gates and opened them to get the recycling cans.

Hannah looked up, worried that the blue curtain would open and Lillian would be watching her. The longer she was outside, the more nervous she got. It was like a bomb that she could hear ticking in the back of her head.

"Do you go to school?" he asked as soon as they headed back down the driveway with their containers. His voice was so loud. "My mom said you're here a lot during the day."

She waited until they got to the end of the driveway to answer him quietly. "I am finish eleventh graduation."

He gave her an odd look. "Sorry?"

She realized she'd just said "graduation" instead of "grade." "Eleventh grade."

"Oh."

"I will study one more year and then I go to college. But I take break now." She couldn't explain that she'd had to drop out a year early because she had to work.

Was that the back door? Her heart beat a little faster. "I must go."

He grinned. "Don't be a stranger."

Was he trying to say she was strange? It couldn't be. "A stranger?"

"You know, like, come by sometime. Don't be a stranger. It's an expression. Like it means you shouldn't act like you don't know me."

She got it. He thought she might act like she didn't know him. Maybe it was because she was rushing off so fast.

She glanced nervously at the walkway next to the house. Tick. Tick. Tick.

"You have to go," he said.

She didn't want to go, even though she knew she should. It was her first time talking to him and she didn't know when she'd get another chance. "We must be quiet," she whispered.

"Okay," he whispered, glancing at her house. "They keep you on a tight leash?"

"Leash?"

"Like a dog, you know, it ties around the neck and you walk it."

"I'm not dog," she said, insulted.

He waved his hands. "No, no, I don't mean that. Just—they watch you."

"Yes." She couldn't say any more. If the neighbors became suspicious, they could report her, and Lillian had made it clear what would happen. She switched the subject to a safer one. "What are your hobbies?" This was a question she knew from English class. Her teacher said it was used for small talk, when people want to become friends.

His face turned red. Why would that embarrass him? "I don't know." He shrugged. "I like video games."

"Your room, you have many sports decorations." Now it was Hannah's turn to be embarrassed. He would know she'd been spying on him—she hadn't meant for it to come out like this.

"My dad keeps hoping I'll turn into an athlete like my brother," he explained, then stopped. "How do you know?"

"The fence," she admitted, stepping backward through the gate to her side of the fence. She pushed on the broken slat in the fence and opened it farther. "It is broken."

He walked down the path on his side of the fence and pressed on the slat in the fence. It opened even more. "Peekaboo," he joked, though he wasn't laughing. He blinked at her through the slat. Then he looked back, into his window.

"I thought I heard—" He stopped. "Did you throw the rock?"

She couldn't lie, not even if he wanted her to pay for it. "I am sorry. It was accident. I wanted only to talk."

He laughed, as if he was relieved. "I thought it was someone from school, you know, like trying to break my window."

"Oh." That was terrible. She didn't know what else to say. "I am sorry."

"It's no big deal." He paused. "Have you looked at me—" His voice cracked and he cleared his throat. "You know, other times?"

If she admitted she'd been spying on him, he might realize she'd seen him after he came out of the shower that time. He might think she was creepy and fix the fence. If she heard him hammering back here, it would break her heart.

"I see not much." She felt so guilty. "I see you drawing."

He nodded but looked down at his feet, refusing to look her in the eyes. He knew she'd seen more than that.

She hesitated. "I see the bag."

He grimaced and stared off through the rain, as if he was thinking of something else. His blond hair was now soaked, flattened to his head, raindrops dotting his bare arms.

"Why are you leaving?" she asked.

He shrugged, looking down. "My life sucks," he said, kicking at the edge of a puddle with his sandal. "Everyone at school hates me and my dad won't even talk to me. He's ashamed of me. It just—" His voice broke and he stopped talking.

"Everyone hates you?" She couldn't believe it.

"Yeah, and they have a good reason too. I mean, they dragged me along to paint up this other school. It wasn't my idea, but I always have to drive because they want to drink. Then they took off and the cops got me. I told the cops all their names like a pussy. It's my own stupid fault."

"What is a pussy?"

He let out a bark of laughter and wiped the rain from his face. "Never mind."

There was a pause and again he looked toward the house, like he wanted to leave her just as much as he wanted to leave his friends and his family.

"You should not go," she said, her heart wrenching. She pressed her hand against the wet, rough wood of the fence.

He looked at her, blinking his sensitive blue eyes at her through the rain. "Why not?"

"I need—" She was going to say that she needed a friend, but it was so desperate and so unlike her former self. In Moldova, she would never have begged someone to be her friend. And what if he said no? She continued, "I need someone, like—" He was staring at her like she was crazy, but still she pressed on. "Someone for talking."

He blinked at her, but he seemed to understand what she was saying at least. After a moment of silence, he said quietly, "Me too."

CHAPTER FORTY-FIVE

The next night, Lillian was still studying in the dining room at eleven and Hannah started to worry. She'd promised Colin she'd meet him at midnight. At eleven thirty, Hannah began cleaning the refrigerator as an excuse to stay in the kitchen and listen for Colin.

At midnight, Colin's back door opened and shut. She heard his footsteps trotting down his back stairs and around his walkway. He'd see she wasn't there and it would look like she'd decided not to come, and then he might leave anyway.

Tea. She'd make Lillian some chamomile tea. It would seem like she was being nice, but it would put her to sleep. Too bad she didn't have any valerian root.

After she'd made it, she knocked on the sliding door. "Lillian?"

"Yes?" Lillian sounded annoyed, but she didn't have that quivering sound Hannah heard in her voice when she was furious.

Hannah opened the sliding door. "I thought you might like some tea."

She gave Hannah a suspicious look. "Why are you still awake?"

"I was staying up for you," Hannah said, putting the tea next to her. "In case you need something."

"I'm studying. What would I need?"

Hannah shrugged. "What are you studying?"

"Microbiology," she said, taking a sip of the tea, eyeing her over the rim.

"The other night," Hannah said, then cleared her throat, hesitating. It was a risk. "You misunderstood."

"What?" There was the fury. Hannah had never known someone's voice to hold so much power.

Hannah stood her ground, even though she was afraid. "Sergey never tried anything with me. He told me you were the most beautiful woman he's ever met, but he said he met my mother when he was younger and I was lucky that I could always remember her because I only had to look at my hair. It wasn't anything. He was just reassuring me because—" Hannah hesitated. She didn't want to say it, but she had to. "Because she's dead."

Lillian's voice softened. "He said I was the most beautiful woman he's ever met?"

Hannah nodded.

A part of the tension that lived in Lillian's face melted away.

"Can you tell me how he knew my mother?" Hannah asked quietly.

Lillian lifted her chin. "Sergey told me he met your mother *and* your father at the Black Sea. They weren't much older than you are now."

Hannah couldn't believe Lillian had actually told her something useful. Her parents had met at the Black Sea, but they'd never mentioned Sergey. She wondered if she'd met him before, when she was younger. He hadn't looked familiar.

Lillian stood up. "That's all I know. I'm going to Paavo's club—Sergey's waiting for me. Stay up until I get back."

Hannah doubted Sergey was waiting for her. She knew he was probably drinking and that it might not be a good scene if Lillian arrived, but there was nothing she could say. Lillian went upstairs, got dressed, and headed out the door. Hannah waited five minutes after Lillian had left, to be sure she was really gone, and went outside.

Before she saw Colin, she could smell his freshly washed hair, but no baby powder deodorant. His face appeared in the fence opening and she smiled, wide, unable to stop herself, before she realized that she was showing her crooked teeth. Quickly, she closed her lips around them.

He grinned at her. "I like your smile," he said.

"Yes?" she asked, blinking.

"Why are you surprised?"

"I no like my tooth."

"Your tooth?"

He hadn't noticed—that surprised her. She lifted her upper lip and showed him the one tooth that twisted to the side, expecting to see him shrink back in revulsion. Americans had such nice teeth.

He shrugged. "You can't see it."

She smiled at him again, showing all her teeth. It was her first American smile. "I bring something from my country," she said, handing him a sirok bar. He opened it. "Coconut," she added proudly, having just looked up the word in Lillian's dictionary.

He swirled the chocolate-covered frozen cream cheese around in his mouth. "Different."

"You like it?"

He nodded. "Yeah," he said, as though he was surprised. "You should come over sometime. I'll make you popcorn. I make a pretty mean popcorn." He let out a laugh.

Something about popcorn. "What is this?"

"Oh, nothing," he said.

He'd said "popcorn." Was he asking her to go to a movie? "Please. Say this again."

"I just said you could come to my house." He pointed at his house and then gestured for her to come. "You know, come over."

She got it. "Now?"

"Not now." He seemed to think she was quite strange. "I mean, sure you can come now."

She didn't know why he was offering and then not offering. "Now is not a good time?" She might not have another chance.

Colin let out a nervous laugh. "I don't know about my mom. It's pretty late."

She understood. It was the same in Moldova. "People do not come to neighbor house in Moldova." Nobody wanted other people to see what they had.

"I just mean, you know, my mom will be weird. She'll want to hang out with us. Maybe we could stay outside in the backyard."

If they stayed outside, she'd hear Michael if he cried. She looked up at Michael's bedroom window—it was open, but not so wide that he could fall out. Hannah hadn't double-checked the front door. But maybe Lillian had locked it when she went out. Hannah imagined Paavo coming into the house. Stealing the children. Was the upstairs light on? She didn't want Michael to fall down the stairs. He'll be fine, she told herself. He was asleep.

"Okay," she said, and walked through her gate, around to his.

Colin opened his gate and waved her in front of him, as if she were a strange animal. His side of the fence was painted white instead of green, and the walkway was paved. She glanced in the first window and saw a large television, two armchairs, and some video game remotes on a side table between the two chairs. She continued down the walkway, past his bedroom and the kitchen. She listened to the sound of his footsteps behind her and felt awkward leading him into his own yard in the middle of the night. She thought of Lillian's accusation and hoped he didn't get the wrong idea.

She stopped. He passed her and gestured at the back porch. She followed him, but when he sat down on the top concrete step and patted next to him, she stared at him in shock.

In Moldova, a boy would never suggest that a girl sit directly on cold concrete—he'd at least offer her his jacket to sit on. It might be an old wives' tale, but they said you'd freeze your ovaries and you wouldn't be able to have babies if you sat on a cold surface. But if American kids did it, she thought, maybe that was silly. She sat down, clenching her knees together to keep her lower parts warm.

A helicopter zipped past above them. She wondered if it was a police or news helicopter. There was the sound of a police siren on

Santa Monica Boulevard. Maybe the police were chasing a criminal. Who was walking down their street. Looking for an open house. Somewhere to hide.

Colin looked up at the sky, ignoring the helicopter. "I guess you don't see the same stars in the sky in Moldova."

Boys said the same thing everywhere. "In Moldova, we have more stars." She cleared her throat. "Do you think there is problem?"

"What? The helicopter? No. They're up there every night. Who knows what they're doing." He grinned at her. "Don't worry."

But he didn't know the children were alone and the front door might be unlocked. "I never see these helicopters in my country."

"They're not everywhere. My mom grew up in Seattle and you never see them there. She says helicopters are the mosquitoes of Los Angeles."

Hannah smiled weakly, wishing she knew what mosquitoes were.

"Do you like Los Angeles?" he asked.

It was a funny question. If she told him how much of Los Angeles she'd actually seen in almost six months, he'd be shocked. "My life here is okay. Some people have bad life in Moldova. I am lucky, I think. But I miss my family."

"You don't talk to your parents?"

She shook her head. "My mother and father are dead." She stopped—had she really just said that? She never said it to anyone, not like that, but in English it was easier somehow. "And my babushka, she cannot call."

A car drove down their street and Hannah listened. It didn't stop, but Sergey and Lillian could be coming back any moment. She stood up. "I must go."

Colin stood up with her. His round cheeks were red and his eyes looked miserable. "I'm sorry," he said. "About your parents."

She nodded.

The back porch door opened and Colin's mom stepped outside. She was wearing red and blue plaid pajamas—a top and a bottom, the kind men wore. "Oh, it's just you," she said, looking down at them. "You scared me half to death. I was sleeping when I heard the siren and then some voices outside. I thought maybe it was your father."

"Nah, it's just me and Hannah."

"Hello, Hannah," she said, her eyes smiling kindly. She walked down to the bottom step and reached out her hand, shaking Hannah's hand firmly. It was her first real American handshake with a real American. She hoped she did it right. "I'm Liz. You two can come inside, you know. We have some cookies."

"Mo-om," Colin said. The expression on his face was pained, and it was so familiar that Hannah smiled. Maybe parents were the same everywhere too.

"Thank you," Hannah said. "I must go." She glanced at Michael's bedroom window, getting more anxious. She'd been gone too long.

Liz ran a hand through her curly hair and studied her with worried eyes. "You don't go to school?" she asked.

"I finish," Hannah said, taking a step back, but not wanting to be rude.

"You don't get out of the house often, do you?" she said.

"No," Hannah said, worried by how many questions she was asking. She heard another car. She couldn't tell if it had stopped or not. What would Lillian do to her if she came back right now and found out that she wasn't in the house? "Nice to meet you. I go now. It is later." She hurried away from them and down the path.

"Hannah, wait," Colin called.

She looked back and saw Colin trotting after her. "You don't have to go," he said.

"The children, they are alone," she whispered. "I am too long here."

His eyes widened. "Oh."

"I see you tomorrow."

"When?"

"Twelve."

He blinked. "Okay."

She turned then, and ran around his pink stucco house, through his gate and her own, along the gravel, around the white house, and through the back door. She hurried across the kitchen and sprinted up the stairs to Michael's room. He was there. Thank God. He'd kicked off his blanket and he was lying on his bed in his train pajamas with his little legs splayed out, his head resting on his pillow, his cheeks flushed, eyelids closed. He looked so peaceful.

She checked in Maggie's room. The bed was empty. The pink sheets and white frilly comforter were all twisted up, but there was no Maggie. She hadn't even really worried about her. Where was she?

She checked the upstairs bathroom next to the office, where Maggie usually went, but she wasn't there. She wasn't in the master bathroom either—or the master bedroom. Hannah tried the door to the office. It was locked. She started to panic. She ran downstairs and searched all the rooms. The garage. Maybe Maggie was waiting for her there.

Hannah threw the garage door open. "Maggie!"

A cold empty garage greeted her. She ran back up the stairs, into Maggie's bedroom, and patted the down comforter, hoping to find her thin body somehow hiding under it. All she found was one of Maggie's dolls, the gaunt one with the frilly yellow dress.

Her stomach heaved.

Then she remembered the time Maggie had fallen off the bed and slept on the floor all night. Lillian had talked about it at the breakfast table. Hannah crawled over the bed and looked down. Sure enough, there was Maggie, curled up on her side, on the hardwood floor, her dark hair fanning out behind her.

Hannah picked Maggie up, put her on the bed, and pulled the white down comforter over her. Maggie chomped with her lips as if she had gum in her mouth. It was such a sweet, little kid thing to do. She really loved these kids. Maybe too much, she thought, as she walked slowly down the stairs, her body shaky from adrenaline.

There was a double beep outside. Lillian's heels came up the driveway. The door unlocked and Hannah met her in the foyer.

Lillian's eyes were red and puffy from crying. She looked terrible, even in the black dress that made her skinny body look even skinnier.

Hannah pretended not to notice. "I was just checking on the children."

Lillian stared at her. "This is all your fault," she said slowly.

It hadn't gone well at the club.

"The children are fine," Hannah said, and hurried away from her, down the hall toward the garage. She felt Lillian watching her.

CHAPTER FORTY-SIX

It was eight in the morning, the last day of school before Christmas break, and Lillian had locked herself in her bedroom. Once again, Sergey had not come home. Over the last few weeks, he'd been noticeable absent on many mornings. Hannah knocked on her bedroom door. "Go away," Lillian barked. "I'm sick." Hannah went to the kitchen to break the news to Maggie, who'd have to miss school.

Maggie waved her cereal spoon in the air. "It's the last day of school before Christmas. There's a party." Her voice was winding up into a panic. "We have a gift exchange. It's the last time I'll see Roberta, until, like, next year! They never let me do playdates during the holidays."

"Go tell your mother," Hannah said, not wanting to get involved again. "She says she's sick, but I'm sure she forgot about the party."

Maggie went upstairs.

Their voices got louder. Hannah heard Maggie yell, "I want Papa!" in English.

Lillian answered, "He's gone to Russia. You might never see him again."

Hannah listened with horror. Lillian had no idea what it was to be a child and hear she'd never see her father again, her father who loved her more than anything in the world. It wasn't true. It couldn't be.

"You're lying!" Maggie yelled. "He wouldn't leave me here with you."

Lillian screeched, "Hannah!"

Hannah hurried out of the kitchen to the bottom of the stairs. "Yes?"

Lillian stood at the top of the stairs, her eyes red from crying. She pointed a finger at Hannah and jabbed the air. "I told you to keep them out of my room."

Maggie squeezed past her mother and rushed down the stairs toward Hannah, her face panicky, her hazel eyes unfocused. Hannah caught her at the bottom and Maggie sobbed into her shoulder. Hannah looked up the stairs and saw a flash of regret in Lillian's eyes.

"It's her last day of school," Hannah explained softly. "They have a party."

Lillian's eyes hardened. "You take her. Go ahead. Walk five miles there and back." Lillian slammed the door. Even at the bottom of the stairs, they could hear the click of the lock.

Maggie burst into tears.

"Shh. Shh. Shh." Hannah stroked her hair, trying to soothe her. Why couldn't Lillian just drive her? Nobody would see what she looked like. She could put on a hat and glasses and stay in the car.

"I'm going to be the only one not there!" Maggie cried.

"I'm sorry," Hannah said, not knowing what else to say.

Maggie looked up, sniffling, and then whispered, "You could take me."

"Oh no," Hannah said, shaking her head.

"She said you could."

Lillian had said it. No matter what, she couldn't deny it.

"Do you know how to get there?" Hannah asked.

"I think so," Maggie said in English, then nodded. "You go down Santa Monica Boulevard. My friend Sophie, she gets a scholarship 'cause she's, like, really smart, and she takes the bus." Maggie grabbed a notice from the refrigerator. "Here's the address. You could ask the bus driver."

"How will you get home?" Hannah asked.

"Roberta's mom can take me."

Hannah thought for a moment. Maybe on the way home, after she dropped off Maggie, she could buy a phone card and call Babulya. No. It was crazy that she was considering this. She'd be in a lot of trouble.

"Please?" Maggie said.

Hannah remembered her last bus trip. It had been so much fun. As long as everyone was okay, Lillian would cool off about it. Eventually.

"Okay," she said. "We'll go."

"Yes!" Maggie said in English. She threw her arms around Hannah's neck and kissed her cheek. "Thank you. You're the best!"

Just for that, it was worth it, Hannah thought. She turned on the television in Michael's room and closed the door, so Lillian would think they were in there. That should buy them some time. Then she wrote a note for Lillian and left it in the middle of the kitchen table. But she hoped Lillian wouldn't get up to read it. If she was lucky, Lillian would just stay in bed all day.

She took some money from Lillian's purse—after all, it was for her children—then grabbed two truffles from above the refrigerator and pulled Michael close. "We're going to play a game," she whispered. "It's the quiet game. We're going to tiptoe out of the house, sit in the stroller, and go down the sidewalk without talking. Whoever stays quiet the longest gets a candy." She showed him the chocolate.

"I want a candy!" he yelled.

"Shh," Hannah said. "First, let's put on your shoes and then we'll go outside."

She put on his shoes and grabbed the extra stroller from the garage. Maggie handed her a white sun hat, which belonged to Lillian. "For your hair," she whispered. Maggie was embarrassed about her hair. Well, she could hardly blame her. She put on the hat and opened the front door. Miraculously, Michael didn't talk and neither did Maggie.

At the end of the path that crossed their lawn, Maggie stopped. "I forgot my present."

It was on the floor in the foyer, inside the house. "Do you need it?"

"Yes!"

Hannah handed Michael a chocolate truffle, ran back into the house, and grabbed the present from the floor. Automatically, she looked for a mirror so that she could turn around in front of it three times to take away the bad luck of returning for a forgotten item. But there was no mirror by the front door. *Forget it*, she thought. *It's just a silly Moldovan superstition.*

An hour later, they were lost.

They were walking down the greenbelt on Santa Monica Boulevard, past the mansions of Beverly Hills, and they couldn't find the school. Hannah had brought a notice from the school with the address on it and the bus driver had told her where they needed to get off, but they couldn't find the street.

"I'm so late, I'll have to get a note," Maggie said, speaking Russian as she always did when she was upset. "My teacher will be angry and they probably started the party already and someone else will get my Secret Santa gift and I'll have to keep Paavo's stupid doll." This was the thing she'd wrapped for the secret gift exchange.

"Out!" Michael said, kicking with his feet. He hated the stroller, but Hannah figured if she took him out, they'd be standing on this spot all day. She pushed the stroller forward.

A black cat walked in front of them. *More bad luck.*

Hannah was filled with a terrible feeling of dread. It sat on her bones like fungus. She turned to Maggie. "We have to go back home."

"I'm not going home!" Maggie whined in tearful Russian and then muttered in English, "Idiot." As if she didn't understand. Hannah bit her lip, surprised by how much it hurt to hear Maggie say this. It was different when it was Lillian.

She watched Maggie march ahead. "Maggie," she said in English, "I am not idiot. We do not find school."

They saw a Latino man pushing an ice cream cart, jingling the bells down the street. "Stop," Maggie yelled, running after him. The man turned and opened his cart. She turned to Hannah. "Can we?"

Hannah nodded. The children chose their colors of flavored ice on a stick, Hannah paid with money she'd found in the laundry, and then, in Russian, Hannah told Maggie to ask him where the school was. Maggie asked in her perfect English.

He gave them a smile filled with holes from missing teeth. He reminded her of people back home. "No English."

Hannah couldn't help but laugh. Just her luck. She showed him the address on the newsletter from Maggie's school and he pointed down the street. "Derecha," he said, and then pointed to the right. It was worth a try.

They turned right, walked for five minutes, and finally, they found the street that was on the paper. "Which way?" Hannah asked.

"That way," Maggie said, pointing to the left.

They kept walking. After a few minutes, a beautiful park came into view with a large wooden play structure that had four metal slides, gymnastic bars, climbing ropes, and a playhouse. Hannah had never seen anything like it.

"Playground!" Michael yelled.

"There it is!" Maggie broke into a run and sprinted ahead, down the sidewalk, toward the park. What had she seen? The park? The school? Maggie was eight years old, and at that age, Hannah had already started taking buses by herself around

Chișinău, but Hannah knew it was dangerous to let any child out of your sight in America.

"Maggie, wait!" Hannah ordered, but Maggie kept running.

Halfway up the block, Maggie ducked behind some parked cars, and Hannah could no longer see her. She imagined her getting hit by a car or, even worse, disappearing somehow. She remembered Rena's sick words that she'd sell Maggie.

Hannah started sprinting down the sidewalk with the stroller. "Maggie!"

Michael dropped his blue ice on a stick and began to wail. Hannah stopped, picked it up, threw it on the stroller's tray, and ran with the stroller, bumping it over the gravel walkway.

"My ice," Michael cried. "Dirty!"

"I'll clean it! Don't touch it," she said, then yelled again, "Maggie! Come back!"

But Maggie didn't reappear.

The wheels of the stroller got stuck in a crack between two concrete slabs that were pushed up by the roots of a gigantic tree. Hannah lifted up the stroller and continued running down the sidewalk after Maggie.

She reached the parked cars where Maggie had disappeared and pushed the stroller into a parking lot in front of a large white building with pillars and double doors in the front. It looked like it could be a school, but it could also be another oversize mansion.

Maggie was standing by a side door, talking to a tall man, probably her teacher. He looked up at Hannah, stepped back into the school, and yelled something. Maggie looked over her shoulder, frightened.

"Maggie? Are you okay?" Hannah called in Russian.

A short black police officer marched out of the building. He looked at Hannah. Her heart jumped in her chest. She was sure she was going to jail.

The police officer pointed at Michael and asked Maggie something. Michael had a dirty blue chin speckled with grass from the flavored ice, which he was still licking. She didn't want to take it away, though, since he'd finally stopped crying. She reached into the diaper bag to get some wipes to clean his hands and face before anyone thought she was neglecting him.

"Maggie!" It was Lillian. Oh my God. She jerked up and dropped the wipes on the ground.

Lillian ran out of the school and swept Maggie up in her arms. She kissed the top of her head a bunch of times before putting her down. Hannah had never seen her give Maggie this much affection, ever.

"I was so worried, my love," Lillian exclaimed in Russian.

Maggie looked up at her mother, stunned. "We got lost," she said in a small voice.

"Everything's okay, then?" the teacher asked, patting Maggie on the back.

"I am sorry," stammered Lillian. "My niece, she does not tell to me anything. I deal with her." She ran her hand over her messy hair, trying to smooth it down.

"Don't worry about it," the teacher said. "Come on, Maggie."

Maggie went into the school with the teacher, glancing back

at Hannah with a worried expression. The officer lifted his finger at Lillian and asked her to wait, saying, "I'll be right back." He followed the teacher and Maggie into the school.

Lillian marched toward Hannah, her face a mask of fury.

"I left a note," Hannah said, stepping back.

"How dare you take my children anywhere without my permission!" Lillian raised her hand and slapped Hannah hard across the face. The skin on skin made a lightning-through-the-sky sound. Hannah lost her balance and fell to the ground. She blinked. For a moment she couldn't see. Her face burned as though someone had just thrown a pot of hot water on it.

The police officer ran out of the school. "Ma'am, ma'am," he said. "You can't do that."

Lillian reached out her hand and helped Hannah up. "It's okay," she said loudly in English, patting Hannah's back.

Hannah stood up and looked at her in confusion.

"Don't say anything to him," Lillian hissed in Russian. "He'll put you in jail."

Hannah pressed her palm against her burning skin. Her eye watered from the pain on that side of her face. Lillian had never hit her before. She'd grabbed her and cut off her hair, but not this. Hannah had no idea she was so strong.

"Mommy!" Michael wailed.

"Shhh, my rabbit," Lillian said. She bent down, spit on her fingers, and tried to wipe off his face.

The officer came up to Hannah, who was still holding her face. His brown eyes were flashing with fury. "Did she just hit you?"

Hannah stared at him, frightened.

"Do you want to press charges?" he asked.

Press charges? Hannah thought that meant she could go to jail. He seemed really angry. She burst into tears. "I sorry," she said in English. "I trying to help."

"Don't talk," Lillian said softly in Russian, like she was saying something kind to Hannah, and she even ran her hand over Hannah's head, which would have looked kind from the outside, but Hannah knew she was trying to smooth her hair down somehow. She wondered where her hat had gone.

Lillian smiled at Hannah, then widened her eyes at her. A warning. She turned to the officer, switching to English. "We are okay. She is my niece. She is seventeen. We are guardians."

"It doesn't matter if you're her guardian; you can't hit her." He glared at Lillian with ill-disguised contempt, then turned back to Hannah, his dark eyes softening now with compassion. "Do you want to press charges? It's assault."

"Tell him no," Lillian said in Russian. "Tell him I didn't hit you."

Finally, Hannah understood. He was angry because Lillian had hit her. Hannah wondered if Lillian could go to jail for slapping her. In Moldova, the police would laugh at you for complaining about something like that. But maybe police here were different—maybe he could really help her. She thought of the police officer who'd brought Colin home and the other one who'd stopped her on the street. They seemed to care.

She hesitated. The officer looked away from her eyes, up to her mutilated hair; maybe he was thinking that it didn't look like something she'd done herself. Hannah saw the white sun hat on the ground a few feet away. It must have fallen when Lillian hit her.

"You want to go to jail?" Lillian asked her in Russian. "He doesn't know you're illegal. If he did, you'd be in handcuffs already."

She was right—he couldn't know. But Lillian did seem nervous. Maybe the laws were different here. Maybe she wouldn't go to jail.

"Do you know what we can do to your family?" Lillian hissed. "To your precious uncle?"

Gulping down her fear, she answered the officer in English, "I am okay. She no hit me."

"Your cheek is red." The officer stepped forward.

"I fall."

"What did she say to you?" he asked.

Hannah shook her head fast. "She is aunt. She is scared for children."

"I going to call their father," Lillian said. "He is worrying."

"You're lucky I didn't witness it." The officer gave Lillian a long look.

"I am sorry for trouble." Lillian actually looked contrite. Her eyes were even a little glassy, as though she were about to cry. Hannah had no idea she was such a good actress. "I am good mother. I think she take my children, maybe do something to them. She have problems. She is poor girl in Russia. We bring her here, we try to help her."

Hannah's mouth dropped open. Lillian was saying Hannah had problems, but that she herself was a good mother. Liar. The officer was staring at Lillian, like he didn't believe her.

Lillian wrapped her arm around Hannah's back and squeezed

her shoulder. "Elena is a good girl. We love her, but she has to learn more. It is hard to living in America."

He nodded. "Be gentle with her. Everyone makes mistakes."

Hannah thought of Vladi and forced herself to smile. "She is good aunt."

Lillian gave her another side hug.

He looked back and forth between the two of them, adjusted his police hat, and finally said, "Well, you take care." He turned and strode toward his police car.

Maggie ran out of the school, looking at Hannah the whole time, her eyes big and scared, and for a moment, Hannah thought she was coming to hug her and say she was sorry.

"Are you okay?" Hannah asked her.

Maggie glanced at her mother, and instead of giving Hannah the hug she was expecting, Maggie ducked down and reached into the stroller for the doll Hannah had wrapped up. Her teacher stepped out of the school and Maggie ran back to him.

At the door, Maggie spun around and yelled in English, "Mom, I don't have a present for Mr. Barnes." Hannah wondered if she was embarrassed about being Russian.

The teacher waved a hand in the air. "Oh, you don't have to—"

"We have it in home," Lillian said in English, her voice as sweet as blackberry jam. "I bring it when I am coming."

The police car drove off.

"Okay," Maggie said. "Bye, Mommy." She didn't even look at Hannah.

"Good-bye." Lillian put on her fake smile. "Sorry for trouble, Mr. Barnes."

"Take care," the teacher said, waving before they disappeared inside.

Lillian bent down and snatched up the white sun hat. "Walk," she said, pushing Michael in the stroller.

Hannah walked beside them, uncertain what she could do to make things better, or at least not make things worse. She felt invisible. If Lillian drove her straight to Paavo, and he stuck her into some horrible brothel, nobody would care. Michael and Maggie would forget her in a week. In the end, children always sided with their parents.

The Cadillac SUV let out its cheerful beep as the doors unlocked. Hannah had loved that sound the first time she heard it, but now it depressed her.

Lillian put Michael in the car, folded the stroller, and heaved it in the trunk. "Get in the backseat. I can't stand to look at you."

CHAPTER FORTY-SEVEN

Back at the house, Lillian jammed the Cadillac into park before it had fully stopped, causing the vehicle to jerk and let out a crunching noise. She swore and jumped out of the car. Hannah unbuckled the straps of Michael's car seat.

Lillian opened the back door. "Did she make you eat a dirty ice pop?"

Michael nodded, his big blue eyes wide.

For months, Hannah had read to him, hugged him when he got hurt, made his favorite snacks, played blocks and trucks with him for endless hours. And this was what she got back.

Lillian picked him up and walked away from the car, calling behind her, "Hannah, I don't know why you're still in the car. Get inside."

At that moment, the front door of the neighbor's house opened. Colin trotted down the steps and walked toward his mom's old red car, farther up the driveway, closer to his house than the Cadillac. Hannah could see the back of his mom's curly blonde hair and her hands holding the steering wheel. The engine was on, so they were leaving. Hannah figured the safest thing to do would be to stay in the car, so they didn't know she was there. She shrank down in the backseat.

"Get out of the car, girl!" Lillian shrieked from the front door of the house.

Colin looked toward the SUV. She had no choice. She climbed over Maggie's booster seat and stepped out on Colin's side. Lillian wouldn't be able to see the signal she gave him—hopefully he would figure it out. Over the last two and a half weeks, they'd met half a dozen times, and talked about everything from the kids at his school to her parents' deaths to his feelings about his younger brother, Jack. She always avoided the subject of Lillian and Sergey, but she figured he knew her well enough to get it. Colin's face lit up when he saw her, but she shook her head quickly to show him that she couldn't talk. He looked over at Lillian by the front door and understood.

Hannah hurried around the SUV, intending to run into the house before anything else happened, but then she heard the low, whirring noise of the neighbor's car window sliding down.

"Hello, Hannah," Liz called.

Lillian spun around by the front door, keys in her hand, mouth open in shock. Hannah stepped back, wanting to delay a slap or whatever Lillian was planning on doing to her.

"Where are you all coming from?" Liz asked, cheerfully, but her eyes were squinting at them as if she sensed something was wrong.

"We have dropped my daughter at the school," Lillian said, smoothing her hair back.

"I met your niece a couple weeks back," Liz said. "She's a lovely girl."

"Yes?" Lillian's mouth pressed together.

Hannah hoped she didn't say what day. She knew she shouldn't have left the children, and she wouldn't have done it if she weren't so desperate. It wasn't her fault.

Liz talked on. "Colin has study block in the morning, so I let him stay home. It's the last day of school before Christmas break anyway. We're going to pick his brother up from school now. Are you doing anything for the holidays?"

"My husband is in business trip until Christmas. We stay here," Lillian answered. "You will stay here in Christmas vacation?" Her voice took on that same fake tone that Hannah had seen at Maggie's school.

"No, no, Colin and his brother are with me until Christmas, but they'll spend Christmas Day and the rest of the break with their father. And I'm going to visit my sister in DC," Liz said.

Hannah stared at Colin while Lillian and Liz talked. Christmas was a few days away, but she didn't know if she'd get out of the house now to see him. Lillian would be watching her and she'd definitely get some kind of further punishment for leaving the children in the house alone.

"This seems to me like nice vacation," Lillian said, squeezing Hannah's shoulder so tight she would have winced if Liz and Colin weren't staring at her. "Say good-bye," Lillian said in Russian, and then switched back to English. "Merry Christmas."

"Merry Christmas to you," Liz said.

Hannah couldn't say good-bye. She wanted desperately to run to Colin's house. But she couldn't. She had to think of other people, not just herself. They had her uncle already. And they'd threatened to take her babushka and Katya. She couldn't take any risks now.

"Go in the house," Lillian said to her in Russian. "Now, *shlyuha*."

Hannah glanced back at Colin. Even though he couldn't understand that Lillian had just called her a slut, he wasn't smiling.

"Is everything okay, Hannah?" he asked, taking a step toward her.

"Yes," Hannah said, and then added, "I talk to you before you go with father, okay?" She wanted Lillian to know that they'd be expecting to see her so that she wouldn't hurt her too much before her anger died down.

Colin nodded, glancing at Lillian, who didn't say anything.

Michael tugged on Hannah's hand. "Trucks?" he asked in Russian.

Hannah looked down at his eager face, gulped down the thick lump of fear in her throat, and followed him into the house. The door shut behind her and Lillian shoved her forward. She spoke in a low, enraged voice. "You were lying all along. What else were you lying about?"

"I wasn't lying. He's just a friend," Hannah cried. "I needed someone to talk to."

"So you can tell him all our secrets?" Lillian shoved her again.

Hannah screamed in pain and Michael started to cry.

Lillian glanced down at him in surprise, as if she'd just realized he was there. "Look what you've done. You've scared him."

Hannah picked him up. "Shh," she said into his ear. "It's okay."

"Get out of my sight," Lillian spat, waving her manicured hand in dismissal. "And take Michael with you."

CHAPTER FORTY-EIGHT

Hannah sat on the sofa in the dark garage, her head in her hands. She didn't feel like doing anything, even though she was supposed to put long strands of red and green tinsel up around the house. It was what Americans called Christmas Eve. In Moldova, some people celebrated on December 25 and the new pro-Western president had even made it a national holiday, but most people still kept to the old ways and celebrated on January 7. New Year's was the big day for gifts, really. When her parents were alive, they used to stay up all night on New Year's Eve, celebrating with neighbors and family. She'd fall asleep at some point and then wake up on New Year's Day to find presents under her pillow from Santa Claus.

In Russia, they celebrated Christmas more or less the same as in Moldova, but it looked like the Platonovs were going to celebrate in the American way, even though they didn't have a tree yet. Maggie had been begging for one all week and Lillian kept saying that they had to wait for their father to come home. Apparently, he was coming home that night, but Hannah wasn't counting on it.

She hoped Colin didn't think she had forgotten about him.

Maybe he'd come over to say good-bye before he went to his father's. Not that Lillian would let her talk to him.

A car came up the driveway. Loud Russian pop music was playing on the stereo. Hannah wondered who it could be. Sergey was gone. Maybe someone was coming to visit and they'd just leave when they saw nobody was home.

Hannah listened to the footsteps up the driveway—a man's steps. She heard the sound of a key in the lock. Maybe Lillian had given Paavo a key. Her throat clenched with fear.

She heard him switch his shoes into slippers. Strange. Paavo's feet were too large for Sergey's slippers. But then who was it? Sergey's flight didn't get in until around five o'clock. The alarm beeped. The person was turning it off.

There were footsteps down the hall and up the stairs. Not toward the garage, thank goodness. Hannah crept out of the garage and down the hall. The alarm was off. She opened the front door and saw Sergey's BMW convertible in the driveway. He'd caught an earlier flight.

She hurried upstairs. Maybe he'd have news of her uncle. She hadn't talked to him since that night when Lillian had cut her hair, when he told her he knew her mother. He'd barely been home since then, and when he was home, he couldn't even look at her, possibly because he was afraid of Lillian, probably because she looked so hideous.

The door to the office was half shut. He was talking fast in Russian, something about a late shipment. She thought of the "AK-47" that she'd seen written on the paper in his office and wondered if he was talking about a shipment of guns. Her guess was he sold guns to the Russian mafia in the United States.

"We are arranging it," Sergey barked into the phone. "Don't go to another distributor."

She'd overheard him talking to customers before, and he never said exactly what he was shipping. He'd say order number five or shipment two hundred, but nothing more. Was he afraid his phones were being tapped?

"Petr Sokolov can go to hell," Sergey said with disgust. "I'm not doing it."

Petr Sokolov. Hannah had heard that name before, but where? It wasn't such an unusual name. Petr was a popular first name and Sokolov was one of the most common last names for Russians. She nearly threw it out of her mind as something insignificant because there had to be hundreds of Russians with that name, but then it came to her. She clapped her hand to her mouth to keep from gasping.

She'd heard this name on the day of the interrogation.

The officers had come to her family's apartment at ten o'clock at night. She'd never forget that knock on the door. She had been sitting with her babushka at the kitchen table, drinking tea and waiting for her parents to come home from the wedding before she went to bed.

There were three sharp knocks at the door. Hannah spilled hot tea down her chin and Babulya jumped up, her weathered hands flying in the air. Even though Hannah couldn't remember the days of the KGB, the secret police who'd ruled the former Soviet Union, a knock on the door late at night still filled anyone with terror.

Babulya fumbled with the key for a few minutes and cracked open the door. She was wearing her nightdress, but she opened it anyway. Four officers stood in the open-air hallway with their hats on.

An older officer with a thick red nose, clearly the leader of the group, introduced himself as Officer Mikhail Baryshnikov. Hannah was pretty sure it was a joke name, because it was the same name as the famous ballet dancer and this man had a round belly and the grace like an aging construction worker. But nobody was laughing.

Officer Baryshnikov asked for their identification. He looked at Hannah's and then nodded once. "We need you to come with us to the police station."

"Why?" she asked, her heart drumming in her chest.

"We have some questions for you." He gave her a look that made her afraid to ask anything more. "Come."

She was glad she was still wearing her regular clothes, jeans and a green button-up shirt. She stepped into her walking shoes, pulled on a sweater hanging by the door, and grabbed her purse with the white tassels. She followed Officer Baryshnikov into the open-air stairwell and to the elevator.

"You stay," one of the other officers was saying to Babulya.

Hannah looked back at the open door. The other officers had gone into the apartment.

"Stop," Babulya yelled. "You can't take her!"

"Hey, leave her alone!" Hannah tried to go back, but Officer Baryshnikov and another officer yanked her into the elevator. She struggled, afraid they were taking her somewhere to rape her, but as soon as the elevator started rattling its way down, they let her go.

They put her in the cab of a police truck and drove through the dark streets, talking about a soccer game, of all things. They stopped in front of what looked like a regular brown house, just one floor high, unusual for any building in Chişinău, especially a government building. It definitely wasn't the central police station. She looked around for a sign.

Officer Baryshnikov pulled some keys on a chain out of his pocket and unlocked the front door. The receptionist's desk in the entryway reassured her somewhat. She followed Officer Baryshnikov down a dark hallway with brown carpets that smelled of urine. The other officer followed her. A fluorescent light flickered at the end of the hall.

Officer Baryshnikov brought her to a room with concrete walls. "Your purse?" he said, holding his hand out for it.

She handed him her white purse with the tassels. Even then, it was looking pretty dingy and worn. "I haven't done anything wrong," she said.

He walked out and closed the metal door without another word, leaving her alone in the windowless room.

"Wait!" she yelled, and shook the door. It was locked.

The room was tiny. She could cross it in five large steps. There was a metal table in the center of the room and one wooden chair against the wall. She moved the chair to the table and sat down. It wobbled. She hated wobbling tables.

She wondered why they'd brought her here. Some bags had recently been stolen from the coatroom at her school. Perhaps they thought she'd done it, though that was ridiculous. She didn't even have classes near the coatroom.

The metal table wobbled, wobbled, wobbled. She swore out loud at the table. Her words rang out in the quiet room and actually made her feel better.

She looked at the fake gold watch on her wrist, a present from her mother for her birthday, and watched the second hand move around its face.

After half an hour, Officer Baryshnikov came into the room, dragging a wooden chair. His hat was off now and she was surprised to see that he had a shiny bald spot in the center of his head. He sat down across from her and asked who'd visited their house recently, why her parents were going to the wedding, and questions about her father's brother in Transnistria, whom she barely knew.

He did not ask her about the bags. Just questions about her family. It had to be her father, she decided. He was always getting drunk and finding trouble. He'd probably started arguing with the wrong person about his radical political ideas. She remembered how Daniil had told her that he thought her father could get himself into trouble if he wasn't careful.

"Why did you bring me here?" she asked. "Please tell me."

He studied her, as if to determine whether she was worthy. At last he said, "There was a bombing at a café. In Tiraspol."

She held her hand over her mouth. "My parents?"

"They are in detention."

She didn't understand at first, but then she realized they were accusing her parents. "You think they did it? Are you out of your mind?"

He gave her a cold stare. "Your father is a suspect."

"He'd never—" She broke off. "Was anyone killed?"

"The Minister of Internal Affairs was killed," he said. "Plus two of his bodyguards, two employees in the café, and two teen-age girls. The girls had just gone into the café for a coffee. They were sixteen."

Hannah's hands fluttered by her face and then pinched on her earlobes. Seven people, including the Minister of Internal Affairs. And two girls her age. Her father wouldn't hurt anyone, especially not two girls her age.

"My father would never do that." She felt ill. "He drinks too much, but he is not a killer."

Officer Baryshnikov cleared his throat. It was one of those disgusting, phlegm-filled sounds. "If you give us information, we'll release your mother," he said.

"My parents were going to my uncle's wedding. It's my father's side. We never see them. They're not close." Hannah didn't know why she was explaining this, except that her mother had said her father's family was a bit extremist in their views and Hannah figured this had to be the reason they suspected her father. "They were supposed to be back today. That's all I know."

"You must know something."

"I don't," she said, opening her eyes wider, pleading with him. She thought about the phone call she'd overheard on the morning before her parents had left for the wedding. She'd just finished washing herself in the cold shower and she was stepping out of the bathroom when she heard her father speaking on a cell phone. She didn't even know he had a cell phone. The other odd thing was that he'd closed the door, which was always open.

She could tell Officer Baryshnikov what she'd heard, but she worried it would seem suspicious. Her father had mentioned a café, but she knew he'd never hurt anyone. He was the kind of man who carried spiders outside rather than hurt them.

The officer gave her a look of distain, stood up, and walked out of the room without another word. He left her there for five more hours, during which she paced the room, stared at her watch, sat down, paced some more, and finally rested her head on the table, drifting in and out of sleep.

When the officer came back, he narrowed his eyes at her as if to see whether he'd worn down her resolve. He sat back down in the chair across from her, holding a silver pen and a small notebook. He opened the notebook to a blank page and clicked his pen. "When did your father start to work for the resistance?"

"He doesn't work for the resistance."

"He was unemployed and then he suddenly started working," he growled. "When did he get the job?"

Hannah remembered the day her father told them he'd finally found work. Her mother had given him that wide, warm smile of hers, and then she'd jumped up, wrapped her arms around him, and kissed him full on the lips.

"A month ago," Hannah said. "It was an office job, I think. He joked that he was an errand boy. That's all I know. But he carried a briefcase." He'd even slowed down his drinking. Things were getting better.

The officer stared at her. "Tell me about the café," he said.

"What café?"

"You must have heard something about the café in Tiraspol. That was one of his jobs for the resistance. His last."

What did that mean? Had he been fired from his job?

"I don't know," she said. Her whole body felt heavy. It was three thirty in the morning and she worried she was going to say the wrong thing and get her father into more trouble. "He's not part of any resistance. He doesn't like the Minister of Internal Affairs, but many people don't," Hannah said. "That doesn't mean he'd do anything to him."

"Tell me what you know," Officer Baryshnikov said, his voice softening. "Perhaps your father did nothing. We are putting the pieces of the puzzle together, that's all."

"I don't know anything," she said.

"Tell me about Petr Sokolov," he said.

"Petr Sokolov?" she stammered.

"Your father talked to him many times on the cell phone. He must have visited your home."

The man her father had talked to on Saturday morning—his name was Petr Sokolov. She hadn't heard much. Just about the café. Then he said, "Thank you, Petr Sokolov. You can count on me. Good-bye." Hannah had waited a couple of minutes before she opened the door to the main room. *Something's wrong*, she thought. Her father's face was red and he looked flustered. "I'm leaving," she said. He told her she should wait for her mother to come home from the hospital, but she lied and told him she'd already said good-bye to her the night before. She hoped her mother hadn't told him that she'd called her *stupid* for grounding her when she wasn't home by ten. She hugged him then and told him Katya was waiting.

"I don't know any Petr Sokolov," Hannah told Officer Baryshnikov. "I've never heard this name."

"You're a slippery Moldovan, aren't you? Just like your parents." As if he was so different from her, just because he had a badge and his clothes were a little newer. "You don't need to protect them. They're dead."

The word hit her like a wooden plank slamming against her head. "What?" she breathed.

"They're dead." He smirked at her like this was a good thing, and then tapped his silver pen on the metal table.

She stuck her chin out, defiantly. It was impossible. "You're just lying to get information."

"I'm not." His face was serious and she almost believed him. Again he tapped the pen. It was loud on the metal and it made her jump. She glared at him.

She'd been left in this little room for hours and all along her parents were dead? She didn't think so. "When did this bombing happen?" she asked.

"I ask the questions," he responded.

"I'm not a fool, you know. My uncle would have called." She looked him up and down, hating him with every part of her soul.

"I never lie about death. Your uncle is in detention. He couldn't call."

She swallowed. "You're lying," she said, tears lacing her words.

"Do you need to see the picture?" he asked.

"Yes," she said, sitting up taller.

He pulled out a snapshot and dropped it down in front of her. "Your mother has no head."

If he'd punched her in the stomach, it would not have been as painful as what she saw in that photo. "It could be any woman without a head," she whispered.

CHAPTER FORTY-NINE

Hannah pushed open the door to Sergey's office. He was gulping down vodka, straight out of the bottle, which was unusual for him. He was wearing a gray suit but no tie. The top buttons of his white shirt were undone, revealing his hairy chest.

"Who is Petr Sokolov?" she asked.

He squinted at her and she saw he was more than a little drunk. "Hannah," he said, staring at her. "I forgot what Lillian did to your hair."

"Who's Petr Sokolov?" she repeated.

"Nobody." He reached into the pocket of his suit jacket and pulled out a prestamped Moldovan envelope. "You have a letter," he slurred. "It came in the mail today."

"A letter?"

"From your family," he said.

He handed it to her nonchalantly, like it didn't matter to him. Surprisingly, it hadn't been opened. She looked down at the scratchy handwriting. It was from her uncle Petru. Babulya's eyes were too weak to write, but perhaps she'd dictated it to him. The envelope was made of thin paper, and it was easy to rip open. She pulled out the flowery stationery, probably Valeria's, though the writing was her uncle's.

> *Dear Hannah,*
> *We have only just received your letters to your*
> *babushka. Unfortunately, there is some bad news.*
> *She's had a heart attack. . . .*

Hannah gasped.

"What is it?" Sergey asked and moved close to read over her shoulder.

She grabbed the envelope to see the date it had been sent, but the stamp was too faint. She held her hand over her mouth as she continued to read.

> *She is in the hospital. I am sorry I could not reach*
> *you earlier, but I did not have your address or a*
> *phone number. Do you have a phone number?*
> *Call us.*
> *Your uncle,*
> *Petru*

A sob rushed out of her and Sergey wrapped his arm around her, reading over her shoulder. "Do you want to call them?"

He picked up his cell phone from the desk and asked her for Petru's phone number. After he dialed it, he handed her the phone. She heard the low double buzz of a Moldovan phone line, different from the single ring she heard when she called Lillian's cell from their home phone. In Moldova, she'd never thought about that double ring, but now it was the most beautiful sound she'd ever heard, and it made her feel as if she were traveling to Moldova over the telephone.

It rang and rang.

Perhaps they were at the hospital. At last, her uncle's groggy voice came over the line. "Hello?"

She realized it was the middle of the night for him. "Petru? It's Hannah."

"Hannah?" There was a pause. Maybe he was sitting up in bed. "We received no news from you for months, and then, all of a sudden, we get four letters, and another one week later."

She looked at Sergey. He had sent them after all. "How's Babulya?" she asked.

"You received my letter?" he asked.

"Yes."

"My dear niece, there is some news." His voice was grim.

"What news?" Hannah asked, gripping the phone.

"Your babushka suffered another heart attack."

Hannah gasped. "Is she worse?"

"She passed away two weeks ago."

Hannah dropped the phone and fell to her knees on the hardwood floor of Sergey's office. She panted, dizzy with grief.

Sergey picked up the phone. "Hello? This is Sergey. Hannah works for me." He was still slurring. "What happened?" He looked down at Hannah and she looked up, hoping she'd heard wrong, but from his face she saw that she hadn't. Babulya was dead.

She reached for the phone and he handed it to her. "Did Babulya get my letters?"

There was a pause. "I'm sorry. We read them to her, but she couldn't hear anything, I don't think. She was in a coma."

Babulya had died thinking that she hadn't written, hadn't sent money, had abandoned her. She'd died with cataracts. Hannah felt her chest constrict with pain, and then she remembered that dream she'd had, the hot wind when Babulya told her to listen to her nose.

"When's the funeral?" she asked her uncle. For some reason, she thought she could go.

"We had it last Friday," he said. "In the church." He recited all the people who'd come. It seemed completely unreal. How could these neighbors have been at Babulya's funeral, while she was here in America, completely oblivious?

She interrupted him. "Was she in pain?"

"Hannah, it was beautiful. She saw the light. And she smiled before she passed away—it was such a smile, something of God, it was so beautiful."

Beautiful. Hannah knew he was just trying to reassure her, but that word made her want to scream. How could he say that? Nothing was beautiful. Nothing would ever be beautiful again. Babulya was dead.

"Hannah?" Petru said.

"Yes?" she asked.

"Do you have some more money you can send?"

Hannah felt sick that he was asking about money at a time like this. Her voice was shaky when she spoke. "I sent fifty dollars in the letter." She worried that a worker at the Moldovan post office had taken it out.

"Yes, but the funeral was very expensive. Valeria is worried about the money, and if you can manage anything more . . ."

You got rid of me, she thought, *and then you didn't even take care of Babulya, your own mother.* "I will send what I can," she said.

He thanked her but didn't ask how she was. Just wanted the money she didn't have.

She hung up the phone, feeling numb.

"They always want money," Sergey said, resting his hot hand on her back.

She nodded slowly, staring down at her hands. Petru was the one who'd given her forty American dollars, a fortune for him, which Volva had then stolen, but maybe he'd only done that because he hoped she'd send him even more.

"Come on," Sergey said, sliding his hands under her arms to help her stand. She wobbled on her feet. The insides of her body had been turned into mashed potatoes. "I'll help you downstairs," he said, and wrapped his arm around her.

When they got to the stairs, she wished he'd just push her. She wanted to feel the *bump-bump-bump* of her body on each stair. She deserved some kind of punishment for leaving Babulya. But Sergey had a secure grip on her, despite his inebriated state, and he helped her down each step, gently reassuring her, telling her everything was going to be okay.

CHAPTER FIFTY

Sergey rested her on the old flowery sofa in the garage. "I'm sorry, Hannah. I know it is hard when something happens in the family and you are here, and not there. It has happened to all of us." It was nice of him to say that, she thought.

"I found your uncle Vladi," he whispered. She looked into his shiny blue eyes. He seemed to be telling the truth.

"You did?"

"He's on his way home."

"Thank you," she murmured, even though she didn't know what to believe. Maybe he was just trying to make her feel better.

He knelt down beside her, kissed her cheek softly, and ran his hand over her butchered hair. His fingers tickled her scalp.

"Don't leave me." She meant that she didn't want him to leave her with Lillian, but it sounded like she didn't want him to leave the room.

He kissed her lips. It was a soft, tentative kiss, and though she didn't kiss him back, she didn't turn away either. "I'll take care of you, *moya lubov*," he slurred. "Don't worry."

She closed her eyes, hoping he'd take this as a sign to leave. She just wanted to curl up in a ball and not move for days and days.

"I love you," he said.

And then he was kissing her face, her neck, her hands, and she didn't know whether she wanted him to stay or whether she wanted him to go. The places where his lips connected were the only places she felt any heat. The rest of her body was cold, as if she'd died with her babulya, the last person on earth who had really loved her.

Sergey said he loved her. In the midst of the fog that filled her brain, Hannah wondered how he could possibly love her. He didn't even know her.

Sergey took off her socks and rubbed her feet. It felt kind of nice. He lifted her arms above her head and tugged off her T-shirt. Her limbs felt wobbly, not her own. His calloused hands glided across her skin. He climbed on top of her. His curly chest hairs scratched against her skin; his heat pressed against her. When had his shirt come off? Then she realized his pants were off too. Her eyes flew open. She was lying on a cold sleeping bag with a married man on top of her and the thing she'd promised herself would never happen was happening.

"Stop."

"You're shaking," he said, squeezing her tightly. "I'll keep you warm."

It was December and the garage was freezing, but she was shivering from more than the cold. At least her bra and the gray sweatpants were still on. He groaned and breathed in her neck.

"Please. I don't want this." She tried to push on his shoulders, but he was too heavy. "I'm a virgin."

He jerked back and gazed into her eyes in disbelief. "You are?"

She nodded. It was almost true.

"I just want to feel your skin," he said, speaking through his teeth, as he did when he was nervous.

"Get off me," she said, struggling to get away.

"Stay still," Sergey murmured. "I won't hurt you. I told you I won't. Kiss me." He pressed his lips to hers and forced her mouth open with his tongue. His mouth tasted of vodka and fish.

She turned her head away. "No!"

"Don't be a tease," he said. "You know you want this. I've seen how you look at me."

"I don't!" she cried, and then wondered if she had been a tease. She knew, or at least sensed, that he was attracted to her, and she might have used it a little to get what she wanted, but she didn't intend this. "Please," she cried, panicking.

"Shh," he grunted, pressing himself into her. "Stay still. I won't hurt you. I love you."

He rubbed himself against her belly but left her sweatpants on. He wasn't going to stop, no matter what she did. She clenched her eyes tight, as if she could make it go away. Tears leaked through her closed eyelids. The house was silent except for the occasional moan that seeped out of him. If Colin were outside, he'd hear Sergey through the thin walls of the garage. *Please don't be outside.*

Sergey was rubbing faster now against the top of her loose sweatpants. He gripped her head with both hands. "Tatiana," he cried.

Her stomach was moist. She wanted to vomit. He rolled off

her. Her hands clapped to her face and she stifled a sob.

He stared down at her. A crease formed between his sharp blue eyes. "What's wrong?"

"I said no," she cried. "I said stop."

He frowned. "I did."

Not enough.

He picked up her monkey T-shirt from the floor and tenderly wiped off her belly.

A blast of anger shot up through her. Did he actually think she'd forgive him? She snatched the T-shirt away from him and threw it on the floor. "Don't you dare," she said.

"Hannah," he began.

"Why did you say my mother's name?"

He shook his head, gritting his teeth together, and shut his eyes, as if it was too painful for him to say. Then he murmured, "You look so much like her."

"Did you have an affair with her?" she asked in a dull, bitter voice that she didn't recognize as her own.

He opened his eyes. "No."

Hannah let out the breath of air she'd been holding. It was such an incredible relief to know that the person she believed to be her mother was real. There were so few things she could count on anymore.

He continued. "I tried, but she wouldn't see me. Not even after your father became a street drunk and shamed her. I came to Chişinău to see her and ran into her when she was walking to the hospital. She was friendly enough, but when I asked her if I could meet her after work, she refused. She said your father would love to see me, but I couldn't stand it. She gave herself to him instead of me and then he threw it away. I hated him."

Hannah glared at him. *You didn't know him. You didn't know his passion. The way he used to read a poem, like there was beauty in the world.*

"Did you plant that bomb?" she asked, keeping her voice even. She had to know everything.

"No."

"You know Petr Sokolov."

He didn't say anything.

She couldn't control herself anymore. "Just admit it," she yelled. "You killed my mother. She refused you and you killed her!"

"I didn't kill her," Sergey said urgently. "Your father was supposed to go to the café alone, where the Minister of Internal Affairs was having breakfast. He was told the minister was on the take and that the briefcase had money for him from the resistance. He was supposed to leave it under the table. That was all he knew. Petr was going to blow it up when he left. Your father would be arrested, and I would be there to console your mother. It almost worked. Apparently, they walked out of the café together, arguing. Your father had her arm, but then your mother broke away and ran back in, yelling that there was a bomb. Your father followed her, and Petr blew up the cafe."

Hannah blinked, taking it all in. Her father had not killed all those people. He thought the briefcase held money, and her mother was the one who'd realized. Maybe she had smelled the explosives. Only then did Hannah realize that a part of her had believed the police when they'd said her father did it.

"Believe me, Hannah, one day I'll get my revenge. For both of us. I loved her too." He paused. "Just as I love you."

"Do you really think I'm going to believe that? All you do is lie. You were never going to let my father live. You knew my mother would never leave him. She loved him. Even when he was drunk and puking all over the place, she used to rub his back and—" Her voice broke off. "You don't even know what love means."

His face reddened with anger. "How about a little gratitude? I've done so much for you, I risked so much. I got your uncle out of the work camp, paid a lot of money, and now you have the nerve to say—" He looked toward the chained doors of the garage. He'd heard something she hadn't. A car.

It drove straight up the driveway as if it was going to ram into the garage and then stopped suddenly. Sergey jumped up and tugged on his pants. He reached into his pocket, pulled out a bill-fold, and dropped a few hundred-dollar bills on the sofa next to Hannah, like a payment.

"Merry Christmas," he said, reaching down to stroke her face. She cringed and he pulled his hand away.

The car door opened. Sergey grabbed the rest of his clothes and sprinted out of the garage.

CHAPTER FIFTY-ONE

Hannah heard Michael and Maggie get out of the car. Maggie asked her mom if she could get another American Girl doll for Christmas and Michael made fart noises. There was the familiar double beep of the car alarm. Lillian's heels clicked toward the front door. Hannah moved slowly, worried Lillian would hear her getting dressed through the walls of the garage.

The three crisp hundred-dollar bills sat on the sofa, but she ignored them, reaching instead for her monkey T-shirt on the floor. It was too disgusting. She tossed it down and looked at her sweatpants. They had gotten dirty too. She tugged them off and hurried to the cardboard boxes that held the rest of her clothes.

What had Sergey meant when he said she should be grateful? He claimed he'd gotten Vladi out of the work camp, but she didn't believe him. She had three hundred dollars now that he'd gotten what he wanted, but before, he hadn't given her enough to fix Babulya's eyes. Her babushka had died thinking Hannah didn't care enough to send her money for a simple operation. *Stop it,* she told herself. She couldn't think of that now or she'd collapse on the floor and Lillian would find her, half-dressed and weeping.

The front door opened. Hannah started to panic. If Lillian came into the garage now, when she was wearing only her underwear and bra and there was three hundred dollars on the sofa, Lillian would think she'd had sex with him for sure.

Maggie called out, "Papa?"

Hannah grabbed the white shirt Babulya had given her on the morning before she left Moldova. The sweatshirt would be easier, but Hannah could not wear their clothes anymore. Babulya had given her these clothes, had chosen them with her own half-seeing eyes, and now she was dead.

She did up each little button with her shaking hands. Her blue slacks from Moldova were tight, but she managed to get the zipper up.

"Sergey?" Lillian was in the house now. "Hannah? Where are you?" Her shoes tapped in the entranceway as she shifted to her hard-soled slippers and then came down the hall toward the garage.

His smell was on her still. Lillian would smell him. She needed a shower to get this stickiness off her belly, to get Sergey off her, but it was too late.

"Maggie," Lillian said sharply. "Bring Michael upstairs and turn on a movie."

Hannah snatched up the money, reached under the sofa, grabbed *Goodnight Moon*, ripped out the documents, and shoved them, along with the money, in her back pocket. Lillian was right by the garage door, in front of the washer and dryer. Hannah could hear her breathing.

Lillian pushed open the door and looked down at Hannah. "Why didn't you answer me?" she demanded. "What are you doing?" She was wearing her black slacks, black shirt, and navy slippers as if she were in mourning.

Hannah hoped Lillian wouldn't notice her bare feet. "Putting away the toys," she said, holding up *Goodnight Moon* as evidence. She walked across the room and shoved it back on the shelf.

In the hall, she heard Maggie and Michael shouting out, "Papa!" He was laughing and Michael let out a screech. Probably he was throwing him in the air.

"Why are you wearing those clothes?" Lillian asked.

Hannah remembered she'd been wearing the sweatpants and the monkey T-shirt when Lillian had left and now they were lying on the ground. "I—um—I wanted to wear this. I missed my grandmother."

Lillian scanned the room like a lizard, as if she sensed a change, and then her eyes focused on Hannah's bare feet. Hannah pressed her shaking hands to the sides of her legs, so that Lillian wouldn't notice them, and waited for Lillian to realize what had happened.

Sergey came to the door of the garage and gave Lillian that tight, nervous smile of his. *"Lilichka, moya lubov."*

Hannah wondered if he felt even a little guilty now as he said these words to his wife right after he'd said them to her. At least Hannah hadn't believed him.

"Why are you home?" Lillian demanded, glancing back and forth between the two of them. She was so convinced that Hannah wanted her husband, she'd never believe the truth.

"It's Christmas Eve," he said, smiling charmingly, holding his arms out to his wife.

You are the terrorist, Hannah wanted to scream, *not my father.*

On the floor, right by her foot, was the dirty monkey shirt. She slid her foot out and kicked it under the sofa. Sergey's eyes flicked down and then back up to his wife's face.

"You were supposed to call me when you got into the airport," Lillian said, her jaw flexing. "I wanted to be here when you got home."

"I wanted to surprise you," he said, grinning, then rubbed his hands together fast, looking at Maggie, who was standing in the doorway. "We need to get a Christmas tree, have a real American Christmas." He stepped across the room toward Lillian when she wouldn't come to him, and pulled her into his chest. Lillian allowed him that but kept her arms hanging at her sides. He continued, in his tight, lying voice, "I bought you something in Moscow in the fashion district."

Lillian didn't say anything.

"Hannah's babushka just died," he murmured.

Maggie looked at her with alarm. "What?"

Hannah's eyes welled up with tears. She couldn't believe Babulya was no longer on this earth, that they would never drink tea together again, that their good-bye had been a good-bye for forever.

Lillian pulled away. "How did you find out?"

"Hannah got a letter," he said.

"A letter? How?" Lillian pulled back, again accusing him.

"She mailed her own," he said, gesturing at Hannah. "Ask her."

"I mailed it when I went for the run," Hannah admitted, hoping to dissolve Lillian's suspicion about Sergey. She'd rather get in trouble for a letter.

Lillian looked at her with disgust. "So now everyone knows where we live?"

Hannah lifted her chin and considered telling her that Sergey had also sent the letters, but figured that despite everything, she still needed him. He was better than Paavo, she thought miserably. At least he said he loved her.

Michael was calling for them. Lillian glanced back at Maggie. "Go see what your brother needs and then bring him upstairs and put on a movie."

"I don't want—" Maggie began.

"Now."

They listened to Maggie's footsteps down the hall and up the stairs. "How'd she die?" Lillian asked Hannah.

"Heart attack," Sergey said.

Lillian squinted at Hannah. "You were close with your babushka, weren't you?"

Did she expect her to lean forward with her neck exposed like a meek deer so that she could clamp down for a bite? Hannah pressed her lips together and looked away.

"Why don't you relax today?" Sergey reached out as if to pat Hannah's shoulder, but then dropped his hand suddenly, perhaps thinking better of it with Lillian there in the room.

Lillian barked, "Did we not agree that I am in charge of what the girl does and does not do?"

"Come on, Lily. Her babushka just died. Have some

compassion." He looked genuinely sad for her, but he was also the best liar she'd ever met.

"Nobody helped me when my father died," Lillian said. "You went off to China to do your *work*." She spat out that last word as if he could hardly call it that. Hannah wondered if she knew that Sergey was still doing that "work."

He raised his hands in surrender and, shaking his head, marched out of the garage. As Lillian stood there, eyeing Hannah, the front door slammed shut, and they heard his BMW start up outside and roar down the street. Hannah was alone with Lillian.

CHAPTER FIFTY-TWO

Lillian was blocking her exit. There was nowhere she could go. Hannah stayed where she was, her leg pressed against the blue and white flowery sofa as if it were her only friend.

"What did you do for that letter?" Lillian demanded, taking a step toward her. "And don't tell me he was just being nice. My husband is not nice. He used to kill people for a living," she added, gloating as if she thought this was going to destroy Hannah's vision of Sergey.

Hannah matched Lillian's calm with her own. "For your information, your husband is still killing people for a living. You're just too blind to see it."

"Don't you talk to me like that!" Lillian raised her hand and slapped her. This time, Hannah barely felt it.

"It's the truth," Hannah said. "I've seen papers on his desk. How do you think I got that book? I've heard him on the phone talking about his shipments. I know about Petr Sokolov. He admitted everything."

Lillian paused. Her eyes narrowed. "You need to get your passport for me."

"I don't have it," Hannah said, thinking about how it was

in her back pocket right at that moment. "It was in my bag. Remember?"

"Your purse, you mean?"

"Yes, my purse." She had to get a hold of her thoughts.

"I've had enough of your lies!" Lillian yelled, shaking Hannah. "Where is it?" Lillian threw her down on the sofa, then dropped down on her knees and swept her hand underneath. Thank God she hadn't put them there. But then Lillian pulled out the dirty monkey T-shirt. Hannah held her breath and hoped she'd just toss it down.

"You don't even clean up your own clothes," Lillian said. Her face turned into one of disgust. "What did you get on this? It's wet."

She couldn't think of any plausible response that Lillian would believe. Her ears heated up in panic. Her breathing stopped.

Lillian looked at it closer. Hannah panicked. Lillian had chopped off her hair for standing in a dark kitchen with Sergey— she wasn't going to wait to see what Lillian did now. She turned and ran.

Lillian lunged at her. She grabbed hold of Hannah's waist, pinning her arms at her sides, and yanked her back so hard that Hannah fell forward. Without anything to break her fall, her nose smashed on the hard concrete floor. Hannah heard a crunch and then a white stream of pain filled her head. Lillian jumped on her back and slapped the sides of her head, again and again, but she was remarkably silent in her rage. Maybe she didn't want the children to hear. Hannah tasted the blood dripping down her face, into her mouth. Lillian had broken her nose.

Don't let her do this. Fight!

Hannah used all her strength to flip around. Lillian fell off of her but got up on her feet fast in a crouched position. Hannah kicked up as hard as she could and got Lillian in the side of the mouth. Lillian cried out and her head jerked to the side. Hannah jumped up and turned to run, but her legs felt gooey, as if she was stepping in thick mud. Her head spun.

Lillian tried to grab her hair, but she couldn't get a grip. It was too short.

Hannah pulled away. She ran through the door, past the washing machine and dryer, almost to the hall. She thought she was free, but then Lillian grabbed her arm and dragged her backward into the garage.

Hannah managed to grab Lillian's shirt and rip it open, but then Lillian shoved her backward. The impact of her head on the floor made a dull thwack. When she opened her eyes, she couldn't see anything but little dots. *This is what they mean by seeing stars*, she realized in the brief moment before Lillian jumped on her, pinning her arms down with her knees. Lillian's shirt was ripped open and her black bra was showing. There was a scratch down her face and her mouth was dripping with blood. It would be swollen and ugly for a couple days, but Hannah wished she'd done more damage.

With a closed fist now, Lillian punched her in the face.

"Mama?" Maggie called from the hall. Her voice sounded frightened.

"Help!" Hannah croaked.

"Don't come in here. Get upstairs!" Lillian screamed at Maggie, clamping her wiry hands on Hannah's mouth. For one terrifying moment, Hannah couldn't breathe. Her nose was stuffed with blood. She squirmed, grabbing at Lillian's hand. Her face heated up with blood. Her lungs burned. "Go!" Lillian yelled.

Maggie ran down the hall and back up the stairs. Lillian lifted her hands.

Hannah gasped. "I didn't do anything."

"You had sex with my husband!"

"He forced—"

"Liar!" Lillian said.

Hannah stared up at Lillian's nose, at the circle of foundation around each nostril. Hannah could still smell her flowery perfume, which was a relief. Even though her nose was bleeding, she hadn't lost her sense of smell.

"You're right, something happened," Hannah panted, hoping this would stop her. "But we didn't have sex. He rubbed himself on—"

Lillian punched her again. No matter what she said, Lillian wasn't going to stop.

Hannah yanked her arms out from under Lillian's knees and tried to use all her strength to get up, but Lillian was tougher and bigger than she was. Even though Hannah had never been in a fight in her life, she never would've thought Lillian could overpower her like this. She'd thought Lillian had had a pampered childhood, but it was clear that this was not Lillian's first fight. She fought like a street kid.

"Get off me, *suka*," Hannah grunted.

"You dare to call me a bitch?" Lillian yelled, her bad breath hitting Hannah in the face.

"You're the worst mother I've ever—"

Lillian smashed her fist down on Hannah's nose. Hannah felt so dizzy, she knew she was going to lose consciousness soon. She tasted blood in her mouth. She lifted her head and spit at her as hard as she could. A bloody gob landed right by Lillian's eye.

Lillian roared and hit her again and again, clawing at Hannah's face and arms. Hannah's eye stung and she felt dizzy. She tried to push Lillian's hands away, but she couldn't focus. Lillian stood up and Hannah thought it was over, but then Lillian started kicking her ribs. Hannah felt a crack inside her. She couldn't breathe.

Please, let it stop.

She managed to get on her hands and knees and started crawling toward the door. She felt Lillian's hand reaching into the back pocket of her pants. Her documents. The money.

"How did you get this?" Lillian waved the three hundred dollars in Hannah's face and then shook her head as if she couldn't believe it. "He gave this to you?"

Hannah tried to find something to say that would save her. But she wasn't fast enough. Lillian swung her leg back. Hannah lifted one hand off the ground two inches. The last thing she saw was the hard sole of Lillian's slipper, coming straight toward her eye.

CHAPTER FIFTY-THREE

Hannah's mouth tasted like the dust on an unpaved road in the village. She opened her one good eye and lifted her head. She was lying on the concrete floor by the door of the garage, freezing. She groaned and looked at the clock. It was seven fifty-five in the morning on Christmas day. Her first thought was of Colin and how he'd probably waited outside for her the night before because they'd said they'd see each other before he left on Christmas.

Once, during the night, she'd woken briefly, but when she'd tried to move, she'd passed out from the pain in her ribs.

Someone was knocking softly on the door to the garage, as if they didn't want anyone to hear. "Hannah, are you in there?" Maggie was whispering in English. "Are you in there?"

Hannah wondered how long she'd been knocking. "Yes," Hannah croaked in Russian. "Help me, Maggie." Her voice would hardly come out.

"Maggie!" Lillian chastised her from down the hall. "I told you to leave her alone."

"But it's Christmas, Mamulya."

"Now!"

Maggie went away. A few minutes later, she heard Lillian's Cadillac SUV beep to unlock the door. Michael and Maggie were outside. Maggie yelled through the chained garage doors, "Bye, Hannah. Merry Christmas!"

"Shh," Lillian reprimanded her.

They got in the car, the engine started up, and they drove away.

Hannah tried to sit up, gasping from the pain. Her chest clenched, like she was having a heart attack. She stopped. Slowly now. Up onto her knees. She panted. The skin on her face was stiff. She reached up and felt dried blood. The entire front of her shirt was covered with brown dried blood. Her nose burned when she moved, as if she'd just opened a cut inside it. She dabbed at the fresh blood with the arm of her white shirt and forced herself into a crouching position. Her chest shifted, making her cry out. Something inside her was broken. She listened to make sure they were gone. The house was silent.

She hobbled to the door, turned the knob, and tried to open it toward her, but it wouldn't budge. Lillian had nailed it shut somehow. She was locked in.

"Help," she called, but it croaked out, barely loud enough for anyone to hear. Her mouth was so dry, and it couldn't open wide enough—it was too swollen. She tried to scream. It was just a hollow gasping sound, not enough to get someone's attention. If she heard someone outside, she'd try it again, but it was quiet out there.

She looked around the room for something to help her with

the door. The hard part was that it opened in, not out, so she couldn't bang her body against it. Her only hope was to find some metal to slide in the door and pry it open.

But she had to pee first. She grabbed a sand bucket and crouched over it. Her pee spilled a little on the concrete floor and she put the bucket down to search for something to wipe it up, panicked over the mess. But then she stopped herself. She didn't need to clean up anything. Not anymore.

She looked at the toys on the shelves, searching for something to help her pry open the door. Everything in the room was plastic or plush. A castle or a stuffed animal wouldn't help.

Her keys from Moldova. They were made of heavy metal. She shuffled toward her tattered suitcase, breathing in shallow breaths, and found them still in the side pocket.

Home. It didn't matter that it wasn't her home anymore. She'd carried these keys everywhere since she was six years old. They were solid and reminded her who she was.

She had to escape before Lillian got back home.

One of the keys, the one for the front lock of her apartment building, was particularly long. She jammed it in the crack and cranked it backward. The door gave, just a little. Her fingers ached, but it had to work. She rubbed them together and pushed on the key again. The wood creaked. Her chest stabbed at her. She tried again. The door opened an inch and then bounced back. She smelled sawdust.

A car drove up the driveway and stopped. She wasn't fast enough. The car door opened and shut, firmly. Heavy steps thumped past the garage. It wasn't Lillian and the kids.

"Sergey?" she called.

No answer. Her heart drummed in her chest. It wasn't Sergey. He would've answered. She stuffed the keys in the front pocket of her blue pants.

The front door opened. The house had been left unlocked. The man's footsteps came down the hall, toward her. There was the sound of ripping wood. The door to the garage opened. Paavo glowered at her, his meaty hands tucked into his sides. She hobbled backward.

He grinned, then spoke in Russian to her, like always. "Lillian was pretty angry, eh? I told Sergey he wouldn't be able to resist." He laughed, a full belly laugh. "Come on. I'll take care of you now. No more cleaning for you. I always said it was beneath you."

A shiver ran through her. Anything could have happened last time if Sergey hadn't shown up. Little had she known that Sergey just wanted her for himself.

Despite her pain, she stuck out her chin. "He won't be happy if I'm gone."

"He'll come visit you, don't worry."

"Where?" she sniffed, wiping her bleeding nose with her finger, hoping Sergey had an apartment where Paavo would take her and then she could find a way to escape.

He studied her with humor, as if she were a funny chimp at the zoo. "We have a place for the girls."

A brothel. "I won't do it."

"Sergey asked me to be good to you. He doesn't want you to

get hurt. You're safer with me than with Lillian, believe me." He nodded at her face as if even he was impressed by the damage. "She'll kill you."

The blood from Hannah's nose was dripping into her mouth. She wiped it on the sleeve of her white blouse, which was already spotted with her blood, and looked toward her belongings in the cardboard boxes, trying to think of a way out.

"You don't need anything," he said. "Lillian will send everything over later."

"Please let me go home." She was begging now and she hated it.

"Home?"

"To Moldova."

He gave her a look like she had to be out of her mind. "How are you going to afford that?"

"I could work when I get home. I'll pay you back," she said.

He laughed. "You can earn money working for me here and be home in a year. And you'll have time to take those English classes you're so obsessed with." He tilted his fat head to the side. "Let's go."

"I don't want to be a prostitute." She tried to stand tall, but she winced at the pain in her ribs and doubled over, her hand on the right side of her chest. "I won't do it."

"We know your family. And your friends. We will tell them you are a whore if you give us problems. And you'll become a whore no matter what you say. But if you come easily, nobody needs to know."

She thought of her uncles and Katya and, worst of all, Daniil hearing this news. She'd wanted to come back and be glamorous and show him that he was wrong for breaking up with her. And now everyone would hear she was a prostitute. She'd never be able to go back, but did it really matter? There was nothing for her in Moldova anyway.

"I won't be a prostitute," she said.

He shrugged. "If you don't behave, I'll take that sweet little friend of yours instead."

Katya. "No!" she said.

"Or you can do this for a year and you will have a future," Paavo said. "You will learn English. From our clients." He paused and then his eyes got hard, as if he sensed she would not go easily. "Let's go. I will not ask again."

She stepped forward. It hurt to move, but she could tell that if she had to, she could run. It was only pain, she thought, that was all. A plan formed in her head. She hobbled past him down the hall, clutching her ribs, moaning with pain. He had to think she was so disabled that there was no way she could do anything.

He opened the door for her and squinted down at her. "Walk normally or I'll give you a reason to limp."

He must be worried about the neighbors, she thought, stepping out of the house. It was another beautiful day in Los Angeles. She felt betrayed by the sun's heat, the chirping of the birds outside, the low roar of a lawn mower down the street, the sweet smell of grass and the laughter from the house next door.

Who was laughing? One of the boys, either Colin or his brother, Jack. Their red car was in the driveway. They weren't gone yet.

Paavo had parked the large black Lincoln in the driveway. He held out his arm and she realized he believed that she couldn't walk normally. She didn't want to touch him, but she had to get his guard down until the moment came. They walked down the walkway toward the driveway and she clung to his fleshy elbow like they were a couple.

He walked around the car with her, opened the front passenger door, tossed his jacket over the backseat, and swept his arm out. "Get in," he said.

Listen to your nose. These were the last words her babushka had said to her as she moved from this world to the next.

She stood next to the car and breathed in through her bloody nose, using it to search the interior of the car. She smelled marijuana—it seemed to be coming from the glove compartment. There had to be a gun in there somewhere. A man like Paavo didn't go anywhere without one. She didn't want to smell Paavo, but she had to listen to her nose as her babushka had told her to do. She smelled cigar smoke on his shirt and a fishy woman's smell on his hands. She smelled a woman's fear and knew it was her own. She would use this fear.

The front door of Colin's house opened. He stepped out wearing a large short-sleeved baseball jersey, and he looked up at her, frightened, probably at the sight of her bloody face. "Hannah?" he squealed.

Paavo grabbed her arm. "Get in."

She wrapped her fingers around the keys in her pocket. She was fast. She could probably get him in the eye, even with her body all broken up. But it would be better to trick him into thinking she was coming.

"Okay," she said, pretending to get into the car. Paavo released her. She ducked under his arm. His fingers grabbed on to the back of her white shirt, but it was slippery and he couldn't get a grip on it. Good old Moldovan fabric, she thought, sprinting around the car toward Colin. Her ribs stabbed her insides as she ran, but she made her legs move as if they were separate from the rest of her broken body.

Colin stepped back into the house, afraid, and it looked for a moment as if he was going to close the door on her.

"Help," she croaked, reaching her hand up to stop him.

"Stop, *shlyuha*, or I'll kill the boy!" Paavo yelled. She kept running. The car's back door opened. Maybe he was going for his gun.

Colin stood, frozen. Hannah ran across Colin's driveway, faster than she'd ever run in her life. She was a child again, sprinting through the sunflowers; her mother and her father were cheering her on. *Bistra! Bistra! Fast, Hannah!*

Hannah's nose started to bleed and the blood ran down into her mouth and tasted like metal, but still she ran across Colin's lawn and up the short set of steps and threw herself into his soft chest. His arms wrapped around her and he stumbled backward. They fell down on the linoleum floor, just inside the house, in the hallway. The pain in her ribs made her scream. Her vision went black and then cleared. She looked behind her. The door was wide open. Paavo had something in his hand. Colin jumped up, slammed the door shut, and turned the dead bolt.

She reached a hand up to him and panted, "He have gun."

"Mom, call the cops!" Colin yelled.

Liz ran into the hallway with a cordless phone. "What's happening?" Her hand flew to her mouth when she saw Hannah's face. "You poor girl! Who did this to you?"

"There's a man outside. Hannah says he has a gun."

"Oh my God!" Liz dialed a number on the phone.

Paavo knocked on the door, two quick knocks, like a door-to-door salesman. He spoke with impeccable English—Hannah didn't even hear an accent. "This is the police," he said. "The girl is illegal and she's dangerous. She was resisting arrest. Open the door."

Hannah looked up at Liz, who started to pull the phone away from her face, uncertain. *She's going to hang up.*

"This is no right," Hannah said, not making any sense, even to herself.

"I have an LAPD badge and her documents here. You can see them through your window," Paavo said. "Hand the girl over and you won't go to jail for harboring a criminal."

Liz looked through the peephole. "He has papers."

"Mom, I *know* her," Colin said. "She's not dangerous."

"He is lying," Hannah said. "Don't open door. Please."

Colin's brother, Jack, stepped into the hall. "What's happening?"

Liz spoke to someone on the phone. "Yes. We have a problem. A man is at our door and he says he's a police officer. We have a girl, our neighbor, and he wants her. But she's very beaten up and I—uh—I don't know." She paused and then gave their address.

Paavo banged again on the door, harder this time. "Give me the girl," he said. "I won't hurt your family."

"One second," Liz yelled.

"Oh my God," Colin said.

Liz helped Hannah up and pushed Colin toward his brother. "Get away from the door, all of you. Go upstairs," she hissed.

"Come on," Colin said, leading them up the stairs.

Hannah grabbed the banister, as her rib stabbed into her, and tried not to cry out with pain.

"Careful," Colin said, glancing back, worried.

It wouldn't help if they went upstairs, Hannah thought. Paavo could easily break a window, climb inside, then come upstairs. It would take him five minutes.

"In the bathroom," Liz said, from behind Hannah. They hurried into a small yellow bathroom upstairs, next to the study. Liz locked the door. It had a tiny frosted window, which Colin cracked open, trying to see out. Hannah had noticed this window before, but hadn't realized it was a bathroom.

"Colin, close it," Liz said.

"He can't get up here," Colin said.

"He'll know where we are." Liz lifted a finger for everyone to be quiet while she listened to the police on the other end of the line. She relayed, "He's not with the police."

"Duh," Jack said.

"Who is this man?" Liz asked Hannah, responding to a question from the police.

"Name is Paavo Shevchenko. He is bad. He have dance club and prostitution."

Liz repeated what Hannah said into the phone and then told them that the police were on the way. The four of them stood close to one another, waiting, mostly in silence, except for Jack, who kept whispering, *"Holy crap."*

They were on the wrong side of the house. Hannah worried that Paavo would enter Lillian and Sergey's house and shoot at them from upstairs. If he did, they might have time to run out of the bathroom. Liz held the phone to her ear. Hannah looked at Colin. He reached for her swollen eye and touched the edge of it.

"Does it hurt?" he whispered.

She nodded.

The operator spoke on the other end of the phone. Liz relayed the information. "They say they have a police car outside. No one's there."

"Tell them there was a car," Colin said. "A large black car. Like a Lincoln."

The doorbell rang.

"The operator says the police are ringing the bell," Liz said.

It was so strange that the police would ring the doorbell. Hannah would have thought they'd break down the door.

"I'm scared," Liz said to the operator. "Can they check the windows and make sure he's not inside?" Hannah wished she hadn't had to involve this nice family in her troubles. She'd never meant to put them in any kind of danger.

"Mom, the guy's gone," Colin said.

"Yeah, Mom. Relax," Jack echoed, though his brown eyes were big and wild.

Hannah stepped forward. "I go first," she said, opening the door slowly. If Paavo was in the house, she'd jump on him and tell them to run.

She led them out of the bathroom, breathing in through her broken nose, searching for any trace of Paavo. But she didn't smell him. She smelled Liz's freshly shampooed hair, the cat's litter box, pine needles on the Christmas tree, fried bacon in the kitchen. She smelled America.

CHAPTER FIFTY-FOUR

Two LAPD officers stepped inside Colin's house, a tall, blonde woman and a medium-build white man with dark hair. They both had their hats on. Hannah wrapped her arms around her body and stared at them, standing between the living room and the room with the television. She'd seen the television room briefly when she passed it to go into Colin's backyard, but she hadn't noticed the homey living room on the other side, with its embroidered wall hangings, afghans, green braided rug, and the Christmas tree with lights and what looked like hundreds of little glass angels.

"This is the girl?" the male officer asked, gesturing at her.

"Yes," Liz said, and began rattling on about how she was their neighbor and they had no idea she was in trouble and she came over one day and sat on the back steps with Colin. She didn't know about all the other times Hannah and Colin had talked between the fence since then.

Hannah's body started shaking. It was warm inside the house, but her teeth began chattering anyway. Her nose ached from the shaking. Her jaw was too tight. She gripped her arms, wondering what had come over her, wishing it would stop.

Colin noticed first. "She needs to sit down," he said, helping her onto a small brown sofa in the living room, next to the Christmas tree.

Liz dropped a quilted afghan over her shoulders and Colin sat down beside her. He patted her back. "You're okay," he repeated, as if he wanted to believe it himself. "You're okay." With him right there, she did feel better. The scent of his baby powder deodorant was comforting.

"She might be going into shock," the female officer said, calling on her walkie-talkie for an ambulance. She put it back in her belt and patted Hannah's knee, kind wrinkles tightening around her eyes. "Don't worry, honey. You're going to be fine."

The male officer dropped down into the armchair across from her and smiled. He was a good-looking man, and he knew it, but Hannah looked down at the braided rug by her feet. She didn't want any more men smiling at her.

Liz gave her some tissues for her nose and mouth, and the officers started asking her questions about Lillian and Sergey and Paavo. They asked her how long she'd been living there, if she'd been paid, what her hours were. The female officer said to the male officer that they needed to call Ice. It sounded like a name of a mean officer who was going to torture her to get answers.

The male officer got up, went into the other room to talk on his phone, and then came back. Hannah heard the hum of the officers' questions to Colin and his mother and brother, but she didn't really listen to anyone except Colin. She heard him tell the officers about the times they'd met outside and how he really liked her and thought it was strange that they had to meet outside, but that he figured that she had a strict family.

"I definitely didn't think they were making her work for free," he said, his voice cracking.

"Like a slave," the male officer added, his voice bitter. "Makes me sick."

A slave?

Colin's eyes filled with moisture as he looked at her. He looked sad, but it wasn't pity, thank God.

Liz said to them, "I can't believe it. Right next door. They weren't very friendly, but I never thought . . ."

The brother, Jack, stared at Hannah from the entrance of the living room like she was a creature from another planet. She didn't blame him. Her shirt was so bloody, she looked like she'd been bitten by one of the vampires in Maggie's book, and she didn't even want to think about what her face looked like. Her eye was so swollen she couldn't open it. Moving hurt and talking made her lip bleed.

She felt bad for ruining their Christmas. The tree was so beautiful, all lit up, with small glass angels dangling from the branches. Only one wrapped present remained under the tree. They must have opened the other ones already. She'd heard American kids got tons of presents.

When the ambulance came, two paramedics in white uniforms entered the house. The female attendant asked if she wanted to go in a stretcher. "I can walk," she said. If Paavo was outside, she didn't want to be strapped to a long board, unable to move. They held her arms and helped her across the living room. With every step, her chest stabbed at her.

Outside, the birds were chirping. Someone was still mowing the lawn. It seemed perfectly fine, but as soon as she walked out of the house, she felt too exposed. Paavo could be hiding. He could shoot her. She froze.

"Hannah, are you okay?" Colin asked from behind her.

"Where do they take me?" Hannah asked, looking back at him.

"The hospital." The female officer came up beside her. "You'll be safe. We won't let anyone hurt you. Do you understand?"

Hannah looked back at Colin. She needed him to tell her it was okay. He wouldn't lie to her. "Colin?" she asked.

"It's okay." He swatted at a tear rolling down the side of his round face.

Hannah gazed into his eyes and realized he blamed himself. She rested her hand on his pale arm, even though the movement made her wince. "You save me," she said.

He nodded, but his bottom lip quivered like he was going to break down sobbing. She tried to think of something, anything, that would make him feel better. Something he'd once said popped into her head and she repeated it now: "Don't be a stranger," she said.

He seemed surprised for a moment and then he let out a bark of laughter, and nodded really fast. "You're cool, Hannah," he said.

Hannah remembered when Maggie had said that to her, and hoped that the children would be okay. She wondered if she'd ever see them again.

"Come on," one of the paramedics said. "She needs to lie down."

Hannah stepped out into the sun. Nobody shot at her. The

neighborhood was still. Next door, in the house where she'd lived for almost six months, the driveway was empty. Did Lillian and Sergey know she'd escaped? What if they came home right now and convinced the police she was lying?

The paramedics guided her down the steps and along the walkway. She stepped up into the ambulance, her ribs stabbing at her. Once she was inside, she felt safer, but she'd feel better when she was far away from here. The female paramedic helped her down onto the semi-prone gurney in the back and stretched a sheet over her.

"Wait!" Colin shouted.

He ran up, holding the single present that had remained under the tree. It was tube-shaped, wrapped clumsily in Santa Claus paper with a lot of tape. He quickly scribbled a phone number on the wrapping paper and handed it to her.

"Call me when you can," he said.

"Thank you," she said, taking the present and cradling it to her chest.

She laid back on the gurney and the ambulance took off down the street. At least five times while they drove, she asked them to make sure they weren't being followed. Every time, the female attendant looked out the small back window and said no. Finally, the attendant tried to reassure her, "The police are escorting us. Don't worry. Nothing's going to happen."

But they didn't know what Paavo could do. Or Sergey. He sold guns and bombs to terrorist organizations. It would be easy for him or Paavo to point an Uzi at the ambulance and blow them all up. Hannah couldn't stop shivering. She felt like a huge moving target.

When they drove up to the hospital's emergency room, the police officers were waiting. The paramedics brought her in on the stretcher and the female officer followed while the male officer stayed outside. If she heard gunfire, she thought, maybe she'd have time to hide.

They brought her into a large room with doctors and nurses and hospital beds and children crying. It wasn't so different from a Moldovan hospital, except that they had a lot more machines and it was bigger.

A Hispanic nurse guided her to a bed and pulled a blue curtain around her. She asked her what parts of her body hurt the most.

"It is hurt more in here," she said, gesturing at her throbbing chest. "I can no lay down." Sitting up was the only way she could cope with the pain, but she didn't know how to explain this.

The nurse adjusted the bed forward. "Is that better?" she asked. "Are you comfortable?"

Nobody had asked her that question for months. She nodded.

The nurse spoke to the police officer. "How old is she?"

"Seventeen," the officer said, looking at Hannah for confirmation.

Hannah nodded.

"Do we have parental consent for treatment?"

"Um, no," the officer said. "She's an illegal. No guardians."

"Okay, I'll speak to the doctor and see what she wants to do," the nurse said, and left her alone in the room with the police officer, who told her they were bringing someone to translate. She asked if Hannah understood.

Hannah nodded. She'd lost her words. She clung to the present from Colin. The curtained room scared her. There were no walls. It would be easy to shoot through the fabric.

She thought of Katya. Maybe Lillian had already made a call to Moldova. "I can use telephone?" she asked the officer.

"It might not be safe for you to use a telephone right now," the officer said. "Relax."

All Hannah heard was that it might not be safe. She started to shiver again.

The officer gazed at her with concern. "Are you okay, honey?" "Honey" sounded so strange coming from a police officer.

Hannah didn't have the words to explain why she needed to use the phone right now. She couldn't think of anything in English. Katya would be sleeping. They wouldn't be able to get to her yet—at least she hoped not. She closed her eyes and hoped the translator would come soon.

It could have been an hour or just five minutes, Hannah couldn't say, but she heard a voice above her, saying *"Privyet,"* hello in Russian. A female voice. Her eyes popped open. She feared she'd see Lillian, but it was a small woman with gray hair and sparkling brown eyes. The woman continued in Russian, "My name is Stephanie. I'm from Uzbekistan and I'm a caseworker here in Los Angeles. I help girls like you." She smiled gently with a closed mouth in the Russian way.

Hannah didn't understand what she meant by "girls like you." Girls who spoke Russian? Whatever she meant, it was a relief to her. For the first time in America, all she wanted to do was speak Russian. The police officer asked her something about Ice and then stepped out of the room.

"Who is Ice?" Hannah asked.

"ICE means Immigration and Customs Enforcement. They're in charge of enforcing immigration laws. They sent me to help you."

She didn't know how a caseworker could help her. But she knew that the immigration police would put her in jail, and she couldn't face being trapped again. Maybe she could escape. She looked at the blue curtain and wondered if she could get out before they grabbed her. The police were already guarding her. They had guns. Lillian had told her that illegal immigrants had no rights. They would take her and rape her, maybe kill her. And then she'd never be able to warn Katya.

"What's wrong?" Stephanie asked.

"Will I go to jail?" Hannah asked.

Stephanie's small dark eyes filled with compassion. "You're not going to jail. You did nothing wrong. I'm taking you to a safe house."

"A safe house?" Hannah was confused. "Not to jail?"

"We have a safe house in Santa Monica," she explained. "It's a place for women and girls like you who've been trafficked into America. It has a guard, but only for your protection—not to keep you in, but to keep out anyone who might want to hurt you."

Trafficked. She'd been trafficked? After everything she'd gone through, she'd never thought of herself as the girl in that poster in Moldova, struggling in the palm of a giant man's hand, with the words underneath: "You are not a product."

From Olga to Ina to Volva to Sergey to Paavo. She had been bought and passed along like cargo. It wasn't her fault. She wasn't going to jail. Instead she was going to a safe house.

She'd be safe, but not Katya. "I must use the phone right away," she said. "They said they're going to hurt my friend Katya. I have to warn her."

"I don't think you have anything to worry about," Stephanie said softly. "They make these threats, but they don't follow through. It's to keep you from running off."

"I must talk to her!" Hannah jerked up, and then cried out from the pain in her ribs.

"Shh," Stephanie soothed. "It's okay. You can call." She pulled a cell phone out of her pocket. "We will get you your own cell phone, but for now, you can use mine." She dialed the numbers Hannah gave her and then handed her the phone.

It was just after two in the afternoon in Los Angeles, so it would be about midnight in Moldova. Hannah gripped the phone, hoping Katya was at home and not out somewhere with friends, where she could easily be snatched. The phone rang that same double ring she'd heard before her uncle told her that Babulya had died. *Please answer. Let it not be more bad news.*

"*Allo,*" Katya answered in her sleepy voice. Hannah cried out in relief. They hadn't gotten to her yet! She was safe, in her bed. There was still time for Katya, still time for her to escape.

"Katya, it's Hannah," she said, then burst into tears.

"Hannah!" Katya shouted. "Are you okay? Where are you? I was so worried—for months and months, we heard nothing from you. Your uncle Petru called me when your babushka died to see if I knew anything. Neither of us had received your letters yet. What's happened to you?"

"I'm okay," Hannah said, even though she was still sobbing with relief at her friend being okay. "I am in the hospital."

"The hospital?" Katya cried out with surprise. "Why are you in the hospital?"

Between sniffles, Hannah explained that the job wasn't what she thought, and the mother beat her up, but she got away. She couldn't tell her about the bad agent. Or Sergey. Or his connection to her parents. Not yet.

"Oh Hannah, I knew you didn't say everything in the letter. Your uncle came by and I showed it to him and he said he was going to send you a letter. He's been worried sick."

"My uncle was worried?" Petru hadn't sounded worried. "I talked to him."

"You did? But Vladi just got back from his work in Russia and you were gone. He said he had to find you."

"Vladi is back?" Hannah yelled, her mouth bleeding from opening it too wide. All along she thought Katya was talking about Petru. Sergey had really done it. This was what he'd been talking about when he said she should be grateful, that he'd risked something for her. "Really? He's home?"

"Yes." Katya sounded puzzled. "He's in Gura Bicului."

The relief Hannah felt about Vladi being released quickly turned to fear. Now that she'd escaped, they could grab him again. Or Katya.

"Katya, you have to be careful," Hannah said urgently. "They said they were going to take you if I tried to run away or did anything wrong. They could be coming to your apartment right now."

"Don't worry about me," Katya said, without a moment's hesitation. "You take care of yourself." She laughed. "I'll get the guys on the soccer team to walk me to school tomorrow."

The guys would probably do it too. Hannah felt the edge of her mouth curling in a smile, but it hurt too much. "Can you ask my uncle Petru to go to the village and warn Vladi? I don't want them to take him again."

"Of course, my friend."

"I don't want you to get hurt."

Katya laughed. "I won't. Stop worrying about me. Just get yourself fixed up."

The nurse came back in the room with a clipboard and waited expectantly for Hannah to finish. "I have to go," Hannah said, promising to call again as soon as she could.

She handed the phone back to Stephanie. It was more reassuring than she ever could have imagined to hear Katya's firm, happy voice.

The nurse spoke to Stephanie. "The doctor says she's an emancipated minor, which means we only need her consent for treatment. I have a form for her to sign."

Stephanie explained and Hannah signed her name, her real name, for the first time in months. She looked down at the clipboard. She was very businessy, this nurse, so unlike Hannah's mother, who had been so warm, she often hugged the patients. Some people said her mother made them feel better by just touching them. This nurse was not that kind of nurse. She asked Hannah what hurt and wrote everything down: her eye, her nose—her whole face, really—her right elbow and wrist, her left hip, and her chest. Then she checked Hannah's eyes, heart rate, and blood pressure.

"The doctor will be right in," the nurse said, and left the room.

Hannah rested on the inclined bed, her chest aching from the exertion of leaning back. She closed her eyes. Her uncle was safe. Sergey had found a way to get him released. Maybe he really did love her, like he said, in his own sick way. Or maybe he was trying to make up for what he'd done to her parents.

A sudden noise made Hannah sit up, and she cried out with pain. But it was only the metal on the blue curtain chattering as the curtain opened and a doctor, middle-aged with short blonde hair, entered. She came up to Hannah's bed and introduced herself, an American name Hannah forgot instantly. Stephanie began translating for her, even though she understood everything the doctor said.

"I'm so sorry this happened to you," the doctor said, looking down at her kindly. "But we're going to get you fixed up." The doctor asked her what hurt and Hannah answered. "We'll check everything out, do some X-rays, and I want you to have an MRI because of the damage to your head. Did you go unconscious?"

Hannah nodded.

Then the doctor asked her some of the same questions the police officers had asked, like who had done this to her, and what her living situation had been like since she'd come to America. And then she asked if Hannah had been raped.

"No," Hannah said, then looked away as she remembered what Sergey had done, the feeling of him on top of her. Maybe he'd figured she owed him.

"You can tell us," Stephanie said.

Hannah hesitated but then told her what Sergey had done. "It was my fault," she added at the end. "I didn't say no at first. He couldn't stop."

"It wasn't your fault," Stephanie said firmly. "None of this is your fault."

Hannah had a hard time believing that, but it was nice to hear. The doctor asked if she'd showered since it had happened. "No," Hannah said, embarrassed at her smell. She'd been stuck in the garage after Lillian had attacked her and then Paavo had come—there hadn't been any chance to shower.

"Good," the doctor said, to her surprise. "We'll take some samples and do an examination in case there was penetration."

"You think she was raped?" Stephanie asked.

"It was no rape," Hannah said to the doctor in English.

The doctor looked down at her sympathetically. "I'm going to check your whole body, and I'll need to do a quick vaginal exam as part of that."

She must have looked frightened, because Stephanie explained softly. "We want to put these people in jail," she said, "for what they did to you."

"Oh." Hannah was confused, but she took off the shiny blue pants and the bloodstained white shirt, and put on the gown with Stephanie's help. Stephanie put the clothes in a plastic bag.

Stephanie held her hand and the nurse came in to help while

the doctor swabbed her stomach and checked her body. Hannah's face and chest and right hip throbbed. But she tried not to think of the pain. She thought of Katya's voice, remembering her laughter when she said the soccer team would walk her home. Hannah couldn't believe how much she had missed hearing that laugh.

Once they were done with the samples, they brought her in for X-rays, and she lay on the cold X-ray machine, shifting with pain. The doctor looked at the large gray sheets and said two ribs were broken. Her nose, too. The doctor numbed her face, poking a needle in three separate spots, pressing her finger to each one, asking if she could feel it, and then she pulled on her nose, one quick motion to straighten it. It was strange to be without pain while she felt the bones shifting numbly inside her.

After that, the doctor stitched up her lip. Hannah breathed in the doctor's minty breath and stared into her blue eyes just inches from her own, noticing the focused yet gentle nature of the doctor's gaze. She was the kind of doctor Hannah wanted to be.

When the doctor was done, she said, "This'll heal up real nice and you'll be good as new." It was nice to hear, even if she didn't quite believe it.

The doctor taped up her chest, providing more relief than Hannah could have imagined. Then Hannah sat in a long white tube machine called an MRI that checked her brain with beeps and squeals. The doctor said she had a concussion and she'd have to be careful not to bang her head, but it would heal within a month.

Finally, the doctor handed her some forms to sign and she was free to go.

Stephanie pulled some clothes from a backpack: underwear, a stretchy cotton bra, and a blue sweat suit, which she said wouldn't put any pressure on her injuries.

"We can keep your other clothes," Stephanie said, "if you want."

Hannah nodded. "They are from my babushka."

At least it wasn't gray, Hannah thought, while Stephanie helped her put the sweat suit on. They brought a wheelchair and Stephanie pushed her through the large white room. Nurses and doctors smiled down at her. She wanted to stay.

The large double doors to outside swooped open automatically. The sun was low in the sky now—it had been high above her head when she'd arrived. The police officer led them toward the police car, which was waiting right by the entrance. The male police officer was gone. Maybe Paavo had already killed him.

"Where is the other officer?" she asked Stephanie in Russian, glancing back at the doors to the hospital emergency room. She could make it back inside if she ran.

"What's wrong?" Stephanie asked.

"Paavo could be here."

Stephanie explained to the female officer that Hannah was worried because the other officer was gone.

"It's okay. He had to go home to his family. His daughter has a birthday party tonight. Don't worry. I've got you," the female officer said, smiling like that would be reassuring. Hannah wished the woman seemed tougher. She wanted her nurses to be soft and her police officers to be tough, not the other way around. There were no female police officers in Moldova, at least none she'd seen. She hoped the woman knew how to shoot a gun.

Stephanie helped her into the backseat of the police car and climbed in next to her. "It's normal to feel nervous. You've gone through a terrible ordeal. But I promise, we won't let anything else happen to you."

How could anyone promise that?

The officer drove down the road, and Hannah looked out the back window while she asked Stephanie the question that had been burning in her. "What will happen to me now?"

"You'll stay in the safe house. They will try to track down Paavo Shevchenko and the Platonovs and proceed with litigation. You'll have to be a witness in the trials if you want to stay in America. And in the next weeks and months," Stephanie explained, "I'll help you go through the legal process of getting your documents, if you want to stay, and help you transition to a regular life. I can also help you go back home if that's what you decide."

Hannah didn't know what regular life was anymore. Even in Moldova, everything would be different. She'd love to see Katya and her uncle, but she didn't want to return worse off than when she'd left, and even though she missed Vladi, she didn't want to live with him in the village. *He* didn't even like living there. Maybe he could come to America. Life would be better for him here too.

"If I decide to stay, I can go to school?" she asked.

"Of course."

"Will I be able to bring family here?"

"Eventually."

"I want to stay," she said firmly.

"You don't need to make any decisions right now."

Hannah looked down at the carefully wrapped present from Colin, which the police officer had grabbed for her on the way out of the hospital. The Santa Claus paper was thick, good quality, and he'd put a lot of tape on it. She wanted to open it, but not here, in the police car. Maybe at the safe house.

She looked out the windshield and saw something shimmering. Like water.

"Is this the beach?" she asked Stephanie, pointing ahead just to be sure that she wasn't seeing things.

"Yes."

"Can we go closer? I've never seen the ocean."

"You've lived here for six months and you haven't seen the beach?"

Hannah shook her head slowly.

"How many times did you leave the house?"

The Russian store. The park with the horses. The run. Maggie's school. "Four times, not including driving from the airport. And I often went into the backyard." Did taking out the garbage count? "One time I went to the neighbor's backyard." She squeezed Colin's present in her hand. It was a long cardboard tube, but she had no idea what it was. Maybe a magazine.

Stephanie shook her head in anger, then leaned forward and asked the police officer if they could go by the beach. They drove down a steep road to a busy highway right next to sand that stretched on and on, until it finally met a bluish-green glistening ocean with long curling waves dotted with surfers, just like in the movies.

The police car pulled into a parking lot and stopped right next to the sand. Hannah asked to open the window, and the officer pushed a button to slide the back window down. The smell of fish and salt filled her nostrils. She closed her eyes and listened to the sound of the crashing waves.

"You want to get out?" the officer asked.

Hannah did want to get out, but she was afraid to leave the safety of the car, even though she hadn't seen anyone following them. She looked back at the road.

"If you're not ready—" Stephanie began.

Hannah felt angry at herself then. Angry at her fear. Was she really going to tell the officer to drive away from the beach, a place she'd dreamed of going for the past six months?

"I am ready," Hannah said in English, and opened the door.

She walked slowly across the sand, holding on to Colin's present. She kept walking and didn't let herself look back, not even when her fear was screaming at her to stop, get back in the car, hide. Her shoes sank down and filled with warm sand. She walked on.

She made it to the edge of the water. The Santa Claus paper on the present was hard to get off with her cracked fingernails, but finally, she removed the tape. Inside the tube was a rolled-up piece of paper from Colin's sketchbook. The ripped fringe was still at the top. She unrolled it and took in a sudden breath of sea air.

It was a black-and-white pencil drawing of her on the day she had thought he didn't recognize her, after Lillian had chopped off her hair. She was framed in the window, one palm pressed against the glass. Her hair came up in uneven tufts and her eyes were desperate and sad, but her chin was held high. Hannah stared at the picture. In it, she recognized her own bravery. Her strength.

She kicked off her shoes, pulled the sweatpants up, and walked into the water. A wave splashed up over her feet and the bottoms of her legs. Cold. Beautifully cold. Like the cold showers she used to take in Moldova.

She squished her toes down into the wet sand and lifted her chin up. Once again, she was a girl with possibilities.

AUTHOR'S NOTE

When I taught English as a Second Language, I heard too many stories about immigrants being mistreated in America. Even though Hannah and all the characters in this book are made up, I based them on real-life people. It saddens me that many children, teens, and adults are slaves today, even in America. Government estimates are that 14,500 to 17,500 people are trafficked into the United States every year. At least half of them are children and teens.

They are hidden in warehouses, brothels, and regular American neighborhoods. They are kept imprisoned not with locks or bars but with words and fear. They are America's modern-day slaves.

If they escape, they rarely go to the police. Often they're too afraid. Sometimes they don't realize that what they experienced was a crime. Mostly they just want to move on and forget what happened to them.

If they do go to the police, they have to be willing to face their abusers in court in order to get a visa to stay here. The traffickers' threats make this a terrifying option for many and could result in retaliation against their families back home. Going home is also not a safe option. As a result, there have been far too few convictions in the United States.

My greatest hope is that we can end slavery in all its forms, including sex slavery and domestic slavery, in this country and around the world. Children and teens should never have to endure this kind of abuse. As a result, I'm donating twenty percent of whatever I make from this book to organizations that help trafficking victims like Hannah. If you'd like to find ways to help girls who are trafficked into this country, go to my website: kimpurcell.com.

Thank you.

THANK YOU . . .

To my husband, Gavin, who believed in this book from the beginning and, most importantly, believed in me.

To my daughters, who provided the inspiration for the children in this book, and who give me so much joy and laughter every day.

To my sisters, Tara and Jenn, my dad, and my mom for their loving support.

To my cousin, Charlotte Dubec, who let me stay with her in Moldova, introduced me to her Moldovan friends, and helped me in endless ways with this book.

To my agent, Kate Lee, for her wonderful notes on draft after draft of this book and for reading it more times than any reasonable writer would hope for.

To my editor, Kendra Levin, for recognizing the promise in this book and the need for people, especially teens, to read a book about modern-day domestic slavery, and for challenging me to stretch myself as a writer.

To writer Jennifer Castle, for reading three drafts (or more) of this book, for giving amazing feedback, and for being such a wonderful friend.

To my early readers and fellow writers Susan Merson, Barbara Bottner, Justine Lambert, Kenneth Nowell, J. R. Hevron, Anna Van Lenten, Molly Castelloe, Dara Schlissel, Delina Codey, Kathryn Purcell, Jake Purcell, Florine Gingerich, Elif Cercil, and Tali Noimann, who gave me wonderful feedback at various stages of this book.

To John Rechy, whose writing workshop and lessons on suspense have been unforgettable.

To Keren Taylor and WriteGirl, who empower teen girls and give them the strength to avoid exploitation and who encouraged me to write this book in the beginning.

To Gurmukh Kalsa, who taught me more than anyone else about how someone overcomes fear.

To the many housekeepers, nannies, Russians, and Moldovans I interviewed for this book, including Ally Fedorov, Vladimir Wexler, Adelina Castillo Garcia, Viorica Damian, Aksana Plotnikava, Alina Radeanu, and Elvira Rusalova-Robles.

To all the nonprofit agencies that combat trafficking, especially La Strada, the Salvation Army, and Safe Horizon, for aiding in my research and for helping so many people like Hannah.